New Horizons

Nick Udall

For Doreen

PART ONE

Ardwick

Chapter 1

They'd waited until quarter to nine before leaving the house and walking the short distance down Armitage Street to the school gates. The rest of the children had already gone into their classrooms and were now on their way to morning assembly. New boy Robert Wilson was a shy lad and his gran worried that it may be unnerving for him to be left alone in the playground, surrounded by strange children. Edna Bloomfield had therefore decided that she would accompany her grandson and hand him over to his new teacher. It would give him time to become familiar with his new classmates, before they went out for morning break.

It was a good plan, but not one appreciated by Miss Morgan. The school secretary was a prim, matronly like figure, her grey hair twisted into a bun. She peered curiously over the top of her spectacles at the woman and small boy who had presented themselves at the school office.

"Well, here he is, all ready for lessons," announced Edna, proudly. "My grandson, Robert Wilson."

Miss Morgan slowly ran her eyes over the aspiring pupil.

"Humph!"

Looking up, Robert wasn't sure whether her response was an observation or a judgement. He thought the latter, as the way she glowered at him suggested that she wasn't impressed.

"It would have been fine to have left him in the playground," said Miss Morgan, sternly. "The teacher on duty would have brought him to us to send on to his class."

"Well, I've saved them a job."

"He's a little old to need you to run about after him, isn't he?"

"It's a big change for our Robert," explained Edna. "He's moved from the edge of Glossop, almost out on the moors. He's not used to Manchester. He lost his dad just after Dunkirk. I wanted to make sure that it went smoothly this morning."

Ignoring Edna, Miss Morgan turned her attention to Robert.

"You're just going to have to toughen up, young man. I know it's hard, but you're not the only child whose lost a father in the War. There are quite a few of you here at Armitage Street."

"And your name is?" Asked Edna.

Robert recognised the hint of menace in his gran's voice. She was unimpressed with the secretary's attitude and lord help anyone who disparaged her grandson.

Miss Morgan was saved by the timely intervention of the school's headteacher, arriving back from morning assembly. Hearing the latter part of their conversation, he intervened quickly to defuse the situation.

"Thanks Miss Morgan. I'll take care of everything now."

His voice was firm, the tone reproachful and the secretary slunk silently back behind her desk. Looking down, she pretended to search through some papers, in an unconvincing attempt to cover her embarrassment.

Turning to Edna, the man smiled and introduced himself.

"Hello, I'm Mr Chandler, the school's head."

He held out his hand to her. Surprised, she shook it warmly.

"Mrs Bloomfield," she replied.

"And this must be …" Chandler paused. "It's Robert. Robert Wilson, I believe. Isn't it young man?"

"Yes," replied Robert, quietly.

"I thought so. I received the letter from the education committee last week, telling us that you were coming and here you are."

Robert nodded.

"So, Mrs Bloomfield, you're Robert's grandma?"

"Yes, that's right. My daughter has a new job in town and she and Robert have moved in with me."

Edna's impressions of Chandler were good. He looked to be in his mid-fifties, an age similar to her own. He was a small, round pleasant man, with a balding head and an engaging smile. He was unlike most teachers she'd come across. Employed in areas like Ardwick, they considered themselves a class apart. Attitudes towards parents were patronising at best; disdainful at worst. Chandler was nothing like that; he regarded her as his equal.

The head was impressed too. Struck by Edna's feisty manner and the confident way she'd dealt with Miss Morgan. She had a twinkle in her eye and he could still see in her features evidence that in her youth, Edna had been an admired local beauty.

"Well," said Chandler, "I suppose we'd better be getting Robert along to his lessons. We've put him in the 'A' class. The report from his old school, says that he's a bright young man. I'm sure he'll do well here."

"Yes, we hope so."

Handing Robert's dinner money over to Chandler, Edna said goodbye to her grandson and made her way outside through the main entrance. As Robert watched her go, Mr Chandler smiled at him.

"Come on Robert. We need to go up to the first floor. That's where your classroom is."

Robert accompanied Mr Chandler along the corridor to the end of the building, where a spacious and well-lit staircase gave them access to the floor above. Quickly, they climbed the stairs and were soon outside the classroom. Knocking on the door, Mr Chandler opened it and walked in. Turning round, he beckoned Robert to follow him.

Chapter 2

The classroom was silent when Robert entered. He looked around and could see that the pupils were bent over their exercise books, writing busily.

"It seems Miss Forsyth, that we have a class hard at work," remarked Chandler. "Excellent!"

Robert thought the head looked very pleased with himself. Even though he had only reached the tender age of nine, Robert recognised that Mr Chandler was one of those unusual adults who believed that praise was the best way to encourage achievement. As such, Robert couldn't help but like him.

"Yes, Mr Chandler. The children are updating their diaries to record what they have done over the weekend."

"That should prove interesting," replied Chandler, with a smile. "Well, as you can see," he continued, "our new boy has arrived. Robert Wilson."

"Hello Robert," said Miss Forsyth.

Robert mumbled a quite "hello." His teacher, having noted his nervous disposition, sought to reassure him.

"You'll soon settle in. Sit there for now," she said, pointing to a desk at the front, "and we'll sort out some books and equipment for you."

Robert sat down behind the desk and waited whilst Miss Forsyth exchanged some quiet words with Mr Chandler. She was young and charming; quite a surprise to him, as his previous teachers had all seemed so old. He was starting to feel more comfortable and after Mr Chandler had left and Miss Forsyth had asked him to write an introduction about himself, the time passed quite quickly. Soon, it was time for break. Before dismissing the class, Miss Forsyth had a question to ask.

"Children. As you know, we have a new boy with us this morning. His name is Robert and it would be nice if someone could take him to the playground and make him feel welcome to our school."

Miss Forsyth paused, waiting for a volunteer. It seemed however, that the boys were reluctant to put themselves forward. Taking a deep breath, she scanned the room, hoping to catch someone's eye. Miss Forsyth preferred not to instruct a particular boy to do it; that risked making Robert feel unwanted. She knew it was no good looking towards the girls. At their age they didn't want to be seen as being too friendly towards any boy. But she was wrong. From the back of the class, a hand went up.

"Please, Miss. I'd like to take Robert."

There was a collective sigh from the girls and a few chuckles from the boys. It seemed that the children were either embarrassed or amused by their classmate's offer.

"Well, thank you Kay. That's very kind. If you can come out to the front and wait with Robert, whilst the rest of you," she continued, addressing the class, "can stand by your desks."

When all the children had pushed their chairs under the desks and were stood quietly behind them, they were released, row by row, into the corridor. Finally, Robert and Kay followed them. Watching, as they made their way to the stairs, Miss Forsyth smiled. She was pleased that Kay had come to the rescue. She couldn't imagine how upsetting it would have been for Robert if, on his first day, he had been left feeling isolated and unwanted.

Out in the playground, Kay took Robert towards the railings alongside Armitage Street, away from the hustle and bustle of the games of football that ranged across the yard. Taking a white paper bag from her pocket she opened it and smiling, offered Robert a sweet. It was an extraordinary act of kindness. It was June 1949 and although sweets had been temporarily taken off ration, with sugar supplies so low, it was difficult to get them.

"Are you sure?" asked Robert.

"Of course," said Kay, firmly. "I wouldn't offer if I didn't want you to have one. Would I?"

"No, I suppose not."

Taking the sweet, Robert looked closely at his new friend, for he knew already that a friend she surely was. Kay was small for her age but he could already see that she had a large and confident personality. She didn't care what anyone said about taking him under her wing. She was pretty, generous and warm hearted. Her light brown, shoulder length hair, parted to the side, curled around and behind her cute, little ears. A light blue ribbon, with a delicate bow, kept her hair tidily in place; a pretty pink neck scarf, complementing her dress. Kay had bright green eyes, that opened wide and a warm, welcoming smile. Robert was suddenly pleased that he had moved here. Otherwise, he would never have met Kay.

Robert was much taller than Kay but slightly built. He had short, brown hair and brown eyes and lips that parted only slightly when he smiled. He was wearing a shirt, with a slightly frayed collar and a blue tie. A striped pullover, short trousers and long, grey socks. Kay smiled when she noticed his knobbly knees. They were relatively free of cuts and bruises, suggesting that Robert wasn't quite as active as most boys his age.

"Where have you come from?" Asked Kay.

"Glossop, in Derbyshire."

"Oh. Why was that then?"

"My mam had to get a new job in Manchester, so we came to live with my gran, here in Armitage Street."

"Whereabouts, on Armitage Street?"

"Just past the wash house. Two doors down from the shop on the corner of Gregory Street."

"That's the opposite direction to where I live."

Kay realised that Robert hadn't mentioned his father. She assumed that he had been lost, like so many, in the War, but made no attempt to find out if this were true. Instead, she went on to tell Robert about her own family. Dad, Ernest Thompson, was a bus driver, based at the Corporation's depot on Hyde Road. Her mam was called Ethel and she had a younger sister Joan, who was also at the school. They all lived at Heywood House, or Bennett Street Flats as they were more commonly known. By the end of break, the two of them were getting on like a house on fire.

"I'll ask Miss Forsyth if I can move to come and sit next to you. That is, if you want me to," suggested Kay.

"Well, yes. But are you sure?"

Kay laughed and shook her head.

"I told you. I don't say anything unless I mean it."

Noticing that Robert appeared embarrassed, Kay felt a little guilty. She realised that he was still uncertain in his new surroundings. He lacked her natural confidence.

"It's okay Robert," she said, softly. "It's nice that you're polite. Not all boys are."

"Well, I would like us to sit together," insisted Robert.

"Well, we will."

And they did. Miss Forsyth readily agreed. Kay was one of her cleverest pupils and they'd been told that Robert was exceptionally bright too. They could only benefit from sitting together. At four o' clock and with lessons over for the day, Kay and Robert said goodbye as they parted outside the school gates. Robert crossed the road and turned right. After a few yards he stopped and looked back along Armitage Street. He watched contentedly as the figure of Kay slowly disappeared into the distance. The day had turned out well. He had met a wonderful friend and was looking forward to seeing her again.

Chapter 3

It was six-thirty that evening and Robert's mam was home from work. Together with his gran, they had eaten their tea and Robert had helped with clearing the table and wiping the pots. His mam had been eager to find out about his day at school and was pleased to know that he had met a new friend. It didn't surprise her that it was a girl. Irene Wilson knew that her son was a sensitive soul and as yet, hadn't taken to the rough and tumble world that most boys inhabited. Being with Kay, who seemed a caring and intelligent girl, was far more to his liking. Irene wondered how far the loss of her husband Billy, had contributed to Robert's character. Unlike other boys, his father had never been there to impart that love of sport; take him to see City at Maine Road, or Lancashire at Old Trafford. There were no uncles or grandfathers to act as role models either. Furthermore, Irene felt unable to do it herself. She felt uncomfortable about the idea of placing herself in such a predominantly male environment. She didn't lack confidence, far from it, but had no wish to encourage the unwanted attention of admirers. Irene was a pretty young widow, just turned thirty, but she was devoted to Billy's memory and could never give her heart to anyone else.

Having helped with the chores, Robert prepared for the family's early evening routine. He would go upstairs to fetch a book from his bedroom, so that he could settle down at the kitchen table to read. His mam and gran meanwhile, would divide the *Evening Chronicle* between them, keen to keep abreast of the local news. Later, they would put on the radio, before it was time for Robert to go to bed. Today, it would be different however.

"I've told Mrs Brown that you'll take Mac out," said Edna, to her grandson. "Mr Brown's on nights and she's hurt her leg and can't get about so well. You only need to go over to the 'Rec'. Mac's getting old now and he doesn't need that much exercise. You don't mind, do you?"

"No, of course not."

"Don't be too long," said Irene. "It'll be getting late soon."

"He'll be all right love."

Edna looked reassuringly at her daughter. She understood that Irene was feeling protective towards him in their new surroundings.

"I'll be fine Mam. Don't worry."

Nipping through the kitchen door, Robert went out through the back yard, into the ginnel, opened the Brown's back gate and walked the short distance to the back door. Knocking, the door quickly opened. Mrs Brown was stood there ready, lead in hand and Mac sat down beside her.

"Thanks cock. Aren't you good helping? I don't know, just lately I've been like a walking demic."

Mrs Brown chuckled.

"It's what happens when you get older Robert. Just wait and see."

Robert looked embarrassed, not sure of what to say. Although of a similar age to his gran, Mrs Brown seemed so much older. Her red hair, streaked with grey, was striking, but wild and unkempt; her features wrinkled. Her smile revealed the absence of two front teeth. But that clearly didn't bother her. Mrs Brown was an effervescent character. Everyone said she had a heart of gold and she had certainly welcomed Robert warmly.

"You don't talk much. There's no need to be shy."

Robert nodded, but remained silent.

"Well, don't just stand there. Here you are."

Robert grasped hold of the lead that was proffered towards him. Looking up, Mac got to his feet ready to walk down the steps.

"Ah, the little love," remarked Mrs Brown, looking affectionately at her canine friend. "You're all ready for walkies, aren't you Mac?"

For a moment, Robert thought that she expected Mac to answer. It was enough to make him smile and in doing so, he felt more relaxed.

"Make sure you keep him on the lead cock. He doesn't know you that well and he might set off home without you."

"I will," replied Robert, quietly.

Mrs Brown smiled, having finally managed to get a response.

"Well, off you go then. I'll see you in a bit."

It wasn't far to the 'Rec'. Robert and Mac walked to the end of the ginnel, turned right down Gregory Street and walking less than a hundred yards, they were at Bennett Street, their destination across the road in front of them.

Bennett Street Recreation Ground was a large cinder field which contained the only football pitch in the area. As such, it was used by all the local schools. It was also a place for kids to play and hang around together. Locals often referred to it as the 'Black Brook'. This was due to the filthy, polluted state of the stream, the Corn Brook, which ran through it. The stream had made its way there through the industrial landscape of Openshaw and Gorton. Throughout its course, dyes, chemicals and other waste products were conveniently discharged into it by local companies, generally unsupervised by the authorities. Along the western side of the 'Rec', just behind the far goal posts, was a large electricity sub-station. On the eastern edge could be seen Brook Forge. Owned by J Garland and Co Ltd, the kids all knew it as 'Judy Garland's Forge'.

As Robert walked Mac through the gap in the railings separating the 'Rec' from the pavement on Bennett Street, his little companion was already beginning to tire. A small black and brown dog with a whippy tail, Mac had short, stumpy legs and they seemed to have been moving at thirteen to the dozen, no matter how slowly Robert had tried to progress. It seemed sensible to stop and offer his companion some respite, a decision quickly appreciated by Mac, as he turned his attention to snuffling his way through the dirt and cinders. Looking around him, Robert could see several groups of children spread out across the wide-open space. It was a pleasant evening; warm and the sky still an inviting shade of blue. It was nothing like the countryside around Glossop, but in its own way, provided a sense of peace in the heart of the city.

Lost in thought, Robert felt a gentle nudge on the bottom of his leg. Getting down on his haunches, Robert stroked Mac's head. It was the signal for his new pal to roll over and Robert quickly obliged him, by tickling his tummy. Mac opened his mouth, almost as if he were grinning, then suddenly he shook his head and got back to his feet. It was the signal that it was time to go home.

Heading back towards Bennett Street, Robert noticed a group of boys stood by the railings. There were three of them and they weren't much older than him. He could see that they were passing round a cigarette. They were trying hard to appear grown-up.

"Ugh, these Park Drive are rotten. Couldn't you have got some others?" asked a ginger haired lad.

"It's what me mam smokes. I was able to pinch a couple when she wasn't looking," replied a dark-haired lad with glasses. "And anyway, what others?"

"Well, Woodbines or Capstan Full Strength."

It was obvious that he was trying to impress, but the third lad in the group quickly ridiculed him.

"Capstan Full Strength. You've never had one of them."

"I have, Keith."

"Have you, heck. You'd spew up if you had one of them. You haven't even been smoking that one properly."

"I have," repeated the boy, but this time he spoke less convincingly.

"No, you haven't. You're blowing the smoke out of your mouth straight away. You're supposed to breathe it right in and then let it out."

The dark-haired lad knew that to save face, he had no option but to prove that he had. Drawing on the cigarette again, he took the smoke down into his lungs. Suddenly he started to cough and retch. His mates burst out laughing, not at all concerned by his continuing distress. Taking the cigarette from his hand, Keith looked at it dismissively.

"You've gone and wet the end. Couldn't you smoke it without slavering all over it?"

Keith was bigger than the others. His words and demeanour marked him out as their leader. He had short blonde hair and piercing eyes that locked on to Robert as he and Mac made their way towards the gap in the railings and Bennett Street. Before he could get there, Keith blocked his path.

"What's your hurry?"

His action wasn't unexpected. Robert had often been seen as a soft target and as Keith watched him, he gave the impression of a predator waiting to pounce. Robert's problem, was how he would respond. He had learned that you needed to think quickly in these situations, but wit and guile were seldom enough to escape a beating. He decided to give a straight response.

"I need to get my neighbour's dog back. It's getting late and she'll be getting worried."

"Oh dear," piped up the dark-haired lad. "Have you missed your bed time?"

The other lads started laughing. Robert looked at them silently.

"Who are you gawping at?" asked Ginger.

He looked menacing, but he wasn't the one who concerned Robert. If anything were to happen, it would be down to Keith.

"Call that a dog," sneered Keith, dismissively. "It's not big enough to bite your ankles."

His mates laughed.

"Yeah. Frightening," added Ginger.

Robert was worried and Mac, sensing his concern, began to bark loudly.

"You need to get that dog under control," suggested the kid with glasses.

"Yeah, or we'll do it for you," threatened Ginger.

His words only induced further barking from Mac. Robert held his lead tightly to restrain him, but his action convinced his little pal that they were in danger. Mac began to growl, determined to warn off the potential aggressors, but he was a small dog and Robert knew that Mac's actions would only provoke the boys further. He was right, as Keith strode towards Mac and lashed out at him with his boot. Too quick for him, Mac dodged behind Robert. As Keith prepared to launch a second strike, Robert dropped the lead. Something snapped inside him. He put up his fists and stared straight at the bully.

"Leave him alone!"

"Oh, yeah. Are you gonna make me?"

Robert couldn't respond; but he didn't have to. His mind had gone. There was no longer any power of reason. Everything had slowed down. The Black Brook, the other boys, had disappeared. There was just Keith and the only sensation that Robert felt was an overwhelming desire to destroy him.

The mind may have been willing but Robert was immediately knocked to the floor. His assailant quickly jumped on top of him, pinning him down and trying to punch him in the face. Robert, able to get his hands free, instinctively raised them in order to deflect the blows. Keith's attack was fierce but with the adrenalin coursing through his body, Robert could feel no pain. Nevertheless, he was now receiving a real beating and his prospects of survival seemed to rest solely in the hands of his assailant and Keith was merciless. Robert had dared to challenge him and as such, he was sending out a message to all those who may consider doing so in future.

Suddenly, the weight pressing down on Robert was gone and as he opened his eyes, the sky was visible above him. Slowly his head began to clear and he became conscious of the sound of cheering and of voices willing someone on.

"Go on! Show him!"

They were girl's voices. Robert didn't understand. What was going on? Slowly he raised himself from the ground, shakily getting to his feet. The noise was getting louder, the shouts of encouragement ever stronger. He turned round and he couldn't believe his eyes. It was Kay and she was sat astride Keith's chest. He was trying desperately to hold her off but her fists were smashing into his face. He began to cry but she wouldn't let up.

"You're nothing but a bully, Keith Clarke. Touch any of my friends and I'll batter you again."

Robert was stunned.

"Kay."

She didn't respond.

"Kay," he repeated, patting her shoulder.

Finally, she stopped and turned her head towards him.

"He's had enough Kay. You can let him go now."

Kay nodded and slowly got to her feet. She stepped back. A crowd of awe-struck youngsters gathered round her. They'd come running from all over the 'Rec', eager to find out what all the commotion was about. Kay, having despatched a feared and hated bully, had achieved heroic status. The girls, in particular, were excited. Kay had struck a blow for female equality.

Meanwhile, Keith had slunk off towards Bennett Street. His nose and lips were bloody and his eyes showed signs of bruising.

He was hurt and embarrassed and he knew that he was finished. He'd lost a fight to a girl; no one would ever feel intimidated by him again. His friends had already deserted him, disappearing once they could see that Kay would be victorious. And Mac? He was stood loyally by Robert's side, the boy who had tried to protect him.

"Are you all right Kay?" asked Robert, as the crowd began to disperse.

"Yes. I'm fine."

No, you're not," replied Robert. "You've got scratches on your leg."

Kay looked down. She could see that there were three short, red lines down the outside of her calf. At the end of one, was a small trickle of blood.

"It's nothing," said Kay, reassuringly. "They'll disappear in no time."

Robert looked at her closely. Her face was flushed from the effort and excitement of the fight. There was a trace of perspiration on her brow and her eyes shone magnificently. She seemed so beautiful.

"I don't understand. Where did you come from?" asked Robert.

"I was with my friends on the football pitch. I thought I recognised you walking the dog and so I came over to say hello and I saw you get into trouble with Keith. When he had you on the floor, I had to do something to stop him."

"But you could have got hurt. You shouldn't have taken the chance."

"And see you get battered? No. Not when I could do something about it."

"You're very brave Kay. Thank you."

Kay was impressed. Robert wasn't at all embarrassed by the fact that he'd been saved by a girl. He was so different to all the other boys she knew.

"So are you, Robert. I heard you; saw what you did. You stood up to him. You wouldn't let him kick the dog. Even though you knew you had no chance of winning. That takes real bravery," remarked Kay, approvingly. "And here he is, by your side."

Robert looked down and saw Mac. In all the chaos, he'd forgotten all about him. Robert was relieved that he hadn't wandered off.

"What's his name?"

"Mac."

"He's lovely," said Kay, bending down to stroke him.

"He likes you making a fuss of him. I suppose I ought to get him home."

Robert picked up the lead, ready to set off.

"I'll walk back with you," suggested Kay.

"It's not far."

"I know, but I'd rather see that you get back all right."

"I will. Don't worry."

The two of them left the field and turned right. Almost immediately they were at the top of Gregory Street.

"Well, I've just got to walk down here and I'll be home."

"It's not like Glossop round here Robert. You have to be careful. Not everyone fights fair."

"What do you mean?"

"You thought that Keith would fight fair. I saw you put up your hands like you were in the ring. We don't follow the Queensbury Rules in Ardwick."

"Queensbury Rules?"

"Yes. They were named after the Marquess of Queensbury. They use them in boxing. When you get in a fight round here though, there are no rules. You have to do anything to win."

"How come you know about them?"

"Dad was an amateur boxer. He fought for his regiment in the Army. He told me all about it. He showed me how to punch too," she said, smiling. "Just in case some boy thought they could push me around."

"Oh!"

Kay smiled. Robert sounded surprised.

"Anyway, you don't have to worry Robert. Keith won't bother you again. I can call for you before school if you like. Two doors down from the shop on the corner, isn't it?"

"Yes."

"Fine, I'll come to the back door at half past eight."

"I'll see you then. Bye," said Robert.

"Bye."

Robert and Mac set off down Gregory Street. It had been an amazing evening and thanks to Kay, he had survived it relatively intact. The image of her sat astride Keith, pounding him into submission, excited him. But he was unsure why. Was it that he was in love? Surely not, he thought. Reaching the ginnel that led home, Mac pulled to the left. Briefly, Robert glanced back along Gregory Street. At the top, he could see that Kay was still there; a guardian angel making sure that he got home safely.

The next morning, Kay knocked on the back door at precisely eight-thirty. Robert was ready and waiting. It was the first time that they would begin the day together, a routine that would continue throughout their time at Armitage Street School.

Chapter 4

By the time the summer holidays began, Kay and Robert had become the firmest of friends. It was an association of which their families approved. Irene Wilson, Ernest and Ethel Thompson, recognised the potential of their children, but felt ill-equipped to help them achieve it. Yet they soon realised that the pair's natural curiosity sparked one another's ambitions to take themselves beyond the limitations that had been imposed upon their parents. The two friends regularly visited the library and would walk down to Oxford Road to view the exhibitions in the Manchester Museum. Sometimes they would go to look at the paintings in Whitworth Park and even into town to the City Art Gallery in Mosley Street. Their receptive minds were always eager to seek out new knowledge and experiences.

Like all children, Kay and Robert were expected to carry out their fair share of household chores and these increased in the summer when they weren't at school. When there were errands to be run to the shops on Hyde Road, the two of them would often go together. It may be that they were getting 'rody' bacon from Wagner's butchers, 'finny haddock' from Tomlinsons, or balm cakes from Sharples bakery. If they ran out of tea or sugar, then it was off to Pye's grocers. Sewing materials would be acquired from Scotts and next door was the radio repair shop, where they would take the accumulator to be recharged for the wireless. If they weren't in a hurry, the pair of them would stare at the second-hand sports cars gleaming in the showroom of Gorton Car Sales, or the brand-new Phillips bicycles in the window of W Ellis. Kay and Robert believed that the latter were there simply to torture their contemporaries, for parents in Ardwick didn't have deep enough pockets to acquire them.

On Saturday mornings, came the hardest and least appreciated task of the week. It was washday and Kay would accompany her mam and Robert, his gran, to Armitage Street Wash House, which had only recently been modernised with the introduction of new appliances. Clothes and sheets were bagged up and off they went. It was a long and tedious process. A sink was paid for in which to scrub the 'whites' and a spinner to remove the excess water, before putting them in the drier. Washing machines could be hired for the coloured items and the driers were used to finish them off. A large, hot press was available to iron the sheets and pillow cases. The hard graft of scrubbing and potentially dangerous use of the press, was carried out by the adults; the children's jobs were to help with the fetching and carrying. Once they had returned home, the items were hung over a wooden clothes rack that was suspended on pullies from the kitchen ceiling. There the items would be aired, before being taken down and put into drawers and cupboards.

Towards the end of the six weeks holiday Kay and Robert were walking down Armitage Street on their way to Ardwick library. Reaching 'Davies and Griffiths' builder's yard on the corner of Hyde Road, they could hear the unmistakable sound of a steam locomotive approaching the bridge that towered above them. Instinctively, Robert stopped and looked up. Trains held a fascination for him that they didn't for Kay, but nevertheless she found herself halting too. As the train rolled towards them, the clatter and squeals of the carriage wheels intensified and the smoke from the engine billowed up and over the sides of the bridge, threatening to envelop the two of them. The unique and peculiar smell of the mixture of smoke, oil, fire and steam, filled the air. As Kay coughed and spluttered, Robert readily breathed in the potentially noxious fumes.

"It's fascinating, isn't it Kay? To think of all the wonderful places that the railways can take us."

"Well, yes. And that one's going to London Road Station," she replied, chuckling.

"You know what I mean. It could be a train going to London or Edinburgh. To Liverpool and then on to a ship to America."

"Is that what you want to do Robert? Leave Manchester and go all over the World?"

"Well, yes. I'd like to see it all. Everywhere. Don't you?"

"I'm not sure. What if you found somewhere else that you'd like to live? Would you leave Manchester?"

"I might. Would you?"

"No. I don't think so. I wouldn't want to leave my mam and dad, or our Joan."

"But you might feel differently when you get older," suggested Robert.

"No, I don't think so. I love Ardwick and Manchester."

"Would you come and visit me, if I lived in another country?" asked Robert.

"Why, do you plan on going right now?" asked Kay, laughing.

She looked at Robert and was surprised to see that he was deadly serious. Clearly her answer was important to him.

"No, of course not. But if I ever did, would you come and see me?"

"Yes, I would," replied Kay, smiling.

"That's good, because I'd always visit you. Wherever in the World I'm living."

Robert smiled. In his young mind, Kay's words were further proof of their friendship. It was a friendship that he had come to depend on and one that had given him a new found confidence. Her support had allowed him to flourish in his new environment, free of the fear of rejection or intimidation. When he'd arrived in Armitage Street, he'd felt alone; unsure of what the future held for him. Kay had seen him through those uncertainties, thrown a protective arm around him and now, the two were inseparable. She had introduced him to 'corporation pop' and 'vimto' lollies. He loved it when she said 'bockle' and 'keckle' and chided him for being 'mard' when he wouldn't climb the trees after they'd walked all the way to Debdale Park. Kay had even got him playing football with her friends on the Rec. Edna had told him off for 'scrawping' his shoes, but had smiled when he revealed the reason why. It was clear that thanks to his friend, the shy boy who had arrived from Glossop, was changing and definitely for the better.

Chapter 5

When Kay and Robert returned to school as members of 3A, they continued to sit together. They were now with Mrs Duncan. Once again, they had a sympathetic teacher who appreciated their talents. Continuing to excel, as the end of the academic year approached, they were called into Mr Chandler's office. He commended them on their progress and advised them to keep working hard, as new opportunities would present themselves if they passed the eleven plus. Getting pupils into grammar school brought far less pressure at Armitage Street, than it did at schools based in the more affluent parts of the city. In those areas, middle-class parents demanded that their children succeed. Pass rates were crucial to how schools were regarded. Ardwick, with lesser parental expectations, put little pressure on its headteachers or staff. None the less, Chandler was keen to see his best students get on and he did everything he could to ensure that they did. Unfortunately, when Kay and Robert entered 4A, their new teacher was to prove far less understanding.

Almost immediately, Robert wished that they still had Miss Forsyth or Mrs Duncan. Mrs Turner, or 'Ruby' as the kids called her, made it plain that the class regime would be rigid. She was in charge and nothing within the classroom; organisation, routines or lesson content, could be questioned. For an able child, it was like being placed in an intellectual straightjacket. Robert and Kay hated it, but were sensible enough to resist the urge to challenge her, aware that in such a situation, she would be the winner. They quickly realised that Ruby's lessons had little to offer, but fortunately Mr Chandler held twice weekly sessions with the class. In these he focused on the exams that they would be taking for the eleven plus and provided projects for them to research at the local library.

For the boys, Ruby's control of the class was problematic. Mrs Duncan, with two sons of her own, could empathise with the high spirits that inevitably materialised as boys moved towards adolescence. This was unlike Ruby, who thought boys disagreeable. As such, she was merciless in her punishment of their most trivial transgressions. Ruby had a drunken and philandering husband, who had caused her much misery and embarrassment. Betrayed and bitter, Ruby developed an aversion to the entire male population, which provided a justification for her punitive behaviour. Perhaps, cracking down on boys without any signs of pity, gave Ruby a sense of retribution for her husband's wrongdoings.   Significantly, Ruby's attitude had created divisions among the girls. There were a few, unlike Kay, who still regarded boys as boisterous and bothersome; strange creatures of little merit. It made them eager to tell tales. Boys who broke the rules, misbehaved in the playground, or on their way home from school, were easy targets. For Robert, it meant that ultimately, he could not go under the radar.

The decisive moment came early in June. By then the children had sat the eleven plus and it was only six weeks before they would leave. It was Monday and Class 4A had just finished their morning bible lesson and Kay and Robert were talking in the playground during the dinner break. In the lesson a boy had questioned whether it could really be true that Abraham had lived for 175 years and his son Isaac for 180. Ruby had insisted that it was; the Old Testament was the word of God and must not be questioned.

"She was talking nonsense," observed Robert, "but the rest of them believed her. I wasn't going to say anything though. I've been punished enough."

"You did the right thing," replied Kay.

"You don't know anything Robert Wilson," claimed a voice from behind.

"No, he doesn't," added another.

Turning round, Kay's heart sank. It was Kathy Smith and Jane Morris, two of Ruby's favourites. It was just like them to be creeping around, looking to get others into trouble. They were bound to tell Ruby what they had heard and Kay was concerned for her friend. Robert however, felt calm. He knew that once they went back into class, he would be in trouble. Yet, the knowledge was enlightening. If he was to be punished, he may as well say exactly what he thought. He rounded fiercely on the girls, ridiculing their gullibility.

"I don't know anything? Really? How many people live to be a hundred? Hardly any. And as for a hundred and eighty! Do you really believe that?"

Kathy and Jane looked at him with contempt. They didn't like Robert and thought Kay peculiar for choosing to be his friend. Their attitudes were aggravated by the fact that Robert continually outperformed them in tests, denying them the opportunity to be top of the class. Before he'd arrived, Kathy or Jane had occasionally beaten Kay to top marks. Now, there was no chance. The problem was that they couldn't dismiss him, like others, as just a stupid boy. If they wanted to satisfy their sense of grievance, they would have to find another way. Robert had now provided them with the perfect opportunity and they weren't about to let it go.

"Yes, I do," replied Kathy, with certainty. "God let them live that long."

"God's special," continued Jane. "He creates all sorts of miracles."

"And how do you know that? What evidence do you have?"

"The Bible," replied Jane.

"Do you believe the World was created in six days then? Because that's what the Bible says."

"Yes. Of course, stupid!" insisted Kathy.

Robert looked at her. She was completely convinced; unable, like her friend, to question anything that Ruby told them. Robert had a sense of the power and influence that a teacher like Ruby could have over her charges. It took a strong and determined mind to stand against the 'truths' that were being handed down to them. And behind all of it was the threat of force. 'Do or believe this, or you'll be punished'. Robert suddenly realised that he'd become a rebel. He was just like Oliver Cromwell or George Washington, two figures he'd borrowed books about from the adult section of Ardwick library. He imagined that he was like them, prepared to risk everything for what he believed to be right.

"Haven't you learned anything from our nature lessons?" he asked. "You know how long it takes plants and animals to grow. An adult or fully grown animal doesn't exist within a day!"

"Not now they don't," replied Jane, "but the first ones created by God did."

"Rubbish. It's not scientifically possible. The Bible's wrong."

"You're saying you don't believe in God," declared Kathy.

It was a sly statement and Kay put her hand on Robert's arm. She wanted him to stop and think about what he would say, but it was too late.

"How do we know that he really exists?" asked Robert. "There isn't any proof."

The girls smiled and walked away. Now, they really had him.

Chapter 6

Ruby was at her desk as the children filed back into the classroom. Standing silently, the pupils waited until their teacher bid them a good afternoon.

"Good afternoon, Mrs Turner," replied thirty-six voices in unison.

"Sit down."

As Kay and Robert settled into their places, they noticed Kathy and Jane approaching the teacher's desk. They were creeping towards her slowly and deferentially, their hands clasped before them, their heads bowed slightly. All pig tails and smiles, their faces writ large with angelic innocence, within them beat a pair of malevolent hearts.

Having gained Ruby's attention, the girls talked quietly, responding to questions that sought further explanations. As the details became ever more incriminating, Ruby shifted her gaze across to Robert, weighing him up and down, a satisfied look on her face. She'd wanted to cut Robert down to size for some time now. It wasn't that he'd done anything particularly wrong, just that he was too clever by half. Those were the kind of boys who needed watching. Thanking the girls for their responsible behaviour, she directed them back to their seats and then proceeded to call the register. Having finished, Ruby called on the class monitor to return the register to the school office and then turned her attention to Robert.

"Robert Wilson. Come out here."

Her words were menacing; sharp and abrupt. They were designed to excite fear. A collective, sharp intake of breath from the class, indicated that Robert's afternoon was about to become very unpleasant. As he moved his chair back and began to stand up, Robert felt Kay place her hand on his knee. He turned towards her and received an encouraging glance; a look that told him to stay strong.

Robert's only advantage lay in the fact that he was prepared. Ruby's summons was not unexpected. Furthermore, he was determined that he would show no fear. If Robert did that, it would mean that regardless of any punishment received, he would win the moral victory. With his eyes staring straight ahead, Robert soon reached the front of the class and stood to the side of the teacher's desk.

The sight before him was far from agreeable. After his mam had met Ruby at a consultation evening, she hadn't been impressed. "Mutton dressed as lamb," she had commented to Edna. Ruby had a skeletal face, her skin hung loosely across her jaw and cheek bones, which were made more prominent by the liberal application of white foundation. Her eyes sat deep in their sockets; heavy mascara applied to her lashes. A trace of light blue eyeshadow and bright red lipstick, gave Ruby the appearance of a woman desperately trying to deny her advance in years. Her short, thin brown hair, with grey visible at the roots, betrayed her best efforts.

Sat in her chair, Ruby leaned back and slowly looked him up and down. Robert knew what was coming. It was how she always dealt with miscreants. A quiet word of censure, a private telling off after the other children had left the classroom, was not her style. Public ridicule and humiliation, was. It wasn't enough to beat down the unfortunate individual, the rest of the class must be taught the value of obedience too and the uncomfortable consequences that befell anyone who annoyed their teacher.

"Robert Wilson," she announced loudly. "Is it true, that you said out in the playground that God doesn't exist?"

Silent, the class was shocked. Most couldn't believe that Robert would have said such a thing.

"No. That isn't what I said," replied Robert. "I told Jane and Kathy that there wasn't any proof that he exists. That's different."

"How dare you!" shrieked Ruby, getting quickly to her feet.

She'd thought that Robert would be cowering before her, but his precise response hinted at ridicule. He was determined to stand his ground, drawing on the conviction that he had done no wrong. To Ruby, this was nothing other than defiance and in all her years at Armitage Street School, no pupil had ever dared do that before. It was crucial that his dissension wasn't allowed to spread.

"I teach children to believe here," she continued. "I don't care where you picked up your terrible and hateful ideas. You will not," she emphasised, "ever repeat them in this school again!"

Getting to her feet, Ruby came out from behind her desk to address the class.

"Children."

A tremor of collective voices weakly filled the room.

"Yes, Mrs Turner."

Turning round, she picked up two books from her desk, before facing the class once more. Taking one in each hand, Ruby held them out in front of her.

"These are all you need to guide you in life. A road atlas to find your way to unfamiliar places and the Holy Bible, to keep you on a straight path through your journey, with the good lord by your side."

Ruby paused, heightening the dramatic impact of her words, before continuing.

"Now you, Robert Wilson. You've got the devil in you and I won't have you filling the good children of this school with your poison!"

Placing the books back down on the desk, Ruby walked over to a large cupboard in the corner. The faint sighs of terrified children escaped quietly into the room, as they watched her opening the doors. Taking out a thin, long cane, Ruby walked slowly and deliberately towards Robert, caressing the fearsome instrument as she did so.

"Put out your hand!"

Robert began to raise his arm, but it wasn't quick enough for Ruby, who impatiently grabbed his hand. Ensuring that it was raised to the horizontal, she'd chosen the perfect position for the class to witness the full fury of the punishment.

Placing the tip of the cane on the palm of his hand, she let it linger. Then, ever so slowly, she raised it slightly and dropped it back against his hand, as if she were marking the exact spot where the blows would be delivered. She was toying with him now, taking a perverse pleasure out of making him wait; playing to the captive audience of children who were intensely watching her performance. After all, this classroom was her theatre and she the star of the show.

Meanwhile, Robert stood proud. Regardless of the pain he would suffer, he had resolved to show no signs of fear or distress. He would refuse to buckle to her will, unlike many before him who'd been reduced to tears.

As the cane swished down, there was a moment where Robert felt nothing. Then a sharp pain seared through his flesh; his hand tingling and burning as the second stroke soon followed. His fingers began to throb, his hand erupting like a fiery volcano.

Satisfied with the surgical precision of her strikes, Ruby looked closely at the young boy before her. But his head was raised, his jaw set firm, his eyes blazed defiance. This wasn't the reaction she'd so confidently expected. Instead of a whimpering wretch shuddering beneath her majestic, terrifying power, she was face to face with a rebel who could, if she weren't careful, assume the mantle of a hero, whose actions would inspire other pupils to similar acts of disobedience. Intuitively, Ruby understood that her authority was on the line.

Sensing her hesitation, Robert withdrew his hand. After all, he knew from experience that two strokes of the cane were considered adequate to bring wayward pupils into line. Yet the drama hadn't played out. It had become a battle of wills and Robert had removed his hand without the permission of his teacher.

"How dare you show me such disobedience. I've not finished with you yet. Put out your hand!"

Groans of despair slipped from the lips of the braver souls within the class. Their hopes for Robert's 'victory', now seemed to have been dashed. After all his steely determination, his resolute refusal to cry out, it seemed that Robert, like all the rest, was destined to fail. Surely, he couldn't take any more. Ruby would break him and with that, their own desperate hopes of tempering her tyranny, would shatter too.

Yet they had reckoned without a saviour, for Kay was about to spring to his defence. For her too, it had become a matter of principle. She was determined that Robert would strike a blow for them all. He must not bend to Ruby's will. But just how much more could he take? Throwing herself into the breach, she jumped from her desk, rushed forward and placed herself between her comrade and their enemy.

"No. Enough! You've hit him enough!" she shouted.

Looking on in amazement, Kay's classmates had no idea from where she had found her courage. Kay was facing down a terrible bully, without a thought for the consequences.

Ruby was astonished too and for what seemed like an age, she stared at her young protagonist. Then, taking a step back, she began to raise her cane. Kay pushed Robert out of the way, preparing to take the blow herself. The class watched on with bated breath. Caning a girl was surely a step too far, even for Ruby, but there were few who doubted that she would do it.

The class were never to find out. Mr Chandler, outside in the corridor, had heard Kay shouting and had looked through the glass at the top of the classroom door as she and Ruby had confronted one another. Entering, he acted quickly to defuse the situation.

"Could I see you outside for a minute please, Mrs Turner?"

Surprised, Ruby turned to see the headteacher stood in the doorway. Lowering the cane, she quickly gathered her thoughts.

"Yes, of course," she replied.

Facing the class, she confidently reaffirmed her control.

"Get your reading books out and get on with them quietly, whilst I talk to Mr Chandler. And I mean quietly! And you two," she continued, looking harshly at Kay and Robert, "stay there."

There was the subdued sound of over thirty desks being carefully opened and books placed on top of their closed lids. Heads were soon bowed over them as the children eagerly showed their compliance with their teacher's wishes. Mr Chandler's appearance indicated that events were seriously out of control. All thoughts of solidarity dissipated, as the pupils realised that now, it was everyone for themselves.

Kay and Robert watched as Chandler held the door open to allow Ruby to enter the corridor. Following her out, he closed it behind them. It was impossible to hear their conversation, but watching them closely through the classroom door, it was clear that Ruby was getting quite animated. The conversation over, she came back into the classroom wearing a satisfied look. Kay and Robert could only assume that she'd convinced Chandler to punish them further.

"Robert Wilson, Kay Thompson. Mr Chandler wants to see you in his office."

Both looked at her.

"Now! Right away!" she added, emphatically.

Leaving the room, they saw Chandler waiting for them just down the corridor. As they approached him, his face showed no trace of either displeasure or disappointment.

"Come on you two," he said, calmly. "Let's go to my office and get to the bottom of what's been going on."

Following him, the friends exchanged encouraging glances. Chandler's words and demeanour suggested that he had by no means accepted their teacher's version of events. Perhaps he would give them a fair hearing. Nevertheless, it wouldn't alter their approach. Kay and Robert had come too far now and weren't prepared to give way. They were determined to air their grievances.

Chapter 7

Stood before Chandler's desk, Robert recounted the details of the conversation in the playground that had led him to be called out before the class. The head listened carefully, only interrupting to clarify certain details. He then asked Kay to tell him about the caning of Robert and explain to him why she had got involved. When Kay had finished, Chandler leaned back in his chair, rubbed his forehead and sighed.

"You've both learned today, what I'm sure you already suspected. Sometimes other people aren't open-minded; as prepared to listen to different views, as we are. It's something that intelligent and inquisitive children like you, have to learn to deal with. Do you know what I mean when I say that 'discretion may prove the better part of valour'?"

The two of them nodded.

"That sometimes you have to hold back on saying what you believe, if it's likely to put you in an awkward situation," explained Kay.

"But we were talking quietly. We didn't know that Kathy and Jane were listening," explained Robert.

"Yes, I know," said Chandler, "which tells you that sometimes you have to be even more careful."

"But if something's the truth, then shouldn't we always be prepared to say it?" asked Kay.

Chandler smiled. How clever and confident, he thought and still only fourth year juniors.

"Sometimes the truth upsets people," he replied. "Perhaps it causes difficulties. It isn't always easy to know when to speak it. As you move on from here, you'll be getting lots of teachers for different subjects. With all of them though, you'll need to work out how far you can challenge them and act accordingly. You've learned with Mrs Turner that she doesn't take kindly to anyone questioning her religion."

"Yes, we have," said Kay, "but it's not the only reason that being in her class is difficult. Mrs Turner is unfair. Especially to the boys. They get far harder punishments."

"Most teachers do the same," replied Chandler. "Boys are seen as more troublesome and of course, more able to take physical punishment than girls."

"It's more than that," added Robert. "Mrs Turner makes them stand up in front of the class. She says horrible things about their clothes, even though she knows their families can't afford to buy new ones."

"Peter Wragg's dad had a really bad accident," explained Kay. "His mam can't work. She has to stay at home to look after him and the baby. They don't have much money, so Peter's clothes are old and tatty. Mrs Turner bullies him; hits him when he's done nothing wrong. It's because he's so poor and because his parents never come to school to stop her doing it."

"Yes. Because Peter's poor, Mrs Turner thinks he doesn't count and it's wrong," insisted Robert.

"I see," said Chandler, quietly.

He looked closely at Kay and Robert. He recognised their innate sense of justice, intensified by the harsh realities of their environment. They weren't just fighting for themselves, but on behalf of their classmates too. Ruby's conduct left a lot to be desired, but it wasn't enough for Chandler to take strong action. The education committee certainly wouldn't have backed him; they would applaud her tough, disciplined approach. The staff would fear more challenges to their authority. Nevertheless, the head felt that he owed Kay and Robert a greater degree of protection. It was his responsibility to find a solution that would keep the school running as smoothly as possible. A compromise had to be found that would suit all parties and Chandler believed he had one.

"It's only a short time now, before you leave us," he noted. "I've been looking at our old school records and I'd like to catalogue them. Get them into some kind of order and follow up interesting events and pupils from the school's past. You two could help me do that over the next few weeks. You wouldn't be in your regular classes with 4A of course and you would be working with the records here in my office. I might arrange with the staff at Ardwick Library for you to go there too. You may have to do some research. Would you be interested?"

Chandler could tell from the way their eyes lit up, that his offer had been well received.

"I'd definitely like that," confirmed Robert.

"Does it mean that we won't be in any more of 4A's lessons until the end of term?" asked Kay.

"I'm afraid so," replied Chandler.

Kay knew that he had played her question with the straightest of bats. He was determined to maintain the pretence that his offer wasn't a device to get them away from Ruby. Her subsequent smile let him know, that she wasn't fooled. Yet Kay made no comment. It was an indication that she had taken his earlier words to heart; when to challenge and when to remain silent.

"Well, that's all agreed," continued Chandler "and your first task, will be to follow up on this chap."

Chandler picked up an old and dusty book from the edge of his desk. He opened it up, flicked through the pages and finding the ones he wanted, laid it back down on the table.

"Now you two have a look at this and tell me what you think it is."

Examining the double page spread in front of them, Kay and Robert could see a long list of names and addresses, together with dates dealing with times of birth, admission and departure. There were also details of parents listed. It related to children in 1898 and 1899.

"It's a school register of pupils at the end of the last century," said Kay.

"Yes, but which school?" asked Chandler, looking at Robert.

"This one."

"How do you know?"

"Because the addresses are all from the streets around here," continued Robert.

"But we aren't the only school around here," suggested Chandler.

"It has to be our school," insisted Kay, "because it mentions Ross Place and Thomas Street in the 'Last School Attended' column. Those pupils came from there to here."

"Excellent! I can see that I've made a wise choice in picking you two to help me. Now, have a look down the list of names. Is there anything that stands out?"

Kay and Robert craned their heads over the register once more and worked down the list of pupils. Halfway down the page, they looked at one another in surprise. There, admitted on January 9th 1899, was the name Charles Chaplin. But was it the famous actor and comedian? They began to talk excitedly to one another, oblivious of Chandler's presence. Looking across the page, they could see that his last school was in London and he only stayed at Armitage Street until February 22nd. They began to discuss ideas about why this may be, before Chandler drew them back to his original question.

"Well, what do you think?"

"It's Charlie Chaplin," said Robert.

"We thought it might be someone with the same name, but we can see that he came here from London, but only stayed a short time. We think it must be him. Are we right?" asked Kay.

"Yes, you are," replied Chandler, smiling. "And you were thinking of lots of good questions to find out more about why he was here. It's always interested me that his address is given as 64 Morton Street. That's over the other side of Hyde Road. It's nearer Ross Place, but his mother brought him here. Just think of all the things he achieved after he left Armitage Street and look on it as a challenge to yourselves. Make the best of your talents like Chaplin did. Great people have come from these streets. There's no reason why living in the less privileged parts of the city, should stop anyone from making their mark."

Chandler hoped that his words would prove as inspiring as his decision to take Kay and Robert out of 4A. Removed from the inevitable vindictiveness of Mrs Turner, they had been given the opportunity to carry out some interesting and valuable work. The decision also went down well with Ruby. To the members of 4A, she declared that their exclusion from lessons, was the severest of punishments. Importantly, she didn't lose face, as none of their peers questioned the logic of her claim. Chandler could congratulate himself for finding the perfect compromise.

On their way home back from school, the two friends went over the events of the day. In particular, they talked about Mr Chandler and his resolution of their situation.

"I think we can say that it's worked out well," said Robert. "We don't have to put up with Ruby anymore and the work that Mr Chandler's giving us, looks really interesting."

"Yes, I suppose so," replied Kay, "although he hasn't really dealt with Ruby, has he?"

"No, you're right Kay. He hasn't. Then again, I'm not too mithered about that now. We can go into school until the holidays and we don't have to worry about a thing. I couldn't put up with Ruby and her lessons any longer. At least in September, we get lots of teachers, so if any of them are like Ruby, you only see them for a short time. You can put up with it."

"The only thing is," insisted Kay, "that Mr Chandler hasn't made Ruby change. She'll be exactly the same with all the kids she teaches for as long as she's at the school. She'll keep bullying boys like Peter and getting away with it."

"That's why I'm happy for us," reasoned Robert. "Mr Chandler wasn't going to be able to do anything about Ruby, but at least he's helped us. He was right. There's a lot of teachers like her and he can't deal with all of them. Lots of people think that kids need a good hiding to make them behave. They'd all agree with Ruby, wouldn't they?"

"What I've learned Robert is that it's daft to believe that people in charge can always put right the things that are wrong. Mr Chandler must have had some idea of what Ruby was like. We've got out of her lessons because you stood up to her. That was the reason."

"You did as well Kay."

"But it was you who made the first move."

"And both of us who complained to Mr Chandler about her. If you hadn't backed me up Kay, I wouldn't have got anywhere on my own."

"Yes and all this tells us that we have to keep standing up for ourselves, because if we don't, then anyone can just walk all over us."

"That's right," said Robert. "I've been thinking," he continued. "When Ruby was going to cane me again and you came out and told her to stop, would you have tried to hold her back, if Mr Chandler hadn't come in?"

Kay stopped. His question had surprised her.

"I'm not sure, but I suppose that I would have done. All I could think about was stopping her from hurting you. She really wanted to, Robert."

"I know that all right," replied Robert, grinning. "My hand didn't half hurt."

"Someone should do it to her," said Kay. "Let her know what it feels like. Then she might not be so keen to do it to others."

"You know Kay, it's the second time now that you've rescued me. It's becoming a habit. I think you've become my guardian angel."

"Don't call me that. Ruby might think we've seen the light. ♫Hallelujah. Hallelujah♫"

Robert joined in with the singing before the two of them finally burst out laughing.

Chapter 8

It was the last Saturday in June. There were just three weeks to go before the start of the school holidays, but neither Kay nor Robert, were experiencing the sense of expectation that normally came at this time of year. The reason was simple. That morning, their parents would receive the letter informing them whether or not they had passed the eleven plus. If so, they would be given a list of grammar schools from which they could choose one to attend. For most of the week, Kay and Robert had felt nervous, regardless of the fact that after taking the exams, they were confident they had done well. They had answered the questions without difficulty, unlike the majority of their classmates. Yet, eager to get to grammar school, they began to fear that something would go wrong. Once again, their friendship was crucial. Sharing the same aspirations and fears, they encouraged and reassured one another through those tense final days, before the envelope containing their fate, would finally arrive.

When the postman delivered the envelope to Kay's home at eight-thirty that morning, there was a mixture of tension and excitement in the air. Ernest's shift didn't start until that afternoon and he was pleased that he would know right away how his daughter had done. He confidently expected her to pass, as did Ethel, but until the letter was opened and it was confirmed in writing, that slight hint of nervousness, wouldn't be dispelled.

Picking the letter up off the doormat, Ethel twisted it in her hands and read the typed address. Now in her early thirties, she felt quietly confident about Kay's prospects, certain that it would prove a landmark day for her family. Ethel was proud of both her daughters who, it was frequently remarked, had inherited her own good looks.

"This must be it," she announced calmly to Kay and Ernest, who had followed her into the hallway when they'd heard the clatter of the letter box.

"Let's go and sit down," she suggested.

Walking through to the kitchen, they sat at the table where Joan was still eating her breakfast cereal.

"Here Ernest. You open it," said Ethel, handing the envelope to her husband.

Ernest looked at his daughter. He could see that she was starting to get impatient, desperate to know her fate.

"Here goes then."

Kay watched as Ernest carefully opened the envelope, ensuring he didn't damage the letter inside. Her heart began to thump in her chest. She felt nervous and uncomfortable. It seemed difficult to breathe. Her dad seemed to be taking an age, until finally he had the letter out, opened it up and then silently glanced at its contents. Seeing a broad smile break out across his face, she didn't need the confirmation of words. It alone told her everything. She had passed.

"She's done it!" announced Ernest, excitedly.

"Oh, love!"

Leaning across towards Kay, Ethel embraced her daughter. Sitting back, she looked at her husband.

"Well, Ernest. Are you going to read the letter out to us?"

Ernest did as she asked. It may have been a standard letter, but the list of schools at the end of it filled Kay's parents with pride. They knew that very few kids from Ardwick passed the eleven plus and went on to grammar school. Their daughter's achievement couldn't be underestimated. They were excited and eager to talk to Kay about which school she should choose to go to. For their daughter though, it was something that could wait. Once Kay knew that she had passed, there was only one thing on her mind.

"Mam, is it all right if I go to Robert's. I need to find out if he's passed too."

"Oh, I'm sure he will have love," said Ethel, reassuringly. "He's a clever lad. Your dad always says so. Don't you Ernest?"

"Aye. He's a bit too clever at times!" he replied, chuckling.

"I just hope so," continued Kay. "I know he'll be really upset if he hasn't."

"Well, you'd best get off and find out love. It's no good hanging about here, worrying yourself sick about it. But mark my words," said Ernest, "if he's not passed, then I'll show my arse on Ardwick Green."

"Ernest! What a thing to say in front of the girls."

"It's all right Mam. I don't mind," said Kay, trying her hardest not to laugh. "Anyway, it's not as if I haven't heard similar things before."

"Oh, really young lady?"

Ethel spoke sternly towards her daughter and Ernest realised that by coming to his defence, Kay had put herself in line for a telling off. Quickly, he attempted to smooth things over.

"Come on love, let our Kay get off. She's made us both proud this morning. It's a day for us to be happy and tonight we can all go to the pictures to celebrate."

"Me as well Dad?"

The question came from Joan. She had sat silently since the revelation of her elder sister's success and she was starting to feel a tinge of jealousy and vulnerability. It seemed to Joan as if she would always be in the shadow of her elder sibling.

"Of course, love. You don't think we'd leave you here on your own, do you?"

"Well, I'm not very good at school like our Kay, am I?" replied Joan, giving her dad a sullen look.

"Don't be like that love. You know that I love the two of you. I'm proud of you both and I always will be."

"I wouldn't want to go, if you didn't come," said Kay, warmly to her sister. "It wouldn't be any fun if you weren't there."

"Well then, it's all settled," said Ernest.

"I suppose it'll have to be," replied Ethel, shaking her head.

Ernest was relieved. He knew that in dealing with the girls, he was prone to sentimentality. Ethel, understanding the female psyche far better than he, thus took the responsibility for laying down the law. Although at times, this did prove frustrating, Ethel loved her husband deeply. Devoted and attentive, Ernest worked long hours and asked nothing for himself. Even though his hairline was receding and his waistline increasing, she saw only the handsome young man in uniform that had charmed her on the day they had met.

Promising her mam that she would look after it, Kay took the letter with her on the way to Robert's house. She told Ethel that she was likely to see many of her classmates and she was eager to compare it to the new schools that they had been offered. That was true, but only by keeping looking at the letter, could she finally accept that she had really passed. It was symptomatic of her unusual state of near nervous exhaustion.

Kay was right, many of her friends were out and about and they too were eager for news of how others had fared. Of those she spoke to, she was the only one given a choice of grammar schools, although a couple of girls had been offered places at Ardwick Technical High School. She was told however, that her old protagonists, Kathy Smith and Jane Morris, had also passed. Kay wasn't bothered if they chose a different school to her though and rather hoped that they did.

Reaching the gate to Robert's back yard, Kay paused to compose herself. Like her dad, she was confident that her friend had passed, but just in case, she wanted to be displaying no signs of excitement or satisfaction in case he hadn't.

Knocking on the door, it opened quickly and Robert appeared before her. For some time, the pair of them stood there, silently looking at one another. For Robert shared Kay's fear of delivering his own good news, should his friend have been unsuccessful. Finally, after what seemed like an age, a voice came from inside the kitchen.

"Come in love. Don't stand out there. We've been expecting you."

It was the unmistakable sound of Robert's gran.

Stepping back, Robert allowed Kay into the room and then shut the door behind him. His mam and gran were sat at the kitchen table and both had a big smile on their face. It was enough to tell Kay that Robert had also passed and instinctively she put her arm around him and gave him a hug. The affection the pair had for one another had always been obvious, but Edna and Irene only now understood how close the two of them truly were.

"I didn't think that either of you were going to say anything," remarked Edna. "It's a good job it's summer or we'd be freezing now with that door open."

"I was worried," explained Kay. "I didn't want to say anything in case I upset Robert."

"That was the same for me," added Robert. "That's why I couldn't speak either."

"What a gormless pair. Have you ever heard anything like it?" asked Edna, turning to Irene.

"No. I haven't," replied her daughter. "And to say that they're supposed to be clever; part of Manchester's finest."

"Well, perhaps in some ways," declared Edna.

The two women began to laugh, but Robert and Kay recognising the pair's good-natured repartee, glanced at one another and simply shook their heads.

As Edna and Irene settled down and began to talk about the future, it was clear to Kay that they were made up with Robert's success. They were excited and proud. Like her own parents, they were already beginning to worry about the choice of school and sorting out the purchase of a uniform, something that hadn't been necessary at primary school. Robert though, was eager to talk to Kay and asked his mam, if it was all right for the pair of them to go out. Smiling, Irene agreed.

"Of course, love. The two of you'll want to get some fresh air. You can put your worries behind you. You've both passed and they can't take your places away from you now."

Heading up Gregory Street, the pair talked excitedly about what lay in store for them in September. By the time they reached Bennett Street and sat on the rails that bordered the 'Rec', the inevitable question could no longer be avoided.

"Why is it, that we have to go to separate schools?" asked Robert.

"Because they only have single sex grammars," replied Kay, bluntly.

"But it makes no sense. All the junior schools take boys and girls, so why not the senior schools?"

"Because the education committee are barmy. That's why."

"And the Government," added Robert.

The two of them stared over towards St Benedict's Church and back along Bennett Street towards Heywood House. They watched as people scurried back and forth, coming or going to the shops on Hyde Road. And from behind them came the excited voices of young footballers, honing their skills from dawn to dusk. Imaginations fired, the 'Rec' transcended and kids transformed. Heroes of City or United. The sun was climbing into a cloudless sky. It was going to be hot and hanging on the breeze, they began to detect the noxious aroma of the Black Brook.

Walking on, Kay returned to their new situation in September.

"It only means that we won't see each other during school. We'll have the evenings, weekends and holidays."

"Yes, I suppose so."

"Well, you know that you're always going to need me around to keep an eye on you."

Kay looked mischievously at Robert. He smiled. They felt comfortable. Attending different schools, although unwelcome, wasn't going to break the closest of friendships.

Chapter 9

The matter of Robert's school uniform was quickly addressed by Irene, for the following Friday night the weekly visit from the 'tick man' was expected.

Budgeting for kids' clothes, especially the new outfits traditionally worn during Whit Week, would have been nigh on impossible without local retailers who extended credit on weekly terms. It was commonly known as 'buying on tick'. The company favoured by many, both in Ardwick and beyond, was 'Stewarts'. They had large showroom premises on the corner of Brunswick Street, where mothers would take their kids to be fitted out. Stewarts were one of the few stores authorised to accept uniform grant cheques. These were issued by Manchester Corporation to the neediest of families. This gave Stewarts a further opportunity to raise their prices, knowing that they had few competitors. Customers received a small booklet in which payments were recorded by a collector who called weekly at the house. Once a family had established its ability to maintain regular payments, more credit would be extended to them.

At six-thirty, as regular as clockwork, a knock came to the kitchen door. When Robert opened it, he saw the familiar figure of George Fitch waiting on the back steps.

"Hello, young man. Is your mam in?"

George knew that she would be. This wasn't one of those families that refused to answer the door; embarrassed at being 'short' this week, or simply wanting to withhold their money.

"Tell him to come in," called out a voice from the kitchen.

"Mam says, come in," repeated Robert, standing back to allow George to get past.

"Thank you."

George walked inside and stood by the table. In the corner, near the sink, Irene was holding a tea towel, in the process of drying some pots. Sat on the settee at the far side of the room, Edna was reading the *Evening Chronicle*.

"Good evening, ladies. Are you both keeping well?"

"Not too bad," replied Edna.

"Hasn't the weather been good? We've been spoiled," continued George.

"It's about time though," suggested Edna.

"Well, that's true," replied George. "I suppose we'll have to take advantage of it whilst we can."

George was a master when it came to engaging in small talk. It was a key tool of the job, necessary to break the ice with new customers and re-engage with his regulars. It created a positive ambience, so important to maintain a healthy relationship with his customers and so encourage them to take more credit. In George's ideal world, he would never lose a customer as they would always turn to Stewarts whenever they needed something new.

A stout man in his early sixties, George always looked immaculate. He wore a fashionable grey trilby, which covered the majority of his fine, white hair. He had a kindly face, clean shaven, with a ruddy nose, that Edna insisted showed his liking for port wine. He wore a stylish beige raincoat, underneath which was a smart grey suit, white shirt and dark blue tie. On his feet were a pair of polished black brogues. George had been with Stewarts for many years, becoming their most trusted collector and particularly successful at finding solutions to help hard pressed customers pay their accounts. Their desire to keep him had resulted in his elevation to management, as the company expanded its operations. Yet, old habits die hard and George insisted on keeping his Friday round, arguing that it kept him in touch with the customers; crucial to keep the business moving as they approached the likelihood of changing times.

Now at the table, Irene invited George to join her. Sitting down, he placed his satchel beside him. Receiving Irene's money, he entered it in the payment book, initialled the entry and handed it back to her.

"You've nearly paid it off now Mrs Wilson."

"Yes, I have. But wouldn't you know it, as soon as you've paid for one thing, you almost certainly need another."

George shook his head sympathetically. He knew what was coming.

"I'm going to have to ask if I can take on some more credit."

"Why's that, Irene?"

"Our Robert. He's passed his eleven plus and he's going to grammar school," she proudly declared.

"Now that's good news. Well done lad," said George, turning towards Robert. "I didn't realise you were so clever."

"Oh, he certainly is that. His dad would've been proud of him."

Robert blushed. Self-effacing, it caused him embarrassment when his mam praised him to friends and family.

"Which school are you going to?" asked George.

"It's not settled yet," replied Robert's mam, not allowing her son a chance to speak for himself. "We've chosen Central from the list they sent us and we're waiting to hear back."

"Oh, I'm sure you'll get it, nearly all the lads who pass from Ardwick end up there. It's the nearest boys' grammar. You're lucky too. We're not official stockists for Central, but they accept boys wearing our blazers, shirts and trousers. It means that you'll only need to buy a blazer badge and sports kit from the approved retailer."

"Who's that?"

"For Central, it's Horne Brothers in town. You'll find them a lot more expensive than us."

"Yes. I've no doubt," sighed Irene.

"I hope I'm not offending you Mrs Wilson," continued George, "but did you know that as a war widow you can apply to the education committee for a uniform grant? It covers the basics, but not everything Robert's going to need and at Stewarts we're authorised to take them."

George knew that his customers were proud. They didn't like to accept any type of assistance if it was seen as 'scrounging'. Yet the small minority of working-class kids who made it to grammar school, were distinctively disadvantaged against the majority of their middle-class peers. The latter's families were far more able to afford the expense of uniform, equipment and excursions. George wanted kids like Robert to get every bit of assistance going.

"Well, at least that's something," replied Irene. "We could do with the help."

"Well, when they confirm Robert's place, I'll write you out a credit note and you can bring him down and we'll sort him out. You'll want him to make a good impression when he gets there; smart in appearance, smart in life."

"That's what I always say," replied Irene "and what his dad would have said too. He was used to all that 'spit and polish' in the Army. Didn't like it, but always said that it set standards and encouraged you to do your best at everything. Only thing is, uniforms don't come cheap and these schools don't give a thought to the needs of ordinary working families, do they?"

"No, they don't, but think of how proud you and his gran will be when he sets off for school on the first day of term."

"Oh, we will be," agreed Edna.

"Remember, the lad's worked hard. He deserves it. And I always tell parents this…"

George paused and looked at Irene intently.

"… that you've got to think of it as an investment. The money you're paying out now is getting an education that opens up a world of opportunities for the lad. Who knows, one day he might be buying you a big house out in Cheshire. Hey, lad?"

He turned and looked at Robert, who was suitably impressed. He recognised that George was sharp; the smoothest of operators and slickest of salesmen. Always ready with the perfect turn of phrase. Polite, almost to the point of being deferential, he rarely dealt in first name terms, no matter how long he had known his regulars. 'The customer is always right', was no meaningless mantra as far as George was concerned; he had built his career on the back of it. He was well-liked by his patrons and the man to go to when special purchases needed to be made.

Getting up from the table, George bade his farewells and then was gone. The matter of the uniform was settled.

Chapter 10

When September arrived and the new term began, Kay and Robert's separation wasn't quite as bad as they'd thought. The education committee had granted their preferred choices. Kay joined Central High School for Girls, whilst Robert would be attending Central Grammar School for Boys. These were adjoining schools that shared the same large building on Whitworth Street, just a short distance from Piccadilly. It meant that Robert would call for Kay at half-past seven in the morning and they would set off for school together. From Bennett Street it was well over a mile to travel, but they usually opted to walk, only occasionally taking a bus. At the end of lessons, they would meet in the small public park with its attractive trees and flowerbeds, sandwiched between the schools and Sackville Street. An oasis of calm amidst the hustle and bustle of central Manchester.

The school building was huge and could comfortably house the two establishments. With classrooms arrayed across five floors, its tall chimneys and ornamental towers accentuated its height. Opened at the turn of the century, it was a reflection of municipal pride; a belief in the importance of education. It had an impressive frontage along Whitworth Street and extended back over a hundred yards along Chorlton Street. Inside, the girls and boys were kept very much apart. Doors on every floor provided access between their respective areas, but these were locked at all times. Outside in the school yard, a high brick wall symbolised the determination to keep the genders apart and woe betide anyone who tried to look out of the upper classroom windows to take a peek at the pupils next door. Only sixth formers were allowed to leave the premises during the dinner hour, when fraternisation with their neighbours was reluctantly condoned.

Unfortunately for Kay's parents, Central High were far less flexible about their uniform arrangements. It meant that they had to buy everything from 'Henry Barry' in St Anne's Square. The location reflected the prices and when Kay had been measured up and all the items off the uniform list had been gathered together, the cost was considerable. Ethel had suggested that she could look for some cheaper, alternative items to meet the school's requirements, but Ernest would have none of it. He wouldn't allow his daughter to stick out in 'cheap clothes' and face the possible ridicule of other girls. Ernest was all too aware of the snobbery of the middle classes, which extended to the teachers too. He hoped that the latter would judge Kay solely on her ability and not on her working-class origins. He hoped that by having the correct uniform, it would make it easier for Kay to fit in.

When Robert called on her that first morning, he was amazed at how different she looked. Seeing the surprise on his face, Kay incorrectly assumed that his opinion mirrored her own.

"I know," she said, with a sigh, "it's this silly hat. I'm going to take it off and not put it back on until we get near the school."

"No, it looks nice, you should leave it on. Anyway, you'll get in trouble if you don't wear it."

"I don't think so," said Kay, dismissively. "Who's going to tell them?"

"You never know," insisted Robert.

"Don't be daft."

Robert thought she looked very pretty in her hat, with her hair curling softly underneath it. And the rest of her uniform too, for he was suddenly aware of a gentle femininity that he'd not observed in the past. Underneath her navy blazer, with its black and green corded edge and MCHS badge on the pocket, Kay was wearing a green gymslip with its pleated skirt, over a pristine, pressed blouse. How differently the outfit was regarded by boys and girls. The latter, especially as they got older, saw it as restrictive, unfashionable and resented having to wear it. It reflected their school's repressive regime. They could never empathise with boys who found the sight of a pretty girl in uniform, so alluring.

It wasn't long before Robert discovered that once he left his own familiar streets, the Central Boys uniform turned him into a marked man. The route to school down Hyde Road, along Ardwick Green, Downing Street and on to London Road, passed through areas where there were few grammar school lads like himself. The secondary moderns, recognising the limited budgets of poorer families, didn't insist on pupils wearing expensive uniforms, so most of their children didn't. Walking back from school, Robert stuck out as a 'posh' grammar boy deserving of a battering. Whilst with Kay, the secondary modern toughs wouldn't attack, but if he were on his own, on the days her class were taken to Hough End to play hockey, he soon found out that he was fair game.

It was a group of lads from the school on Mansfield Street that were the biggest problem. At first it was name calling. Pretending not to hear them and hurrying along the pavement, seemed to be enough to keep him safe. Kay advised her friend that merely intimidating him wouldn't be enough for these lads and she told him to catch the bus home when she wasn't with him. Yet Robert ignored her advice and then found that he was being surrounded and jostled; derided for being too 'stuck up' to talk to them and he knew that matters were coming to a head. He thought hard about what he should do. Deep down, he knew that Kay was right, but he wanted to prove to himself that he could confront them. It was time to stand up to the bullies.

The next time, there were four of them. He reckoned that they were one or two years older than himself and his plan was to pick out the one he perceived to be the weakest. That seemed obvious, as there was a thin, sickly-looking lad who seemed to be hanging back a little more than the rest. Suddenly, Robert stopped on the pavement and dropped his satchel.

"Okay, you win," said Robert suddenly. "But one against four's not right."

"Ha. It speaks," observed the tallest.

The other boys laughed, responding to their leader's quip.

Robert looked at him. He was sporting a black crew cut and a chipped front tooth that was revealed as his lips curled into the inevitable sneer. He looked mean and there was nowhere to run. Yet Robert was determined.

"Yes," he continued. "I'll take one of you on. Right now."

He turned and looked directly at the sickly kid.

"How about you?" he asked. "I'll fight you."

"Why not me?" said the leader, smiling with evil intent.

"What's wrong with him? You're all older than me. Doesn't he fancy it?"

Robert had put his intended opponent in an impossible situation. If the lad let his leader take the fight, the others would see him as 'mard'. He'd never be allowed to forget it.

"I'm ready anytime," said the lad, with real bravado. "Let's go."

Robert took off his blazer and tie and put them on his satchel. Stepping away from them, he faced his opponent whilst the other lads placed themselves around them. At that moment, he felt a sense of satisfaction. He had thought quickly on his feet and he'd forced the lad into doing what he wanted. Or so he thought. For, putting up his fists, ready to fight, he was suddenly rushed by all four boys who quickly knocked him to the ground and proceeded to kick him. Instinctively he curled into a ball to protect himself the best he could. Fortunately, the blows ceased. He heard shouts and the sound of rapidly retreating footsteps and then felt a reassuring hand on his arm. Raising his head he saw a young woman, who asked him if he was all right. Getting gingerly to his feet, he checked himself over.

"No real damage done," said Robert, bravely.

The two were then joined by the lady's husband. He had seen the confrontation and had chased the boys away. Thanked by Robert, they walked with him to the corner of Hyde Road to make sure he was suffering no ill effects.

After tea, when Robert went to see Kay, he related his experience and found that she was unsympathetic.

"I told you to take the bus when you were on your own," she admonished. "But you didn't listen, did you?"

"But the four of them attacked me when they'd agreed to it being one against one."

Noting his bewilderment, Kay began to laugh.

"Well, thanks a lot for the sympathy."

"Don't sulk," replied Kay, firmly. "Only you could have been so gormless as to think that those lads would fight fair. Don't you remember me telling you that they don't follow the Marquess of Queensbury rules in Ardwick?"

"Or Chorlton-on- Medlock too," added Robert.

Once more, Kay burst into laughter. This time Robert joined in. She had been tough on him, but she was right. He accepted that what had happened was almost inevitable. He should have taken the bus and it would all have been avoided. Yet Robert still felt the need to justify himself.

"Just for once," he explained, "I wanted to show that I could stand up for myself. That I could fight off the bullies."

"Show who?" asked Kay.

"Well, myself and …"

"And me?"

Kay looked at him closely. Embarrassed, he turned away, but when she spoke, her words were reassuring.

"When it comes to fighting, you don't need to impress me or anyone else. I said, when you stood up for Mac and challenged Ruby, that you showed different types of bravery. I don't think any less of you because you'll never be the 'Cock of Ardwick'. In fact, you're my best friend because you aren't like that. Boys who want to prove themselves by fighting all the time, don't impress me. And Robert Wilson, you're cleverer than that."

Robert looked at her sheepishly. He realised how stupid he'd been. It wasn't through his fists that he would escape the limited horizons imposed by his environment, but through his intelligence.

"The main thing is that you didn't get badly hurt," said Kay, at last showing some sympathy.

"I suppose so."

"What are you going to do in future when you're on your own?" asked Kay.

"I'm going to catch the bus."

Robert smiled and once again, the pair set off laughing.

It wasn't long before they had another girl from Kay's class accompanying them on the walk to school and it was a name that was surprising. Jane Morris, their old adversary, had gone to Central High without her old friend Kathy Smith. The latter's parents had moved to Burnage and had insisted that their daughter go to nearby Levenshulme Girls Grammar. It had come as something of a shock to Jane, who arrived at Central on the first day, feeling rather nervous. As the new girls had gathered in the school hall to be allocated their forms, Kay had noticed how timid and isolated Jane appeared. When it became apparent that the two of them would be in the same class, Kay offered to sit with her. With Kay's forgiving nature, everything that had happened in the past was forgotten and the two girls became the firmest of friends. It inevitably meant that Jane became friendly with Robert too and as they got older and advanced through their respective schools, Kay found it amusing that Jane, once so hostile to Robert, was becoming increasingly affectionate towards him.

Kay had found Chandler's advice about how to deal with different teachers useful, as there were certainly more than a few strange ones in her time at Central. Detentions could be easy to acquire and rules were rigorously enforced by most of the staff. At the first assembly, the pupils were warned about wearing their hats. Roberts fears about informants quickly proved true, as the headmistress called out girls in subsequent assemblies who'd been reported for uniform infringements. The intimidating atmosphere in the school hall was such, that girls would step forward to admit their guilt, even when there was no evidence against them. Kay however, took it all with a pinch of salt. She knew that in return for all the regimentation, she was getting a very good education. Throughout it all, her parents were a constant source of encouragement and she was determined to repay the faith that they had shown in her. Consequently, although Kay stood up to her teachers if she felt it right to do so, she was never going to become a rebellious student.

The established routine of working together in Ardwick Library, continued for Kay and Robert. Being in separate schools made no difference. Robert would call for Kay after tea and off they would go. The pair found it interesting to see the different approaches to the common topics they studied and to explore others not covered by their own teachers. Relying on one another for encouragement and inspiration, they had a shared enthusiasm for learning. The pair were investing heavily in each other's progress. It wasn't long before they had mapped out their ambition to progress into the sixth form and on to university.

At weekends and during the holidays, Kay and Robert were invariably together. It may just be hanging around the flats or on the Rec. Perhaps a walk to Debdale Park, or their usual trips to the museums and galleries. Once they were thirteen, the pair quickly got part-time jobs. On Saturdays Kay worked at Scotts on Hyde Road. Thanks to his mam constantly badgering George Fitch, Robert was taken on by Stewarts. The money helped them go to the pictures or dancing, as Kay especially loved jiving. At first, Robert was a poor dancer, but Kay refused to let him give up. As his confidence increased and he became more proficient, Robert found that at youth club dances some of Kays friends, especially Jane, were prepared to take the floor with him. For Kay, there was never a shortage of partners. Dancing at a competitive level, there were lots of boys eager to perform with her. Yet she never stayed with any of them for long. It may be that they had 'tried it on', or that they were big-headed. Mainly, it was because she wanted to keep improving; finding ever better partners to challenge and develop her skills.

When he and Kay had left Armitage School, Robert had been worried that it would lead to a decline in their friendship. His fears however, had proved groundless. Well into their fourth year at grammar school, the two of them had remained inseparable; a source of strength and support for one another. Whilst most of their primary school contemporaries were preparing to leave school and take employment, Kay and Robert were working towards their exams. They were Ardwick kids who were following a different path. Yet regardless of what the future may hold, Robert couldn't imagine it without Kay being with him too.

Chapter 11

Although surrounded by so many pretty girls, as Robert moved through his adolescent years, he increasingly doubted his ability to experience real intimacy with any of them. He'd met girls at youth club dances and even stolen a kiss from one or two, but that was as far as it had gone. School friends boasted of encounters with girls who were willing to let them go 'all the way', but no one really believed them. Nevertheless, this didn't dampen Robert's own fantasies of sexual fulfilment, regardless of the fact that he doubted whether they would ever become a reality.

Just after his sixteenth birthday, everything was about to change. It was because of his friendship with Bert and Johnny. Seventeen, they'd been working for two years as apprentices at Beyer Peacock Engineering in Gorton. There, exposed to the pranks and wit of the factory floor, the lads had quickly turned into a pair of likeable comedians. It was thanks to Kay, who knew them, that they'd adopted Robert as their friend. Crucially, they provided extra protection against the bullies. Once it became known that he was a pal of Bert and Johnny, the threats and intimidation stopped. One Saturday morning in May, the three of them were sat at the bottom of a stairwell at Heywood House, contemplating what to do with the rest of the day.

"I don't fancy yours much," said Bert, as a couple of girls walked past them.

"She's not mine," replied Johnny. "I'm with her friend. That's right, isn't it love?" he asked, looking at a slim, freckle faced girl with a tidy ponytail and a pretty smile. Her pleated skirt hugged her waist and billowed daintily down towards her ankles.

Stopping, the girl turned towards Johnny and smiled. Her friend, not as pretty, but certainly not unattractive, looked at her disapprovingly.

"Come on Rose. We need to get on."

"Don't be like that love," said Bert. "I was only joking."

"Well, I don't think it's funny."

Robert, watching on, was intrigued. Although the other girl was pulling on her arm, Rose had yet to decide whether she'd follow.

"We are going out tonight, aren't we?" asked Johnny. "What time shall I pick you up?"

Rose giggled and smiled.

"Well, I'm going if you're not."

Her friend, clearly frustrated, started to walk away.

"You didn't tell me what your name was," said Bert, as he started to follow her.

Stopping, the girl turned around.

"Get lost!"

"Oh, come on. Don't be mean. You'll like me once you get to know me. Everyone does."

Bert smiled. Robert could see that the girl's attitude was softening. Yet, he suspected that she wouldn't want to lose face, by proving susceptible to his charms. He was right. The girl looked at Bert rather haughtily, threw back her head, turned on her heel and tutting, continued to walk away.

"I suppose, I'd better get after her," said Rose, disappointed.

"You don't have to," suggested Johnny.

"I do. She's my friend and I can't leave her."

"Well, I live up there," said Johnny, pointing. "The one with the blue curtains on the second floor. Now you know where I am, you can call for me anytime."

"We'll see."

Rose smiled and Robert watched her longingly as she walked away. She was a pretty girl and he envied Johnny for his confidence when talking to her.

"How do you get away with it, Johnny?" asked Robert.

"Get away with what?"

"You know. That girl. She was lovely and you asked her out without any hesitation. A nice girl like that would belt me one if I dared say what you did."

"Poor kid, he's all frustrated," said Bert, sympathetically.

"We can't see him suffer like this. What can we do about it?" asked Johnny.

"I wonder," replied Bert, stroking his chin, deep in thought.

Robert assumed that they were ribbing him. It was what lads did and although it was good natured, he couldn't help but feel embarrassed. After all, he knew that Bert and Johnny had experienced what he hadn't. Robert was desperate for real intimacy with a girl.

"I know," said Johnny. "We'll get you in with Pauline."

"Ah. 'The initiation'. Good thinking," observed Bert, nodding his approval.

Robert looked confused.

"The initiation?" he asked.

Bert and Johnny smiled, exchanging knowing glances.

"You're a bit slow, aren't you kid?" remarked Bert.

"Slow?"

"Yes. Gormless in fact," added Johnny, for good measure.

Robert's face was blank. He didn't have a clue what they were talking about.

"Well," said Bert, turning to Johnny, "she'll certainly be able to put him straight on a few things."

"Has done for quite a few of us. Nothing wrong there though."

"No, definitely not."

They looked at Robert and laughed.

"Pauline's everyone's first experience …" Johnny began.

"Well, not everyone's," insisted Bert.

"Yes, but you know what I mean," continued Johnny.

The penny had dropped. Robert understood.

"She isn't on the batter, is she?" asked Robert.

"Why, would that make a difference?" asked Bert, grinning.

Robert hesitated. He wasn't sure.

His friends burst out laughing.

"Oh dear," said Johnny. "You really are desperate, aren't you?"

Robert could feel his cheeks going crimson. He was embarrassed and involuntarily looked away. It was all to the further amusement of his friends. Gradually however, their laughter subsided and they moved to reassure him.

"No," said Bert, quietly. "She isn't. Pauline is eighteen and she likes men."

"Oh, yes, she really likes men!" emphasised Johnny, smiling.

"You don't have to pay for it, if you know where to look," continued Bert. "Not all girls care about their reputation. They'll let you go much further than just a quick fumble, although I doubt you've even had that, have you?"

Robert's silence confirmed the fact.

"Well, luckily for you, Pauline always wants to cop off with a virgin. She loves it when it's your first time," said Johnny.

Robert was nervous, but excited. He felt sure that they weren't having him on, yet assuming it was true, he still wanted to know more about her. He wasn't sure he could just go with anyone.

"What's she like?"

"To look at?" asked Bert.

"Yes."

"We thought you were that desperate, you wouldn't care."

Robert observed his friends. With their deadpan expressions, they were giving nothing away. It seemed that they were keen to prolong his uncertainty. There was a long, silent pause, until Bert finally smiled.

"You're all right kid, she's not bad."

"And well endowed," added Johnny. "You won't be disappointed."

They watched as a faint smile flitted across Robert's face. His sense of relief was almost palpable.

"Well, erm, how do we go about setting it up?" asked Robert, uncertainly.

"You just leave all that to us," replied Johnny. "She lives near Bert. He'll sort it out."

"But where will we ..."

Robert's voice tailed off. He couldn't help feeling embarrassed about what they were planning, but needed to be sure that everything would run smoothly. He didn't want to be caught in a compromising situation, or have his family find out what he'd been up to.

"You'll go to her place. She lives with her mam on Exeter Street. It's the other side of Devonshire Street. It's well away from here," said Johnny.

"But what about her mam?"

"She works nights cleaning offices in town. You'll be all alone. You've nothing to worry about."

“It’s your big chance,” added Bert. “You’re not going to cry off now, are you?”

“No.”

Robert’s forthcoming liaison, was all agreed.

Chapter 12

The following Saturday, Bert informed Robert of the arrangements. On Wednesday evening, he would take him to Exeter Street at seven-thirty and then leave him in the capable hands of Pauline.

Until then, the plan had seemed rather fanciful, one that deep down, Robert felt would never come to fruition. Now a reality, Robert found his emotions in turmoil. Excitement, trepidation and fear impacted on him in equal measure. Yet most powerful of all were the cravings of desire which, as he anticipated the fateful appointment, threatened to overwhelm him.

He'd arranged to meet Bert outside St Matthew's Church. Waiting there, Robert suddenly panicked. He realised that he was stood almost opposite the bus depot. For a few moments he was afraid that Kay's dad would suddenly drive his bus out and see him there. Then, he gathered his wits about him. What if he did, he thought, how could he possibly know what I'm up to? Then, his mind began to speculate about the task before him. He was suddenly struck with the fear that the evening would end in personal failure; that he'd be unable to adequately perform. Dissatisfied, Pauline would tell Bert of his shortcomings and then he would become an object of ridicule to his friends. Robert began to think that it was perhaps better that he went home, but his friends had gone to a lot of trouble to organise the evening for him. It would be too difficult to back out.

Unsurprisingly, Robert felt relieved when he finally saw Bert walking up Devonshire Street towards him. There was no more room for doubt. He would simply have to go through with it. As they walked towards their destination, Bert put him at ease by making general conversation. As they entered the ginnel leading to Pauline's back yard, Robert suddenly stopped.

"What's the matter?" asked Bert.

"I've not come prepared. I don't have a …"

Robert was flustered, embarrassed to use the word.

"Don't panic. Pauline takes care of that. Do you think she wants you to get her up the duff?"

Robert shook his head. He was relieved, but felt stupid.

As they approached the steps to Pauline's back door, Robert's heart was pounding. He gulped in the air, desperate to calm down. His mind seemed to be racing at a hundred miles an hour. He was aroused and excited. He wondered if he was heading for a seizure. Watching him closely, Bert stopped and placed a hand on his arm.

"Robert, relax. Just listen to Pauline and you'll be fine."

Robert nodded his head.

"Okay then," said Bert. "Let's do it."

Mounting the first step, Bert knocked on the door. It wasn't long before it started to open. Stepping down, he moved aside and indicated that Robert should move forward. Approaching the step, Robert looked up. Stood in the doorway, was Pauline.

"Hi Pauline, this is Robert."

Pauline smiled.

"Yes, I can see. He's quite fit, isn't he?"

Bert laughed.

"Well, I'd best be getting off. I'll catch up with you later, Pauline."

With that, he was gone.

Pauline looked down at Robert. It was indicative of the understanding between them. She was, for the evening, unquestionably the senior partner. Yet Robert was by no means disappointed. Pauline was far more attractive than he'd expected. Her long, black hair framed a pretty face with attractive brown eyes and rosy lips. She was wearing a simple blouse and knee length skirt, both of which hugged her ample figure. Wearing heels, he could see her firm calves and slim ankles. Even if he hadn't been aware of the reason why he was there, as Robert's eyes eagerly drank in every detail of Pauline's alluring body, it would have been impossible for him not to feel the powerful stirrings of arousal.

"Well Robert. Are you going to stand there for ever?"

"Oh. No," replied Robert, hesitantly.

"Come in then."

Pauline smiled and stood aside. Her calm, confident manner, was reassuring. Robert found himself walking quickly up the steps and into the kitchen. As the door closed behind him, he knew that everything would be all right.

Chapter 13

It was Friday night. Robert had arranged to meet Bert and Johnny, his friends eager to hear about his experience. Robert had considered whether he should tell them. He remembered his assumption that if Pauline was prepared to go with him, then she couldn't have been at all attractive. He'd been too quick to accept the stereotype that portrayed a young woman who enjoyed sex outside marriage, as being no better than a 'pro'. Yet Pauline was indeed attractive and she had treated him with kindness and understanding. Even though he certainly wasn't her first, Pauline had still made him feel special. Nevertheless, intelligent as he was, there was an immaturity about Robert that, as the clock ticked by, made him eager to brag about his exploits. When he arrived at the flats to call for Johnny, he found Bert waiting there too. Making their way down to the bottom of the stairwell, they sat down, ready to discuss his night with Pauline.

To Robert's surprise, Pauline had beaten him to the punch. She had already given Bert a pretty detailed account of their night together.

"Well, you did all right, didn't you?" said Bert, with a smile.

Robert looked at him, confused.

"She was well satisfied. I have to admit, we weren't sure that you had it in you."

"That's right," Johnny added. "We were a bit worried that you might run away!"

Robert blushed, temporarily embarrassed, but their approval of his performance pleased him nonetheless. Yet he found it ironic that whilst he'd considered that it may be disrespectful to reveal details about Pauline, she had shown no such reticence in talking about him. She had turned the tables. She didn't care what anyone thought. Pauline enjoyed her liaisons and treated men in exactly the same way as they treated her. For a moment, Robert had the slightly unpleasant feeling that she had used him; that he had been her conquest. His ego soon recovered however, with the cheery comments and backslapping of his pals.

"That's it now," remarked Johnny. "The first time. No need to be nervous anymore. You've got your confidence. Pauline's shown you what you need to do. That was your initiation and there'll be no stopping you now."

And it was true. It wasn't long before Robert paid another visit to Pauline and following that there were encounters with other girls. Not all were prepared to give him what he wanted, but it never stopped him from trying. Without realising it, he developed a cavalier attitude towards girls and their feelings. For Robert, it was a game and once he'd taken everything he could get, he would cast them aside. His friends, responsible for setting him on his path, were surprised by the changes they witnessed. No longer shy or embarrassed, Robert would openly discuss his intimate encounters. Any thoughts about respecting the confidentiality of the girls he went with, were well and truly left in the past. "Crikey, is there any stopping you," Johnny had asked, in exasperation. "You need to tie a knot in it!"

All the while, Kay and Robert remained best friends. He would have liked to keep his encounters hidden from her, but it was inevitable that Kay would find out about his intimacy with other girls and in particular, his attempts to get amorous with some of her school friends. "He's just a randy get!" one of them explained, "but he's still cute."

As she got older, Kay sensed that Robert's feelings towards her went further than just friendship. He was always attentive and considerate, unable to disguise the fond and admiring glances he cast in her direction. When she had become aware of his dalliances with her friends, Kay had facetiously suggested that if he ever tried it on with her, he would receive short shrift.

"I know. You'd knock me into the middle of next week, if I ever did. I don't want to end up like Keith Clarke!"

The pair of them had set off laughing but it was clear that into their teenage years, the dynamic of their friendship would continue to be challenged. It was unusual for a boy and girl to be so uncommonly close, without them being romantically involved. There would surely come a time when one, if not both of them, would find a loving relationship with someone else. And when that happened, would it put their friendship on a lesser footing?

What Kay couldn't possibly understand, was just how deeply Robert's feelings ran for her. It didn't matter how many girls he'd already experienced, several of whom he'd been intimate with, only Kay did he truly desire. Robert loved those occasions when she put her hair into a simple ponytail. When they were out, he would endeavour to walk slightly behind her. Without Kay noticing, he would watch, almost mesmerised, as it swished from side to side, exposing the beautiful nape of her neck and the teasing loose strands of hair that danced across her beautiful, smooth skin. How he longed to bend forward and press his lips against it. Yet, he would never do such a thing without her permission.

Robert had placed Kay on a pedestal. He was unable to develop any real feelings for the girls he went out with; there were to be no lasting attachments to anyone else. No one, he believed, could possibly compare to his wonderful Kay.

Chapter 14

In August 1956, Kay and Robert were notified that they had passed the 'O' Levels needed to enter their respective sixth forms. The news was enthusiastically received by Ethel and Ernest, as well as Irene and Edna. Although they had always recognised the ability of their children, success on such a scale had, for so long, seemed unthinkable. What Kay and Robert had achieved was exceptional for youngsters from their background. It was only natural that until it actually happened, their families couldn't quite conceive of the idea that their loved ones could study 'A' Levels and go on to university. Ernest felt almost in awe of his daughter, whilst Irene took Robert's success as somehow justifying the sacrifice that his father had made, in helping to defeat the Nazis and bring forth a better world. Regardless of the strain of keeping their working age children in school, both families were convinced that the struggle would be worth it.

Kay and Robert were appreciative of that support. Bright, working-class scholars were invariably encouraged to leave school and find employment at the earliest opportunity, even before sitting their exams. A short-term contribution to the household finances, was seen by many parents as preferable to the long-term opportunities that lay in further education. Kay and Robert were well aware of this and helped their families the best they could. Working at weekends and taking other jobs during the holidays, meant that they were able to buy many of their own clothes, as well as pay for their entertainment and personal items.

To celebrate their exam success, the pair arranged to go jiving with some of their classmates at the Ritz. When Robert knocked on Kay's door, she was ready and waiting. He was stunned by how beautiful she looked. She was dressed simply. Functionally in fact, for Kay took her dancing seriously and wanted to move effortlessly around the dance floor. Kay was wearing a white blouse, unbuttoned at the top to display a pretty silver necklace that lay around her smooth, slender neck. Over her blouse, Kay was wearing a short, white, fitted cardigan. Kay's pale blue and white skirt hugged her slender waist and then billowed around her as it reached to just below her knees. The colours suited her perfectly. White ankle socks and black pumps, completed her outfit. Kay's choice of clothes emphasised her stunning figure and with her hair brushed back into a ponytail, Robert's eyes were drawn to her perfect cheekbones, cute nose and soft lips. Wearing just a hint of make-up, there was a freshness to her complexion. When she smiled, she simply sparkled.

"Do I look all right?" asked Kay.

Robert wanted to tell her that she looked beautiful, but that would only have made things awkward, so for a moment he was silent.

"Well?" asked Kay.

"Yes," replied Robert. "Your clothes look lovely."

It sounded like the response of a dispassionate observer, but when he looked at her again, he betrayed his true feelings. Robert could feel himself blushing and he was forced to turn away. Kay was pleased to note his reaction, but surprised too. She acted quickly to spare him any further embarrassment.

"I made the skirt at school," said Kay, rather matter-of-factly. "It's a pleated swing skirt. I used lots of material, so that it would billow out and swirl around when I'm dancing. It has to taper in at the waist so that it can do that. I was able to get the material from work. Mr Scott wouldn't let me pay for it. He said that I should consider it a thank you for being so reliable."

"That was good of him."

"Yes. He's very kind," replied Kay.

Setting off, they walked down to Hyde Road and then caught the first bus to Piccadilly. They had intended to get off at the junction of Whitworth Street and London Road. Kay however, was keen to have a memento of the day. Consequently, they travelled to the bus station on Parker Street and then walked across Piccadilly Gardens. It was after five, but the shops were still open and their destination was Woolworths and its photo booth. Robert couldn't help notice the growing number of young men, who eyed Kay up as she passed by. He suddenly felt proud that he was the one who was by her side.

Inside 'Woolies', they reached the booth and prepared to take their photos. Drawing back the curtain they squeezed in together with Kay sat on Robert's knee. Before putting in the money, Kay told Robert what they must do.

"We have to take two sensible photos. Be very still and hold the pose for both of them."

"Why?" asked Robert.

"Because we need a good copy for each of us and I don't fancy having to pay again to get another set."

"Well, you'd best make it three. Just in case one of us blinks," suggested Robert.

"Good idea," noted Kay. "It's annoying when the photos come back and someone has their eyes shut. And Robert, that still leaves you one photo to make a silly face. Because I know that's what you're planning to do."

"Was it that obvious?"

"You're always that obvious," replied Kay, shaking her head.

Robert received a look of mild disapproval. Over the years, she had given him many. He likened it to that given by a mother to a wayward child.

The photographs successfully taken, Robert put the black and white strip carefully into his wallet, making sure not to bend it. He and Kay then walked the short distance to Portland Street and followed it to the junction with Oxford Road. Turning left, they passed the St James Buildings and reached the Palace Theatre. Crossing over Oxford Road, they were at the corner of Whitworth Street West. To reach the Ritz they had to walk alongside St Mary's, the sight of which, brought a more serious tone to their conversation.

St Mary's was a maternity hospital and Robert and Kay knew of several girls who'd already had babies there; teenagers who'd been forced to get married once they knew they were pregnant.

"I can't imagine what that must be like," observed Kay. "At sixteen or seventeen, to have already given up your childhood. Serious responsibilities if you're a boy and stuck at home looking after a house and a baby, if you're a girl."

"I've no sympathy," replied Robert. "Lads should take precautions and girls shouldn't go with them if they don't."

"But when they get pregnant, they have to grow up so quickly and not everyone's as responsible as you Robert."

Hearing her words, Robert felt a twinge of embarrassment. Nevertheless, he understood that Kay wasn't being judgemental, but was showing her approval for his prudence.

"No, I suppose not. But we're different Kay. We know what's at stake; the chance to do something else and not just accept the place we've been allotted. I've worked hard at school because I want the chance to see what's out there. All the kids that went with us to Armitage Street, hardly any share our ambitions. I don't want to be saddled with a kid and lose the chance of a better life. I suppose for others, it's not so important."

"Even more so for girls," replied Kay. "The grammar schools see domestic science and sewing as every bit as important as the secondary moderns do. We're encouraged to be good wives and mothers. In fact, I suspect that they only see the value of girls being well educated, as being to provide perfect hostesses for middle-class husbands when they're entertaining. A lot of our teachers are spinsters. It seems to tell us that we can't have a career if we get married, for it interferes with looking after our homes. So, how surprising is it that girls get pregnant? They're expected to be mothers anyway, so why not get there sooner rather than later and achieve the ambition that's been laid out for them."

"I've never really thought about it like that."

"Why should you? You're a man. Read Betty Friedan if you want a woman's perspective."

"I don't need to. I've got yours. And I understand that it's far harder for you to fight against expectations, than it is for me."

Kay smiled. There was a clear dichotomy between his lack of concern for the girls he went out with and the deep respect that he always showed to her.

Chapter 15

Approaching the entrance to the Ritz, Kay and Robert spotted their friends waiting for them. Exchanging greetings, they all went inside. The Ritz Ballroom had been built back in the Twenties and once opened had quickly established itself as Manchester's premier dance hall. The reason was down to its superb, sprung floor; the movement and flexibility of which reduced stress on the dancer's joints and legs. Professionals loved it as it meant they could perform for longer and with less chance of injuries. The regular customers enjoyed the strange, bouncy sensation as they moved across the floor. For Kay, it was perfect, for she wanted to dance all night and there was no shortage of prospective partners. Robert's friends, already impressed by how pretty she looked, were soon captivated by her movements on the dance floor. Light on her feet, swaying her hips, her dress swirling around her, she danced with one after another.

Robert was dancing too. Several of Kay's school friends had come along and Jane Morris was particularly keen to share the floor with him. The girl that Robert had known at Armitage Street, was a distant memory. Since Kay had befriended her, she had changed into a kind and warm-hearted young woman who, during her teenage years, had become quite pretty. Fresh faced, with freckles, blonde hair and blue eyes, boys were eager to go out with her. Notwithstanding, Jane had developed something of a crush on Robert and was desperate to become his girlfriend. Accordingly, she turned down numerous suitors, only to find that Robert, though always of a friendly disposition, was disinclined to regard her in a romantic light. Trying to create the spark that would ignite his interest, Jane started going out with other boys. She knew of Robert's reputation and reasoned that it would make him see her differently; but it didn't. Desperate, Jane had approached Kay, prior to the night at the Ritz.

"What should I do, Kay? How can I get him to ask me out?"

"I'm not sure what to say," Kay had replied.

"But you know him better than anyone. You've always been so close."

"Maybe so, but I don't interfere in that part of his life."

"It's because he thinks I'm frigid, isn't it?"

Jane had looked pleadingly into her eyes. She had been desperate for an answer, but Kay had remained silent.

"It's why I went out with the other boys. I wanted him to see that I wasn't. I'm not daft Kay, I know all about Robert's reputation and I don't care."

Kay had been surprised by her revelation. She thought Jane was foolish, but didn't want to appear judgemental. Consequently, she chose her words carefully.

"There are lots of boys who'd love to go out with you Jane. You don't need to wait around for Robert. You have to watch them though. All this talk of being frigid. Don't be daft. Boys put that into girls' heads, so they can have their wicked way with them. And if you really fancy a boy, never let him know it. If you do, the chances are that they'll just try it on. Don't ever let a boy do that. They won't respect you and you'll lose your reputation."

"That's easy for you to say. You can have the pick of any of them."

Jane's petulance had led Kay to become frustrated.

"It makes no difference. I keep them at a distance. Even my dance partners can get 'fruity' and as soon as they do, then they're gone. No boy is worth getting worked up about. It's barmy to get like that. Face it. You might be looking for love, but most boys are just after a leg over!"

Jane was mistaken when she thought that Robert wasn't interested in her. As she had grown older, he had noticed how pretty she had become and especially how her figure had pleasingly filled out. Bert and Johnny had seen her around and they were certainly impressed. When they found out that she and Robert often travelled to school together, they couldn't believe that he hadn't made a move on her.

"Oh, he's finally slowing down," Bert had remarked. "What's up? Or isn't it!"

He and Johnny, broke out into howls of laughter. Watching them, Robert couldn't help joining in. He was no longer the shy and embarrassed boy of just over a year ago.

"It's not that I wouldn't," Robert had explained, "but she'd be thinking engagement rings and wedding bells."

"So what?" Bert had replied. "You just chuck her. What can she do? She's not going to tell anyone she's been with you. You don't owe her."

"You're not going all soft, are you?" asked Johnny

"Don't be daft. The problem is that I'll see her every day and she's the type who'll be clinging on to me every chance she gets and I'll have two years of it to put up with."

His answer was certainly convincing, but later he acknowledged to himself that considering Jane was a friend, his conscience wouldn't rest easy if he were to take advantage of her vulnerability.

Back on the dance floor, Kay finally had a partner whose skills could match her own and Robert was surprised to see that it was one of his friends from Central. Already, other revellers had moved back to give them room. They watched the couple in admiration as they completed a series of skips, twists, hops and jumps in perfect co-ordination. Their movements were fluid and flawless. Kay was soon twirling around her partner, who flung her over his back with consummate ease. Swaying her hips seductively, a radiant smile on her face, Kay had the rapt attention of every man in the room. It was breath taking and exciting. Robert, though thrilled, suddenly felt a tinge of jealousy, realising that on the dance floor, his friend was taking Kay to heights of pleasure, that he himself could not.

Sensing his frustration, Jane took him by the arm. Well aware of Robert's feelings for Kay, she saw the opportunity to take advantage. When Robert turned towards her, she pulled him close and whispered in his ear. He looked at her and nodded, following her off the dance floor, through the foyer and outside. Dusk was descending, but the glare from the lights on the signage of the Ritz, hadn't yet penetrated the gloom. There were few people around as they walked a short distance down the street and then up the steps and into the entrance of a nearby building. Here, out of sight, the two embraced. Robert was shocked, he'd never known a girl as willing. She was kissing him passionately, thrust her tongue into his mouth and pressed her hand tight against his groin. Where had she learned to do such things?

Nonetheless, he was aroused, but although it was Jane that was responsible for his pleasure, closing his eyes, he could only see images of Kay sensually shimmering around the dance floor. And somehow, he knew that it wasn't right. When Jane tried to slip her hand inside his trousers, he pulled quickly away.

"What's wrong? What've I done?" asked Jane, gasping for breath; imploring him for an answer.

"Nothing. You've done nothing."

"But something's wrong. I felt you. You can't deny it. You wanted me."

Her words were emphatic, her eyes flashed fiercely. She was a woman scorned and she wanted answers. Breathing deeply, Robert fought to gain control of his senses. Tenderly, he took Jane's hand.

"I don't want to take advantage. It's not right. You're better than this."

"You're not taking advantage. I want to."

"You don't know what you want and if you do something you regret, it'll be too late."

"But we can still go out together. Can't we?"

She was pleading with him, a situation he'd wanted to avoid. Weakness of character wasn't a quality that would endear any girl to him. He realised that he'd been right to stop. If they'd gone any further, he'd never have been clear of her. Robert tried to let her down gently.

"You should wait. Think about what you want. There are better lads than me out there."

"That's just what Kay said."

Robert was quiet.

"That's it. It's Kay, isn't it? You want her, but she doesn't want you. But I do …"

Jane's voice tailed off. She was quiet. Robert could see that she was upset, but there were no words that could mollify her now. Although it hadn't been his intention, Robert knew that she felt let down; humiliated even. Inevitably, the tears began to flow and before he could stop her, she had stepped back on to the pavement and was running towards the Ritz. Trying not to draw the attention of the doormen, Robert followed her slowly back inside, concerned to see that she was all right.

Searching the dance floor, he finally found her. Jane was at a side table with Kay and having placed a consoling arm around her, the latter was offering some words of comfort. Clearly though, she was still upset. Robert approached them tentatively. Jane, her head bowed, didn't see him, but Kay nodded, mouthed the word 'okay' and then indicated that he should leave them.

It took quite some time before Kay could begin to question her friend about what had happened. Several times Jane seemed to be on the verge of telling her, but she was too distressed and kept breaking down. Eventually, the tears abated and Kay could begin to investigate why Jane had come to her in such a state.

"You're not hurt, are you?" asked Kay.

Jane shook her head.

"You're sure?"

"Yes," replied Jane, quietly.

"Can you tell me what happened? Why you're so upset."

"It's Robert."

Kay's heart sank. She hadn't been sure if Robert's appearance was simply because he'd seen Jane in distress, or whether he was somehow its cause. She now knew that it was the latter. Kay understood that she must proceed carefully. She had no wish to do either of her friends an injustice. Her questioning had to be precise and fair.

"Can you tell me what happened?" she asked softly. "Right from the start."

Jane began to recount what she and Robert had done from the moment they had left the dance floor together, to her return alone in tears. As she spoke, Kay could see how difficult it would be to get to the truth of the matter. It was clear that Jane had been willing to go outside with Robert, but she was saying little about what had happened when they did. Kay found that she had no option but to push her further.

"There has to be a reason why you're so upset Jane. What happened? Did Robert do something?"

Jane was silent. She clearly had no wish to go into details. Kay was puzzled. She couldn't understand why that was the case. If something had upset her so much, why wouldn't she tell her?

"You don't need to worry. I won't repeat anything, if you don't want me to."

Still, there was no response.

"Did Robert touch you? Is that it?"

Jane bowed her head and remained silent.

"He must have said or done something. Mustn't he?"

"I thought that he'd want me."

Jane's voice was barely a whisper. Kay took her hand.

"Go on, tell me."

"We went in a door way and kissed …"

Jane was hesitant, still reluctant to explain further.

"Go on," prompted Kay, quietly.

"We held one another …"

"And did it go any further?"

"He didn't want me."

Kay was confused.

"Didn't want you?"

It was just three words. Yet the power of the question broke down Jane's stubborn resistance, releasing the pent-up anger that lay behind her anguish.

"No. He wants you, not me. I was willing to give him anything, but all he cares about is you."

Kay was shocked; momentarily stunned.

"He's made a fool of me. I hate him!"

Kay felt a sense of relief. She was sorry that Jane was upset, but it was clear that it was only her pride that had been hurt. Robert had refused to take advantage of her when clearly, she had wanted him to. Most importantly, there was no suggestion that he'd acted improperly. Jane's claim that Kay was the only one that Robert wanted, intrigued her. She had however, no intention of pressing for a further explanation.

By now it was getting late and Kay's friends had come to join them before they set off to the bus station together. It gave Kay a chance to find Robert, who had endured a long and nervous wait since she had sent him away. Robert knew that Jane felt slighted and he was concerned at what she may say about him. He feared that Kay may believe her and turn against him. As she walked towards him, his heart was in his mouth.

"Is she alright?" asked Robert.

Kay looked at him. His concern for Jane seemed genuine.

"She will be, but I think it best that you don't catch the bus back with us."

"Oh?"

"Yes. Give her longer to get over it. If she sees you, it might set her off again."

Robert looked concerned, assuming that Kay was being critical of him.

"Don't worry," she added, reassuringly. "Jane told me what happened. She's calmed down quite a bit. It's just that she feels embarrassed."

Robert nodded. He was silent. He too was embarrassed, fearing that Jane hadn't held back in revealing all the intimate details of their encounter.

"You'll call tomorrow after tea, won't you Robert?"

"Yes. Of course."

"Right, I'd best get back to Jane. I'll see you tomorrow."

With that, she was gone and slightly relieved, Robert left for home, without a word of goodbye to his other friends. It had been an awful end to a day that had promised so much. Most importantly though, his relationship with Kay remained firm and for that, he was grateful.

Although, Kay didn't breathe a word of what Jane had told her, it wasn't long before the other girls at the Ritz, decided what had happened. Having previously indicated her desperation to go out with Robert, it appeared to them that Jane had tried and failed, to entice him into a relationship. Their attitude towards her was harsh and judgemental, for they could only regard her as foolish. When Robert called on Kay the following evening, she greeted him warmly. The incident with Jane was never mentioned again. It would have been as if it had never happened, but when they returned to join their respective sixth forms in September, Jane was nowhere to be seen. A couple of weeks later the word came through that she had transferred to Levenshulme Girls Grammar.

Chapter 16

After passing the eleven plus, Kay and Robert had come to appreciate that although they continued to progress through the educational system, they were essentially outsiders. Their backgrounds made them so. Grammar schools were essentially middle-class institutions. The emphasis was on being aspirational, not only to access the higher salaries found in business, management or the professions, but to assume middle-class values too. Coming out of relative poverty, working-class pupils were certainly attracted to the former. However, many rejected the latter. Nurtured within communities where notions of loyalty and solidarity were inculcated from birth, education was seen as a tool to improve the lives of everyone and this didn't sit well with the selfish individualism of the middle classes. As Kay and Robert gained a greater understanding of the world around them, so did their political consciousness increase. By the time they entered the sixth form, both were ready to act.

The issue that prompted them to do so, came with the emergence of the Suez Crisis at the end of October 1956. The Soviet threat to invade Hungary, had already grabbed their attention and Kay and Robert had been avidly reading the daily accounts of that emerging crisis, in the newspapers at the library. It was an issue in a distant land however and it wasn't clear if, or how, they could express their support for Nagy's reforms. When news of Israel's invasion of Egypt broke on October 29th, the rumoured collusion of Britain and France created a national controversy. The following day the leader of the opposition, Hugh Gaitskell, made it clear that the Labour Party wouldn't support the prime minister if military action was taken to protect the free passage of shipping through the Suez Canal. When British and French planes bombed Egyptian airfields on October 31st and troops were sent into the canal zone, demonstrations were arranged throughout the country. Learning that students from the university planned to hold a march to the Town Hall,

Kay and Robert had an opportunity to join the protests against Eden's Government.

The only obstacle to their participation was that the event was to take place the next day, on November 1st. It was a Thursday, a school day and their absence from lessons was certainly not going to be sanctioned by their respective head teachers. There was an additional problem too. Both Kay and Robert respected their parents and although Robert was certain that his mam would support him if he decided to attend the march, Kay wasn't quite as sure about her parents.

"Mam will be fine about it," noted Robert. "She'll see me as being like my dad, standing up against aggression."

"I think dad will be okay with it, but I'm not sure my mam will be," replied Kay. "She'll worry about what the school might say."

To have gone without their family's approval was unthinkable. Kay and Robert had no desire to upset their parents or challenge the social expectation that until they reached the age of twenty-one, they would consult them on all important matters.

Returning home, with Robert accompanying her for moral support, Kay told her mam and dad about the march and why she wanted to go on it. As she spoke, Kay directed her comments towards Ernest, for she knew that he was more likely to prove sympathetic.

"It's terrible, Dad. The RAF are bombing innocent women and children. We've no right to be there and Eden's told our representatives at the UN to block any attempt to arrange a ceasefire. More people will die, British soldiers too, unless we stop it. Eden's no better than Khrushchev. The Soviets can do anything they like in Hungary now and it's all because of this."

It was an impassioned plea and Ernest was impressed. He'd been reading about what was going on in the *Chronicle*, but he had to admit that he didn't understand events as clearly as Kay. Many fathers would have felt inadequate, but Ernest was delighted to have such a clever daughter.

"The only thing love, is that really, you should be in school tomorrow, shouldn't you? You don't want to land yourself in trouble."

"Dad," replied Kay, firmly. "If people don't protest, the killing is just going to carry on."

"Surely there'll be enough people protesting without you having to join them," said Ernest, who was remaining very reasonable.

"We need as many as possible. It lets the soldiers in the canal zone know that people at home don't agree with what they're being asked to do."

"That won't matter love. When you're in the army, like I was, you have to do as you're told. Soldiers can't disobey orders."

"But if it's the right thing to do, they should. It's not the same as fighting Hitler, like you did. You were standing up to evil, but now our boys are being asked to be just like the Nazis. When we protest, they'll understand and the Government will have to bring them home. Skipping a few lessons is a small price to pay Dad. And you know, both Robert and I work very hard. We'll easily catch up anything we've missed."

Ernest smiled. His daughter spoke so passionately; believed so much in her cause. He couldn't bring himself to deny her.

"Well," he said with a sigh, "If you are going to be able to catch up and like you say, it is for a good cause, then I suppose it'll be all right."

Whilst, Kay and Ernest had been talking, Ethel had kept her own counsel. Now that she had heard her husband's verdict, it was time to give her own opinion.

"I don't know," she said, shaking her head at Ernest. "There you go, being soft, as usual. And this is where it gets us. With you so fond of encouraging her, there isn't any wonder that our Kay will end up getting in trouble."

"I know love, but that's what she's stayed on at school for, isn't it? To improve her mind by thinking about things."

Ernest smiled at Ethel, but she wasn't having any of it.

"And, don't doubt it, that mind is going to get her and Robert into a lot of bother!"

"Oh no, Mrs Thompson," said Robert, hurriedly. "Kay hasn't encouraged me at all. I already believed that we had to do something to stop Eden and the Establishment, well before we found out about the march."

"Oh, it's the Establishment then, is it? And who are they supposed to be when they're at home?"

Ethel looked at him mischievously. He appeared rather sheepish and she knew that he wasn't going to reply. Nevertheless, it pleased her to see how he had tried to defend Kay against her accusation that she'd led him astray. Coming to his rescue, Kay proceeded to explain to her mam what Robert had meant. Ernest turned proudly to his wife.

"Do you see what a clever girl you've given us? She knows her stuff, doesn't she love?"

"Well, I suppose I've no choice then," said Ethel, with a feigned look of resignation. "She'll have to go then, there's no point me saying anything about it. She's got a bee in her bonnet all right and you'll let her do it anyway."

"Thanks Mam."

Kay smiled and gave Ethel a hug.

For all she'd claimed otherwise, Kay knew that if her mam had put her foot down, Ernest would have given in to her and she wouldn't have been allowed to go. Nevertheless, Ethel concluded the conversation with a word of warning.

"You may as well smile. Just don't come running to me when you're in trouble at school and get a week of detentions for going."

It was a mother's role. The serious voice of reason that kept everyone's feet on the ground. Kay and Robert looked at one another. They both knew that Ethel was right. Once their schools found out that they had skipped lessons to go on the march, retribution would be swift.

Chapter 17

Kay and Robert arrived early at the students' union. It was a substantial four storey building and it had stood along Oxford Road, sandwiched between Lime Grove and Burlington Street, since 1909. It was by no means as grand as the combination of buildings that lay next to it. The original Owens College, the great towered entrance, the adjoining museum and Whitworth Hall, were all designed by Alfred Waterhouse. The Oxford Road frontage of Whitworth Hall combined oriel windows, round and pointed arches and Perpendicular tracery; an impressive example of the Gothic Revival. Yet just how stunning the buildings had been in their original state, was lost to the contemporary observer. The stonework had been blackened by the thick patina of sooty deposits, that had been laid upon it over the passing years.

Kay and Robert knew that before the march took place, there would be a meeting to vote on a resolution to condemn the actions of the British Government. Unsure as to whether they would be allowed into the debating hall, they had worked on disguising their relative youth, by attempting to blend in with those around them. They had dressed conservatively. Kay was in a navy blue, two-piece suit that she had borrowed from her mam. Over it she wore her long, grey winter coat. Robert was wearing a beige raincoat, tweed jacket, shirt, tie and trousers. Carrying their home-made placards, declaring 'Eden Must Go', they were greeted by a smiling young woman, carrying a clipboard.

"You're here for the demonstration, I see."

"Yes," replied Kay.

"Well, I'm collecting the names of any students who are interested in helping us to organise other events, but looking at you two, I don't think that applies."

Robert and Kay looked disappointed.

"I suppose it is that obvious, isn't it?" asked Kay.

"Yes. Just a bit," replied the young woman, smiling. "I'm Elizabeth, by the way."

"Kay and this, is Robert," she replied.

Elizabeth turned towards Robert. Their eyes met, but quickly he looked away. His slowly reddening cheeks betrayed his awkwardness. Elizabeth was exciting; an 'older woman' and one who was very pretty. She had an almost continental look. Wearing a beret, she had short black hair, full, red lips and long eyelashes which fluttered enticingly at him. She oozed sophistication. She was far removed from the girls that he could so easily pick up, as and when he wanted. He knew that if he were around her for long, she would be at the centre of his fantasies. But now, Robert needed an excuse to hide his embarrassment.

"I'll just go and find somewhere safe to leave these," he said, waving the placards.

"Leave them around the corner near the entrance to the men's union," suggested Elizabeth.

Robert had no wish to turn and acknowledge her, for fear that she would see that he was still blushing. Consequently, he pretended not to hear her. What he thought to be a clever ruse proved unconvincing however, when he immediately followed the instructions that she had given him. Kay found it hard not to laugh.

"You'll have to excuse him, Elizabeth. He seems to have become all hot and bothered."

Elizabeth began to chuckle and Kay couldn't help joining in. After they had both calmed down, Elizabeth asked a question.

"If you don't mind me asking Kay, how old are you and Robert and where are you from?"

"We're both sixteen and doing our 'A' Levels. I'm at Central High and Robert at Central Boys Grammar. We live locally in Ardwick."

Elizabeth seemed impressed.

"Are you planning to come to Owens after you finish in the sixth form?"

Owens College was the precursor of the Victoria University of Manchester and had remained the familiar and favoured name for the institution among administrators, staff and students, as well as with most Mancunians. Kay was thus familiar with its use.

"Yes, we'd like to. Of course, we'll have to work hard and make sure that we get good grades. We don't want to have a problem getting our county scholarships. We'll need them. Part-time and holiday jobs won't be enough to get by. Our parents have helped us this far, but they're not well off and it wouldn't be fair to expect them to do it any longer."

"You seem to have it fairly well worked out. I've been spoiled Kay. My parents are well off and I'm lucky that they can support me. In fact, as you'll find out when you come here, most students are from similar families. I am unusual in one way though, as I've come up from London. Most students at Owens are from Manchester, or the surrounding towns in Lancashire and Cheshire. It's an advantage being local I suppose, as it's easier and cheaper to live at home and you can be close to all your friends. I wanted to feel a bit more independent and come to a different part of the country. There's so much going on at university. You can broaden your horizons, whatever your background."

"There's one thing that bothers me though. You mentioned the men's union. Does that mean there's a separate one for women?" asked Kay. "I don't like that idea."

"Yes. The union building is divided. We can come together in the debating hall and there's an occasional dance, but two distinct unions exist. Don't worry, it won't be for too much longer. As you can see," Elizabeth pointed towards a building site on the opposite side of Lime Grove, "the new union building will be finished next year. The men's and women's unions have decided to federate and run it together. It's going to be far more integrated."

"Good," said Kay.

Having taken care of their placards, Robert returned. Now composed and confident, he explained to Elizabeth that they had 'wagged off' school because he and Kay felt that it was important to register their protest against Eden's actions.

"But won't you both end up in trouble?"

"Yes. Most likely," replied Robert.

"But we reasoned that it was worth it," added Kay.

Elizabeth was visibly impressed.

"It's good to see your enthusiasm …"

Pausing, she stepped to the side and craned her neck to peer down Burlington Street. Smiling, she raised her arm and began waving.

"Simon!" she shouted.

Kay and Robert followed her gaze and saw a man raise his arm in return. Beckoned over by Elizabeth, he walked briskly towards them.

"I think I may be able to get you into the hall for the debate," observed Elizabeth. "Simon is on the committee. I'm sure he'll agree."

Simon fitted perfectly the image of the dashing revolutionary. He seemed in perpetual motion, as he strode purposely towards them. Wearing a narrow brim, brown fedora, a scarf draped around his neck, his long, open overcoat, flapped around his legs. Reaching them, he stopped and Kay noted his handsome, angular features and the trim black beard, reminiscent of the power and intellect of Vladimir Ilyich. Kay was impressed.

Yet other students looked askance at him, as they passed along the pavement. Negative, muttered comments, suggested that Simon wasn't necessarily a popular figure.

"Don't worry about them," said Elizabeth. "They don't approve of us missing lectures or tutorials in order to demonstrate."

"Oh," said Robert, surprised. "I thought most students would be sympathetic."

"Not so," remarked Simon. "Most of them wouldn't dream of getting involved in any political issues."

The key fact for the friends from Ardwick however, was that Simon readily agreed to get them into the Men's Union Hall, where the resolution against the Government would be debated. They were certainly fortunate, for the room was packed and it was probable that some students, who'd been interested in attending, had been turned away. Once the speeches began, it was clear that the balance of opinion lay heavily on the side of those who condemned Eden's actions. Speakers from the Labour and Liberal Clubs, as well as the Socialist Society, railed against the prime minister. Norman Selwyn condemned him for trying to act as an international policeman, asserting that the conflict between

Egypt and Israel, was a matter for the United Nations. Chairman of the Socialist Society, Paul Rose, went further.

"This is a violent and flagrant violation of international law. Britain and France acted hypocritically after deprecating the movement of Soviet troops into Hungary just a few days ago."

Kay and Robert cheered loudly, clapping enthusiastically with the majority of the audience. Bringing his speech to an end, Rose urged members to pass the resolution and march to the Town Hall to lay it before Manchester's Lord Mayor, Councillor Harry Sharp.

There was some opposition, but unlike the support for the resolution, it wasn't broad based. It focused on the Conservative group, who wanted to defend their party leader. Nevertheless, just like at Westminster, there were some dissenting Tory voices. They were clearly uneasy about the possible repercussions of the Anglo-French action, especially given the negative reaction of the Americans.

It was therefore no surprise when the vote was taken, that out of the four hundred students present, only around fifty voted against. Carried along by the wave of enthusiasm, Kay and Robert had also raised their hands in support of the resolution, the only non-students to be given such a privilege.

Flushed with excitement at having so dramatically made their first political statement, Kay and Robert waited patiently as the hall began to empty.

"I hope that our resolution and protest will come to something," said Robert. "Eden and his cronies don't strike me as people who are likely to listen."

"It will," replied Kay. "These protests will continue all over the country. You saw it here; some of his own Party are starting to turn against him. The Government won't be able to ignore the opposition. And remember," she declared proudly, "we in Manchester are leading the way."

Chapter 18

Back outside, Kay and Robert collected their placards and took their places towards the back of a procession of over three hundred students, that stretched in double file along Oxford Road. As one of the organisers, Simon was near the front, where he would be close to Paul Rose, the leader of the march. Elizabeth had stayed with Kay and Robert. There were a number of police officers accompanying them, helping to make sure that they were safe from the traffic, given that they were walking in the road. The demonstrators were orderly and well behaved and the authorities expected no issues in terms of public order.

The placards were numerous but the message was focused, with the emphasis on three simple slogans: 'No War over Suez'; 'Stop Aggression' and 'Eden Must Go'. The latter two phrases were combined to fill a large banner that was held by those at the front. It was a busy route that the marchers were taking. As they proceeded down Oxford Road, into Oxford Street and through St Peters Square, they were passing lots of busy shops and offices. As such there were lots of people hurrying along the pavements and although there was a natural curiosity aroused by the unusual presence of the protestors, Kay and Robert were disappointed to note that there weren't too many shouts of support and encouragement. Many older Mancunians believed that a student's life was an easy and privileged one and more than a few comments could be heard criticising 'irresponsible time wasters' who should get back to their studies. Elizabeth smiled, pointing out to her young companions that it was the messengers rather than the message, that were bringing such a lukewarm response.

Moving into Peter Street, the marchers were flanked by the Midland Hotel on their left and the Central Reference Library on their right. As they reached the rear of the latter, they turned down Mount Street and followed it the short distance into Albert Square and drew up outside their destination; Manchester Town Hall. More speeches followed and then, the Mayor and Council left in no doubt about the strength of feeling against the Suez invasion, it was finally time to disperse and for farewells to be said.

Having been joined by Simon, his duties over for the day, Kay and Robert were able to express their gratitude to both of their benefactors.

"Thanks for getting us into the meeting," said Robert. "It was pretty exciting."

"Yes," affirmed Kay. "We really appreciate it. I have to admit, we did worry a little that because we're still in the sixth form, there was a possibility that we might not be allowed on the march. To end up getting into the debate as well, was great."

"Ah, but you were determined," replied Simon. "You showed initiative and there aren't many your age that would have done so. Keep that spirit and you'll go far. Perhaps you'll be helping to organise demonstrations here in a couple of years' time," he added, smiling.

"How are you feeling about Owens after today?" asked Elizabeth. "Has it made you more determined to come?"

"We were fairly set on it anyway," replied Robert," but I've seen how different it is here. How you can express yourselves. In the sixth form, we're not given the chance to voice our opinions if the school takes exception to them. They just won't listen. We're sixteen and old enough to go to work. Some of our friends have held full time jobs for almost eighteen months. They're being treated as adults, whereas we're still regarded as children. I know we'll have far more freedom when we get into university."

"And it's the opportunity to get a degree and a chance to use it to help make a better world here in Manchester," added Kay. "It's not just in Suez where there's injustice."

The following day, Kay and Robert were back in school. They knew it was likely that their respective headteachers would already know about the reason for their absence. Too many of their classmates had found out about their plans and there would always be someone who would pass the information on to the staff. What they weren't aware of however, was that the leaders of the two schools had already met to decide on how they would approach the matter. Robert was therefore surprised when he was asked to accompany his headmaster to the office of Central

High's headmistress. When he arrived, Kay was already there waiting. She was shocked to see him, but smiled reassuringly. Taking a seat, the headmaster joined his colleague behind her desk. The miscreants were left standing.

Robert looked closely at Kay's headmistress. She seemed formidable. Her greying hair had been tightly squeezed into a bun and she wore a heavy, dark tweed jacket over a Victorian blouse. Her small, round glasses exaggerated her sharp, piercing eyes, which sat deep within a sour, scowling face.

"We know where you were yesterday," she stated, disapprovingly. "I think you owe us an explanation. Don't you?"

When physical danger threatened, it was Kay who would naturally spring to their defence, but in these circumstances, Robert confidently seized the opportunity to respond.

"We found out about the protest march on Wednesday afternoon marm. Both of us feel strongly about Suez and there wasn't any chance of informing either of you about our intention to go…"

"Oh. So, you just assumed that it would be all right, did you? Don't you understand that as members of these two schools, your obligation is to attend lessons?"

"If we hadn't gone, Kay and I would have been ignoring our consciences. The Government's actions are wrong. People are dying and as school has taught us that we should always stand up for what is right, we assumed that there wouldn't be any disapproval of our actions."

There was silence. Kay knew that Robert's final point was untrue, but she admired how he had attempted to gain the moral ascendancy. She saw a hint of a smile on the face of Robert's headmaster, but her headmistress was far from impressed.

"Sheer impertinence young man! You knew very well that we wouldn't have agreed. The march was for students at the university, not for sixth formers at Central High or Central Grammar. In fact, you were nothing but a couple of interlopers."

"Excuse me marm," replied Robert, politely. "The organisers knew where we were from and they were very welcoming. They allowed us into the Union Hall for the debate and were keen for us to go on the march."

The headmistress was disconcerted. She had assumed that her fierce response would have doused the dying embers of rebellion within this troublesome young man, but he was making it abundantly clear that he would not bend to her will. Sensing an opportunity to defend themselves further, Kay made an observation.

"The reporter from the *Chronicle* didn't seem to find it unusual that we were there. I'm sure he would have said something to us if he did."

Robert's headmaster glanced at his counterpart. They looked concerned. The mention of journalists was the last thing they wanted to hear. It wouldn't be good for either school's reputation if it emerged that their sixth formers, rather than attending lessons, were participating in political demonstrations. Having to explain that to the education committee, was a situation that neither of them wished to face. A compromise was going to have to be found and it was Robert's headmaster, who'd been silent until this point, who was best placed to secure it.

"I think I can say for both of us," he began, "that this episode has been rather unfortunate. It would have been far better and good manners, if we'd been alerted to your intentions earlier. We respect your strong feelings over events in Egypt, but I have to say that if a similar event were to occur in the future, we wouldn't be so generous if you did anything without discussing it with us first."

He looked sternly at Kay and Robert and then nodded his head towards his colleague. His words were impressing her in the way that he desired. He was eager to assure her that he was just as unhappy with their behaviour, as she was. Of course, he wasn't. Unlike her, he was no stickler for the rules and he had to admit that he rather admired their independent spirit.

Kay liked him. He was a kind looking man with a high forehead and neatly trimmed moustache. He wore a brilliant white shirt, navy and white spotted tie and a smart suit. Unlike his colleague, he had carried a sense of style into his later years.

"Now, in view of your genuine and laudable concerns for the potential sufferings of others," he continued, "it seems reasonable that we draw a line under this whole business. You have to understand though, that as rules have been broken, consequences have to be faced. Therefore, you will both carry out a detention after school on Monday. Do you understand?"

"Yes, sir."

"Off you go then."

Kay's intuition had been correct. Robert's headmaster had worked hard to convince his counterpart that the issue should be quietly forgotten. Yet in return, he had to agree that neither Robert nor Kay would be given posts of responsibility when they entered the upper sixth. Whereas this was unlikely for Robert, Kay had been seen as having the potential to become head girl. Having demonstrated her independent spirit however, she was no longer seen as a 'safe pair of hands'. Be that as it may, the situation held little concern for Kay. Status didn't interest her. She would never take any position, if the cost of acceptance would mean a betrayal of her principles.

That evening, Kay and Robert discussed the experiences of the last two days. It had turned out well for them. Neither Kay nor Robert had expected to be treated with such leniency. Their bravery in standing up for what they believed in, had been vindicated. Moreover, their short exposure to student life had reinforced their intention to gain a place at Owens.

"I'm more determined than ever to get there," declared Robert.

"Yes. So am I. It's a different world and I'd love to be part of it."

"There's one thing that's bothering me though," remarked Robert.

He was trying hard to look serious, but Kay was unimpressed and ready for the inevitable witty remark.

"Go on then," she sighed, "tell me what it is."

"When we get there, Elizabeth will have already left."

A cheeky grin broke out across Robert's face and he started to chuckle. Kay shook her head and laughed too.

"No Kay," said Robert, who had settled down and was now sounding more serious. "I'll be made up if both of us can get there together."

"And we will," replied Kay. "We'll always be here for one another and nothing is going to stop us."

Chapter 19

In the months that followed, neither Kay nor Robert had provided any reason why the staff at their respective schools would be dissatisfied with their conduct or progress. Both had performed excellently in the exams at the end of the lower sixth and when they had taken their 'mocks' in the following January, they had both achieved top grades. When they had applied to Owens, Kay to study for a BA in Social Administration and Robert a BA in History, their schools had given them glowing references. Invited for interview, both of them were confident that it had gone well. Nevertheless, they still had to endure a nervous wait before finally receiving confirmation that they would be offered a place.

Kay and Robert had already realised that any university offers they received, would be contingent on them securing high 'A' Level grades. Although they had always worked hard, it was agreed that nothing could be left to chance. They therefore decided to increase the time that they spent studying together at Ardwick Library. Their routine quickly became familiar. Arriving home from school, they would eat their tea, help with the washing up and then make their way to the library to meet up and study.

At just after half past five on Thursday February 6th, 1958, Kay was feeling slightly perplexed. She had just walked to the end of Bennett Street and was waiting for a break in the traffic, so that she could cross Hyde Road to get to the library. On the way, she had passed several groups of men. Their heads were bowed and they were huddled closely together on the pavement. It was an unusual sight, but there was no obvious indication as to why it was so.

Having crossed, Kay walked quickly along Hyde Road. She passed several newsagents but eager to reach her destination, didn't read the headlines on the display boards, as she would normally have done. Hyde Road was a busy thoroughfare, bristling with shops and people. It was therefore understandable that she failed to notice the knots of men, young and old, gathered along the pavement. Kay was soon at the junction with Syndall Street. On the opposite corner, immediately before the library, stood the 'Clarence'. An Ind Coope public house, it looked prominent in black and white. Its front was set back from Hyde Road; a small open area before it's entrance. This time, as she crossed over, Kay couldn't miss the group of men who'd gathered outside. At first, she assumed that they were waiting for the pub to open at six. Yet they didn't seem to be interested in drinking, for just like those she had seen on Bennett Street, they were silently looking at the floor. They seemed like a collection of desperate and lost souls.

As she walked by, Kay's attention was drawn towards an elderly man. Wearing a cloth cap and long overcoat, he was holding a copy of the *Manchester Evening News*. Staring straight ahead, tears were rolling down his face. Kay was shocked. She had never seen a grown man cry. Stopping, she asked him if he needed help.

"I've seen them all you know, right back to Billy Meredith. He was a good 'un. But some of these lads could have been even better."

Kay didn't understand.

"But is everything all right?"

"No love. It's not. Here."

The old man handed her his copy of the *Evening News*. It was the 'Final' edition and the headline was harrowing: UNITED CUP XI CRASH: "28 DIE." The aircraft carrying the United team home from their European Cup tie against Red Star Belgrade, had crashed on take-off at Munich airport. It was too soon for the German authorities to have released the names of the dead and injured, but it was clear that the toll on the famous 'Busby Babes' would be heavy. Handing the newspaper back, there was little Kay could do to assuage the old man's sadness. With a sympathetic nod, Kay said farewell and walked the short distance to the library steps and made her way inside.

Placing her books and pens on the desk, Kay found it hard to concentrate. She had felt the despair of the old man and now realised that it was the events at Munich that had brought the groups together on Bennett Street. When Robert joined her, he too had lost his appetite for study. He'd seen similar scenes outside the 'Crown' and the 'Junction' at the bottom of Clowes Street. Feeling that it was pointless to remain in the library, Kay agreed to Robert's suggestion that they should go back to his house. They could get some fresh air, clear their heads and then study together in his gran's front room.

Walking back, it seemed quieter than usual. As they approached the Marsland Hotel, next to the wash house on Armitage Street, they could see a number of men and youths gathered outside. Passing by, Kay and Robert heard someone calling to them. Looking round, they recognised Bert and next to him was Johnny.

"You've heard, you two. Haven't you?" asked Bert.

He and Johnny looked sad and downcast, far from the genial jokers with whom they were so familiar.

"I can't believe it," said Johnny. "It's just not right. It shouldn't have happened."

"Perhaps, it won't be as bad as they think," suggested Kay. "They haven't released any names yet."

"The *Evening News* said it was twenty-eight killed," replied Johnny. "There's bound to be lots of players included."

"I would think the police in Germany are holding back the names until they can let the families know," suggested Robert.

The others nodded.

There was a peculiar atmosphere. It was eerily quiet, even though there were so many stood around them. It was as if those present had an inexplicable need to be with others who understood and shared their despair. A collective depth of feeling, that could only come from those who had experienced the passion and loyalty that existed on the terraces.

From the huddle of bodies, a young man emerged. Kay recognised him at once. With his shock of red hair and scarred face, Jim Smith couldn't be mistaken. His bluish skin was a legacy of his work at Beatties coal yard, where continual, hard graft had sculpted a lean, but powerful frame. A fanatical 'Red', Jim enjoyed the banter with his City counterparts, especially Johnny and Bert. Today however, the football divide had closed. Red and blue were bound together in grief. Jim extended his hand and Bert and Johnny shook it warmly.

"It's good of you City lads to come out for us."

"Of course, pal," replied Johnny. "It's Manchester's loss; City's as well as United's."

Saying their farewells, Kay and Robert continued on towards the corner of Gregory Street. Neither of them felt much like studying now and they agreed that Kay would go home and they would see one another again tomorrow morning.

The next day, the full details of the casualties were released and the United team had paid a heavy price. Geoff Bent, Roger Byrne, Eddie Colman, Mark Jones, David Pegg, Tommy Taylor and Liam Whelan had all been killed. Duncan Edwards and manager Matt Busby, were on the critical list and the former would not survive. Two other players, Johnny Berry and Jackie Blanchflower, would never play again.

Like so many others, Kay's dad had taken the news particularly hard. Alone with her in the kitchen on Saturday morning, Ernest reflected on what had happened.

"It's such a waste. So many young men with incredible talent. They had so much to offer and now we'll never get to know how good they could have been. It's the sadness of it all, Kay. I thought that losses like this had been left behind in the War. Back then, I saw so many young lives being taken and I thought I'd never see it happen again. But I suppose that's life. None of us can ever know what's going to happen in the future."

Kay was surprised. Her dad was invariably cheerful and optimistic and it was unusual to hear him sound so glum.

"It's a terrible thing," he continued, "to see real promise go unfulfilled. You have to make sure Kay, that you never let your talents go to waste. Always be grateful for the chances that you're given and take them with both hands."

"I will, Dad."

"I know," replied Ernest, nodding. "I didn't really need to say that to you, did I love?"

"It's all right Dad. I understand. What's happened has affected everyone. The shock of it is bound to make us stop and think."

"Yes. I suppose it's just because I'm feeling a bit sad."

The disaster and especially the reaction to it, from people all over the city, made a great impression on Kay. It had underlined the importance of community and the benefits of coming together in order to care for one another. Kay already saw her future as one in which she would work with the most vulnerable. Taking a degree in social administration would enable her to work as a children's officer. To achieve that aim, everything would now depend on how well she performed in her exams.

Chapter 20

Once their exams were over, Kay and Robert had quickly found themselves jobs for the summer. They were both working in the offices of Manchester Corporation's Transport Department, which were located at the bus depot on the corner of Hyde Road and Devonshire Street. Their role was to cover for members of staff who were absent on their holidays. Based at the depot, Ernest had tipped Kay and Robert off about the vacancies before they had been advertised in the student's union at Owens. The tasks that they were carrying out were varied, interesting and made enjoyable by the fact that they were working together. Most importantly, the extra money would help meet the expenses they would incur when hopefully, they started their degrees at the end of September.

When leaving the exam hall for the final time, Kay and Robert had felt a sense of relief. They had been working hard for a considerable length of time and they now needed a period of relative calm. As July turned into August however, the release of the 'A' Level results inevitably approached. It soon began to weigh heavily on their minds, no matter how much they tried to pretend to one another that it didn't. The pressure also increased because they were so emotionally invested in each other's success. In fact, if either of them wasn't able to attain the grades required by Owens, it would be considered a failure for them both. For so long their ambition had been that they would go together. Neither of them could bear thinking about the consequences if they couldn't.

Kay and Robert had decided that when their results arrived in the morning post, they would bring their envelopes to work and open them together during the dinner break. The café that they went to for their dinner was close by. It was located back along Hyde Road, on the corner of Marsland Street. Robert always felt a sense of history when they went there. The café was next to the railway bridge that crossed over Hyde Road, the scene of the Fenian's attack on a police van to release two prisoners in

September, 1867. It was a notorious day in Manchester's history, given that it resulted in the death of Sergeant Charles Brett. He was the city's first police officer to be killed on duty. In November, William Allen, Michael Larkin and Michael O'Brien were executed for the murder. As the evidence against them was questionable, Irish nationalists referred to them as the 'Manchester Martyrs'. Hung before a large crowd at Salford Gaol, it was the last public hanging in the Manchester area.

The café was popular locally, as well as with its regular clientele of travelling salesmen, van and lorry drivers, who would pull over whenever they were in the area. It opened at the crack of dawn, providing a hearty fried breakfast for workers coming on and off shift. Dinners and teas were served up in abundance and a hot meal could be purchased at any time throughout the day. Kay had taken Robert there shortly after they had met, for it was the summer and the café offered a variety of ice lollies that could be bought for a penny, tuppence or thruppence. Of course, they never chose other than an orange jubbly or Vimto lolly. Now, signs at the tops of the windows advertised 'Players Weights', 'Craven A', Park Drive' and 'Senior Service' cigarettes.

It had been natural for them to choose the café as the place to spend their dinner break. It was not long however, before Kay was finding it necessary to tell him off. Robert had been fascinated when he watched lorry drivers pouring hot tea from their cups into a saucer. It cooled the liquid so that they could drink it more quickly. He wouldn't have dared imitate them had his mam or gran been present, but alone with Kay, he decided that he would. Yet as he was about to lift the saucer to his mouth, he received a stinging rebuke.

"Just what do you think you're doing!"

Robert immediately placed the saucer back on the table. Sheepishly, he looked back at her. Silent, it was clear that he didn't have a clue what to say.

"You're showing yourself up and me too."

Kay wasn't amused. Robert's proposed experiment had gone badly wrong.

"You're just like a kid. What is it? Do you think it tastes better out of the saucer? How utterly gormless."

Thankfully for Robert, Kay began to chuckle.

"Or are you trying to be just like a rough, tough lorry driver?" she continued. "It'll take more than that to put hairs on your chest."

Once again, she started to laugh. Robert was embarrassed. He felt the need to justify himself.

"No. You know I wasn't."

"Oh," replied Kay, "then I suppose it's some misguided attempt to try and prove that you're still part of the working classes."

"I am part of the working classes," insisted Robert.

Kay sensed an opportunity to tease him further.

"Well, I'm not too sure about that. Perhaps you were Robert, but you need to consider the facts. You've become an intellectual. You're leaving your working-class roots behind."

Kay spoke calmly; her face, expressionless. Robert was convinced that she was serious and responded accordingly.

"Well, so were Marx and Engels. They were intellectuals and for that matter, Lenin and Trotsky too."

"And that just makes my point," replied Kay. "All of them were members of the bourgeoisie. They weren't workers at all."

"It doesn't matter," said Robert, clearly getting frustrated. "They created socialism. What could be more working-class than that?"

"But you know Engels. He mixed with Manchester's finest. He rode with the Cheshire Hunt and was a patron of classical music. Mark my words, Robert. You'll end up just the same. There'll be no more Elvis, or sneaking in the side door at the ABC. Your working-class roots will be long gone."

She looked at him. He seemed shocked.

"Yes," she continued, shaking her head. "That won't be a pretty sight. Not pretty at all."

Robert was quiet. He began to rack his brains for a witty rejoinder, but try as he might, he was unable to think of one. Finally, Kay broke into a smile.

"I really had you going there, didn't I?"

"No," he replied, tersely.

"Ah, poor Robert. He's all upset."

"No, I'm not."

"Oh dear, he's starting to sulk."

"I'm not."

Robert looked at her. She had a beautiful smile and she was teasing him mercilessly and suddenly, he loved it. Smiling himself, he started to chuckle.

Yet there could be no such jollity when they were sat in the café clutching their unopened results envelopes in their hands. The moment of truth had arrived and there was no escaping it.

"It's okay if you make it and I don't," said Kay.

"You'll be fine. We both will be."

Robert's words, meant to be reassuring, lacked conviction. Nerves had clearly got the better of both of them.

"Well, come on," said Kay. "Let's do it. After three."

Both counting to three, they quickly opened their envelopes and pulled out the letter. There was no attempt to read through the contents, their eyes immediately fastening on to the bold letters that indicated their grades. Kay and Robert had achieved their offers, but each of them was concerned that the other may not have. Consequently, neither of them showed any signs of relief or satisfaction, for fear of upsetting their friend. For what seemed like an age, the two of them stared at one another. Finally, Kay spoke.

"You've done it. Haven't you Robert."

"Yes," he replied, quietly.

"Oh, brilliant!" exclaimed Kay, her face lighting up.

It was all Robert needed to see. It told him that she would be going to Owens too.

"It would have been okay, if you'd have made it and I didn't," said Kay.

"Well, I would never have forgiven you, if I'd failed and you hadn't," joked Robert.

The two of them began to laugh; the tension had finally been broken. They had both got the 'A' level results they needed and their places at Owens were secure.

"We've both worked so hard," said Kay. "I think we deserve our success. I can't imagine the despair I'd have felt if either of us hadn't made it."

"But we did," replied Robert "and we were always going to. Anyway," he continued, "talking about working hard, we'd best be getting back. We've a transport department needs running."

Getting up from their table, the friends left the café and returned to Hyde Road Depot. In less than six weeks, a new chapter would open in their lives. The working-class kids from Ardwick were on their way to university.

PART TWO

Owens

Chapter 21

The day had arrived, Monday September 22nd, 1958. Robert was feeling nervous, but excited. So were his mam and gran. Irene had arranged to go into work later that morning. Her boss had been sympathetic, understanding her desire to see her son off to his first day at university. For Irene, it marked the fulfilment of a dream; he'd achieved the impossible. That morning, her first thoughts were of her husband Billy and how proud he would have been of their son's achievement.

As Edna and Irene fussed around him, their attention threatened to become a little overbearing, but Robert remembered just how much they had sacrificed for him. Without their unstinting support, this day could never have come. Robert therefore did all he could to put them at ease. Even though he was full to bursting, he ate all of the 'proper' breakfast they'd cooked for him. Neither did he complain when they adjusted his tie and collar and had him stand in the centre of the kitchen for what seemed like an age, as they checked his jacket for loose threads and gave it yet another, final brush down.

"There. You look fine," said Edna, who'd worked as a machinist and was judged to have the finer eye of the two women, when it came to the question of clothes and presentation.

"Yes, very smart," added Irene, with an air of satisfaction.

"I'm sure I do," remarked Robert. "I don't think you need to make quite so much of a fuss Mam."

"I'll be the judge of that," replied Irene. "We're not having any of them snobby types looking down their noses at you. You might be from Ardwick, but we've got standards too and you've got to let them know it."

"Oh, I'm sure it won't be like that Mam."

"It'd better not be," said Edna, "otherwise I'll be down there and they'll have me to deal with!"

"Yes," added Irene, for good measure. "Don't let any of those posh types try to put you down."

"I'd never do that," insisted Robert. "I'm working-class and proud of it. I don't care who knows."

Edna and Irene looked at him with satisfaction.

"I always say, you can take me as you find me…" began Edna.

"Or leave me alone!" completed Robert. "I know gran."

"Well, it's right love."

Irene and Robert nodded. Her logic couldn't be questioned.

"Well, I'd best get off. It's eight o'clock and Kay's expecting me."

Kissing his mam and gran goodbye, Robert noticed that they had tears in their eyes. He understood that it was difficult for them to avoid sentimentality but feeling a little awkward, he tried to make light of it.

"Looking at the pair of you, anyone would think that I'm on the way to my execution."

"Get off with you, you cheeky monkey! I'll give you a good hiding, if you're not careful," warned Edna.

"When have you ever done that?" asked Robert, smiling.

"It doesn't mean I won't. You might think you're all grown up, now you're at university, but to me, you'll always be a little squirt with a runny nose and scrawped shoes. So don't get cocky!"

Irene and Robert burst out laughing. Edna shook her head.

"Go on then," she said. "Have a good day and we'll be expecting to hear all about it when you get home."

"And give our love to Kay," added Irene, "and tell her we're thinking about her."

Knocking on Kay's door, she was ready and waiting. Her mam was at home, as usual, to see them off, but Ernest, working the early shift, had been gone since five o' clock. Like Edna and Irene, Ethel couldn't avoid becoming emotional when she bade them farewell.

"You both look so grown up," she said, haltingly. "And to think of when you were together for the first time at Armitage Street, all those years ago. Who'd have thought we'd have ever seen a day like today?"

"Well, we have."

Kay put her arm around Ethel and squeezed her softly.

"Thanks Mam."

"What for?"

"For you and Dad believing in me and giving me the chance to stay on at school."

"Don't be daft love. It's all down to you. We didn't pass the exams."

"You know what I mean."

As they set off down Bennett Street, Kay and Robert realised that they'd probably got through the trickiest part of the morning; reassuring their families that everything would be all right on their first day at Owens.

"I hadn't realised just how much getting to university meant to my mam and gran," said Robert. "I don't think that until today, they really believed it was true."

"Yes, my mam and dad are the same. What we're doing is unusual though. Who do we know around here that's managed it? I can't think of anyone."

"It does feel like we're carrying their hopes too. They're desperate for us to settle in and do well."

"But they've always wanted that," replied Kay.

"Yes, I know, but I can't stop thinking," continued Robert, "that as they've done so much for us, we owe it to them to do the best we possibly can."

"You'd do that in any case."

"I suppose so," agreed Robert.

"When I went for my interview," said Kay, "one of the lecturers commented on my address and complimented me on having the ambition to get to Owens. He said that there were too few working-class students at the college, but those that were demonstrated a hunger to succeed that few other students could match. He thought it was because we had to fight so hard for our places and would never take them for granted, unlike many middle-class students who'd been brought up to expect that they would go to university."

"I suppose he had a point," replied Robert.

Smiling, he looked at her mischievously.

"Then again," he continued. "How old was he?"

Kay was well aware of where the conversation was leading and pretended not to hear him.

"Well?"

"Well, what?"

"How old was this lecturer?"

"I don't see what that has to do with anything."

"Ah, I see," said Robert, smiling. "He was one of the younger ones. No doubt he fancied you and was making a good impression for when you arrived."

"Don't judge everyone else by your own standards, Robert. It might surprise you, but not all men are out there on the pull."

"Neither am I. I was being serious," said Robert, trying to appear shocked.

"My, you are a good actor, Robert. You should think seriously about signing up for the drama club this week."

"Now that's just unfair."

Robert sounded hurt.

"There you go again," observed Kay. "Another Oscar winning performance."

The two of them began to laugh. Robert was well aware of how far the jesting could go and if he ever did overstep the mark, Kay would put him firmly in his place.

It wasn't a long walk they had to take, shorter in fact than their previous one to Central. Happily chatting away, they had soon reached the end of Hyde Road. Crossing Stockport Road, they then followed Brunswick Street across Upper Brook Street and down to Oxford Road and the university. Arriving outside Whitworth Hall, it was time to register and collect their termly scholarship cheques. That task complete, it was then off to the Arts Building to complete the induction process for their respective departments. Before separating, Kay and Robert agreed that at twelve, they would meet up for dinner in 'Caf', the students' refectory.

Chapter 22

History was a popular degree at Owens. The department had long had a strong reputation and so attracted students from all over the country. It was for this reason that when Robert arrived at the departmental office, he met the young man who, next to Kay, was destined to become his closest friend.

Arriving together, they were given details about the courses they would be taking, the weekly timetable of lectures, the essay and exam requirements and information about the library. Once these had been received, the two of them were taken to the room of one of the lecturers in order to be welcomed to the department. The word 'welcomed' soon seemed inappropriate however, as what followed seemed more akin to an interrogation.

Sat behind a desk, sprawled in his chair, the lecturer gave them but a cursory glance when they entered the room. Leafing through a sheaf of papers, he muttered and sighed and then, throwing them down with an air of disdain, he finally fixed his eyes on the new students who had been brought before him.

Robert looked at him calmly. He'd noticed the nameplate on the outside of the door and it was impressive too. They were in the presence of Professor Franks. Since Robert had been young, the title had always conjured up pictures of grey-haired old men who were kind, but absent minded. It soon became apparent that whereas the first two descriptors could be quite accurately applied to Franks, the latter were clearly wide of the mark.

His hair was certainly grey, what was left of it, for he was completely bald on top and only small tufts of hair remained around his ears and the back of his head. Yet this was rather compensated for, by his long bushy eyebrows and the untrimmed hairs that were growing out of his nose and ears. He had fierce eyes and cruel, thin lips. He didn't talk, but growled and it was clear that he thought that the youngsters of today had it far too good.

Franks opened proceedings with his idea of a pep talk.

"Now I know you young chaps have escaped your national service and you probably think you've got it easy now, that you've got away with it, but that's not the case. Let me be very clear about it; you're here to work hard, damn hard! Do you understand?"

Robert was dumbfounded. It was like he was back at school. He glanced to the side of him and he could see that his companion was astonished too. The pair were silent, but it seemed that Franks' final words were a statement of fact, rather than a question to which he demanded an answer.

"So, who have we got here then?"

Franks looked directly at Robert's companion.

"Well?"

"Laurence Foster."

Franks picked the papers back up off his desk and looked through them.

"Ah, yes. Here you are."

Franks took a few moments to read through the information before continuing.

"King's, Canterbury. A fine school. Like it there, did you?"

"It was all right, I suppose."

"Only all right? Well, seeing these exam results, it can't have been that bad. Grade As in your 'A' Levels and you sat three 'S' Levels and achieved three 'distinctions'. You should never take a good education for granted young man."

He paused and looked the King's boy up and down. It seemed that despite the exam results, he wasn't sure if he approved of the young man. Robert was certainly impressed though. He had received two grade A's and a B in his 'A' levels, but had only taken one 'S' Level paper and that in history. Unlike Laurence, he had received the lower grade of 'merit'.

"I assume that as you took three 'S' Levels," continued Franks, "you applied to Oxford or Cambridge."

"Yes, Cambridge. I received an offer from Sidney Sussex, but I decided that I wanted to come to Manchester."

"I see."

It wasn't apparent whether Franks approved of his decision, but it was clear that Robert was impressed. He'd not been certain what to make of Laurence at first. A softly spoken Southerner, he seemed friendly enough, but Robert was always wary of the traditional class enemy and Laurence certainly seemed to come from that particular camp. Now, with his preference for Manchester, Laurence's stock had risen immeasurably.

"And what about you? What's your name?" asked Franks, turning to Robert.

"Robert Wilson."

Franks once more consulted his list.

"Ah, yes. One of our Mancunian brethren. And you're from Ardwick. A bit rough round the edges I shouldn't wonder, but no doubt from proud working-class stock."

Robert couldn't work out whether or not Franks comment had been a compliment, but he was determined to emphasise the fact that he was indeed, a proud working-class lad.

"Yes, and I attended Central Boys Grammar, a fine school run by Manchester Education Committee."

"No doubt," replied Franks, somewhat dismissively.

It was obvious that he didn't see the state grammar school system as having any particular merit.

"Now," he continued, "are there any questions that you would like to ask me about the course?"

Laurence, eager to escape, shook his head, but Robert was keen to take up the offer.

"Yes, I'd like to please."

Franks looked surprised. Rarely did any of the new students seem eager to prolong their meeting.

"Yes?"

"I've looked through the course details and there's mention of the topics that are covered and the exams we have to take, but there's no mention of students carrying out their own research projects. When will they take place?"

"They won't."

"Oh."

Robert sounded surprised and disappointed.

"I thought that when I came to university," he continued, "we would be given the chance to carry out our own research. Our studies this year seem no different to what we were doing in the sixth form. I know we have to take exams, but I was hoping to have some freedom to carry out my own enquiries."

"You have to earn the right to do that," replied Franks. "When you've proven to us, through excellence in your essay work and top marks in the exams, that you have the capacity to take it on, then and only then, will you be considered for post-graduate research."

"If I want to carry out research then," continued Robert, "I'll have to wait until after I've graduated."

"Yes."

There was a pause, before Franks wound up the meeting.

"Now, as long as you both work hard, we're unlikely to come across one another until you reach the third year. I'm not involved in teaching any of the courses until then, but I do monitor the progress of those students who we feel are underachieving."

Franks paused and looked at them closely, his eyes fixing on each of them in turn. He was ensuring that his message about working hard had been received and understood.

"Well, I think that's all," he continued. "Good luck. Close the door on your way out."

With that, the meeting was closed.

Chapter 23

Having left the Arts Building, the two of them sat on a nearby bench. Laurence breathed a huge sigh of relief.

"It's good to get some fresh air."

"Yes," agreed Robert. "It was a bit stuffy in there."

"When he said we wouldn't get him for the first two years, I felt like cheering," continued Laurence.

"So did I," replied Robert, laughing.

"I felt uncomfortable when he was questioning me," noted Laurence, "but it didn't seem to bother you, Robert. You weren't intimidated at all, were you?"

"Well, no. But then again Laurence, I've had a good teacher."

"Call me Larry. Everyone does."

"Okay. What are you going to do now?"

"Well, I thought I'd go to the library and get started on finding some of the titles on the reading lists."

"Don't you want a drink and something to eat?" asked Robert. "Come with me and you can meet my friend Kay. She's from Ardwick too and the one who taught me how to deal with bullies like Franks. I'm meeting her in 'Caf' at twelve and it's nearly that now. It's just over there."

Robert pointed to a chapel like building which was attached to the rear of the old students' union opposite.

"Thanks. I'd like that," replied Larry. "Besides you, I haven't really met anyone yet."

"Where are you staying?" asked Robert.

"In lodgings on Palatine Road. My landlady is expecting a couple more students, but they're third years and not arriving until next week."

"It's nice in Withington," noted Robert "and you're all right for the buses."

"Yes, lots of them come straight down Oxford Road."

Noticing Kay coming out of the Arts Building, Robert waved and called out to her. As she walked over to them, both he and Larry stood up ready to greet her.

"Have you had a good morning?" asked Robert.

"Yes," said Kay. "The staff were very nice and everything was well organised."

"Not like for us then," replied Robert, chuckling.

"Well, Robert. Aren't you going to introduce me to your friend?" asked Kay.

"Yes, I'm sorry. This is Larry."

"Hello, I'm Kay."

Kay smiled and held out her hand. Larry took hold of it gently. Her skin felt soft, but her firm hand shake suggested a real strength of personality. Kay struck him as warm and friendly and it was impossible to ignore the fact that she was exceptionally pretty.

"Come on then," she continued, "are we going to get something to eat?"

Walking over to the entrance to 'Caf', they went inside. Their first time in the building, they couldn't fail to be impressed. 'Caf' was originally St David's Welsh Church and had been completed in 1899. It had been designed and built in the Early Perpendicular style out of red brick, with Ruabon terracotta dressings. It had a nave and aisles, with a chancel and vestries on its south side and it contained a number of pointed arches. Large, light and airy, it was a wonderful space. Deconsecrated in 1935, it had been purchased by the university and turned into a refectory.

Sat with their tea and sandwiches, the conversation flowed quickly and easily. Kay was impressed with Larry. Under his dark black hair that swept across his forehead, he had a pleasant countenance. He also possessed a laudable sense of humour. When amused, his brown eyes would open wide, his lips would part and break into a grin that revealed his brilliant white teeth. He was articulate, clearly very clever and listened attentively to what she and Robert were saying. Yet she also felt a sense of sadness within him and at times he seemed a little unsure of himself. It was clear that he came from a privileged background and Kay wondered how he would adapt to life in a Northern industrial city. It didn't concern her too much though, for she had already decided that, together with Robert, she would be on hand to help him make the necessary adjustments.

"I have to say that it's very pleasant in here," remarked Larry. "It's quite strange to be drinking and eating in a chapel."

"And most importantly, it's a cheap place for dinner," remarked Robert.

"Oh, they serve dinner as well, do they? I thought that most students went home, or back to their lodgings for their evening meal."

Kay and Robert began to laugh. For a moment, Larry looked confused, then his eyes lit up and he began to smile.

"Oh, you meant lunch. It's a good place for a cheap lunch!"

"No," replied Robert. "We meant dinner. You're in Manchester now lad and it's dinner!"

"Don't tease him, Robert. You're not being fair. He'll need time to mend his Southern ways. Isn't that right Larry?"

Kay looked at him and smiled.

"You're the one teasing me now," replied Larry.

"Yes, but you don't mind, do you?"

Kay looked at him mischievously. Once again, she and Robert started to laugh. It wasn't long before Larry joined in. He felt comfortable; appreciative of how warmly they had welcomed him. Larry had only known them for a short time, but Kay and Robert had already extended the hand of friendship to him.

"Why did you choose to come to Manchester?" asked Kay, once the hilarity had subsided.

"Yes," said Robert, "especially as you told Franks that you'd been offered a place at Cambridge. Why didn't you take it?"

"I suppose part of the reason was down to the fact that going to Cambridge was just expected of me. That would have been the easy option. Yet when I went to look around and returned for my interview, it seemed too comfortable and privileged. I thought if I came here, that I'd be able to live and study in a completely different environment. I've spent all my life in rural Kent and all my education in an independent school. That hasn't given me a balanced perspective on life. That's why I'm here."

"I see," said Kay. "You're like Robert, you see yourself as a bit of a rebel."

"No. My teachers and some of my friends saw it that way, but I didn't. I just wanted to broaden my horizons by coming to a real city with real people."

"Oh, you'll certainly see that here," said Kay.

"And that means of course, that we're going to have to make sure that we show you around," noted Robert.

"When we do," added Kay, "you'll find that working-class life doesn't quite fit with the romantic notions you may have about it."

"Oh, no. You've got me all wrong," insisted Larry, concerned. "It makes me seem condescending. I'm not naïve. Human weakness exists among all social groups, rich and poor. People are good and bad everywhere. Yet I've also learnt enough to know that society isn't fair and I believe that I have a responsibility to help change that and I can only do it by understanding the lives of working people. That won't happen if I sit in a library in Cambridge reading books. I've already led a far too sheltered life, especially by spending seven years at King's."

"I see what we've got here," remarked Robert. "Our friend Larry is part of the tradition of liberal minded, upper class 'toffs'. He's determined to do his bit for the downtrodden workers. He aspires to be a latter-day Gladstone or Disraeli."

Larry looked closely at Robert, but he couldn't discern any trace of emotion. He was uncertain how to respond.

"You two are always ribbing me, I never know when you're being serious. Are you?" asked Larry.

"No. He's just being daft," replied Kay, smiling. "We wouldn't joke with you if we thought you couldn't take it. Isn't that right Robert?"

"Oh. I'm not sure about that," declared Robert, grinning.

Larry broke into a smile.

"I see," he replied. "You're just giving this soft, Southern 'toff', a sample of your good old working-class wit and repartee."

"That's better," said Kay. "Give it him back. You mustn't be too serious Larry. And you shouldn't be embarrassed about your background or apologise for the public school that you went to. Where we come from, most people don't care about that. All they want to know, is that your heart is in the right place. They'll take you as they find you."

"I understand," said Larry, nodding. "I have to say though that I feel like I've been well and truly told off."

"Oh, you'll find that Kay's very good at that," suggested Robert.

"Well, considering how gormless you are, I can't help getting plenty of practice, can I?"

Kay's quick response, stunned Robert into silence and Larry found himself starting to laugh. Yet, the general sense of hilarity, didn't disguise the fact that here before him, was a very special young woman. Kay possessed feminine qualities in abundance; she had grace and beauty, was kind and considerate, quick witted and intelligent. Yet she also impressed him as tough and uncompromising; a steadfast friend. It was obvious why Robert held Kay in such high esteem, even referring to her as his 'teacher'.

Over the following weeks, Kay and Robert's friendship played a crucial role in ensuring Larry's comfortable transition to life in Manchester. Although he had assured his family that the city was the best destination for him, in reality he wasn't quite so confident. In fact, Larry felt nervous after he had first arrived at London Road Station. Taking a taxi out to Withington, the city was bustling with people and vehicles. He could see that it was a tough, hard environment; one so unfamiliar. On that first night in his student digs, he had felt alone. Meeting Robert and Kay changed everything. They showed him around and their families invited him into their homes. Their support ensured a successful start to his studies and helped him to feel part of the city too.

Chapter 24

Larry's first evening venture into the centre of Manchester was certainly not without incident and proved just as educational as the lectures he'd been attending. Just before Christmas, Kay suggested that they should go to the pictures and after they had looked through the entertainments page in the *Evening News*, it was decided that they would go to see Alec Guinness in 'The Horse's Mouth' at the Odeon on Oxford Street. It was a unanimous decision given the rave reviews that the film had received and the admiration all three of them had for the Oscar winning actor.

As they would be going on Saturday night, it was arranged that Larry would take the bus from his lodgings down to Parker Street, in order to meet Kay, who had just taken on a Saturday job at Lewis's. The two of them would then wait for Robert in the nearby 'Wimpy'. Still employed at Stewarts, Robert would be making his way to them from Ardwick Green.

Kay had told Larry to be outside the store just before six. When he stepped off the bus, it was a dismal evening. There was a light, but persistent drizzle and a thin haze that hung all around, accentuated by the glare of the glowing street lamps and the headlights of cars and buses as they circled around Piccadilly Gardens. Approaching Lewis's on Market Street, Larry could see its large, bright windows displaying an array of attractive gifts. Above them, on the narrow ledge that ran the length of the building, were a series of large decorated fir trees representing the season of goodwill. From top to bottom, the building was festooned with decorations.

As the drizzle began to intensify, Larry decided to move away from the main doors, so that he could take shelter inside Lewis's Arcade. Stood under its canopy, he could keep popping his head out and look back along Market Street to see if Kay had emerged. As the shops were closing, there were fewer people around now, but Larry noticed a woman rapidly approaching him. Standing back, to let her pass, she stopped and smiled.

"Hello love. Lost your way, have you?"

"No," replied Larry, "I'm just waiting."

"That's what I thought," she replied, smiling.

Larry looked at her closely. She was wearing a long, beige raincoat, that went almost to her ankles. Her belt was pulled tightly around her waist, so accentuating her figure. On her feet she had an attractive pair of brown heels. As far as he could tell she was in her late thirties, but her bleach blonde hair, blue eye shadow and black mascara, suggested her desire to appear somewhat younger. When she turned into the light, the lines on her face couldn't be disguised, yet she certainly wasn't unattractive. Unsure of how to respond, Robert didn't understand why she had approached him.

Seeing his confusion, the woman laughed.

"Well, you're a shy one. Don't worry love. I'll look after you."

The woman smiled and put her hand on his shoulder. Larry felt apprehensive. He pulled away and quickly glanced around him, thinking that there may be a nearby accomplice, ready to attack and rob him. Seeing the fear in his eyes, the woman looked disappointed.

"There's no need to be like that. If you're not interested, just say so."

"Interested in what?"

For Larry, the penny still hadn't dropped.

"Oh my," laughed the woman. "You really don't know, do you? And here I was, thinking there weren't any innocent fellas left. You're a right turn up for the books, aren't you cock?"

The woman began to walk down the arcade and breathing a sigh of relief, Larry quickly returned to Lewis's entrance, no longer concerned about getting wet. Kay emerged almost immediately.

"Hi Larry. Have you been waiting long?"

"No. No. Not at all," replied Larry, somewhat hesitantly.

Kay looked at him. He seemed distracted.

"Are you all right, Larry?"

"Yes, of course. I'm fine."

Larry smiled, keen to convince her that he was. The incident with the woman had made him feel uncomfortable, but he preferred not to mention it to Kay, for fear that he would appear rather foolish.

Arriving at the 'Wimpy', Kay and Larry found Robert already sat inside. They still had plenty of time to make it to the cinema, so decided that they would have something to eat. When Kay went over to order the food, Larry quickly told Robert about the woman and her strange behaviour.

"And this was in Lewis's Arcade, was it?" asked Robert.

"Yes."

"And you've no idea what it was all about?"

"No, or I wouldn't be asking you."

Suddenly, Robert began to laugh.

"What's happened?" asked Kay, who had now returned to the table.

"It's our country cousin here."

"What's he done?"

"He's only gone and had an encounter with 'one of Lewis's'. The only thing is, he didn't know it."

"And when was that?"

"Whilst he was waiting for you."

Kay looked at Larry, who stared blankly in return. He had been listening to his friends' conversation, but was clearly mystified as to what they were talking about.

"You're going to have to tell him Robert. He's got no idea."

"Larry. She was on the batter."

"What?"

"On the game; a prostitute," continued Robert, wondering if his friend was ever going to understand.

"Oh," said Larry, quietly. "I really didn't know."

"And if you had," asked Robert, mischievously. "Would you have been tempted?"

Larry blushed and although Kay tried to control herself, she found it impossible not to laugh.

"She may have been from around our way Larry," added Robert. "There are a few of them on the dilly. We might be able to track her down and give you a formal introduction."

Larry wasn't amused, particularly as his friends' laughter was drawing the attention of nearby customers. Gradually however, calm was restored and Larry was able to express his surprise at being propositioned in such a prominent part of town.

"It's been like it for ages," replied Robert. "You'll find them in Piccadilly, down Market Street, York Street and other places too. They're always touting for business, especially when it goes dark."

"She probably approached you Larry, because she thought you were loitering and trying to pick someone up," added Kay. "It can be awkward for women too. I was waiting to meet a friend further along Market Street and one came over and told me to clear off her patch. It's happened to quite a few girls I know."

"Don't the police do anything about it?" asked Larry.

"They occasionally round a few of them up, but generally they leave them alone," replied Kay.

"Perhaps for favours rendered," suggested Robert, laughing.

Moving on to the Odeon, the film lived up to expectations, making for an enjoyable night. As they arrived back at Parker Street to catch their respective buses home, Larry prepared to say farewell.

"Thanks for the night out. I'll see you both on Monday morning."

"Hold on," said Robert, "we'll come to your stop with you. Make sure you get on the bus all right."

"It's only just there," replied Larry, pointing along the bus shelter.

"Well, you can't be too careful," said Kay.

Larry looked at his friends. They were deadly serious.

"No, honestly. I'm fine. You might end up missing your bus."

"No, it's too early for the last one," said Robert.

"And we'd rather walk back, than risk anything happening to you. We'd never forgive ourselves," added Kay.

"Especially if your lady friend comes back."

Kay and Robert began to laugh. Larry shook his head and smiled. He had no alternative, for their serious demeanour had fooled him completely.

"We had you there, didn't we?" asked Robert.

"Yes, I suppose you did."

"Nevertheless," said Kay, "I'll be a lot happier if I see you safely on the bus. I'm not sure that you've got wise to living in Manchester yet."

No, honestly. I'm fine. You get off," insisted Larry.

"There's no point arguing," said Robert. "You know Kay always gets her way."

Reluctantly, Larry agreed, but not without a grumble.

"I feel like a child, being told what to do."

"Well as far as being in Manchester late at night is concerned, you are like a child; you do need looking after."

Kay looked at him sternly. Larry knew that there was no point arguing further and deep down, he was appreciative of Kay's concern.

Getting on the bus, Larry took a seat on the lower deck, on the side nearest the stop. He looked out of the window and waved at Kay and Robert. He expected them to walk off, but they stayed. Only when the conductor had rung the bell and the driver started to pull away, did they give a final wave and then set off to catch their bus.

"You do worry about him, don't you Kay?" asked Robert, on the journey home.

"Yes, just like I worry about you Robert. The two of you are my closest friends and I'll do everything I can to make sure that nothing bad happens to either of you."

"Most people would find it very strange; a young woman like you looking out for us. They'd think it should be the other way around."

Robert smiled.

"Yes, they might. But who cares? You and Larry don't."

"No, that's true."

And it was. Kay had been looking out for him ever since that first day at school and now she had taken Larry under her wing too. For Robert, it had become a fact of life and he couldn't imagine that it would ever change.

Chapter 25

Together at Owens, Larry and Robert soon discovered that they had a common interest in journalism and consequently approached the office of the student union journal, the *News Bulletin*, to offer their support. Initially charged with administrative tasks, their enthusiasm led to them being given the opportunity to interview members of the college administration and write short pieces on matters of local interest. Both came impressively through the challenge. They could produce succinct and interesting articles to tight deadlines. Soon they were writing reviews and features and both were seen as future members of the editorial team, as the graduation of the existing members would inevitably leave vacancies to fill.

As the second year at Owens began, Robert approached the offices of Hammer Films. They were producing a movie, starring Stanley Baker, called 'Hell is a City'. The film was being shot on location in Manchester and Robert was pushing for an interview with the leading man. To his surprise, Hammer accepted his request and invited him down to watch the filming of the final scene at the Refuge Assurance Building on Oxford Street, before interviewing the actor at the nearby Midland Hotel.

When Robert told Kay and Larry, they were impressed, but a little surprised.

"And they knew that you were from a student journal and not one of the nationals?" asked Larry.

"Yes. They said that they could fit me in between the interviews they already had planned. They seemed to like the idea of the film being taken seriously in academic circles."

"I'm not sure we're that," said Larry.

"I know, but I wasn't going to argue. The film's director, Val Guest, made his reputation in comedy and he's never been taken that seriously by the critics. Perhaps, that's part of the reason they were happy to oblige."

"But he directed the 'Quatermass Xperiment' and 'Yesterday's Enemy'. They were brilliant films," replied Larry.

"Well, I suppose it's difficult to change perceptions, once you've got started in the business."

"You're really lucky getting to interview him, Robert. I wish I had the chance. He was lovely in 'Violent Playground' and 'Blind Date'."

It was evident that Kay was quite taken with the popular, handsome movie star, yet neither Robert nor Larry would dare suggest it to her.

"Well perhaps you can come too. We can get you a camera and pretend you're my photographer," suggested Robert.

"Do you think so?"

"Why not? All the other journalists will have one with them."

"I'd have to learn how to use it."

"It's easy. We can use one of those in the office."

On the afternoon in question, Robert and Kay presented themselves at the entrance to the Refuge Assurance Building, where they were met by a young member of Hammer's publicity department. They were both nervous but for different reasons. For Robert, it was the first big interview he'd ever done and he was desperate for it to go well. If he were successful, it would surely prove impressive to future, prospective employers. Robert had thoroughly researched his subject's background and career, devising a series of questions that he hoped would reveal details about the real man that lay behind the star. Kay's concerns were more straightforward. When they ended up meeting Stanley, she was desperate not to appear star-struck.

James, their host, explained that filming was taking place along the tops of the Refuge Building and India House next door.

"The cameras have been set up to film a chase across the roof and a final fight scene between Stanley and the villain, played by the American, John Crawford. It's a bit dangerous to have you up there, so I'll take you outside so we can watch the action from ground level."

Walking to Whitworth Street, they crossed over and stood by the corner of the Palace Theatre. It was now approaching five-thirty.

"Isn't it a little late to start filming?" asked Kay.

"No. Mr Guest wanted to be able to shoot the crowds down on the streets reacting to the scenes on the roof. He chose to film at this time because he knew it was rush hour and there would be lots of people making their way home from work. They would be bound to stop and gather to see what was going on."

"Clever," said Robert. "And the shots will appear spontaneous and authentic."

"It should certainly give an interesting view of the city from up there," added Kay.

"Yes, that was Mr Guest's intention. He wants Manchester to be constantly in the background. We've been shooting on location all over the city, trying to give the film a hard, Northern edge."

The director was right. A large crowd had gathered around them and there were others on the opposite side of Oxford Street too. The action had been visible from below. The struggle between Baker and Crawford, which had the latter dangling over the edge of the building, was realistic enough to convince some of the onlookers, that either one or both of them, would end up hurtling to their death. When finally, the filming had finished, James handed Robert a couple of passes and a letter that would give them access to Stanley for their interview.

"If you show the letter and passes to the staff on the reception desk at the *Midland*, they'll take you to the suite we've booked for the interviews. Our team will handle all the arrangements from there."

Walking down Oxford Street, Kay and Robert soon arrived at the entrance to the *Midland*. Ascending the gentle flight of steps, they went through the hotel doors and into the lobby beyond. Faced with the finely decorated and furnished interior, the two of them paused to take in their splendid surroundings.

"I didn't expect to be coming here for a few years at least," remarked Robert.

"If at all," replied Kay.

Manchester's grandest hotel, the *Midland* wasn't designed for the likes of the pair from Ardwick. It was the location where the great and the good came to stay when visiting the city, or perhaps met to strike a deal; just like Henry Rolls and Charles Royce had famously done in the early days of the establishment. It seemed the natural place for a production company to choose for its popular star to hold court before a collection of eager journalists.

"Well, we're definitely here now and I suppose we'd best go and report at reception."

"Be confident Robert. Don't let them condescend to you."

"I won't."

Kay needn't have worried. Even though still a young man, Robert's time at Owens had made him far more assured. He mixed easily with his middle-class contemporaries and he had developed a demeanour that fitted neatly into the stereotypical picture of a *Midland* guest. As such, the reception team were eager to help and one of them took Kay and Robert directly to the suite booked by Hammer.

Welcomed on their arrival, they found themselves in a large room with comfortable chairs in which a number of journalists were already waiting. To the side were a couple of long tables covered in white table cloths. They contained a large array of food and refreshments. Focused on their approaching interview, neither Kay nor Robert chose to avail themselves of any of the items on offer. With journalists being escorted from the room every twenty minutes, Robert realised the need to keep focused for when their turn arrived.

Eventually, Kay and Robert were the only ones left in the room and they realised that they would carry out the star's final interview. That was hardly surprising given that they represented the publication with the smallest circulation. Robert realised that Stanley must be tired by now, but he was counting on two factors to help keep him engaged once the interview began. Firstly, Robert realised that it was inevitable that the actor would have faced similar, repetitive questions from those who had gone before. After all, most publications were chasing the same readers, whose interests were focused on Baker as a celebrity. On the other hand, Robert's audience were intelligent young adults with a range of interests. That had allowed him to compile a set of questions far more interesting and challenging for his subject.

Should that not be the case, Robert was confident that Kay's presence would help rescue the situation. When he had first offered to bring her with him, it wasn't just because he knew she was eager to meet the actor. He also expected that Stanley would be charmed by her good looks and pleasant personality. He was sure too, that Kay wouldn't hesitate to ask searching questions of her own, should she feel the impulse to do so. In fact, Kay may prove more adept at eliciting revealing responses from the star, than himself.

Entering a small side room, the aspiring journalists were greeted warmly by Stanley, who rose from his chair, advanced towards them and shook their hands. He was dressed casually in a tweed sports jacket, shirt and tie and Kay wasn't disappointed in the man she saw before her. Stanley was just as he appeared on screen. Almost six feet tall, he was powerfully built and ruggedly handsome. A firm jaw, strong cheek bones and dark brown eyes that suggested strength and sensitivity in equal measure. When he'd taken her hand, his touch was soft and delicate. Inexplicably, she felt a thrill of excitement and for a moment she felt like a giddy, lovelorn schoolgirl, who longed for the actor to sweep her up in his arms and pull her close to his chest.

Motioning towards three comfortable chairs placed around a low table at the end of the room, Stanley invited them to sit down. He clearly felt relaxed and picked up an open packet of cigarettes from the table, offering one to Robert and Kay, who both declined. Lighting one for himself, Stanley sat back in his chair. He was the first to speak.

"I don't recall being interviewed by anyone from a university publication before. Why the interest?"

"Students are as curious as anyone when it comes to the life of a well-known actor," replied Robert. "Quite a few have ambitions to enter the profession themselves and all of us are interested to find out how someone from your background has, you could say, broken the mould and brought authentic, gritty, working-class characters to the screen. And of course, the new production is being filmed in Manchester. That brings a fascination in itself."

"Well, I can't disagree with that," said Stanley, smiling.

"About your background Mr Baker, did you find that coming from a mining family held you back in the early days?"

"I've said it before; it gave me a determination to succeed that I might not have had if my family had been well off. After my father's accident, I was determined that I wasn't going to follow him into the pits. But tell me, how hard have you two found it?"

"What do you mean?" asked Robert.

Stanley smiled.

"Well, with those Mancunian accents, it's quite clear that you're both from working-class stock. How did you find it, getting to university? I don't suppose it was easy?"

Stanley turned towards Kay.

"Sorry, I didn't catch your name."

"It's Kay."

"Well, Kay. How difficult was it?"

Stanley looked at her closely. He was waiting for an answer. Kay had certainly made an impression when she'd walked in carrying her camera. Wearing a fetching pale blue and white two-piece suit, it perfectly complemented her light brown hair, green eyes and fresh complexion.

"I think it's down to the support of those around you," replied Kay. "We both had to work hard and we helped one another, but without our families being prepared to let us take our exams, we wouldn't be here. There weren't many at grammar school from backgrounds like ours and of those, most left at fifteen or sixteen, as their families needed them working."

"Yes," replied Stanley, nodding. "My teacher, Glynne Morse, encouraged me to act and my parents never stood in the way of me pursuing a career on the stage. It would have been easy for me to have become a local tearaway. You could say I already was."

Stanley laughed and Kay smiled. She felt comfortable in his presence. He certainly carried none of the pretensions suffered by other high-profile stars she'd read about. Kay sensed that he was quite enjoying their interview. It was probably because he felt it unnecessary to be so guarded. After all, their publication wasn't part of the entertainment media.

"You must have been sympathetic to Johnnie Murphy's situation in 'Violent Playground'. Did you see a similarity between that character and yourself?" asked Kay. "Coming from similar backgrounds, it could just as easily have been you, or Robert here, who ended up falling foul of the law."

"That's a tricky question Kay and here I was thinking that you were just the photographer."

Stanley laughed, but nevertheless he was impressed with her knowledge of his work.

"You're right. It's easy to go off the rails when you're brought up in poverty, but Johnny's a pretty desperate character and I'm like Jack Truman, who I play in the film, in thinking that his actions can't be justified. But also, as Truman tries to do, I believe that we need to find ways to help boys like Johnny find a purpose in life. And of course, we have to remove the poverty that leads to desperation."

"We know that you're a strong supporter of the Labour Party," said Robert, "but as you've become a successful box office star, is there a danger that you'll lose touch with the working man?"

"That's a brave question. What you're actually asking me, is whether or not I've betrayed my roots."

Robert felt concerned. The interview had been going so well and now he feared that he had overstepped the mark. Stanley noticed the worried look on his face and was quick to reassure him.

"It's fine. A legitimate question. I do think about that. I don't see my wealth and position as providing a contradiction though. It enables me to fight with more influence for what I believe in. I've not turned my back on Wales, my family, my class or my heritage and I never will. But we should use the talents we are given and follow our vocation as far as we can. We have to live in the real world, hoping that we can create our ideal one. I'm sure you'll soon be facing similar choices yourself Robert. You'll probably find that you won't always be living in Manchester."

"We haven't asked you about your popularity with the female audience," said Kay, changing the subject. "You've played several tough characters who pretty much dominate the women in their lives. Are you concerned that you might end up with that image yourself?"

"My characters can be violent and aggressive; excessively masculine you could say. I'll often have a twisted sneer on my face, fighting or making love as if I hated the human race. It seems to fascinate and repel women at the same time, especially as my leading ladies battle against that excessive virility."

"Perhaps that's a reflection of the fact that more women are starting to question the perception that they should naturally be subordinate to men."

Stanley smiled. He paused for reflection before responding to Kay's suggestion. She was clever and pretty and was challenging him to reveal what he, not his characters, really thought about the relationship between men and women.

"I believe that most women long to be dominated, but that some of them fight against this instinct."

A part of Kay felt that Stanley's answer could be construed as condescending, yet she appreciated his honesty. Furthermore, having met the star, Kay had found him fascinating and she was certainly attracted to him. It was often said that you should never meet your heroes, for they will only disappoint. As far as Kay was concerned, Stanley certainly hadn't.

"Going back to your question about my image," continued Stanley. "Although I'm grateful for the exposure and rewards I've received, the trouble about playing tough roles is that's what people think I'm like in my private life as well. In fact, nothing could be further from the truth."

At that point, an assistant approached and indicated that it was time to bring the interview to a close.

"You must take some pictures Kay," said Stanley. "You'll need them for the article. I think this photography business is a little new to you, isn't it?"

"Yes," admitted Kay. "I've not done it before."

"Well, let Robert take care of it and if you like, he can also take one of the two of us."

The photos taken, Robert and Kay shook hands with Stanley and in no time at all had descended the steps from the *Midland* and were making their way past the Odeon to the 'Oxford Snack Bar'. Sat inside, tucking in to their sandwiches, they reviewed the day's work.

"I have to say that I liked him," said Kay, enthusiastically. "He was genuine; down to earth. Not at all arrogant. For all that he plays the tough guy, he has a soft, sensitive side which is evident when he talks to you."

"I could see that you were impressed," replied Robert. "Perhaps too impressed. You seemed enthralled with the man."

"But he isn't just any man, is he? He's a famous actor."

"What difference does that make?"

Kay sensed that Robert was getting jealous, but he was trying hard not to show it. She decided that she would tease him further.

"The movie cameras don't flatter him, do they? He's very handsome and he's fit; in good shape. I suppose he still boxes. It's said that he was a very good amateur and could have turned professional."

"I don't know," said Robert, barely hiding his irritation. "Anyone would think that you were a love-struck teenager."

Kay laughed.

"Well, I can't help finding him attractive now, can I? Most women in Britain do."

"Hmm, no doubt."

Robert was quiet. He was jealous. Kay had never looked at him in the way she had at Stanley.

"But you must respect him," said Kay. "His background is just like ours and he's done very well for himself."

"Yes, I agree," replied Robert. "What he said about my having to leave Manchester to follow my vocation. You and I have already talked about that. I don't want to settle into the first job I get after we graduate. I want to go as far as I can. It's logical. You and I have already overcome so many obstacles and I want to keep on going. For us, there'll always be another barrier, but I'm going to break through them all. Stanley's reached the top. He's got a smart house in London, a villa abroad and flash cars. When he was our age, he could only dream about it. But he's done it and so will I."

As he spoke, Robert become more animated. His final revelation was something of a surprise.

"That's what Joe Lampton in 'Room at the Top' would say," observed Kay. "I hope you don't ever become like him."

"It's just a film. It's not real," observed Robert.

"No, you're wrong. It has a serious message. Lampton sacrifices everything, even his own happiness, in order to pursue success. I'd hate to see that kind of ambition change you, Robert. You mustn't lose touch and turn your back on the past and the community that helped make you."

Noting her concern, Robert reached across the table and patted her shoulder.

"With you around, I'll always have a conscience, won't I? I'm sure you'll do your best to keep me in check."

"Well, just so you know."

Kay did her best to raise a smile. She had enjoyed the day's experience and was grateful that Robert had invited her along. Hopefully, he would heed her advice, but a whole new world had opened up for both of them since arriving at Owens. For a poor lad from Ardwick, the desire to equal and then surpass the material achievements of his so-called 'betters', may become an obsession that would be hard to resist.

Chapter 26

At the end of October, Robert was aware that his gran's birthday was rapidly approaching. He had kept on his weekend job at Stewarts and had been putting money aside from his wages so that he could treat her. Knowing her enthusiasm for wrestling, it seemed the obvious decision to take her to the King's Hall at Belle Vue. Sat with Kay and Robert during dinner in 'Caf', he told them of his plans.

"Oh, she'll be made up," said Kay. "She loves her wrestling."

"Yes, but gran can't afford to go that often," replied Robert, "so I thought it'd be nice for me to take her. The reason I've mentioned it, is because I wanted to see if you two would be interested in coming too."

"Of course," replied Kay. "We'd love to."

Larry smiled, amused at how she had simply made the decision for him.

"You do know what wrestling is, don't you Larry?" asked Robert.

"Of course, I do. They have it all over the country. It's just as popular in London, as it is here."

"Yes, but with you being a 'toff', I bet you've never been before, have you?"

Robert smiled, eager for the banter to continue.

"I think it's become your favourite hobby," said Kay, looking sternly at Robert.

"What has?"

"Tormenting Larry."

"No, it's all right Kay. I'm just waiting for a chance to get even."

Larry smiled and Kay shook her head.

"You're as bad as one another."

"Anyway, Robert's right. I've never been before, so I'd be interested to see it."

"Yes, you can find out how the other half lives," said Robert. "You can see some good old, working-class entertainment. None of your tennis or polo."

"I don't have a horse. How could I play polo?"

"Of course, you don't," replied Robert, with more than a hint of sarcasm.

"Can you two pack it in!"

The lads went quiet. Kay had spoken and when she was irritated, they both knew it was as well to listen.

On the following Saturday, at quarter past five, Kay and Larry arrived at Robert's house. The entertainment didn't start until seven, but one of Edna's neighbours, was part of the management at the King's Hall and had arranged for Edna to meet Billy Two Rivers, the famous wrestler, before the bouts began. Robert's gran was understandably excited and pleased that Kay and Larry were on time. Before they set off however, Kay had a card and a gift for her.

"Happy birthday Mrs Bloomfield. We've brought you a card and some 'Black Magic'."

Edna's eyes lit up at the sight of the box of chocolates.

"They're my favourites. Oh, that's lovely. But you shouldn't have love. And you too Larry."

Throwing her arms around Kay, Edna gave her a kiss.

"Well, they could try taking them back," suggested Robert.

"You cheeky ..."

"Ah, ah, Gran," said Robert, grinning and shaking his head. "We've got visitors."

"I'll give you visitors. Watch out lad."

Edna gave her grandson a reproachful look, but it was clear to them all that she wasn't the least bit angry with him.

"Anyway Gran, we'd best get a move on if we want to make sure we meet Billy Two Rivers."

"Billy Two Rivers?" asked Larry.

"Haven't you been to wrestling before love?"

"No."

"Oh, you'll really enjoy it," continued Edna. "Billy Two Rivers has just come over from Canada. He's a real Red Indian, you know. Not a fake like some of them love."

"Oh."

"Yes," continued Edna. She talked quietly, her hushed tones emphasising Billy's authenticity. "He's a real Mohawk Indian with a native hairstyle; bald at the sides, with a thick mane of black hair down the centre of his head. I can't wait to see him in his headdress and if we're lucky, he'll do his war dance and use his tomahawk chop."

Despite his Mohawk heritage, it sounded to Larry as if Billy was setting out to create a parody of himself. Whether the audience would see it in that way, was questionable however. Yet, did it really matter? The reality was that if he really wanted to understand working-class culture, he should simply relax and experience the excitement and emotions that would be generated by the events in the ring.

Belle Vue was a relatively short distance from Armitage Street. The complex, along Hyde Road, was a huge site that covered one hundred and sixty-five acres. The original zoological gardens were established back in 1836. By the turn of the century, a famous amusement park had also developed. Visitors now flocked in by train from all over the country and beyond. A Christmas circus was added along with exhibition halls, cafés and restaurants. The King's Hall had become a venue for sports and music and there were also greyhound and speedway tracks, the latter the home of the Belle Vue Aces.

Reaching the zebra crossing at the junction of Belle Vue Street, Larry could see the impressive main entrance and the kiosks for admission at the side. Along the top of the latter were large letters spelling out the words 'Belle Vue' and rising behind them into the gloomy Manchester sky, was the huge framework of the world famous, hair-raising rollercoaster, 'The Bobs'.

Presenting their tickets at the kiosk, they entered through into a tree lined walk leading down to the King's Hall, a range of animal enclosures extending to their left and beyond. All the while however, they could hear the ratchet of the chain cog mechanism, hauling the carriages up the steep climbs on the 'Bobs'. Then, the whoosh and rattle of the cars, as having reached the top, they hurtled down and around the twists and curves of the track, their occupants screaming. With a reputation for danger and acknowledged as one of the World's fastest roller coasters, the ride inspired fear, fascination and admiration in equal measure. It was a point of honour among young Mancunians to ride the 'Bobs' and there was a fatalistic approach to doing so that overcame the terror it inspired and so kept a constant stream of victims queueing to take their place on board.

"I don't think we'll have time to get on the 'Bobs'," said Robert, who'd noticed Larry looking towards them.

"No, we won't. We're here for the wrestling," said Kay, sharply.

"I know," replied Robert, "but I wouldn't expect you to go on them anyway. You never have."

"No. Because I've got far more sense than you. It doesn't make you a tough guy if you have. Certainly not in your case," added Kay, smiling.

"Why are they called the 'Bobs'?" asked Larry.

"It depends on who you ask. Some people say that the carriages are like bobsleighs and so 'Bobs' is an abbreviation. Others say it's because it used to cost a shilling, 'a bob', to ride on them. The one thing I find interesting though," continued Robert, "is that my old school has moved to a new site off Kirkmanshulme Lane, at the back of the zoo. I can imagine some of the kids finding it a bit of a distraction, with it being open when they're in lessons."

Larry looked shocked.

"What? Do you mean that they might play truant?"

"It's called wagging school here," said Kay "and yes, some will. Not many grammar school kids do, as they're too afraid of the consequences and know that they have exams to pass."

"Yes," added Robert. "When I was at school, only those who didn't care, would do it. They didn't mind getting the strap if they got caught and they usually did. Their reputations meant that the school would always check up on them when they were absent."

They were now outside the King's Hall and Edna could see her neighbour waving to her. It was time to go inside and meet Billy Two Rivers.

Chapter 27

Bob Preston was a jolly and rotund middle-aged man, with thinning hair and a large personality. Since leaving school at thirteen, he had been employed for over thirty years at Belle Vue and had gradually worked his way up to a position on the management team at the Kings Hall. It had given him close access to the stars who appeared there and he was delighted to occasionally introduce his friends and family to them.

"He's a lovely lad, Billy. You can't go wrong with him Edna. Ask him anything you want and he'll be straight with you."

Bob took them inside the vast arena and led them down to the ring, located at its centre.

"It's strange to see it empty like this. It's so quiet."

"It'll soon liven up when everyone gets in. Especially with you here Edna," added Bob, laughing.

"Can I get in the ring?" asked Edna.

"Yes, of course you can. And you youngsters too."

Bob climbed the steps at the corner of the ring and held open the ropes so that his guests could climb through. Following them in, he chuckled as he saw Edna bouncing up and down on the centre of the ring.

"Isn't it springy!" she exclaimed.

"Of course," said Bob, "the floor needs to give when wrestlers are thrown to the canvas. If it didn't, they'd soon get badly injured."

"But it must be difficult to get your bearings."

"No, you soon get used to it," came a voice from behind.

The words were softly spoken and the accent unfamiliar. Edna turned round. Her eyes opened wide; amazement was writ large on her face. She was face to face with Billy Two Rivers. Dressed casually in a loose-fitting suit, he held out his hand. Tentatively, Edna reached out towards him and shook it. Robert smiled. His gran was finding it hard to believe that Billy was really with them.

"Hello Edna, it's nice to see you," said Billy. "I've something for you."

Clutched in his other hand was a signed photo with a personal dedication to Edna.

"Oh, that's lovely. You shouldn't have."

Robert and his friends smiled. It was exactly what she'd said when given the box of 'Black Magic' earlier.

"The ring seems bigger, when you get inside it," remarked Edna. "I can see why it's not so easy for a wrestler to reach the ropes, when they're in trouble."

"That's right Edna and if you're fighting a villain and they've got you pinned down in the middle and the referee's distracted, they've got you at their mercy."

"Oh, I know," said Edna. "That Jackie Pallo and Mick McManus, they get up to some right shenanigans, don't they love? It must be hard playing fair when they keep getting up to all those dirty tricks."

Billy smiled. He was the consummate professional and wasn't going to undermine any of her illusions concerning the world of professional wrestling. Edna was a committed fan and like so many of her fellow aficionados, believed wholeheartedly in wrestling's authenticity and integrity. Her three young companions however, soon demonstrated a more critical approach towards the sport. Walking over to a corner of the ring, Kay examined the protective pad that covered the metal post which held the ropes. Hitting the cushion with her hand, she expressed her surprise.

"It's soft. I expected it to be firm. When wrestler's get thrown against it, they always get hurt. They either fall to the floor, or are dazed and can't defend themselves."

A faint smile flitted across Billy's lips, but he made no reply. Walking over, Robert slapped the pad with his hand. His reaction was similar to Kay's, except it went much further.

"You're right Kay. It's really soft. There's no way that anyone can get hurt being thrown against one of these pads. It's just a big con."

"Robert!"

Edna was mortified, concerned that her grandson's thoughtlessness had upset their host.

"I'm sorry Billy," continued Edna. "I don't know what's happened to his manners. Robert's not normally like this."

"Yes," said Robert, looking suitably chastened. "I'm sorry Billy, I wasn't thinking. I hope I didn't offend you."

"Is that because I'm a dangerous guy, or because you don't really think wrestling's a con?"

Billy smiled, but he was a powerful looking athlete and Robert began to look distinctly uncomfortable. Kay and Larry could see the fear in his eyes and both had to try hard to contain their mirth.

"I know," suggested Billy, "let's see whether this wrestling game really is a con. What do you say Robert?"

"What do you mean?" asked Robert, uncertainly.

"Well, just step over here and the rest of you," Billy gestured towards the others, "if you go and stand over in that corner, Robert and I will put on a little demonstration."

Bob, Edna, Larry and Kay, did as he asked. They were fascinated to know what was going to happen next and Billy, the great showman, wasn't going to disappoint. Suddenly, he grabbed Robert under the shoulder and with ease picked him up and swung him back into the air, the two of them sailing to the floor. As the canvas bounced to receive them, the effects could be felt by those at the edge of the ring.

"That wasn't too bad, was it Robert?" asked Billy. "You can't get hurt on a nice springy canvas, can you?"

Robert, prostrate and effectively pinned to the canvas, found it hard to respond. Eventually, he produced a grunt.

"What's that Robert. It's all a con?"

Holding on to Robert's arm, Billy sprang back to his feet.

"Come on Robert, let's get you up."

Shocked and confused by his somersault through the air, Robert got slowly to his feet.

"Let's see if this hurts then Robert, but I'm sure it won't."

Standing in front of his 'opponent', Billy put his right arm behind Robert's head whilst his left arm moved under Robert's right. Placing his left hand on Robert's shoulder, Billy pulled him forward. As Robert had no alternative but to stoop down, Billy turned to the side, his left arm firmly holding Robert's right.

"That's what we call an arm lock Robert," said Billy. "But of course, it doesn't hurt, does it? We're just conning Edna and your friends, aren't we?"

Kay and Robert watched as Robert's face went a deeper shade of red. Edna, mesmerised by Billy's close-up demonstration, had forgotten all about her grandson's welfare.

"It doesn't hurt, does it?" repeated Billy.

"Yes! Yes!"

Billy reduced the pressure, but didn't release the hold.

"No Robert. You're just acting. Be serious. Tell them it doesn't."

"It does! It does! Submit! Submit!"

"But we haven't done the bit where my knee slams into the side of your head. We're set up for it now. Come on. It's the best part of the act. Don't disappoint everyone."

"No! No! It isn't a con. Honest!"

"Oh," said Billy, sounding disappointed. "I thought it was."

Releasing his hold, Billy stepped away from Robert and smiled.

"Well, there you are folks. It seems as if it isn't."

As Robert moved gingerly towards them, Kay and Larry burst out laughing. Billy had certainly made his point. Wrestlers were skilled practitioners of their craft and not just celebrities. As Billy had demonstrated, they had the ability to inflict serious damage on one another. Regardless of whether the action was contrived or not, those who participated were in a dangerous business.

Rubbing his arm, Robert received no sympathy from his gran.

"It serves you right for acting the goat."

"But…"

"No buts," said Edna, dismissively. "You shouldn't have been rude to Billy."

Billy smiled.

"Well Edna, it's been nice to meet you. I must go and prepare for tonight."

With their farewells ringing in his ears, Billy made his way to the changing rooms.

"Well, I'd best let you out again," said Bob. "You've still got time to get something to eat before we start at seven-thirty."

Sat in the cafe with her young companions, surrounded by tea, cake and sandwiches, Edna couldn't stop talking about how wonderful Billy had been. Robert wasn't quite as enthusiastic, but nevertheless had begun to appreciate his rather quirky sense of humour.

"That photograph, it's a belter, isn't it?" asked Edna. "I'm going to get a nice frame for it and I can put it next to Robert's on the sideboard in the front room."

"Are you sure you shouldn't move mine so that you can see Billy's better?" asked Robert.

"Don't be so gormless," replied Edna, shaking her head. "Any one would think you've got a cob on, because Billy had a bit of fun with you."

"A bit of fun? He had me in an arm lock and it hurt."

"Well, we thought it was fun," said Kay, laughing.

"He's always been a big softie. Haven't you love?"

Edna patted Robert reassuringly on the shoulder.

"Never mind," said Kay, "he's got us to look after him, hasn't he Mrs Bloomfield?"

"That's right," agreed Edna "and it's a good job that he has."

Robert shook his head. They were ganging up on him, but he knew that what they said was true. Billy, Edna and Kay had put him well and truly in his place.

Chapter 28

It really was an education. Larry had never witnessed anything like it. Warmth and passion, anger and hostility; an intensity of excitement that washed around the arena. All eyes were focused on the wrestling gods, as their titanic struggles swung one way and then the other, providing all the drama of a Hollywood epic.

Yet at first, it had all seemed rather tame. The opening bouts involved skilled practitioners whose abilities were warmly applauded by an appreciative audience. A whole range of moves and holds were being expertly demonstrated, but there was nothing to get the fans on their feet. It was too clean, too sporting; almost polite. The fans had grafted hard all week. They needed something to ignite their emotions. As the early contests came to an end, it was all about to change.

There were two types of wrestlers who really counted; the heroes and the heels. These were characters with a story to tell and a reputation to uphold. Billy was, of course, a hero. He fought fair, was honest and just. But he also had that unique Mohawk identity that set him apart; his trademark headdress, tomahawk chop and triumphant war dance. The antithesis of Billy were grapplers like Mick McManus and Jackie Pallo. They were mean and nasty; villains who fought dirty. For these men, the rules didn't matter. Winning, by whatever means possible, did.

It could all so easily have descended into comic farce. Nevertheless, it didn't and the reason was due to the sport's unpredictability and its capacity to tap into the working-class psyche. It was good versus evil, but with a twist. Unlike in the movies, the hero didn't always win. And the audience could understand it, for they had all been cheated and exploited by a landlord or a boss. So often, right had been on their side, yet they had still lost. Their heroes were like themselves, fighting on with their values intact. Doing it the right way, even though they knew that that when they met a McManus or a Pallo, they could be cheated of victory. Larry didn't fail to see the irony of it all. The fans' sympathy for the 'gallant loser' reflecting the old public-school adage that it wasn't important whether you won or lost, but how you played the game.

Regardless, many fans still developed a grudging admiration for those heels who somehow, some way, would always seem to grasp victory from the jaws of defeat. The more these wrestlers prospered, the more eager the fans became to see them finally receive their comeuppance. The promoters loved it, for nothing could be more guaranteed to keep the box office merrily ticking over.

In the early matches, Edna's response to the action had been quite subdued. She'd clearly been enjoying herself, but everything so far was just a warm-up for the final couple of bouts. That was when Billy would be appearing, before Jackie Pallo, 'the man they loved to hate', topped the bill.

Billy's opponent was Bill Howes. Well known on the circuit, he was a tough, uncompromising opponent, famed for his 'backbreaker' and 'Boston Crab'. Nevertheless, Edna had few fears for her favourite when he entered the ring, resplendent in his long, magnificent headdress. Taking it off, he stood proudly, a powerful figure acknowledging the cheers of his fans. At first the match ran smoothly, both wrestlers taking stock of their opponent in the opening round. As the action continued into round two however, Billy's superior skills began to have his opponent in trouble. Dazed in the middle of the ring, Howes was open to a perfectly delivered tomahawk chop that sent him crashing to the floor. Following up, Billy quickly pressed his shoulders to the mat and after a count of three, the referee confirmed that Billy had achieved the first of the two falls he needed for victory.

Billy's success brought an immediate change of approach from his opponent. Howes, when under pressure, wasn't beyond turning to the dark arts in order to increase his chances. From the moment the bell rang for round three, he was looking for an opportunity to get on the blind side of the referee and deliver an illegal blow to his opponent. Successful, the fans howled in protest at the referee who, as convincingly as possible, indicated that he'd seen nothing wrong. Yet as a stunned Billy was pulled on to the ropes, it was time for him to step in and pause the action. Howes merely swept him aside and proceeded to twist the top and middle ropes around Billy's head and shoulders. Having trapped his opponent, Howes then delivered a series of forearm smashes to Billy's face and chest before finally, the referee pulled him away. As Billy was slowly released from the ropes by his cornerman, the referee lectured Howes in the centre of the ring. The audience, including Edna, was now baying for his blood and at the very least, his disqualification. But that wasn't part of the plan; good must have its chance to defeat evil.

As the referee signalled for the bout to continue, the MC announced that Howes had received a 'public warning'. It was no punishment of course and as Billy was still dazed in the centre of the ring, Howes had soon knocked him to the canvas and manoeuvred his limp body into a position to put him in a backbreaker and gain a match tying submission. As Billy was helped back to his corner, it seemed touch and go whether he'd be able to continue. Larry watched Edna, concern writ large on her face, but willing her hero to go just one more round. Billy did, but straightaway he was in trouble, slammed against the post and drop kicked to the floor. Back on his feet, he received a barrage of forearm smashes. Surely, he was finished and Howes was gleefully getting ready to issue the coup de grace. Then, out of nowhere, came the recovery. Drawing on all his proud Mohawk inheritance, Billy straightened up, beat his chest and launched ferociously into his opponent. Caught off guard, it was now Howes turn to be stunned. Unsteady on his feet, he had no answer to another crunching tomahawk chop that sent him crashing to the mat. Pinning him once more, Billy had his victory. Getting to his feet he gleefully performed his famous war dance as his vanquished opponent lay prostrate on the canvas, his fans dancing up and down and cheering uncontrollably.

There had been times during the bout when Edna had almost lost control. Larry suspected that it was only because he and Kay were with her, that she had managed to restrain herself from rushing to the ring in order to confront Howes. It was clear though, that Billy's victory had left her in quite an emotional state and Larry wondered whether witnessing the final match of the evening, with 'the man they love to hate', would finally tip her over the edge.

For all that Jackie Pallo was hated by the fans, none of them could deny that he was a tremendous showman. His extreme cockiness in the ring, his blatant cheating and illegal moves, the way he would hold up the action to joke or remonstrate with hostile members of the audience, made him a star attraction. Everyone wanted to see him lose, but he rarely ever did. Tonight, the promoter had thrown him a young, naïve prospect. The lad was outrageously talented but crucially, lacked the vicious cunning of his wily opponent. Despite all of their hopes, few in the audience felt that Pallo would be defeated.

Nevertheless, the lad started well, throwing Jackie around the ring and slipping his attempted counters. In fact, frustrated because he couldn't get to grips with his young adversary, Pallo began to complain to the referee that his opponent wasn't fighting fair.

"Get off with you, you mard sod!" yelled Edna.

Larry was shocked. He couldn't believe what he'd heard. Yet looking around him, he could see many other old women on their feet, shaking their fists and shouting expletives towards the ring. All the while, Jackie was smiling, identifying those nearest the ring to whom he could give a response. It was pure theatre as Jackie worked the emotions of the fans. The prospect, inexperienced in such an atmosphere, stood waiting for his opponent to get back to the business of wrestling. His naivety cost him dear as without warning, Pallo launched an attack, knocking his opponent to the canvas. Dragging him to his feet, Jackie applied an arm lock and then forced him once more to the floor. Blindsiding the referee, Pallo delivered a couple of rabbit punches to the back of his opponent's head, then turned him on his back and pinned him down for a count of three. Leaping to his feet, Jackie strutted arrogantly around the ring.

The arena was in uproar and Edna was furious.

"The dirty bugger! Let me get at him. I'll show him."

Larry stood open mouthed in amazement and although he felt slightly embarrassed for her, Kay and Robert just couldn't stop laughing. Edna hadn't noticed any of their reactions, she was oblivious to everything other than giving Jackie a piece of her mind. Before anyone had a chance to stop her, Edna was at the corner of the ring, remonstrating with Jackie.

"You're nothing but a cheat Pallo. A bad 'un. You couldn't beat the lad if you fought fair."

"Now, don't be like that missus," replied Jackie, smiling. "I always fight fair. He's the one trying to run away all the time."

"Look at the poor lad. Just look at him!" said Edna, pointing to the young opponent sat groggily on his stool. "You should be ashamed of yourself. You're just a bully and if I get hold of you …"

Edna didn't get chance to finish. An attendant laid a gentle arm on her shoulder and suggested that she should return to her seat. Suddenly realising where she was, Edna let him lead her gently away, a cheery farewell from Jackie ringing in her ears.

Pallo loved the fans' participation. He understood that it was part of the spectacle and provided the drama that made the sport so appealing. Moreover, he had the confidence, character and experience to play the crowd like a fiddler with a Stradivarius. Whenever emotions threatened to get out of hand, he could hold them at bay by slipping back into passages of more orthodox wrestling.

Back in her seat, Edna was calm. Her anger had peaked following her outburst at Jackie and the bout seemed effectively over. Yet her mood improved as Pallo, appearing just a little too arrogant, relaxed enough to give his opponent the chance to come back strongly.

"Go on love, pummel him," shouted, Edna enthusiastically.

"He's no chance gran," said Robert. "Pallo's too good. He's just toying with him."

The situation however, suggested anything but, as a stunning dropkick sent Jackie to the canvas. Seizing the opportunity, his opponent pinned his shoulders and suddenly the bout was level.

Edna jumped up and down clapping enthusiastically and turned triumphantly to Robert.

"There, lad. You're wrong."

"We'll see."

Robert felt confident. He knew the script. The promising novice would be given an equalising fall and the fans would dare to believe that he could slay the monster. Then, just as it seemed likely that he would succeed, the heel would recover to snatch the victory from his grasp.

And yet, for a time it really did seem as though Pallo had met his match. Three times, Jackie was just one count away from defeat and only a desperate, but successful lunge for the bottom rope, enabled him to avoid submitting when his opponent had him in a Boston Crab. Robert, as cynical as he was, began to wonder if their moves really were being choreographed, for Jackie's desperate situation certainly seemed convincing. His defeat inevitable.

Edna turned again to her grandson.

"He's had it now. He's finished!"

"It's not over yet," replied Robert.

And it wasn't. With the referee distracted, Jackie lashed out a kick into his opponent's stomach, bending him double. Grabbing his legs and turning him upside down, Jackie completed a text book piledriver. Knocked senseless, his opponent couldn't resist having his shoulders pinned to the canvas. It was the winning fall and 'the man they love to hate' was victorious once again.

It was as if the air had suddenly been expelled from a balloon; the arena fell flat. Hopes had been crushed and there, prancing proudly in the centre of the ring, was Pallo. As he was declared the winner and stood contemptuously saluting the audience, the Kings Hall reverberated to the sound of boos and catcalls. Despite having railed against him throughout the fight, Edna didn't join in. Instead, she looked at him admiringly and with a slight giggle turned to Kay.

"Do you know what Kay, for all that he's a dirty so and so, he's a fine specimen of a man, isn't he?"

"Who?"

"Jackie Pallo, of course."

"Yes, I suppose he is," chuckled Kay.

"It's a real shame about the young lad though," continued Edna. "If it hadn't been for Pallo's dirty trick, he would have won."

Robert, hearing her comment, shook his head.

"Come off it, Gran. You know it's all a fix. Pallo was always going to win, because he's got to. That way everyone hates him even more and they'll pay their money and fill up all the seats, hoping to see him finally get beaten."

"Don't talk daft Robert. Of course, it's real. You saw how he hurt that poor lad. And I don't care what you say, if he hadn't cheated, he would have got beat."

Looking towards the ring, they could see that the 'poor lad' was now slowly getting off the canvas. Still in pain, he was stoically refusing all offers of help.

"And your appreciation for the loser," boomed the voice of the MC.

Hearty applause swept over the arena. Despite the result, the fans could still take heart from the performance of the gallant loser.

"Never mind love," shouted Edna. "You'll beat him next time."

"No, he won't," said Robert.

"Robert! You might be a clever bugger at university, but let me tell you. You don't know everything."

Robert, trying hard not to laugh, appeared suitably chastened and looked down at the floor.

"I know. I'm sorry Gran."

"That's alright love," said Edna. "Come on. Let's all go and get a drink."

Chapter 29

Early on Monday evening, just before Christmas, Robert made his way round to Bennett Street flats. Both he and Kay were working over the vacation and he hadn't seen her for several days. It was Joan who answered the door. She told Robert that her sister was out with her mam and dad, taking presents to friends and relatives. Joan indicated that Kay wouldn't be too long and suggested that if Robert wanted, he could come in and wait for her.

"I'm not sure," said Robert. "I've got some reading that I should be getting on with. It's probably better that you tell Kay that I'll come tomorrow at about the same time."

"That might not be a good idea, Robert. Lewis's are really busy at the moment and they might offer our Kay some overtime in the stock room. She'll have to turn it down if she knows you're coming."

"Ah, I see."

Robert hesitated. He knew how important the money was to Kay.

"She'll not want to miss you, Robert. She'll be disappointed if you don't wait for her. I'm sure that she won't be too long."

Joan's insistent, but gentle persuasion, finally achieved its purpose.

"Okay then Joan. I suppose I might as well."

Joan smiled and stood back from the door as Robert entered. She was now almost eighteen. No academic, it was over two years since she had left school and she had matured quickly in a more adult environment. As such, she was aware that for some time, Robert had been taking an increasing interest in her. It wasn't surprising. Like her sister, Joan was very pretty. Unlike Kay, whose appearance suggested modesty and restraint and whose sexuality was accentuated by the sense that she was unattainable, Joan actively encouraged men's attention by her flirtatious behaviour and sense of style.

Joan made far more use of make-up than her sister, a fact which had risen quite naturally out of her employment at 'Boots' on Market Street. At first, Joan's new appearance had drawn concerned advice from her mother. Ethel warned her that she needed to watch out that young men didn't gain the wrong impression and take her "for one of Lewis's." Yet such comments were perhaps unfair, for Joan applied cosmetics skilfully. Her complexion was unblemished, her lips soft, red and full, her mascara and eye shadow highlighted her warm, hazel eyes and all was complemented by her long brown hair, curling away from her beautiful face. At work, Joan's appearance hadn't gone unnoticed. She had been moved on to the cosmetics counter and somewhat unusually for one her age, had already been told that in future she would be trained as a beauty adviser. How lucky she was, the manager had said, for only the prettiest girls are given such an opportunity.

Tonight, Robert couldn't fail to be impressed. His host was wearing a low-neck light blue cardigan, which tapered in to her waist. Underneath was a pretty white blouse that, unbuttoned at the top, teased his eyes with the revelation of soft white skin, above the promise of her hidden, but well-formed breasts. Wearing a long, flowing skirt, pinched into her waist by a black waspie belt, Robert found it hard not to admire Joan's hour glass figure. Aware of the impression she had made on her visitor, Joan smiled.

"Well, don't just stand there Robert. Come and sit down."

She motioned over to the settee and smiled again as, knowing she hadn't failed to see his admiring looks, Robert blushed and then tried to cover his embarrassment by turning away and attending to his coat.

"Can I hang this somewhere? I think it's a little damp from the cold outside."

"Of course. Give it here."

Handing Joan his coat he felt his hand brush against hers. Unconsciously he looked into her eyes and then saw her mischievous smile. And once again, he blushed.

"Go on then, sit down," ordered Joan.

Breathing deeply, Robert made his way to the settee. Sitting down, he tried to compose himself. He was shocked by his reaction. Confident around young women, intimate with many, he always felt in control. Yet now he felt like a novice. Joan clearly had his measure. Glancing at her as she hung up his coat, he felt a shortness of breath and a stirring of desire. He tried to rationalise why he should feel this way. Perhaps because Joan was Kay's sister, it was simply that she was the forbidden fruit; to make love to her would be so deliciously exciting and dangerous too. Under such circumstances, it was no surprise that he couldn't help but become aroused.

Returning, Joan sat beside Robert on the settee. Crossing her legs, she smoothed her dress down carefully with her hands and looked closely at Robert.

"It seems ages since I last saw you, Robert."

"I'm sure it's not been that long. I have been round."

"Well, I suppose I'm out at work a lot and with you being busy with your studies, I must have missed you. It's not like when you were at school though. You were always calling round to take our Kay to the library."

"Yes, it was different back then. Now we have everything we need in the university library."

Joan nodded.

Robert smiled. The conversation was falling into the realms of the unremarkable; a typical exchange of pleasantries that hinted at no sense of intimacy. Robert felt a little relieved, given that his amorous feelings had begun to subside. All signs of his previous embarrassment were seemingly forgotten. When Joan sat close to him, he had been afraid that he would reach out to her, but he had managed to resist the temptation. Now he hoped that it wouldn't be long before Kay and her parents returned.

"So, how's it going at work then? Are Boots treating you well?"

"Yes. I'm on cosmetics now. I'll soon be a beauty adviser."

"Oh."

"I love it. I have to make sure I'm made up and dressed nice for work. The bosses insist."

Joan looked directly into Robert's eyes and smiled.

"What do you think about women and make up Robert? Do you like us wearing it? Some men say they don't."

The question caught Robert by surprise and he struggled to respond. Sensing his confusion, Joan gave him another mischievous smile and continued.

"I'm sure it makes my eyes look more mysterious and my lips far more inviting. Don't you think so, Robert?"

Her voice, now soft and husky, played seductively on Robert's emotions. Once again, he felt aroused. His mind struggled desperately to overcome his desire, but he sensed that it was a losing battle. Desperate, he reminded himself of Kay. She had always been his best friend and Robert hoped that someday she would become even more. If he allowed something to happen with Joan, then surely Kay could never love him in the future.

"Clothes are important too. Don't you agree, Robert."

Joan stood up, stepped back, straightened her cardigan and moved her hands towards her belt.

"This cardy fits lovely. Snug at the sides and with this waspie belt, shows off my waist and figure."

Standing nimbly on her tip-toes, Joan raised her arms like a ballerina and pirouetted slowly on the spot. Laughing, she looked at Robert, who seemed mesmerised by her actions.

"Well, I hope you don't think it's a 'waist' of time," she joked.

"No," mumbled Robert.

"Well then, do you like what you see?"

Giving him no time to respond, Joan sat back down on the settee and turned towards him. Looking expectantly into his eyes, she reached for his hand and moved it against her arm.

"Feel how soft the wool is. It's lovely, isn't it?"

As Joan released his hand, Robert gently squeezed her arm.

"Go on Robert. It's okay."

Hearing her soft and reassuring words, Robert was no longer able to restrain himself. He moved his hand across her and down the outside of her leg. He could feel the outline of her suspenders and the fabric of her cotton skirt gliding over her nylon stockings. By now, he had lost all semblance of control and pressed his lips up against hers, Joan responding eagerly as the two of them shared a deep and passionate kiss. Separating, Robert took in a deep breath as he watched Joan lie down on the settee. Her eyes sparkled and beckoned to him and he could not resist following her down. With Joan's body so tightly pressed against him, he was filled with excitement and desire. The thought that at any moment they could be disturbed, was gone. All Robert knew was that he wanted her right now. Pulling up her dress his hand moved up between her legs and pressing against her, Joan could feel his arousal. Breathlessly, she tried to pull away from him.

"No, we mustn't," she protested. "I shouldn't. I can't."

If it had been any other girl, he wouldn't have stopped. But she was Kay's sister and then again, he knew that he was unprepared. He hadn't expected that he was going out 'on a promise' and he slowly came to his senses, realising that he had no intention of ruining his future by getting any girl pregnant. Sitting up, he allowed Joan to come out from under him. Pulling her dress back over her knees, she was wide eyed and breathing heavily. She looked down at Robert's lap and laughed gently.

"I think you might need me to do something about that. Wait there, I'll fetch a towel."

Once more she made him blush and for just a moment the thought crossed his mind that Joan may not be as innocent and inexperienced as he had assumed.

"No. No. It's okay. I'll manage. I just need to calm down," he sighed.

"Was it good?" asked Joan, mischievously raising her eyebrows.

"I said, I need to calm down!"

Joan sensed the irritation in his voice and fell silent. She couldn't be sure if it was because of his frustration, or if he'd already begun to regret what had just happened between them. Yet she didn't care. In her eyes she had succeeded in seducing him and that was all that mattered.

Getting to his feet, Robert collected his coat. Putting it on, he made his way to the front door.

"Aren't you waiting for Kay? I'm sure she won't be much longer."

"No. I'd best be off and if I were you, I'd check your clothes and fix your hair."

Opening the front door and without a word of farewell, he was gone.

Chapter 30

It was early in the new year. A Tuesday evening. Ernest was at work and Ethel was getting ready to go with her friend Maisie to the bingo. As usual, she was feeling guilty about not being there to put out the tea for her daughters. Joan had yet to arrive home, but Kay had already prepared the vegetables for boiling and was just about to start reheating the meat and potato pie that Ethel had made that morning.

"Now Kay, you won't forget to warm the pie thoroughly, will you?"

"No, Mam."

"I'd wait a bit longer to light the oven. You don't want to risk ruining it. You know how late our Joan can be."

"It's okay Mam. I'll make sure I keep checking it."

Kay smiled. Like most mothers, Ethel took her domestic responsibilities very seriously. No matter how old her daughters became, they would always be her little girls in need of her constant guidance.

"You need to be getting off soon Mam, so just concentrate on getting ready. We're going to be just fine."

Ethel sighed and began to check her hair and apply some make-up in front of the big mirror over the fireplace. Pushing out her lips, she applied some bright red lipstick and smacked them together softly, trying to ensure an even covering. Her head bobbed comically back and forth as she attempted to get a close, then long range perspective, of how she looked. Kay, who never tired of watching her mam's weekly performance, chuckled quietly to herself.

Almost satisfied with her appearance, Ethel turned to her daughter.

"Do I look all right love?"

"Yes Mam. Lovely. My dad's going to think there's a beautiful new woman in the house when he gets home."

"Get off with you. Don't be daft!"

Yet Kay couldn't fail to notice the flicker of a smile that crossed her mam's face. One that made it clear she was pleased with her daughter's compliment.

"Right. I'm ready then. I'll just get my coat and shoes and I'll get off to Maisie's."

Finally ready, Ethel moved towards the back door. Just before she reached it, it swung open. Joan was home from work.

"Oh. Hi Mam. Are you just off to bingo?"

"Yes love. I've left you a nice meat and potato pie. Kay's getting it ready now."

"Oh good. Thanks Mam."

"Well, just make sure you eat a proper amount. You need feeding up in this cold weather. Dieting's for summer."

"Yes Mam. Good luck at the bingo." .

"Oh no," gasped Ethel. "That's done it now!"

"What do you mean?" asked Joan, surprised by her mam's reaction.

"Well, I won't win, will I? You never do when someone wishes you luck. It puts the mockers on it."

"Oh. I'm sorry Mam. I didn't know."

"I might as well not go now," replied Ethel in a sad, dispirited voice.

"Oh, go on Mam" said Kay, reassuringly. "It's your night out and you and Maisie look forward to it."

"Well, I suppose so," sighed Ethel. "And I don't want to disappoint Maisie."

"That's right," said Kay.

Opening the door, Ethel's good humour had returned, so much so that Joan couldn't resist a parting comment.

"Anyway Mam. Just think about all those times you've gone and no one's wished you luck. I can't remember you ever winning then."

Ethel turned to her youngest daughter.

"You cheeky little mare!"

But there was a smile on her face as she walked off to meet her friend.

Chapter 31

Closing the door, Joan turned to her sister. The two of them burst into laughter, but the jovial mood wasn't to be extended very far into the evening.

It was the first time that the two of them had been alone together since Joan's intimate encounter with Robert and she was determined that Kay was going to hear every little detail about it. Her motives for doing so were entirely vindictive and rooted in envy. For so many years she had felt herself to be in the shadow of her sibling. Kay had passed her scholarship, made it to grammar school and then had been accepted into Manchester University. There were so few children from their background who achieved this and it cut her to the quick every time her father complimented Kay to his friends. It didn't matter that Ernest lavished equal praise on his other beautiful daughter. With the dark thoughts that inhabited her mind, she felt nothing but resentment for her sister, convinced that her parents loved her sibling more than herself.

For some time now, Joan had seen her relationship with Kay as a competition and one that her sister had been winning. Yet her employment at Boots had filled her with self-confidence. It also confirmed what she had learned from her teenage years in school; that the opposite sex found her attractive. As a young woman, she had learned how to dress, style her hair and apply her make-up to embellish her already beautiful face and figure. It was no surprise that she was surrounded by men vying for her attention. Joan felt sure that few could resist her charms and so the idea took shape that she would take away from Kay, the young man who clearly idolised her. Joan would set out her stall for Robert. The opportunity that had presented itself before Christmas had been taken and now, to complete her victory, Kay would have to be told.

As Kay finished preparing the tea, Joan set the table and the two of them sat down to eat. There was the usual small-talk. Kay asked her sister how her day had been and Joan, as always, remarked that she would know herself when she too began full-time work. It was a point she liked to make; a suggestion that Kay had it easy at university. It was however, just another ill-disguised indication of her jealousy and as usual, Kay accepted her comments with good grace. After all, both she and Robert were used to them. Although many of their friends were pleased that they had the opportunity to look beyond the world of their parents, others were not. Some accused them of arrogance and a betrayal of their class. Others dismissed their studies as worthless; that passing exams didn't mean that they were practical or had any common sense. Such critics were confident that once outside the sheltered precincts of Owens, the two of them would have a rude awakening. They would be unable to cope with the harsh demands of the real world. In reality, such hostility emerged from an inverse snobbery born out of anger and frustration. Unable to leave these streets themselves, the critics resented anyone else who looked like doing so.

Having finished their meal, Kay cleared the table and washed the pots, whilst Joan made them a cup of tea. Sat with their drinks, Joan now had the opportunity to raise the subject of Robert. Looking straight at her sister, she smiled.

"Well? Has Robert told you anything?"

Kay was puzzled.

"About what?"

"Ah," replied Joan, "he hasn't then."

There was a hint of satisfaction in her voice and Kay noticed a faint smile flicker across her lips.

"Well, I suppose he might not want to upset you."

"Upset me?"

"Yes. After all, you've always been so very close. Haven't you?"

Joan's words were slow and deliberate. She was carefully teasing them out. Almost as if she wanted the process of revelation to last as long as possible. Kay suspected that whatever she was about to tell her, Joan was going to enjoy it.

"Yes. You know we are."

Joan now hesitated and took in a deep breath, indicating that she was having second thoughts about continuing the conversation. Yet her efforts made no impression on her sister.

Kay was convinced that her sudden reticence lacked sincerity. And she was right. Joan was taking every bit of pleasure in prolonging what she assumed would be, her sibling's agony.

"Come on Joan," continued Kay, calmly. "It must be important, so tell me."

"I'm not sure now that I should. I'm sorry, I don't want to upset you. If Robert wants to tell you anything, then it's up to him."

Joan averted her eyes and looked down at the table. It was mere simulation, for Kay knew that she was simply waiting to be asked again for an answer. It seemed that Joan was intent on playing a game. She'd made clear that her revelations about Robert would be upsetting, yet Kay's discomfiture could only be extended by Joan's current silence. Kay needed a response. She had to do as her sister desired.

"No, I don't think it is Joan. If it wasn't important, you wouldn't have said anything. I should like to know now please. If Robert has got into any trouble, he may be too embarrassed to ask for help. I …"

"Oh no! It's nothing like that," interrupted Joan. "It's something good."

She hesitated and then continued.

"Well, to me it's good."

Kay looked at her mystified. She still had no idea what Robert could have done.

"If it's something good, then surely you have no reason not to tell me."

"I suppose so," replied Joan, quietly.

"Go on then."

"We made love."

The words were out, but Kay was finding it difficult to grasp their meaning.

"You made love?"

"Yes, me and Robert."

"When?"

"That night before Christmas when he came to the house and you, Mam and Dad were out. It's why he didn't wait for you coming back. He was embarrassed and couldn't face you."

Joan watched her sister's face carefully for a reaction, but her features were giving nothing away. Perhaps she needed more time for it to sink in.

Inwardly, Kay was confused. She was well aware of Robert's reputation with women, yet she was finding Joan's claim hard to accept. Kay had no reason to believe that Robert would have set out to seduce her sister, but she wasn't naïve and knew that Joan was no innocent. Attractive and flirtatious and left alone together, perhaps Robert had fallen for her charms. After all, she finally reasoned, why would her sister lie? What had she to gain by doing so? Kay therefore decided that she would proceed on the assumption that there was at least an element of truth in what she'd been told.

"Why should he be embarrassed, if it's what he wanted?" asked Kay.

"Because he knew he'd let you down."

"How has he let me down?"

"Because you were always his girl, but now he wants me and he doesn't know how to tell you."

Kay could hear a slight tremor in her voice. Joan stared at the floor. Her actions suggested her regret over what had happened.

"I feel so guilty," she continued. "Robert loves you and now I've stolen him away. But I never meant to do that. He just wanted me so much and I couldn't resist him."

Joan continued to look down. Kay was quiet. She was unconvinced by her sister's protestations of regret. Rather than indicating that their actions were either inappropriate or reprehensible, Joan's words seemed rather a celebration of their encounter.

Moving her hand across her face, Joan indicated that she was wiping away a tear. Finally, she raised her head and looked sadly at her sibling.

"I hope you can forgive me Kay."

"There's nothing to forgive. If you and Robert want to be together, then you should be."

Joan couldn't hide her surprise. She was clearly unprepared for Kay's response. In fact, events weren't unfolding anything like she had expected. Her sister had remained calm; she spoke without any hint of passion or anger. What Joan had told her about Robert hadn't proved devastating at all. Determined to hurt her sister, it seemed that she had failed utterly.

"You're right when you say that I love Robert," continued Kay, "but it's a different kind of love. It's like the love I would have for a brother. Robert has gone with many girls on the flats and he's been out with women at Owens. I've always known. We're best friends; always have been and always will be. But nothing more. I'm sure that if the two of you are serious, he'll not hesitate to tell me."

Kay's comment was revealing. It indicated to Joan that she hadn't necessarily accepted her version of events. It was also a clear sign from Kay that, as far as she was concerned, the matter was closed and no longer up for discussion.

"Come on, let's sit on the settee and see what's on the telly. I've got assignments coming out of my ears at the moment. I need to sit down, relax and forget about them for a while."

Determined to hide her disappointment, Joan smiled weakly and joined her sister. The evening hadn't worked out as she'd planned. Yet she wasn't necessarily satisfied by Kay's claim that Robert was nothing more than a friend. And in that respect, she was undoubtedly correct.

Chapter 32

The relationship between Kay and Robert was nothing like how she had described it to Joan. There was no doubting that they were the closest of friends, inseparable since the day they had met in the playground at Armitage Street School. Yet Kay's claim that there were no feelings of intimacy between them, wasn't entirely true. Just how complex their relationship had become, was apparent when they were taking a break in 'Caf' just a few days later.

"I've been wanting to talk to you for some time now," said Robert.

"Really. Correct me if I'm wrong, but don't we talk together every day?"

Robert was silent. Kay realised that her playful response had missed its mark. Her friend obviously wanted to raise a matter of some concern.

"Okay Robert. What is it?"

Robert coughed nervously and took a sharp intake of breath.

"It's your Joan."

"What about her?"

"I've been foolish. I came to see you before Christmas, but Joan told me that everyone was out and asked me in. We were sat on the settee talking and then it just happened."

Robert paused. He was feeling awkward.

"Take your time. It's okay."

Kay gave him a smile, encouraging him to continue.

"Joan asked me if I liked how she looked. We ended up lying on the settee together and it all got out of hand."

He paused and for a moment Kay was concerned.

"How far did it get out of hand?"

"Oh no, not like that!" he exclaimed. "There was some kissing and touching, but nothing more. As far as I'm concerned, Joan's virtue is very much intact."

"I thought it was. She's not said differently."

"What do you mean?"

"Joan's already told me about what happened."
Robert was confused.
"Why haven't you mentioned it before?"
"Because I was giving you time to tell me yourself. I'm not daft Robert. I know what our Joan's like. I wouldn't just accept what she's told me."
There was a pause as Robert mulled over her response.
"I suppose that's good then?"
"I suppose it is," replied Kay.
"But I'm not proud of what I've done," continued Robert. "I've not come to the house, because I'm worried that Joan might tell your mam and dad. I'd not want them to feel bad about me."
"I wouldn't worry. Mam already thinks our Joan's no innocent, so she'd never say anything. She'd be too worried that they'd try to stop her going out."
"I don't blame Joan. I should have known better. I'm ashamed of what I've done."
"Why should you be? You didn't let things go any further."
Robert was silent. He looked uneasy. Kay thought it was ironic. Usually so cavalier in his treatment of women, this time he clearly regretted his actions. Yet by referring to her parents, he wasn't being honest. In reality, his feelings of remorse were centred on Kay herself.
"It's all right," continued Kay. "What's happened doesn't change my feelings for you. We're still best pals."
Kay smiled and squeezed his hand.
As Robert looked up, a shaft of sunlight shone down through the high chapel windows, illuminating Kay's beautiful face. With her hair brushed back and her pretty, delicate features, it seemed as if he were staring into the face of an angel. As she raised her hand, attempting to shield herself from the glare, Robert was drawn towards her soft, green eyes. He no longer had any sense of time or space; nothing but an appreciation of the beauty he saw before him. Capturing his glance in hers, Kay instinctively sensed his passion. Then as quickly as it had appeared, the sunlight was gone and the spell it had cast was broken.
For a short time, the two sat in silence, but she couldn't forget that look. Kay knew that she must now take their conversation deeper than Robert would find agreeable.

"I'm not about to judge you, Robert. I've always known that you've been with girls on the flats and here at Owens and that's okay. What you have to understand though, is that it's different for girls."

"How's that?"

"Well. Me for instance. I might like someone and think they're really handsome. Unlike you though, I have to be careful. If I go out with anyone, I've a reputation to consider. You men don't have to worry about that. Society doesn't judge you the same as us. A single man has sex and it's almost condoned. It's simply 'sowing your wild oats,' good to 'get it out of your system,' before settling down. If a woman does the same, then they're worse than a pro, because 'at least pros get paid for it.'"

"No. That's not right. It's not like that anymore Kay. There are women at Owens going out with different guys all the time. And from what I've heard, let them do anything they want."

Kay leaned slightly forward and looked directly into his eyes. "Only heard?"

Robert, feeling uncomfortable, ignored her question.

"The point is Kay," he continued. "They don't seem to worry about their reputations."

"Well, more fool them. Perhaps they think that with their middle-class, liberal backgrounds, their indiscretions won't matter. They're deluded. If they came from Ardwick, they'd know different."

"No, I'm sure you're wrong Kay."

"Really? Do you think I don't know the nickname that your friends have given me."

"Oh?" said Robert, looking embarrassed.

"Don't come it. You know very well. They call me Elliot Ness. Why's that Robert?"

"I don't know."

"Yes, you do and so do I. So go on, I want to hear you tell me."

"Because," replied Robert, rather hesitantly, "like Elliot Ness you're one of the 'untouchables.' No one's ever going to get a chance to get amorous with you."

"And that underlines my point. For the sake of her reputation, a young woman, unlike a man, has to remain a virgin."

"Well, I think it's a mark of respect for you Kay. All the guys do. They all fancy you like mad. Yet they know whoever you choose, they're going to have to make an honest woman of you first."

"Oh. It seems that I'm quite the topic of conversation," replied Kay, angrily. "Do you enjoy sharing your little fantasies with one another?"

"No! Never!"

Robert was shocked that she could think such a thing.

"I would never do that. There's no one in my life who I care more about. I've even threatened to punch guys for making inappropriate comments about you."

"What, you Robert?"

Kay started to laugh.

"Yes, me Kay."

"I suppose that would be another fight I'd have to come and rescue you from."

"Well, I did."

Kay shook her head. Her reaction to Robert's comment had lifted the tension somewhat.

"You'll never let me live that little matter on the Black Brook down, will you?" sighed Robert.

Kay smiled.

"No. Of course not. You're always going to owe me for that one, Robert."

Noting her good humour, Robert felt able to return to their conversation.

"I regret what happened with Joan, but all the other girls Kay, it didn't mean a thing."

He paused. He looked at her expectantly, seeking some kind of approval for the many dalliances he'd had with girls in the past. Unfortunately for Robert, her response fell short of what he hoped for.

"It has to mean something. You've made those choices. No one forced you. You must have wanted to."

"But it really doesn't."

Robert was insistent; determined to defend his position. He was eager for her to understand that she was the only woman who mattered to him. The only one he truly wanted. To win Kay over, he was determined to lay himself bare before her; reveal his innermost thoughts and feelings.

"I didn't want anything to happen with Joan. It felt wrong from the start and I had to get away. It's made me realise that when I've been with other girls, all I got was immediate satisfaction. I never once experienced any lasting feelings of love or fulfilment."

Kay understood his sincerity, but she couldn't accept that his feelings of emptiness would lead to a sudden diminution of his voracious sexual appetite. After all, he had always chased after girls and he still did now. In his mind he may believe that he wanted to change, but she suspected that the hormones raging inside him, would prove far more difficult to contain.

"That's easy to say Robert, but it's far harder to do anything about it."

"Kay," he pleaded. "Listen to me. I have to tell you."

He paused and took her hand. He had a look of determination about him and Kay knew that he was going to tell her that he loved her. She couldn't deny that sometimes she had entertained thoughts about the two of them becoming a real couple. Kay had never been as close to anyone else. She never tired of his company and he was the first one she would reach out to in adversity. Yet now, at this moment, she knew that the time wasn't right.

"No, Robert. Don't say it."

"I have to Kay, for I really do love you. I don't want to lose you."

"But how can you? We'll always be a part of one another's lives. I can't imagine you not being there for me."

"Yes, Kay. But that's as a friend. I want more. It's not enough for what I feel for you."

"Don't you understand?" asked Kay, softly. "If we went out together, it would all go wrong. You could never guarantee you'd be faithful and I couldn't accept that. I value our friendship too much. I won't risk it by doing as you ask."

Robert's head dropped. He was clearly devastated. It hurt Kay to see him that way, but she knew that it was for the best. This way, he would always remain part of her life.

"Come on Robert," she said quietly. "Let's go out and get some fresh air."

Raising his head, Robert nodded.

"Yes, let's."

"Best pals?" asked Kay, managing a smile.

"Yes. Always and forever."

Chapter 33

March 28th, 1960 was a special day. Gene Vincent and Eddie Cochran were beginning their week-long engagement at the Ardwick Hippodrome and Robert, Larry and Kay were in the second house that began at eight-forty. The two Americans had been in the country since January. Impresario Larry Parnes had promised them enthusiastic audiences and generous contracts. Gene was on $2500 a week and Eddie, a thousand. It reflected the deep respect and fascination that British teenagers had for authentic American stars. In his own home-grown roster of young, rock 'n' roll artists, Parnes paid no one more than £20 a week. Although Gene was touted as the headline star, it was Eddie who was grabbing the headlines and he was the one that Robert and Larry really wanted to see.

An astute businessman, Parnes made sure that the Americans worked hard. In just under three months, they were scheduled to make 108 live appearances, along with several radio and television engagements. Parnes own stars were also on the bill. Billy Fury, Joe Brown and Marty Wilde had their rock 'n' roll credentials enhanced by appearing with Gene and Eddie.

The tour proved a bruising schedule for its participants, with the Hippodrome being one of the final venues. Even so, you couldn't tell it from Eddie's performance. With his back to the audience, the 'Wildcats' playing the opening bars of 'Somethin' Else', Eddie suddenly wheeled around and launched into his opening lines. Stood confidently behind the mike, his head bobbed rhythmically to the beat, his hips swinging in perfect time. As the set progressed, his rhythm playing was crisp, percussive and biting. It was driving the music on and his lead breaks were innovative and outstanding. The songs were varied. There were driving rockers like 'What'd I Say', ballads such as 'Have I told you Lately' and the favourites, 'Twenty Flight Rock' and 'Summertime Blues'. His voice was powerful, with inflexions of Elvis. Eddie was every bit the star and his appealing soft drawl, pleasant personality and good looks, only further endeared him to an enthusiastic audience.

"We have to get an interview," said Larry, after Eddie had left the stage.

"Of course," replied Robert, "but you do know we'll have a problem getting it past the editors."

"No, surely not."

"Of course, we will. Rock 'n' roll isn't cerebral enough for them. They think it's trashy; music for the ignorant."

"I don't see 'trad jazz' as being particularly sophisticated," remarked Larry, "and that's the type of music the student fraternity seems to go for."

"What do you think?" asked Robert, turning to Kay.

"About rock 'n' roll, trad jazz or Eddie?"

"Eddie of course."

"I think he's lovely."

"Lovely?" asked Larry.

"Yes. He's got great hair, he's handsome, seems to have a nice personality and he's an excellent mover. I'd love to see him on the dance floor at the Ritz."

"You're getting star struck again, aren't you?" suggested Robert.

"Well, you both wanted my opinion and I've given it."

Kay was going to add that she thought Larry and Robert were getting jealous, but thought better of it.

To get access to Eddie, the boys realised that they would have to go through Larry Parnes. Contacting his London office, it proved relatively easy. Eddie was attending a photo signing on Friday at twelve-thirty at 'The Record Shop' on the corner of Hilton Street and Stevenson Square. Arriving early, there were already lots of fans queuing to see the young star. His arrival didn't disappoint as he swept into Stevenson Square in a sleek American Cadillac. Emerging from the vehicle, Eddie, wearing dark glasses, made his way into the store. It seemed a stylish look, although the girls present would have preferred to see him without them. What they didn't know was that he wasn't trying to look cool, but covering up the black eye he'd received play fighting with Gene. Given the demands of the fans, it was only possible for a brief exchange of pleasantries, but it was agreed that Robert and Larry would accompany Eddie back to his lodgings, where an interview could take place.

Milverton Lodge was a hotel on Anson Road in Victoria Park. Gene and Eddie were staying in a small annexe behind the main building. On their arrival, they were joined by teen idol, Billy Fury. Eddie soon excused himself. He needed to make a phone call and left Larry and Robert in Billy's care.

"He'll be on to Sharon," explained Billy. "The time difference is eight hours and she'll only have just got up."

"Sharon Sheeley?" asked Larry.

"That's right. They're making arrangements for her to come over. Eddie's missing her. He's always on the phone to California. It must cost him a fortune."

"Wouldn't it be great if they were to write another hit together when they were over here," suggested Larry.

As they chatted it was clear that Eddie had made a huge impression on the English members of the touring party. Billy, Joe Brown, Marty and the Wildcats, loved his sense of fun and had huge respect for him as a musician.

"He practices with the guys all the time. Passes on knowledge and tips. Eddie told Joe to swap his G string for an unwound B and tune it down to G. It's what Eddie does and it means you can bend the note a full tone. No one over here has ever done that."

"What's Gene like?" asked Larry.

Having been effusive in his praise of Eddie, Billy was more restrained when talking about his compatriot.

"He's not too like Eddie, although they both drink Jack Daniels neat from the bottle! The guy's in a lot of pain from his accident. It must make it difficult for him."

"We heard a rumour," said Larry, "that Gene's got a friend called Henry and that it's actually a switchblade. Is that right?"

"Come off it, lads. I'm hardly going to talk about anything like that."

"It's off the record. We wouldn't print it," said Robert.

Billy shook his head. It was clear he felt that any revelation would be betraying a trust and seemed relieved when Eddie made his way back into the room, ready for his interview.

Since his performance on Monday, Eddie had been suffering with laryngitis.

"It's the weather. It's so cold here. Not like back home," he explained. "I hope I didn't sound too croaky last night."

"No, you were fine Eddie," said Billy. "The fans loved you."

"We caught the show on Monday," noted Robert. "You certainly went down a storm then."

"Yeah, everywhere the fans have been warm, just like your English beer," replied Eddie. "I'd just love a cold one. We need some refrigeration around here."

Robert and Larry laughed. Already Eddie's fabled sense of humour was coming to the fore.

"You know, back home I'm used to watching all night tv. Not having it has taken some getting used to. And do you fellas know where I can get hold of some proper comic books?"

"It's difficult Eddie," replied Larry. "They've only just started importing them officially from the States. They are around, but not many newsagents stock them. They prefer to stick with the British comics, which they can always sell."

"Yeah, I've tried some of those, but they're not the same."

Eddie sounded disappointed. Robert and Larry weren't surprised. The British economy had started to pick up and there was a growing affluence among the middle classes, but the country wasn't that long out of rationing and austerity. Life in Britain must have seemed fairly dull compared to warm and sunny California, with its booming consumerism. Nevertheless, Eddie was on a mission to spread his music and regardless of the strange environment he found himself in, there was no disguising his enthusiasm when it came to playing and performing.

"You've done tv and radio work whilst you've been over here Eddie. How does that compare to performing in theatres?" asked Larry.

"I much prefer working live before an audience. I prefer to be looking out at real people, rather than staring into a camera."

"How did you find Manchester and the Hippodrome?"

"Well, we'd already been here for recording sessions at Granada Studios."

"Yes. The shows for 'Boy meets Girl'. We saw them. You were great."

"We don't really get a chance to look around," continued Eddie. "Travelling, rehearsing and performing takes up most of our time. The audiences here in Manchester have really appreciated us and the press reports have been generous too."

"It was good that the *Evening News* and *The Chronicle* were so positive," replied Larry. "There's still a lot of hostility towards rock 'n' roll. A fear of juvenile delinquents. 'The Blackboard Jungle' has a lot to answer for."

"I think you and Gene have proved on this tour, that rock 'n' roll is alive and kicking," added Robert.

"They said, straight after Elvis made it, that it wouldn't last," said Eddie, "and they've said it every year since. We're still here though and the music isn't going away. But there's no formula; I write and play what I feel."

The interview over, Larry and Robert walked the relatively short distance back to Owens, where they spent the late afternoon in 'Caf', working up their final draft. Robert's interview with Stanley Baker had been given the prior approval of the editorial team. This time however, he and Larry had acted on their own initiative. It remained to be seen whether others at the *News Bulletin* would have the same enthusiasm for their subject, as the boys themselves.

Chapter 34

On Monday afternoon, an editorial meeting was taking place to discuss the content for the next edition of the *Bulletin*. Robert and Larry had arrived feeling confident about the merits of their article. As Larry provided typed copies to members around the table, Robert talked about their visit to the Hippodrome, the Record Shop on Hilton Street and their interview at Milverton Lodge. Whilst Robert talked, Larry saw indications that their piece on Eddie wasn't going to prove an easy sell. Few of those seated around the table had given other than a cursory glance at the document in front of them and the disinterested expressions on several faces, indicated a lack of enthusiasm for the feature. Larry's fears were confirmed when Terence, the editor, provided an initial response.

"You've worked hard lads, but I just wish that you'd had a word with me about your intentions beforehand. I have to be honest. I can't see where we can fit this in. I don't think it's particularly relevant to the community at Owens and it doesn't strike me that it covers an important matter of local interest."

"You were happy enough with the feature on Stanley Baker," replied Robert. "Surely this article is comparable in its scope and content?"

Terence leaned back in his chair and breathed in deeply. It seemed clear that he wanted to bring an end to the matter, but without upsetting Robert or Larry.

"Yes, it was an excellent piece, but the subject was important. Stanley Baker's well known and admired by most students. The interest in him is undeniable. It's not quite the same with this Cochran chap now, is it?"

Trying to be reasonable, Terence had in fact appeared condescending. Robert's mood wasn't helped by the murmurs of agreement coming from those around the table.

"You couldn't be more wrong," insisted Robert. "Your perspective is blinkered. I know the relevance of Eddie and rock 'n' roll to the kids of Manchester. Unlike those around this table,

I'm part of that community. It might surprise you, but not too many youngsters in Ardwick get enthused by trad jazz."

"Well perhaps they should," suggested Mike, a final year student and long-standing contributor to the *Bulletin*. "It might broaden their musical horizons."

"Well now," said Larry. "At last, it's out in the open. The times are changing, but like so many students at Owens, you don't want to move with them. If our article is rejected, it merely underlines the fact that we're an elitist middle-class institution, out of touch with the youth of this city."

Larry's comment was forceful and incisive, but Mike treated it with contempt.

"You can't for a moment suggest that rock 'n' roll contains anything of artistic merit. It's nothing more than a poor man's twelve bar blues. Every song's the same. There's no justification for giving any column inches to this character."

"A poor man's twelve bar blues! You've justified Larry's point," said Robert, angrily. "You hate rock 'n' roll because of its popular appeal. You can't intellectualise the music; you have to feel it. That's something that you, with your bourgeois hang-ups, can't do. You're desperate to look down your nose at the music and dismiss it as being for 'oiks' like me."

"Yes, that's right," insisted Larry. "It's snobbery and class prejudice."

"And you should know," replied Mike, with a sneer. "There's no one here more privileged and bourgeois than you!"

"Steady on," said Terence, finally feeling the need to intervene. "It's all getting a little too heated. We need to treat one another with a little more respect."

There were several sympathetic nods around the table. The meeting had developed an intensity that was on the verge of becoming unpleasant. Nevertheless, Larry was determined to respond to Mike's jibe.

"I can't deny that Mike's right and it's why I made the decision to come to Manchester. I wanted to get away from all that. I thought that here, in a tough Northern city, I'd experience different attitudes and broaden my outlook. I have to say that the city and its people haven't disappointed me, although many of my fellow students have. Surely by coming here, it becomes part of our wider education to try to understand and reach out to, the people whose community we're a part of. Yet, if we're honest, that doesn't happen anywhere near enough. Through our article, Robert and I are trying to help our fellow students understand what matters to their working-class contemporaries. That's why I think it has merit and should be included."

Larry had spoken in calm, measured terms. The mood in the room was now more relaxed and Terence was quick to offer an olive branch, indicating that he wouldn't reject the article altogether. If the opportunity arose, an abridged version could be used in a future edition. Moreover, Terence offered them some advice.

"In July lads, you'll be the ones editing the *Bulletin* and then it's your responsibility to decide on content. You'll find that you're going to have to handle a lot of criticism and deal with many conflicting interests. It's not always an easy place to be."

Although frustrated that all their hard work may have been in vain, Robert more readily came to an understanding of Terence's decision than Larry. The latter remained insistent in his belief that the article should be published, whereas Robert had become far more realistic in terms of his expectations.

"He had to make the decision he thought was most suited to the readers," explained Robert. "No matter how much we might love Eddie, a lot of students don't. A successful newspaper has to please its readers; to sell copies, you have to give them what they want."

"What about the duty of the press to inform and provide opinions?" asked Larry. "Where's the freedom for the journalist if they can never write anything other than what they're told?"

"I think you're exaggerating. It's not quite that bad. If we get into the business, we'll have to learn to compromise. Proprietors all have an agenda and editors have to enforce it. The trick, I suspect, is learning how to bring them round to your point of view. I should have realised that Terence was a trad fan. If I'd seen him before we met Eddie, I could probably have persuaded him to print the article before we did all the hard work."

"I see your point Robert, but if you have to keep compromising, you'll lose the ability to think independently anyway," insisted Larry.

Resigned to not seeing their feature in print, events in the early hours of Sunday, April 17th changed everything. Having finished the final night of his UK tour at the Bristol Hippodrome, Eddie was killed in a car crash in Chippenham on the A4 heading to Heathrow Airport. Within a few days his final recording, 'Three Steps to Heaven', was released, making its way to number one on June 23rd. Suddenly, Larry and Robert's feature had become newsworthy and Terence asked if they would amend the article so that it would serve as an obituary for Eddie. The lads agreed, but they had mixed feelings about the heightened interest in their musical hero.

"It's the macabre fascination with untimely and violent death that has brought all this interest," remarked Larry. "It's sad to see. Those of us who are true fans of Eddie respect 'Three Steps to Heaven' as a great song, whilst the rest buy it because of its novelty value."

"I understand what you're saying," replied Robert, "but I think you're being a little too cynical."

"I'm not. Just think about Buddy. The same happened with him. They released 'It Doesn't Matter Anymore' just after he was killed and it soon made it to number one. It's not a coincidence that neither Eddie or Buddy had a number one before they died. People are morbid; fascinated by tragedy."

"Yes, I get that Larry, but don't forget you've got two very good songs there and Eddie's lyric is really clever. Okay, perhaps both of them wouldn't have reached number one, but they would have definitely made it on to the charts."

"What's sad, is that we saw Eddie just a few weeks ago," noted Larry. "He was a great guy and a phenomenal talent. All that's gone. It seems such a terrible waste and I'm finding it difficult to accept."

Robert looked at his friend, who was visibly upset.

"No, Eddie's still with us. Not physically of course, but as part of the legacy he's left behind and especially over here. Just think of the influence he's had on the British musicians he's met and played with; Billy told us that. And what about all those kids in skiffle groups who've been to see him at theatres all around the country. He's inspired a whole new generation of musicians. I tell you Larry, Eddie's spirit lives on and before too long, the likes of Mike and his trad jazz cronies will find themselves firmly in the dustbin of musical history."

"Long live the rock 'n' roll musical revolution!" shouted Larry.

"Amen," replied Robert.

Chapter 35

He couldn't help but notice her. She had been one of those around the table when he and Larry had presented their article on Eddie and was in the office again when they went to put their final touches to his obituary. She was tall and graceful. Her silky, long black hair, brought to life her gorgeous green eyes. Robert was fascinated and couldn't help glancing at her as she sat writing on the far side of the room. Deep in thought, she raised her eyebrows and pushed out her bottom lip. It was an action that reminded him of Kay; a trigger that Robert could hardly resist. Rising from his seat, he walked over to her desk. Watching him go, Larry shook his head. Once more, his friend was on the prowl.

"Is everything all right? You seem a little worried."

Lifting her head, she examined him closely.

"Yes, I'm absolutely fine."

She was softly spoken. Her words were perfectly enunciated, with a suitably neutral accent that came unmistakably from the Home Counties.

"I'm Robert by the way."

"Yes, I know and you don't have time for 'trad' and those who like it. So where does that leave me?"

The question took Robert by surprise. Noting his confusion, she smiled mischievously.

"I'm Caroline," she continued "and don't worry, you'll find that I'm quite forgiving."

Robert was relieved. His chance with her seemed to have gone, even before he'd got started. Now Caroline had let him know that she was definitely interested.

"What are you working on?" asked Robert.

"Oh, nothing important. I'm far more interested in your interview with Eddie. I thought that Terence was wrong to turn it down. There's more support for rock 'n' roll here at Owens, than he realises."

"Well, why didn't you say so at the time?"

"Oh, that it could be so easy!"

"Well, surely it is."

Caroline shook her head.

"You are naïve. Try being the only woman on the paper. You know that you're here on sufferance and the last thing you want to do is to draw attention to yourself and have the boys' close ranks against you."

"Do you think you're the only one treated differently?" asked Robert. "Try coming here from my background. You've got to stand up to narrow-mindedness and find ways around it."

"Yes, you're from Manchester, aren't you?"

"Of course. Ardwick and proud of it."

His words thrilled her. She had been searching for a man who was authentic and in this blunt, working-class Mancunian, she believed that she had found him. Sensing a connection between them, Robert moved quickly.

"Do you fancy taking a break and going to 'Caf'?"

"What about your friend?" asked Caroline, looking over towards Larry. "Aren't you supposed to be working with him?"

"No, I've done my bit. Larry always prefers to give it one final run through himself."

To underline his point, Robert called over to his friend.

"Hey, Larry. You're okay to wrap things up, aren't you?"

"Yes, of course," replied Larry, more than willing to support Robert's latest romantic adventure. "There's no reason you can't get off now."

"There you are," said Robert, turning to Caroline. "There's nothing to stop me. So shall we go?"

"Well, in that case, of course."

A few minutes later they were sat in 'Caf', the conversation flowing easily between them.

"I kept my copy of the piece on Eddie. I thought it was very good."

"You must have been the only one who read it then," replied Robert, laughing.

"No, seriously Robert. It was good and I was shocked that no one else was prepared to even look at it. I feel like apologising for them all, but I don't think you need me to do that, do you?"

"No, because I've got used to it. You don't get given anything in this world and you just take every setback as a challenge.

There's always going to be someone like Mike crawling out of the woodwork. You just have to remember: 'don't let the bastards grind you down'."

His language surprised her. He'd met her for the first time and he'd defied convention, for no man swore in the presence of a lady. It was clear that he didn't care. He was a handsome, rough-hewn character and she knew that she wanted him. Yet Caroline was unconventional too. Aware in the office that he'd been observing her for some time, she knew that Robert found her attractive. Caroline was convinced that she would soon have him desperate with desire and that would put her in control of whatever may happen. For all that Robert proclaimed his pride in being working-class, Caroline saw a young man who appeared to be carrying a huge chip on his shoulder. She was sure that deep down, he wasn't quite as confident as he wished to appear.

"What you say may be true, but it's not always quite so easy," suggested Caroline. "When others have the power to shape our lives, it may not be sensible, or possible, to stand against them."

"I don't see it that way if you're young," replied Robert. "Perhaps if you've got a family to support, you might be inclined to allow the bosses to push you around. If you're single, you can tell them to stick it and get a job somewhere else."

"You can't tell one of the lecturers to 'stick it' though, can you?"

"Well, that's different. You wouldn't need to."

"I suppose so," said Caroline. "Not being ground down though," she continued, "I'm not sure that your contemporaries in Ardwick would feel so strongly about it. More likely, they're full of inhibitions and uncertainty. They're scared to challenge conformity. Satisfied to marry their first serious girlfriend and settle into an average job and a dreary, unexceptional life. The thought of passion and excitement terrifies them. What about you Robert?" she asked, flirtatiously. "Are you afraid of opening up to the possibilities of liberating yourself and being truly free to experience everything you can?"

Caroline looked into his eyes. Her eyelashes fluttered fleetingly, her moist lips parted slowly and seductively. Subtly, the conversation was becoming more suggestive, as Caroline waited for Robert's response.

There was no doubt that Caroline intrigued him. Robert knew that he was being propositioned and that the rich girl, with her liberal attitudes, was testing him to see if he was equally liberated in his thinking. She needn't have worried. Robert had been with many girls, but never one who oozed social class; privileged and Southern too. Her accent, her fine clothes and of course, her good looks, set her apart. She was the kind of trophy that the ambitious lad from Ardwick, was eager and determined to possess.

"I don't know about the others," replied Robert, "but I've no inhibitions and for me, uncertainty doesn't exist."

Moving his hand across the table, he wrapped his fingers softly around hers.

"You have to live life to the full," he continued, "and I've never turned down an opportunity to do so."

Robert looked at her intently. His message was unequivocal. He wanted her too and it was clear that she understood.

"Well, Robert. I suppose we're going to have to see what we can do about finding that opportunity, aren't we?"

Robert smiled. Once again, he was on a promise. This time however, it was different. Once he would have thought her out of his league. In fact, he would have been unlikely to meet anyone like her. But now, everything had changed. Attending Owens had allowed him to move among his so-called betters. Robert didn't have their money or social connections and he suspected that most of them, unlike Larry, would never truly accept him. Yet the background that they so disdained, the terraces and cobbled streets of Ardwick, had given him the wit and intelligence to survive and would prove priceless if he wanted to succeed in the cut and thrust of the world of journalism and business. Caroline was right, he did have a chip on his shoulder and it made him all the more determined to make his mark on the world and partake of every pleasure that it was able to offer.

Chapter 36

Caroline began her relationship with Robert, fully believing that she was in control. After all, he was still, despite his exposure to the more cosmopolitan environment at Owens, somewhat unrefined and she sensed that he was flattered by her attention. Uninhibited in expressing the intensity of his emotions, she recognised that he was already sexually experienced. Nevertheless, she was confident that the local girls he'd already been with, wouldn't have the allure of a sophisticated young woman like herself. Caroline had already led many others a merry dance and regardless of whether she had allowed them intimacy with her or not, they all remained desperate to possess her. Already responding eagerly to her advances, she was confident that Robert would be the same.

They had been out on a couple of dates, frustrating affairs as it was clear to them both that they had no way of satisfying their ardour. For Robert it was unbearable. When he took her to the pictures, Caroline had teased him mercilessly. The summer was approaching, the weather was warm and she had worn a soft, white cardigan, over a fetching yellow swing dress, stockings and white heels. She was a vision of beauty and femininity; a collector of admiring glances. Inside the cinema, they had chosen seats to afford them some degree of privacy. When the lights had gone down, she had taken his hand, tracing her finger softly around his palm. A simple act, the sensation was thrilling and Robert struggled not to feel aroused; an impossible task when she placed his hand on the top of her thigh and moved it down along the line of her suspenders. His heart pounding in his chest, he gulped in the air as Caroline whispered softly in his ear.

"Calm down, we've all night yet."

Moving her hand towards his groin, she touched him softly.

"Naughty boy. I thought so. The rise and fall of Robert Wilson!"

Caroline chuckled and then her lips brushed his cheek with the gentlest of kisses; the starkest of contrasts to the hard, smouldering desire beneath her hand, that was so desperate to be released.

Robert thought that he was experienced, but this was something new. After losing his virginity, he would always initiate foreplay. But now, it was Caroline in charge and she was enjoying Robert's frustration at not being able to achieve satisfaction. Uninhibited, she didn't seem to care where they were. She had a raw sexuality that belied her genteel appearance. Caroline had held out the promise of a new, liberating relationship, but he'd never believed that it would be quite as exciting as this.

There was to be no relief for Robert in the stalls at the cinema, or in the cafés and pubs that they visited. Caroline may be liberated, but she was still refined. Robert knew that he couldn't find release with her, as he had with other girls, on the basis of a quick 'knee-trembler' down some quiet back alley. The longer the situation continued, the more frustrated he became. And he was sure that's what she wanted; teasing and tantalising him to a point where his desperation to make love to her, became almost painful. It was then that finally, Caroline seemed satisfied that the time was right. In the Kardomah cafe in St Anne's Square, she decided to reveal her plan to Robert.

The choice of location said much about their different backgrounds. It was one in which Caroline was clearly more at ease. Sat at their table, they were approached by a smart and polite waitress in her black uniform and starched white apron. Ordering a coffee, Caroline was surprised when Robert asked for tea.

"Aren't you having a coffee too?"

"No. I prefer tea."

"But you must want a coffee. How can you not, when you can smell such a wonderful aroma."

"No. Tea's fine."

He was adamant. Caroline looked at the waitress and shrugged her shoulders.

"Well, a tea and coffee it is and two tea cakes please."

It wasn't long before the waitress returned with their order.

"You're more at home than I am in places like this, aren't you?"

"What do you mean?" asked Caroline.

"Well, for starters, we're in the posh part of town and freshly ground coffee, is for the middle-classes."

"But all types of people come in here."

"Yes, they do. But I know a couple of girls who work in the shops around here and they only come in to treat themselves when its pay day. I think you'll find most locals regard the place in the same way. It's just a bit too fancy, isn't it? Waitresses in uniforms, jars of coffee beans on the counter and the smart tiles and decorations."

"Well, I thought you'd be all for the uniforms," replied Caroline, with a cheeky smile.

"Well," he replied, "just as long as those in them aren't too old."

Robert laughed. He couldn't help it. Caroline sighed, shook her head and pretended to admonish him.

"You really do have a one-track mind, don't you?"

"It's not my fault. You're the one encouraging me."

"Well, be that as it may," replied Caroline, "I don't think it's any different here than it is at the Lyons cafés. Their 'nippies' wear uniforms, don't they? You wouldn't say that they were posh establishments."

"No, you're right. I wouldn't. They're tea houses though and like Orwell says, in 'Road to Wigan Pier', cups of tea provide comfort for the troubled working-classes. Mind you, he is a bit of a condescending 'get'."

Caroline was confused.

"Git," explained Robert. "In Manchester, we say 'get'.

"Oh. I see."

"Anyway," continued Robert, "the only kind of coffee you'll find in a working-class home is 'Camp Coffee' and I bet you don't know what it is, do you?"

Caroline shook her head. She was finding out that she knew very little about the peculiarities of Mancunian life.

"It's not really coffee but it's cheap and allows poor families to pretend that they can indulge in luxuries too. It's a brown syrupy mixture that contains about a quarter of chicory essence and less than five per cent coffee extract. It smells of chicory; there's no wonderful aroma of fresh ground coffee, like there is here. If you put it with warm milk, you can have café au lait," he continued, laughing. "Mostly though, you can't afford the extra milk, so you just put it with boiling water. My gran thought we'd become fashionable and bought a bottle once. It was bloody awful and it stayed in the cupboard unused until she had to throw it out."

"You wouldn't recommend that I try it then?"

"Well, not unless you want to know how the other half lives."

Caroline smiled and then looked straight into his eyes.

"Will you tell me Robert. Is the real reason why you refused to have a coffee, because you're moody as you're feeling so frustrated?"

"What do you mean?" asked Robert, clearly surprised by her question.

"You know what I mean."

Robert knew very well what she was referring to, but preferred not to respond. He was anxious to try and establish some control over their relationship. She had been calling the shots and exciting as it had been, it was damaging to his ego.

"That's all right," she continued, with a smile. "I like the silent and moody type, so much so, that I've got a nice surprise lined up for you. And rest assured, you're not going to be feeling frustrated for very much longer."

Caroline paused. Her eyes opened wide as she ran the tip of her tongue suggestively across her lips. Robert's heart began to pound in expectation.

"Every Friday, my landlady goes into town. She's there all afternoon and Alice, her other lodger, is going home this weekend. We can have the house to ourselves."

It was the opportunity for which he'd been waiting for so long. Robert suddenly felt exceptionally calm.

"It's said that all good things come to he who waits and it sems that for you Robert, it's going to come true."

At that moment it seemed that Caroline was very much in charge of their relationship. However, once she had given Robert what he so desperately wanted, how long was that likely to continue?

Chapter 37

Caroline's digs were out on Palatine Road in Didsbury. It was a large, rambling house owned by an elderly widow who, wanting some life put back into her home, had approached the accommodation office at Owens and offered to take a couple of female students. Not needing the additional income that they provided, she was more than generous in her provision of varied, good quality meals and all-round access to hot water. Laundry was included too. Caroline and Alice had certainly fallen on their feet.

When Robert got off the bus at noon and walked up to the house, he was in a state of growing excitement. Caroline had insisted that he arrive early so that they could take advantage of every possible moment together. As he knocked on the door and waited for an answer, he suddenly realised that he hadn't prepared for the possibility that her landlady may have decided to stay in. Quickly, he began to think of an explanation as to why he had turned up in the middle of the day. As the door opened, that now seemed unnecessary, for there, stood before him, was Caroline.

"She has gone out, hasn't she?"

"Yes, don't worry."

"What about the neighbours, they're not looking out for the house are they?"

"Look around. We're set back from the road and hemmed in by trees and bushes. You can't see the neighbours and anyway, what would they say? I am living here. You are allowed to call for me. Honestly, you are silly!"

Caroline laughed. She was surprised that Robert seemed a little nervous. She had expected to be hard pressed to hold him back and that he would be eager to be shown to her bedroom.

"Well, I'm only thinking about you," said Robert, attempting to justify his hesitation. "It's a fancy billet you've got here and I wouldn't like to mess things up for you."

Caroline wondered if it was more than that. This was one of Manchester's most sought-after locations and perhaps the usually confident working-class lad, wasn't quite so sure of himself in these surroundings.

Ushering him through the front door, Caroline closed it behind him. They were stood in a wide entrance hall. It was beautifully decorated, with gold flock wallpaper and ornate, sculptured coving around the ceilings. Two large landscape paintings, increased the elegance even further. Robert let out a soft whistle.

"Wow, I'm impressed. This hallway's bigger than our kitchen and front room put together. Very nice."

"Are you here to review the décor, or would you rather go upstairs?"

Following a few steps behind, Robert gazed in admiration as she began to climb gracefully up the stairs. Reaching the landing, Caroline took him into her bedroom and closed the door. Standing by the bed, she pointed over towards the marble fireplace.

"Over there," she whispered, enticingly.

Almost shaking in anticipation, Robert obeyed.

"Let's see how much you want me. Take off your clothes."

As he started to remove his jacket, Caroline watched him carefully. Dropping it to the floor, he received a stinging rebuke.

"Don't make a mess! Place it on the back of the chair."

He looked at her confused.

"You'll do as you're told!"

Her wish to dominate was exciting and Robert was eager to play along. Taking off his shirt, trousers, vest and socks, he put them neatly on the seat of the chair.

"And those," demanded Caroline, pointing to his underpants.

She had him naked now and there was no hiding his desperation. Yet Caroline was still teasing him; she hadn't removed a single stitch of clothing. Getting on the bed, she lay on her side. Robert looked at her hungrily, his eyes tracing the curvaceous profile of her stunning body. Pleased by his reaction, Caroline moved on to her back and rested her head on the pillows.

"Come here," she directed. "Lie next to me."

Getting on the bed, Robert pressed tightly against her. He sighed in satisfaction as her skirt and stockings rubbed against his bare, sensitive skin. It was the strangest of sensations, his nakedness leaving him vulnerable to her every whim. Aching with desire, he wanted her completely and Caroline sensed that he could wait no longer. Whispering for him to wait, she raised herself from the mattress and hitched up her skirt. Lying back down she looked at him expectantly, ready for him to take what she had promised.

Their appetite for one another was insatiable; their love-making continuing throughout the afternoon. Robert had finally found release from the pent-up frustration of the last few weeks and as Caroline hoped, his passion and ardour satisfied her completely. The privileged young woman had fantasised that only a man from the streets could take her to the very limits of pleasure and Robert hadn't disappointed. Yet they couldn't go on forever and finally, noting the time and the impending return of her landlady, Caroline reluctantly advised Robert that it was time for him to leave.

After the two of them were dressed, Caroline gave Robert a quick kiss and they hurried down the stairs to the front door. Then, he was gone. Caroline hadn't registered his lack of tenderness after they had made love. Perhaps she was just relieved that her landlady hadn't caught them together, but more likely it was because she saw their relationship in terms of physical, not emotional, significance. It was certainly how Robert viewed the situation and as long as they both felt the same way, neither of them was likely to get hurt.

In the following weeks their appetite for one another continued unabated. Their liaisons in Didsbury became more daring, as they sought new peaks of excitement through dangerous games of risk and reward. Caroline had smuggled in her lover when Alice and her landlady were asleep. It had been so delicious as they struggled to control their moans of delight, as they worked themselves into a frenzy. On Friday afternoons they had ignored the clock and continued to make love. It was the intoxication of danger. Risking the shame of discovery, electrified the intensity of their lovemaking. Once, they had almost been caught and Caroline had giggled as he stumbled around the room, struggling to get into his clothes. She had quickly gone downstairs, leaving him stranded in the bedroom until finally, he could safely escape.

Eventually however, the dynamic began to change. With each passing week, Robert began to feel more empowered. At first, it was as if he was held in thraldom. She had teased and tormented him; liberated his thinking, but under her control. He felt complete sexual fulfilment. Caroline had taken him much further than any girl he had been with before. Yet once he sensed that he had taken charge, could make her moan with delight and beg for more, the sexy, pretty, posh girl began to lose her exclusivity. Almost inevitably, Robert began to look around for his next potential partner.

At the same time, Caroline believed that their relationship was at a crossroads. She had gradually developed feelings of affection for her lover and it seemed the right time to put their relationship on a more serious footing. Her fatal assumption was that Robert had the capacity to change. The fact that he didn't, would soon lead her into emotional turmoil.

Chapter 38

They had only been together a matter of weeks and Caroline could already sense that Robert's enthusiasm for their arrangement was beginning to wane. Her instincts had always led her to take the maximum pleasure out of the men she collected, for as long as the satisfaction lasted. Once gone, there would be a parting of the ways and no looking back. Now, she found herself changing the rules. She was intent on fighting to win Robert's affection and had decided that she would enlist Kay's help in doing so.

The College Hotel, better known to its patrons as the 'College Arms', was located opposite Whitworth Hall, on the corner of Brunswick Street and Oxford Road. It was a pub frequented by students and lecturers and it had the added attraction of having local residents as 'regulars,' providing the establishment with a Mancunian complexion. The relief sculpture of a phoenix at the top of the building, indicated that the premises had originally belonged to the Phoenix Brewery. Now owned by the Cornbrook Brewery, its beer had always been seen as superior to that served in the students' union. It was here that the *Bulletin* editorial team had arranged to meet and Robert and Larry would be attending. Accompanying them were Caroline and Kay, who had the chance to talk privately until the meeting was over.

It wasn't the first time that the two women had met and as Robert frequently referred to Kay in conversation, Caroline was well aware of his attachment to their friendship. Not at all naïve, she also understood that Robert's feelings for Kay went deeper. In fact, if Caroline had any chance of a long-term relationship with Robert, it was only because Kay had rejected his romantic advances. The irony of the situation didn't escape her. Caroline had been arrogant in her dismissal of working-class girls; confident that they were dull, uninspiring and lacking in sophistication. She had been guilty of creating a stereotype which, once she had met Kay, was shown to be ridiculous. Now she found herself prepared to ask for Kay's advice in order to help her hang on to Robert.

"Kay, you've known Robert for a long time, haven't you?"

"Yes. Since we were kids."

"So, I suppose you know him better than most?"

"Well, yes. I suppose you could say that. But why do you ask?"

Caroline hesitated. She looked closely at Kay. It was clear that she was uncertain about resuming the conversation. Kay remained silent, showing no inclination to push for a response. Finally, Caroline continued.

"I didn't think that I'd develop any real feelings for Robert, but I have and I'm not sure that he feels the same way about me. I don't want to tell him if it's likely to push him away. I know he's had lots of girlfriends, but none for any length of time. What do you think I should do?"

Kay was surprised by her request. When they'd met in the past, Caroline hadn't provided any indication that she felt strongly about Robert. Furthermore, Kay was uncomfortable discussing him behind his back. Unsurprisingly, her answer was non-committal.

"I'm sorry Caroline, but I never get involved in the details of Robert's love life. I've always considered that it's none of my business. It's one of the reasons why we've remained such good friends."

"But you understand him, Kay. You must have an idea of what I should do."

Kay took a deep breath. She could see Caroline waiting expectantly. It seemed clear that she would have to say something.

"You have to think carefully about yourself; what is it that you really want? Whether it's Robert, or anyone else for that matter, then surely you have to tell them."

"But that's my fear. If I tell Robert how I feel about him, will it just drive him away? And if it doesn't, do you believe that he's capable of providing me with a long-term commitment?"

It was an awkward question, for Kay's own rejection of Robert's advances was because she believed him incapable of sustaining a monogamous relationship. Kay would never share that judgement however; it would be nothing short of a betrayal of her best friend. Furthermore, Kay was aware of Caroline's promiscuous reputation and doubted whether she was actually prepared for a serious relationship. Yet Kay was unwilling to introduce such thoughts into the conversation and so, once again, she responded in general terms.

"It seems to me that you have two choices. You can leave things as they are and see what happens, or you can tell him exactly what you feel. Perhaps, because you haven't been together that long, the first choice is the best one at the moment."

"Yes," replied Caroline, "but if I hesitate, it may mean that it's all over before I'm able to tell him what he really means to me."

"I don't know what more I can say. It has to be your decision, Caroline. No one can make it for you."

Frustrated by Caroline's continued uncertainty, Kay was relieved to see Larry and Robert making their way towards them. It meant that she could finally relax in the company of her friends. Although Caroline didn't yet know it, the fate of her relationship with Robert would shortly be resolved.

Chapter 39

At the end of the evening, Larry and Caroline had gone to catch the bus on Oxford Road, whilst Kay and Robert had set off along Brunswick Street towards Hyde Road and home. As they walked, Robert asked Kay how she'd found Caroline.

"She's very pretty and seems quite pleasant," replied Kay.

"Just that. Nothing else?"

"What else is there? Surely, it's what you think about her that's important."

"Yes, I suppose it is," replied Robert. "What did you talk about?"

"Oh, nothing much."

"You must have talked about something."

"Only women's things," replied Kay, sounding disinterested.

"You, talking about women's things. I don't think so."

"Well, it doesn't matter what you think. You shouldn't be nosy, should you?"

Kay looked at him disapprovingly. Robert knew better than to push her any further on the matter and for the rest of their walk home, his girlfriend ceased to be a topic of conversation. As such, Kay had no idea that Robert was intent on ending his relationship with Caroline.

When Robert had met Caroline, she had seemed different and exciting. She was feisty and confident, qualities that Kay had in abundance and it was therefore natural that he would be attracted to her. She had given him real sexual satisfaction and for a time, he couldn't get enough of her. But it couldn't last. If Caroline were to win his affection, that wouldn't be sufficient and Robert soon realised that she was nothing like his beloved Kay. The gloss had worn off their relationship and he had become bored with her. From then on, it was only a matter of time before Robert's roving eye took a shine to someone new.

When they had parted at the 'College Arms', Caroline and Robert had arranged to meet one another in 'Caf', at dinner the next day. When Caroline arrived, she found Robert waiting outside. When he failed to return her smile, she sensed that something serious was on his mind.

"I thought we could sit there," said Robert, pointing to a bench over near the Arts Building.

"Can't we talk in 'Caf', whilst we have some lunch?" asked Caroline.

"I think you'd prefer it if we were on our own."

His words seemed ominous. Caroline suspected that he was about to end their relationship. It was a new experience for her. Usually, she was the one who ditched her boyfriends. For a moment, Caroline thought about striking first. She could simply feign indifference, or tell him to 'get lost' and walk away. After all, she had her pride. Yet she had fallen for Robert and wasn't prepared to give him up without a fight. Yielding to his request, she followed him to the bench and sat down. Without hesitation, Robert came straight to the point.

"I think you see things the same as me. It's been a bit of fun and we've both enjoyed it, but it's time to move on."

"A bit of fun!"

Caroline had originally thought in those terms, but now she was angry that Robert could be so dismissive of everything that had happened between them.

"Yes, a bit of fun. You know it was. It was never meant to be serious."

His words cut her to the quick. Caroline should have realised that any feelings he had for her were gone, but she still didn't want to give him up.

"It's not like it was a one-night stand, Robert. Surely, what we've had together means more than that."

Robert was surprised by her attitude. He'd assumed that she'd be content for them to go their separate ways. Frustrated, he became brusque and impatient.

"Come off it, Caroline. We never meant anything to one another. You wanted the sex, just like me. In fact, more than me."

"Oh, don't flatter yourself Robert. Do you think that you're the only one who can give pleasure to a woman? Well, I can tell you now. You're not the best."

"Huh. Well, you should know."

"And you've got no room to talk, either. Have you, Robert?"

Angry, Caroline had fought back, but her words had provoked a cruel response. She realised that her liberal, feminist views about sexual freedom for women, weren't shared by her working-class lover. Caroline sensed that by giving herself to him, she had lost her claim to Robert's respect. Society hadn't progressed as far as she had hoped. Education couldn't overturn long-standing social expectations. The scholar from Ardwick had made it plain that it was still a man's world.

"I don't understand why you're angry," continued Robert. "From the start you wanted no commitment and that's what you've got. I can only think it's because you're not able to control things in the way you thought you would."

"What do you mean?"

"You had the idea that if you went with me, I'd be your grateful loyal lapdog, to do with as you wished. I was your little experiment. Your chance to have someone rough and ready, only it hasn't worked out the way you wanted. You felt that I'd be eternally grateful for allowing someone like me to make love to you. Yes, the sex was great. But then again, you're not that special, are you?"

Caroline looked down at the floor. Robert's words were cruel, even if his observations contained a kernel of truth. Slowly, Caroline raised her head. Robert could see the tears in her eyes, yet remained oblivious to her pain. Not for an instant did it elicit any sympathy. Nevertheless, Caroline still tried to reach out to him.

"Perhaps, at first, what you say is true, but that was before the times we've shared together. I've come to care for you Robert and I can't believe it when you say that you don't feel anything at all for me."

"But I don't. It's finished. Walk away with some dignity."

It was a blunt and vicious response, but Robert didn't care. He wanted rid of her; he'd had enough.

"You're a complete bastard," replied Caroline, angrily. "You've used me."

"But when we started out, you thought you were using me."

"That's not fair Robert. It's not how things are."

"Well, chalk it down to experience in your ongoing search for liberation."

With that, Robert rose from the bench and walked off towards the library.

Chapter 40

It had been Larry's idea. Relaxing with Kay and Robert in 'Caf', their end of year exams over, he had suddenly sighed.

"Well, I don't think that I can put it off any longer. I suppose I'll have to go home and show my face again."

"Well, so you should," remarked Kay. "You couldn't have got here without your parents' help and they care about you. I'm grateful that I'm at Owens. I can't imagine how it would feel studying halfway across the country and unable to see my mam and dad for such a long time."

"Ah, the emotional voice of the concerned female."

It was a flippant remark, one Robert soon regretted, as it inevitably brought a stinging rebuke.

"I'm serious Robert. You should know better. Don't you love your mam and gran? Wouldn't you miss not seeing them?"

Kay frowned. Robert, duly chastened, averted his eyes.

Surprised at Kay's reaction, Larry explained his concerns about returning to Kent.

"It's not that I don't care about my parents, I do, but they've asked me to go whilst Bernard is on leave. I was hoping to visit when neither of my brothers were there, but Mother's insisting that she wants us together for a family dinner. I'm afraid I can't see any way out of it."

"Haven't you written to tell her that the three of us have got vacation jobs at Belle Vue?" asked Robert. "Use that as an excuse. Then you can go and see her just before the new term begins in September and avoid your brothers."

"I wish I could. Only problem is that I've already told her that we don't start work until the school holidays begin."

"Oh well," replied Robert, disappointed. "It looks like there's no way out of it then."

"Well, I'm so sorry for you Larry. Isn't it a shame that you're going to have to see your horrid family and spend time with them?"

It was now Larry's turn to be the target of Kay's displeasure and he found it difficult to withstand her biting sarcasm. Meekly, he again tried to defend his position.

"Bernard's ten years older than me. He's an officer in the Royal Engineers; a real action man, qualified to serve with the 'paras' too. Norman's twelve years older and a partner in Dad's firm. Before you say it, no he didn't get it because he was the boss's son; Dad made him work for it. I'm not driven like them. I don't have my life mapped out in front of me. I suppose they mean well, but they can't avoid picking me up on my 'lack of direction.' They still can't believe that I didn't choose Cambridge and that I came to Manchester, to 'wild and woolly land' as they call it."

"Sound like right bloody Southerners!"

Larry had primed the gun and Robert, ready to pull the trigger, was about to launch into one of his furious tirades about the betrayal of the North by the Establishment in the South.

"Present company excepted of course," added Kay, quickly.

"Yes. Well, yes. Of course. I don't consider Larry one of them anymore. He's getting to be like one of us now."

"No offence taken," replied Larry. "I came here to get away from there."

"So, what are you going to do?" asked Robert.

"Well, I've thought of an idea, but it all depends on what you both think about it."

Hesitating, Larry seemed unsure as to whether he should continue.

"Go on then," prompted Kay.

Both she and Robert looked at him in anticipation.

"You could both come with me," suggested Larry.

"But what would your mother say?" asked Kay.

"Oh, she'd love to have you. Honestly. I've told her all about you and it'll give you a chance to see how the other half lives."

"I bet it's no 'garden of England' down there. I bet that's all bull."

Besides a couple of day trips to Blackpool, Robert hadn't ventured very far outside his native city, but he was convinced that he didn't need to in order to form a judgement. Like the good

Northerner he was, Robert had an ingrained and healthy suspicion of the South.

Kay shook her head in dismay.

"You really are so open-minded, aren't you Robert?"

"Of course," he replied, ignoring her sarcasm. "I'm just dealing in plain facts."

"Well, if you both come with me, then you'll be able to find out."

Larry was trying hard to persuade them.

"You'll only need the train fare," he continued. "We've got plenty of spare bedrooms and our meals will be laid on. You'll enjoy the break. Something different."

"Okay, I'm keen," said Robert. "What about you Kay? It won't be the same if you don't come."

"Yes, go on Kay," added Larry, "I'm sure you won't regret it."

Kay could sense the pressure of expectation as both Robert and Larry turned towards her, eager looks on their faces.

"It doesn't seem as though I've got much of a choice."

Kay shook her head and sighed as they both let out a cheer.

"We're just like the three musketeers," remarked Larry. "All for one and one for all!"

"Or the three stooges," quipped Robert.

"No, definitely just the two stooges and Kay to sort us out," replied Larry.

"I should think so!" noted Kay.

There was however, little point in her pretending to be annoyed. Unable to disguise the smile that came to her lips, her friends knew that she had been amused by their reaction when she had consented to go with them. And she had to admit that the idea of travelling to London and on into Kent was appealing. She was sure it would be quite an adventure and no doubt, educational too.

Chapter 41

On the following Friday morning, July 15th, Kay and Robert arrived early outside London Road Station. Waiting for them was Larry, who had already collected their tickets to Faversham. London Road had been undergoing development for some time now. British Railways had initiated a programme to remodel the station for the future of electrification. The transformation wasn't yet complete, but the station was already looking very different to the one Kay and Robert were used to. Much of the imposing Victorian entrance building had been demolished and already rising in its place was the imposing Rail House, a ten-storey office block. It certainly was all change; a conscious attempt by British Rail to project a modern and technological image. Management hoped that it would convince the doubters that their services were entering a bright new era. And it would only be another few weeks before the metamorphosis would be complete, for London Road would be no more. Henceforth, the station would be known as Piccadilly and so, as the technocrats desired, the break with the past would be achieved.

Inside, the expectant trio checked the departure boards before proceeding to their train's designated platform. Making their way to the barrier they were confronted by the ticket collector. An elderly, bespectacled chap, he was a combination of moustache, cap and uniform. As Kay approached, he observed her carefully. She looked charming in her blue two-piece suit, white gloves and heels. Standing respectfully to the side, he had no intention of checking the ticket that she offered to him.

"That's fine love, just go through. Have a nice journey."

"Thank you," replied Kay, with a smile.

Held at the barrier, Robert and Larry had to wait as the ticket collector gazed admiringly at Kay walking down the platform. Turning back towards them, his face was transformed. Serious and officious, he insisted on carefully checking each of their tickets in turn, before somewhat reluctantly allowing them through to their train.

"Another conquest you've made" said Robert, with a chuckle, as he and Larry caught up with Kay.

"What do you mean?"

"Back there. The ticket collector."

"Don't be daft!"

"I'm not. Why didn't he ask to look at your ticket then? He did ours."

"I assume because you strike him as a pair of pretty desperate characters."

"Oh, thanks very much."

"Well, you did ask."

Larry burst out laughing.

"Well, yes. Perhaps. But I think maybe you're getting a little embarrassed Kay."

"About what?"

"All these hearts you're breaking; both young and old."

"Shut up! The pair of you are being completely gormless!"

The fierce response came straight from Bennett Street; a clear signal to Robert and Larry to desist.

"You could have just said 'balleys'" replied Robert, trying to lighten the mood.

"Balleys?" asked Larry, confused.

It was now Kay's turn to laugh.

"Yes, balleys," she said, eventually.

"Oh, no. Not another bit of Mancunian!"

"Afraid so," replied Robert. "We did it at school. When kids were mithering you in the playground, you could cross your fingers, shout 'balleys' and they'd leave you alone."

"Well, they were supposed to," added Kay. "But it didn't always work."

"Oh," said Larry, surprised. "We never had anything like that when I was at school."

"Well, you're not as civilised down South, are you Larry?" replied Robert.

"Balleys!" shouted Larry, holding up his hands and crossing his fingers for extra effect. "Leave this poor Southerner alone."

Kay and Robert burst out laughing, then noticed the frowns on the faces of several of their elderly, fellow passengers, clearly not impressed by their general exuberance.

As they waited to board their train, the signs of reconstruction work were going on all around them. Outside the main part of the station, above Fairfield Street, completely new platforms had replaced the old and a new entrance was being constructed on the road below. Everywhere, new electric cables were being installed overhead, whilst under the spectacular arched roofs of the four Victorian train sheds, could be seen the rubble from the old platforms. In their place, were the frameworks of pristine, new concrete constructions.

Finally boarding the train, the trio took their seats either side of a small table and settled down for the long journey ahead of them. They had made sure that they were well prepared with reading material; a selection of magazines and newspapers to share between them. Yet, unlike Larry, Kay and Robert had never been on a long-distance rail journey and the two of them soon found that there was something exceptional about sitting on a fast-moving train, that leads one almost unconsciously to peer out of the window. It was as if they were mesmerised by the scenery flashing by.

Eager to engage his friends in conversation, Larry drew their attention to the fact that the journey to London would take them the best part of four hours. This was forty-five minutes longer, he noted, than the time proposed for the future electrified service. It was a saving of time that made little impression on Kay.

"And what would anyone do with the time once they had it?" asked Kay. "Surely the journey is part of the process that helps to build up expectations before reaching London and its attractions?"

"Yes, definitely," agreed Larry. "Even now, I still find long train journeys something of an adventure; almost magical. Just like when I was young."

"Well, I disagree," remarked Robert. "I think that keeping an eye on what they're doing in Westminster, becomes easier if its quicker to get down there."

"You're just being argumentative," replied Kay, dismissively.

"No, I'm not. We need development here; the whole North-West does. Old industries are declining and Macmillan and his cronies couldn't care less."

"And I don't know that, Robert?"

"Of course, you do. I'm just saying Kay."

"Well, you needn't bother. Don't waste time preaching to the converted."

"You're right about the Tories," said Larry. "But it needs more than fast trains to change attitudes in the capital. And I should know."

Robert nodded and turned back towards the window. A proud Mancunian, he was no more passionate about the prospects for his city than Kay. Yet restrained and less demonstrative, she had been far more successful at winning over fellow students to the Northern cause. Robert all too often failed to realise that his acerbic manner was often unappealing and so effectively undermined his arguments. Reaching across the table, Kay smiled and patted his arm reassuringly.

"Come on. We're going to enjoy ourselves. You need to relax a little after all the hard work with exams and the like."

"Yes. I know Kay. I'll try harder."

"But not too hard," said Larry, with a chuckle. "Your observations on the South are going to be quite educational and no doubt, pretty amusing."

"Huh. You might not think so once I start laying into you 'toffs.'"

"I don't know, what are we going to do with you?" asked Kay, shaking her head. "Here, read this magazine and behave."

Like a naughty boy, Robert did as he was told. Looking on, Larry smiled. He was so pleased that his friends had accepted his invitation to Kent. Witty, confident and assertive, their working-class, Mancunian upbringing had given them an authenticity that he'd never experienced with people in the South. They were straight talking and fun to be with. He was confident that the weekend would turn out to be a far more pleasant occasion, now that they were with him.

Chapter 42

Arriving at Euston, their next destination was Victoria station, from where they would catch the train to Faversham. It meant that they would be travelling on the tube and as Larry took responsibility for leading his friends to the station below, he initially failed to appreciate how disorientating a first visit to the underground can be. Euston was a deep level station and it would require them to descend two escalators and traverse a labyrinth of passages, in order to reach their platform.

As they made their way beyond the barrier, Robert was clearly fascinated by the strange new environment around him. Kay, on the other hand, immediately felt uncomfortable. All she could sense was confusion. There were so many travellers moving with determination; ploughing on relentlessly, regardless of anyone who was in the way. Yet others were floundering. Suddenly, they would change direction or turn on the spot, desperately trying to find their bearings. Yet this was central London and there was little chance of anyone stopping to help them. Kay was pleased that Larry was with them and she instinctively reached out and took hold of his arm. Looking round, Larry could see the expression of anxiety on her face and moved quickly to reassure her.

"Don't worry Kay, it's not as bad as it looks. It won't be too long before we get to Victoria. Let Robert take your case. You won't get lost if you hang on to me."

As they rode down the first escalator, Kay felt a little more comfortable. The movement of the staircase providing uniformity and regulation to her journey once more. Nevertheless, she could see why Larry had directed her to one side, as numerous others hurried by on the other, not content with their rate of progress.

"Are you alright?" asked Larry, turning towards her.

Kay nodded and breathed in. The air seemed stale and the deeper they descended, a distinct smell, much like the one she associated with garages or engineering works, became more noticeable.

"It's just like a series of tunnels we're travelling down," she observed. "Semi-circular mine shafts and the smell of machinery. That's what it is."

"Yes, I can see that," replied Larry. "I think the electric rails the trains run on, give off an odour similar to a welding shop."

Leaving the escalator there was still some way to go as they negotiated another series of passages. As they progressed, Kay became more conscious of a drop in the temperature. The sounds of people moving and talking now seemed muffled and echoey. Reaching the top of the second escalator, she was shocked to see that it descended an even greater distance than the first. As they travelled down, they could feel and hear the sound of the wind from the tunnels, drawn through by the moving trains. Reaching the bottom, there were still passages to negotiate before they finally emerged on to the platform.

Standing well away from the edge, Kay observed the round curvature of the station walls. Looking to the right and left, she noted that the rails disappeared from sight as they entered into the blackness of the tunnels, the dull station lighting unable to penetrate their interiors. Although the platform had seemed fairly deserted on their arrival, it wasn't long before it seemed full of people. Afraid that the press of numbers may force her closer to the platform's edge, Kay instinctively tightened her grip on Larry's arm. Sensing her discomfiture, he moved her firmly but carefully, to the rear of the platform. Clear of the melee, Kay let out an audible sigh of relief. Larry smiled, pleased to have come to her rescue; a chivalric knight, rescuing a damsel in distress.

And then Kay heard it. A low rattle at first which grew ever louder. Facing towards the sound there was nothing to see but the darkness of the tunnel, but then the rattle became a rumble and the glare of headlights poked through the gloom and the train raced alongside the platform. Before the doors had time to open, a throng of people surrounded them. Kay wondered whether it would be possible for anyone to leave the train but somehow, they all did.

"Come on, let's move along. There are plenty of seats in the other compartments."

Kay was happy for Larry to lead her quickly along the platform and towards an open carriage. The 'swoosh' of the doors opening had concerned her; she was worried that they would trap her before she could enter and she would be pulled along the platform and crushed in the tunnel. Suddenly, she remembered her other friend.

"Robert. Where's Robert?"

"Don't worry, I'm right here," came a voice from behind.

Turning, Kay was relieved to see Robert's smiling face. He could tell that she was anxious and it was so unlike her, but then being in the underground was something she'd never experienced before. Sitting down, Kay expressed her fears.

"I was worried that we'd get trapped in the doors, or that you Robert, would get left behind."

"You can't get trapped in the doors Kay," said Larry. "There's a guard in the last carriage and he steps out on to the platform and makes sure that everyone is clear before he shuts them."

"And if we get separated," added Robert, "I can soon follow the maps and catch up with you both at Victoria."

Kay sat quiet for a few moments and then sighed.

"I suppose I've made myself look a bit silly, haven't I?"

"No, of course not," replied Larry, generous as ever.

"Well," said Robert mischievously. "You might be able to handle the terrors of the Black Brook, but the London Underground has definitely got you beaten."

The three of them burst out laughing. It was just what Kay needed to put her recent tribulations behind her.

Chapter 43

Having taken the Northern Line to Charing Cross, it was then necessary to change to the District Line in order to get to Victoria. Larry had planned to give them the option to break their journey at Westminster, so that they had an opportunity to look at the Houses of Parliament. Given Kay's recent experiences however, he decided that it would be best to avoid any further, potential difficulties and once at Victoria, they were soon sat on the train to Faversham.

As they proceeded out through London and into the Kent countryside, the sun was shining brightly. It was a beautiful day and the temperature, though hot, wasn't unpleasant, as the opened windows allowed a refreshing breeze to pass through the carriage. As they left the Medway towns behind them, the scenery was more obviously agricultural and when the train came to a temporary halt, both Robert and Kay began to notice a faintly spicy and herbal aroma.

"What's that smell, Larry?" asked Kay.

"Hops."

"For beer?"

"Yes. Weren't you aware that the 'Garden of England' was a key producer?"

"Should I be?"

"Well, I suppose not. As I've spent most of my life in Kent, I take it for granted that everyone knows."

"I do," said Robert.

"Well, that's not a surprise, given all the time you spend in the 'College Arms'!" replied Kay.

"She's got you there," said Larry, laughing. "If you look out of the window you can see them just behind that hedge. You can smell them because it won't be long before they're ready for harvest."

Looking out, Kay and Robert could see a mass of tall, green stems covered in leaves and large, acorn like flowers. They reached up from the ground along strings attached to a wooden framework.

"They're huge," remarked Kay, as the train slowly began to move again.

"Yes, as much as eighteen to twenty feet. They're grown on a framework of strings, attached to the chestnut hop poles. They train the young shoots on to them and they grow upwards and then spread out. The flowers come out early in July and are ready to harvest by September. That's becoming increasingly mechanised now, although there are still some 'hoppers' coming down from London to do the work. As well as Romanies of course."

"Yes," said Robert. "I know about the 'hoppers.' I've read George Orwell's account of working in the hop gardens back in the 'thirties.' He says that it's no better than slave labour."

"Well, it's definitely hard work," replied Larry, "but most Londoners who come down have always treated it as a holiday. They're out in the country, breathing fresh air and the women and kids are earning extra money. I don't think it's going to last for too much longer though."

"And I reckon that won't only be down to mechanisation," noted Robert. "People aren't as daft as they used to be. They expect better conditions and adequate recompense for all their hard work."

"Yes, there's that as well. The worst part of it I've seen growing up though, is how hostile many Kent people are to the 'hoppers.' 'Foreigners' they call them. Shopkeepers serve them from separate counters in the village shops and most landlords won't let them drink inside the pubs when the men come at the weekends to visit their families. They all have to stay outside, separated from the locals."

"They're obviously quick enough to take their money off them though," replied Robert. "Typical bloody Southerners."

"Will you shut up, Robert." Kay was far from happy. "We didn't come down here wanting to upset everyone we come across. If you haven't noticed, we're on a train full of Southerners."

"It's okay," laughed Larry. "If he carries on, it's going to make it quite interesting."

"And no doubt I'll be the one who's going to have to get him out of trouble. Yet again!"

"Oh?" asked Larry, intrigued. "When was that then?"

"Never mind. Kay's just being daft," said Robert, with a tinge of embarrassment. "Okay, you don't have to worry. I'll make sure I watch what I'm saying from now on."

"Just make sure you do," replied Kay.

Robert was quiet now, chastened by the stern look that she had cast in his direction. Observing them, Larry couldn't help but smile. Ever since he'd known his Mancunian friends, it was clear that Kay was in charge; Robert almost always prepared to bow to her judgement. Yet she was loyal and devoted to their friendship too and it was obvious that she wasn't going to embarrass him by revealing to Larry the details about any awkward incidents from his past.

Chapter 44

Arriving at Faversham, it was now late afternoon and Kay was feeling somewhat tired. She wasn't used to long journeys and her experience on the Underground had proved trying. She was eager to reach their destination and have time to rest and recuperate. Emerging from the station, Kay assumed that they would be taking a taxi, but was then surprised as Larry called out to a man waiting next to a car parked across from them.

"Who's that?" asked Kay.

"Bernard. My brother," replied Larry. "I let my mother know the time we were arriving and she told me there would be someone here to meet us."

Waving in acknowledgement, Bernard quickly approached them.

"Bang on time. I've only been waiting a few minutes."

Bernard smiled at both Kay and Robert and then looked expectantly at Larry, who appeared confused.

"Well," prompted Bernard, "aren't you going to introduce me?"

"Yes, sorry," replied Larry, slightly flustered. "These are my friends, Kay and Robert."

"Hello. I'm Bernard. Larry's brother. It's very nice to meet you."

Shaking hands with Robert, Bernard then turned to Kay. Extending his hand towards her, she took it firmly, looking straight into his eyes. His manner and appearance pleased her. The hand shake was a mark of respect; an acknowledgement of her as an equal. He was pleasant; smiling and friendly. Confident and assured too, given his military training and command of men in dangerous situations. He had an unmistakable air of authority, as well as being exceptionally handsome. His rugged, chiselled features complemented his soft, brown eyes. The faded remains of a scar on the top of his cheekbone, hinted at the danger and excitement of his chosen vocation. When she thought of men in Bennett Street and those at Owen's too, Kay hadn't any use for the word 'dashing.' Yet, if any man could fit that description, she was sure that it was Bernard.

Seeing Kay's case, beside her on the pavement, Bernard walked towards it.

"Can I take that for you, Kay?"

"Yes, thanks."

She smiled, pleased to accept his help.

Leading her to the car, Bernard stopped to open the boot. He then placed the case inside it, joined by those of Robert and Larry. As he closed it, Larry commented on their vehicle.

"I see you've brought the old man's P5."

"Yes. I'm afraid so."

"Not very flash for you though," replied Larry, with a chuckle.

"Well, I'd hardly be able to get you all into the MGA now, would I?"

The pair of them laughed, unaware that their conversation had little relevance to their guests. For Kay, Robert and their families, car ownership remained out of reach. There were few parked in Ardwick; a blessing for the kids who could continue to play safely in the streets. Yet any car was fascinating for those who couldn't afford one and the P5, although spoken of so dismissively by the brothers, seemed magnificent to their Mancunian visitors. Shiny and polished, its chrome grille, bumpers and headlights dazzled in the sun, highlighting the long and impressive green chassis. Inside were wonderful and inviting plush, leather seats with a polished wood dash board. With its Rover badge emblazoned on the steering wheel, as the car pulled away from the station, Kay and Robert felt that they were riding in the lap of luxury.

It wasn't long before the streets of the small market town of Faversham were left behind and they were heading out into the countryside and the hinterland of small villages. With the windows down, the warm July air filled the car with the scents of summer. Everywhere they could see orchards full of fruit. There were apples, pears and cherries and fields of wheat and hops. Turning into a narrow winding lane, Bernard took his foot off the accelerator and slowed the car.

"Always have to go carefully down here," he commented. "I need to be ready to pull over at a moment's notice."

They could see why. The hedges were tall, their foliage resplendent and a succession of bends reduced visibility considerably. At any moment, Kay expected another vehicle to emerge in front of them, yet she had no fears, certain that Bernard would react quickly to keep them safe. Then she saw a break in the hedge, followed by a wooden railed fence. The car slowed down, almost to a stop and then Bernard pulled hard on the steering wheel. There was a welcoming sound of gravel crunching together, as the wheels of the P5 advanced down the driveway. Sweeping around a long bend, edged with small trees and flowers, the house emerged impressively in front of them. It was huge. For all that Larry had told them about it, neither of his friends could have imagined how imposing it actually was. Pulling up in front of the main entrance, Bernard turned off the engine.

"Well, here we are. Let's get you inside. You must be ready for a drink and something to eat."

Enthralled by the sight before them, Kay and Robert were silent. Bernard got out of the car and opened the door for Kay. He smiled, understanding that Larry's friends were somewhat bewildered by their unfamiliar surroundings.

Standing on the drive, Robert surveyed the sprawling grounds around them. There were several large outbuildings, flower beds and vegetable plots; the latter almost like a series of allotments. Most striking was the enclosed grass tennis court that he could see in the distance. Robert let out an involuntary whistle.

"Whoa, so this is how the other half lives!"

Kay, embarrassed, dug him in the ribs with her elbow, eliciting a muffled groan. Bernard, observing her reaction, was quietly amused, before responding thoughtfully to his comment.

"Yes, we're lucky Robert and you can be sure that we do appreciate it. Growing up out here in the countryside and in the fresh air, we had opportunities denied to most children our age. I'm sure you already know how strongly Larry feels about it. Admittedly, I don't share the sense of guilt that he does. Perhaps, Larry and I differ in the sense that I would like to see a levelling up of society; everyone having the potential to live in a place like this. Larry thinks that's impossible and so he believes that levelling down is the only fair solution to inequalities."

Larry was quiet. He didn't disagree, but normally he would have been quick to join the conversation; to at least elaborate on his views. Kay now understood why he was keen for them to be there. Although he'd never admit it, Larry was in awe of his brother and probably of Roger, the eldest, too. She and Robert would provide him with moral support. Nevertheless, Kay had to admit that she could detect no hint of ridicule or condescension in Bernard's voice. If anything, he had shown genuine affection towards his brother. Kay suspected that Larry's anxiety was fuelled by a desire to match his siblings' success and at the heart of this, was a sense of insecurity.

Eager to change the subject, Kay directed her attention towards the house and its peculiar layout.

"Your parents' house is beautiful Bernard. From here, it seems to have at least five sections to it. And what's this strange construction?"

Kay pointed towards a round section of the building, topped with a steep, tiled conical roof.

"That's an old oast house Kay. It was where they would light fires to dry off the hops before they were used for brewing. There's another one behind it. Other buildings have been added over the years, giving the current house its unusual design. If you come over here," continued Bernard, "you'll be able to see it better."

Walking towards him, Kay stopped and followed his gaze upwards.

"You can see that the oast house has been divided into three floors. The windows make it light and airy. The top floor is a bedroom in the roof itself and it's where you'll be sleeping. The boys will be in the cottage at the far end of the house. It's self-contained, so when guests stay, they can have some privacy."

"Bring them inside Bernard," insisted a voice from behind. "Don't leave them out any longer, when they've been travelling all day."

Looking round, they could see Larry's mother. She'd been waiting eagerly for their arrival and was keen to make them comfortable after their long journey. Approaching her guests, she introduced herself.

"Hello, I'm Violet. You must be Kay and so you must be Robert," she observed. "It's nice to meet you."

"It's very kind of you to invite us," said Kay.

"It's the least we can do," replied Violet. "You and your families have been so kind to Larry. It's certainly brought home to us the generosity of Northern hospitality. I'm afraid that you won't always find that it's the same in the South. But hopefully, you'll enjoy your stay."

Violet was well spoken, but her voice was welcoming; soft and assured. Like her sons, there was nothing ostentatious about her. She was wearing a plain blue, long-sleeved dress and simple, flat shoes. Her short, wavy hair, framing a small, but delicate face, had long since turned grey. If it hadn't been for their surroundings, thought Kay, there was little to distinguish Violet's appearance from her own mother's.

"Come on Kay, we'll get inside. The boys can see to the cases. Can't you?"

The three of them nodded in agreement.

"Once you've done that, come to the breakfast room. I'll have some tea and cakes ready for you."

Kay smiled. For all that her husband and sons had achieved, inside the family home, Violet's authority was unquestionable.

"I'm sure you'd like a drink, wouldn't you?" asked Violet, turning her attention back to Kay.

"Yes, that would be nice. Thank you."

Led into the oast house, Kay was amazed by the unusual features of the room before her. Circular in shape, the internal brick walls rose above a patterned, tiled floor. Around them was a wooden spiral staircase reaching up towards the first floor and then climbing to the bedroom nestled under the roof above. Beautiful, framed pictures of landscapes and famous racehorses followed the curvature of the stairs, whilst antique chairs and occasional tables were strategically placed around the entrance hall and landing, made more impressive by the contrast of the bare bricks behind them.

Walking through to the kitchen and adjoining breakfast room, Kay found it hard not to stare. She was sure that all of their home in Bennett Street would be swallowed up by the cavernous space in front of her. The kitchen was full of tops, cupboards and appliances; incredibly modern. She couldn't conceive of how much money it must all have cost.

"What would you like Kay, tea or coffee?"

"Tea's lovely, thanks."

"I thought young people were coffee drinkers now."

"That's mainly when we go to the cafés in town; to sit and chat and pretend that we're being very bohemian. I actually prefer tea."

"So, do I. Will that suit Robert too?"

"Yes. Is there anything I can do?" asked Kay.

"Well, whilst I finish the drinks, you can help by taking these plates through to the table in the breakfast room."

Violet indicated a number of plates on the side, containing an array of sandwiches, cakes, tarts and biscuits. She watched as Kay began ferrying them into the adjoining room. Violet had quickly warmed to her guest. Kay was polite, helpful and friendly and seemed very sensible. She was also very pretty and it was no surprise that Larry had spoken and written so much about her since he'd gone to Manchester.

With the tea brewed, the final trays were carried in to the breakfast room and Kay had a proper chance to look around. The table was large and substantial. Made of oak, it was surrounded by six hand carved chairs. What caught her eye however, were the two Welsh dressers, each of which housed a fine, porcelain dinner service. Noticing her interest, Violet walked over to the nearest and picked up one of the plates and brought it across to the table.

"Here. You can take a closer look at the pattern."

"Are you sure?"

Kay was nervous. Her Mam had a couple of pottery dogs proudly displayed on the fire place at home and all the family knew that they must never touch them. The porcelain on display here had to be far more valuable and Kay had no wish to damage it.

Violet smiled. Understanding Kay's fears, she quickly reassured her.

"Yes, of course. Take a seat and I'll put it on the table. Nothing will happen to it."

Placing it down, Violet walked over to the second dresser and brought across a plate from the other set, joining Kay at the table. The first plate had a swirling, gold foliate design on top of a cream background. It was a rich and stunning pattern; splendid for a house such as this. Turning the plate over, Kay could see that it had been made by Royal Worcester.

"Can you see the three interlinked circles and the dot?" asked Violet, pointing closely at the back of the plate.

"Ah, yes. Now I can," replied Kay.

"Well, that tells you that this set was made in 1933. It was an anniversary present from Norman."

"It's beautiful."

"Yes, I think so too, but this other set is actually my favourite."

Kay followed Violet's hand which rested on the second plate. Its colouring was far more vibrant than its predecessor; lots of different coloured flowers bursting from a basket against a pale green background.

"It's from around the same time as the Worcester plate," explained Violet. "It's made by Clarice Cliff; their Green Ophelia service."

"They're very different. Equally attractive, but in different ways," suggested Kay.

"Yes. The Worcester set is more formal; but the Clarice Cliff, more fun."

Kay smiled. It could be considered somewhat strange for an Ardwick lass to be discussing the merits of different types of expensive porcelain. Yet the conversation seemed so natural. In fact, since she had arrived in Faversham, Kay hadn't shown any hesitation in her approach to either Bernard or his mother; her words were spontaneous and from the heart. She felt no need to 'mind her p's and q's', as her mam had advised and knew that her dad would be proud if he could see how confidently she was handling herself.

"You see Kay," he'd said to her that very morning, "trips like this, are a reward for all the hard work you did at Central. Owens has opened doors for you. It's given you the chance to mix with the types of folks who me and your mam would have no chance of meeting. Take people as you find them; give everyone a chance. There's some decent types out there and for those that aren't, always remember that you're just as good as anyone else. Larry's a fine lad. He mucks in and he's got no airs and graces, so I'm sure his parents are all right. They wouldn't have invited you there otherwise."

Further consideration of the plates would have to wait however, as 'the boys' noisily entered the kitchen. Calling them through to the Breakfast Room, Violet quickly had them sat down and then she and Kay distributed the drinks. Taking his plate, Robert's eyes opened wide at the vast selection of food in front of him. Without thinking, he turned to Violet.

"Is it someone's birthday?" he asked. "I'm sorry, we didn't know. Larry never told us."

Immediately Larry and his brother burst out laughing.

"Boys! Your manners!"

Violet looked reproachfully at her sons. The laughter subsided as quickly as it had begun.

"No Robert," said Violet, softly. "I just wanted you to have something nice after your journey and Larry's not been home for a while, so he's getting spoiled."

"Oh, I see."

"Well, get stuck in then," said Bernard, eager to put Robert at ease, "take whatever you want. We won't be having dinner until later on."

Robert needed no second invitation, quickly filling his plate with a selection of items and joining in the excited chatter around the table, as the three students answered an array of questions about their studies and their lives together in Manchester. Listening to their laughter and enthusiasm, Violet felt happy and relaxed. Whilst at school, Larry had caused his parents much anxiety. They had worried about how he would get on alone at Owens. Today had confirmed what he had told her in his letters; he had two good friends who would care and look out for him. It was everything that a mother could ask for.

Chapter 45

She had slept well; right through in fact and it took some time for Kay's mind to register the insistent ringing of her little, travel alarm clock, placed on the cupboard beside her bed. The brightness of the early morning sun was already beginning to penetrate through the thick beige curtains that covered the two large windows in her roof top bedroom. Beginning to stir, Kay slowly drew herself up, stretched her arms above her head and breathed in deeply. The air was fresh and the twittering of the birds drifted in through the partly open windows. Throwing back the covers, Kay leapt nimbly out of bed and was soon washed and changed. Dressed very much for the countryside, she was wearing a pretty white blouse, a thin, light blue cardigan, beige slacks and moccasins. For now, Kay had placed her hair in a ponytail. It was a style that emphasised her youth, but the fact that it revealed more of her pleasing face and soft, delicate neck, suggested the classical beauty that she was destined to become.

Making the bed, Kay opened the curtains. How different to the view from Heywood House. There she could see the rows of terraced houses, the high tower of St Benedict's reaching up to the sky and people moving busily up and down the pavements. Here, there was just trees and vegetation and the sounds of birds and animals. It was strange, but Kay was thrilled to be here, eager to explore everything this strange, rustic world had to offer.

Descending the stairs, Kay soon found her way to the kitchen, where she was greeted warmly by Violet, busy preparing the breakfast.

"Did you sleep well?"

"Yes, as soon as my head hit the pillow."

"Well, you must have been very tired. You had a long journey yesterday."

"Yes, I suppose so, but I think the fresh, country air had something to do with it."

"You may be right. I remember that I used to think the same when we first moved down from London. I've been rather spoiled by it all since then. No London smog to suffer anymore."

"As we still do in Manchester."

"Yes. The Clean Air Act hasn't done its job yet, has it?"

"I'm afraid not," replied Kay. "What can I do to help?"

"Well, if you can take through the plates, dishes and cutlery to the table and then get on to the toast, I can finish off the bacon, eggs and so forth."

The two women got on busily with the task, chatting as they went along. Kay could see that Violet was keen to make their stay as enjoyable as possible and so was eager to play her part too. It wasn't long before they had almost finished, when they were joined by Bernard. Smartly turned out in his neatly ironed shirt and trousers, his smile beamed across the room as he greeted the two women. Giving his mother a peck on the cheek he turned towards Kay.

"Good morning, Kay. Did you sleep well?"

"Yes. I was just telling your mam. I'm sure the fresh air put me into a deeper sleep than usual."

Bernard smiled. She had no idea how the little quirks of her accent made her more endearing to him. It gave her an authenticity that most officer's wives or girlfriends lacked. He knew that Kay would always be true to herself, whatever her surroundings. She was witty, clever and exceptionally pretty. He had noticed too, that there were no romantic attachments in her relationships with Robert and Larry. Bernard wondered what impression she had of him. Regardless, he knew that this weekend, he would enjoy his time with her.

"Can you go and hurry the boys along Bernard and tell them that their breakfast is ready and getting cold?"

"Yes. To be fair, I suppose they're taking it easy because they feel like they're on holiday."

"That may be so, but it hasn't stopped Kay from being up and helping me with the breakfast, has it?"

"No that's very true," replied Bernard, laughing. "I think that the chaps in our company would get quite a shock if you were to take over."

Kay laughed, soon joined by Violet, who then shook her head and sighed as Bernard went off to fetch them.

With Larry and Robert in attendance and having completed breakfast, Kay began to clear the table ready for the washing up. Directing her friends to help her, they had soon moved everything into the kitchen.

"That's fine," said Violet. "Alice and I can take care of everything now. She'll be here shortly. Larry, take Kay and Robert outside and show them around. Bernard's going to pick your father up from the station. Remember that Roger, Barbara and the children will be here about two o clock, so we'll be eating shortly after that."

Outside, the sun was shining brightly and as it moved into mid-morning, the temperature began to rise correspondingly. The grounds were extensive and beautiful, tall privet hedges provided the boundary along two sides, whilst the lawns extended seamlessly into a hop field on one side and an apple orchard on the other. In front of the latter, was an enclosed grass tennis court, marked out and with its net in situ and ready for action.

"Who's Alice?" asked Robert.

"She's a lady from one of the local villages," replied Larry. "She's been with us since my parents moved here before the War. She helps Mother around the house. When my brothers and I were younger, she would baby sit. Sometimes we'd stay at her house, with her family. It wouldn't be the same without her being here. She still insists on coming on her bicycle, even though father always offers to arrange a taxi for her."

"I suppose it's a way of establishing her independence," suggested Robert.

"Yes. I suspect you're right," replied Larry. "But mother never asks her to do anything that she wouldn't do herself."

"I'm sure of that," said Kay. "I've seen how hard your mam works. I've got a lot of respect for her. She has the means to act like a lady of leisure; too exalted to get her hands dirty. But I can tell that she would never do that."

Larry smiled. He was pleased that his friends could see that despite their affluence, his family had retained their sense of human decency.

"Neither of you play tennis I suppose?" asked Larry.

"No, it's a toff's game," said Robert dismissively. "But I still reckon I could beat you at it."

"Oh, could you now?"

"Of course. Northern superiority. Only problem is, I haven't got any kit."

"You don't need it. We can play as we are. I thought all you Ardwick lads learned to play cricket and football in the streets. Wait there whilst I go and fetch some balls and rackets."

Larry walked to the far corner of the court and opened a small hut, re-emerging with the necessary equipment. Kay was grinning. She knew that Robert would now regret the fact that he had talked himself into a game. He couldn't lose face by backing out now. She was sure that not having played before, 'Larry the toff,' was going to inflict a sorry defeat on him.

"Well, you'd better explain the court to me," insisted Robert. "I don't want you trying to cheat."

Having painstakingly explained the rules and checked the height of the net, Larry finally prepared to take the opening serve. Without being able to move, Robert watched the ball whistle past him.

"Hang on. I wasn't ready."

"I'm sure you were," replied Larry.

"No. Serve again," insisted Robert.

Larry served once more. The result was exactly the same as before.

"Fifteen, Love."

"What?"

"Fifteen, Love."

"What kind of a score is that?" sneered Robert.

"It's how you score a game in Tennis," replied Larry.

"You mean it's how you 'toffs' in your fancy public schools and tennis clubs do."

"No. It's the scoring system used all over the World. You must have heard it at Wimbledon."

"Never been there."

"But there are always clips of games in the news reels at the cinema. You must have seen them."

"No, I'm sure I haven't."

Kay understood Robert's plan. He knew his only chance of avoiding a dismal defeat lay in either frustrating his opponent and putting him off, or dragging the game out so long that they wouldn't be able to reach a conclusion. Unfortunately, Larry was having none of it.

"Right Robert, change sides. You need to receive my next serve from out of the other box."

Robert had no option but to oblige his opponent.

"Thirty, Love."

The ball had bounced hard and whooshed past Robert's head. Yet again, he'd been unable to move his racket in response.

"Perhaps you should stand back a bit, old chap," suggested Larry, mimicking an upper-class accent.

He was enjoying being on top; turning the tables on his friend. It was now his turn to irritate his opponent. Robert responded by stepping back to the base line. This time he was able to attempt a swing before the ball had passed him by, but it was a mere waft into thin air and the effort led to Robert almost losing his balance and staggering in to the fence at the side of the court.

"Ah! Bad luck old boy. I'm afraid I put a bit of swerve on that one. Never mind. Damn fine effort, what?"

Kay was trying desperately not to laugh. The sight of Robert's face, flushed with effort and anger was a sight to behold. She knew that Larry's 'toff' accent was driving Robert to distraction, but it was clear that he wasn't going to admit it. That would be tantamount to saying he'd been beaten. She was sure however, that if she hadn't been there, the game wouldn't have assumed such competitive significance. How stupid young men could be, she thought, when there were women around to impress.

"Well, it's game point now I'm afraid," continued Larry, preparing to serve.

Concentrating all his attention, Robert finally laid his racket on the ball. Yet there was no success, as it fired uncontrollably off the side of the court.

"Game to Foster. Foster leads by one game to love. First set."

"It's this racket. You've given me a dodgy one," pleaded Robert in mitigation for his dreadful performance.

"We can swop if you like?" offered Larry.

"No, you keep it. I wouldn't want you to have a ready-made excuse if I start winning."

It would have been advisable for Robert to cut his losses, but he was stubbornly determined to carry on. He seemed convinced that somehow, his game would fall into place and he'd be able to wipe the smile off his opponent's face. But it didn't happen. If anything, it got worse. Dropped rackets, stumbles, missed serves and an ever increasing crescendo of curses, as Robert succumbed rather weakly to a six-love drubbing in the first set. Fortunately, rescue was at hand, as Bernard had returned with his father who had come over to greet his guests.

"Good to see the court getting some use," remarked Bernard. "Robert, Kay, this is my father."

"Hello. I'm Norman. It's good to see you. Larry's told us all about you."

Kay smiled and looked carefully at their host. Norman must have been in his late fifties but was sprightly for his age. He still had a full head of hair, although greying, a strong forehead and jaw and a moustache that made his associates remark that he had more than a passing resemblance to Neville Chamberlain. He was an astute lawyer and businessman, his success reflected in their splendid surroundings. Yet there was no hint of ruthlessness about him and when Kay looked into his eyes, she could sense only kindness.

Offering his hand to Robert and then Kay, Norman was impressed by the firm handshake he received from the latter. She was certainly a confident young lady and Norman understood why she had made such an impression upon his son.

"Is this the first time you've been in the South?"

"Yes," replied Kay.

"It's actually the first time we've seen anything of London," added Robert.

"And what do you think?"

"Well, it's not Manchester," replied Robert.

"And is that good?"

"Oh no," replied Robert. "It's different."

Norman laughed.

"A very diplomatic answer young man. You're not looking to go into my line of work by any chance, are you?"

"I've pretty much got my heart set on journalism."

"Yes, just like Larry. You two work together on the student newspaper, don't you?"

"That's right. We're hopeful that it will help us get into the industry after we graduate."

"I'm sure it can't hurt," replied Norman. "The pair of you are doers not talkers. All businesses like to see commitment and practicality in the people they employ. And being in Manchester, you're really at the heart of the newspaper industry, aren't you?"

"We certainly are."

"And you Kay? What are you planning to do when you graduate?"

"I'm studying for a BA in Social Administration. I'm hoping that I'll get taken on as a children's officer for social services. There are plenty of local authorities around Manchester, so opportunities should be available. I've already carried out voluntary work with children for local churches and through the university."

"I'm sure it's an area that's going to expand," replied Norman. "Children still suffer so much hardship in this world. I've no doubt that you and Robert see it every day. We're well clear of post-war austerity now. I can't see how governments of any political persuasion, can continue to underinvest in the young."

"Well, I'm not convinced Father."

"You may be right Larry," replied Norman, "but I'm more optimistic than you."

There was a pause. The conversation had taken a slightly depressing turn, at odds with the lighter mood that had preceded it.

"I suppose that I'd better get back inside and make sure that I pass muster with Mother. I'll see you all later."

As Norman wandered off, Larry and Robert continued half-heartedly with their game, giving Bernard and Kay the opportunity to talk quietly on a bench outside the court. Kay felt a little nervous. It was unusual for her to feel such an emotion when close to any man, but Bernard was different. She wasn't naïve. She could tell that he found her attractive, but he was older than her usual admirers; far more experienced. A real man who made Larry and Robert seem like boys.

"Would you like to play tennis?" asked Bernard. "I think we need to come to Robert's aid. Larry's showing no inclination to ease up on him."

"Well, Robert's only got himself to blame," replied Kay, laughing. "I've no idea how to play."

"Don't worry. I can show you. It won't be serious. We'll just knock a few balls over the net."

It was agreed and Bernard led Kay on to the court. Waiting for the end of a rally, Bernard suggested that Larry and Robert should take a break, so that he and Kay could have a chance to play.

"Well, I suppose so," said Robert. "I think Larry's about had it, anyway."

"I don't think so!"

"Come on, you know you have. Anyway, I'd like a drink. I'm pretty thirsty now."

With an air of reluctance, Larry agreed and the two of them set off back to the house, leaving the rackets and balls behind.

"Which racket would you like?" asked Bernard.

"Either's fine."

"Well, take this one. It's lighter than the other."

Kay took hold of the racket and waited for further instructions.

"It can be a tricky game until you get the hang of it, but if you can master the forehand, you should be all right."

"Oh," replied Kay, confused.

"Yes. If you watch me, I'll show you how to do it."

Dropping a tennis ball to the side of him, Bernard's arm swept in one continuous movement past his body, knocking the ball over the net in front of them. Passing her a tennis ball, he asked her to try and follow his example. Yet it was all to no avail as twice, Kay dropped the ball beside her only to miss it with the sweep of the racket.

"Oh dear. I haven't a clue."

"If you don't mind me helping Kay, I can see where you're going wrong, but I'll need to guide your arm through the shot. If that's all right?"

"Yes, of course it is."

Kay had no intention of refusing. Bernard was behaving like a perfect gentleman and she could not conceive of him having any ulterior motives.

"If you stand sideways on to the ball, I'll come behind you and guide your racket through the swing."

Positioning himself, Bernard reached around her and lightly put his hand on hers. For a moment she felt a thrill of excitement racing through her body and involuntarily she took a deep breath. Bernard had felt the sensation too, but reacted quickly to avoid the potential for any mutual embarrassment.

"Relax your arm Kay and let me take you through the swing."

Doing as he asked, she could feel his hand guiding her towards the ball. She felt a satisfying thud and watched as it sailed over the net and into the court beyond.

"Did you feel that, Kay? Your arm swinging in one continuous movement at an equal distance from your body. It's all about getting sideways on, keeping your eye on the ball and then swinging through it. Here, try again."

Once more he helped guide her through the process. She was concentrating now, eager to please him. He was a good teacher and she was sure that he showed equal patience and encouragement to the men in his unit. Kay realised that he was making a big impression upon her. It was something she hadn't expected to happen.

Satisfied that she was mastering the basics, Bernard suggested that they try hitting the ball to one another across the net. Going round to the opposite side of the court, he lobbed a tennis ball slowly across to her, happily expressing his pleasure as she successfully returned the ball to him.

"You see Kay, you're rather better at this than you realise. I think we've got a budding ladies champion on our hands."

"I think you're getting carried away," replied Kay, laughing. "Any one would think that you were puddled."

"What?" asked Bernard, in amazement.

"Puddled."

Kay saw a blank stare of confusion looking back at her and burst into laughter. Feeling at ease, she walked up to the net and looked him in the eyes.

"You know. Puddled. Daft. Barmy."

Finally, he understood.

"Oh. Of course. Yes. I see."

"Do you really, Bernard?"

She stared at him with intent. She was teasing him and he knew it. They had only spent a short period of time together, but there was clearly an affinity between the two of them.

"Yes, I do."

"Well, that's good then," replied Kay, smiling. "Isn't it about time we were making our way back inside? We have to get ready for dinner."

"Dinner?" asked Bernard, before correcting himself. "Ah, lunch."

"Well, not in Manchester. I think I'm going to have to learn some of your Southern words, aren't I? 'When in Rome.'"

"No, you mustn't. It's a beautiful dialect."

Kay blushed, his compliment both welcome and unexpected. She turned away, hoping that he'd failed to notice, but he had. Yet Bernard gave no hint of the fact. Looking at his watch, he acted quickly to put her at ease.

"Yes Kay, the time is getting on, isn't it? I suppose we'd best be getting along."

Walking towards the house, the conversation continued. The sun was shining, the birds were singing and it was a perfect summer's day. The omens seemed good. There could be no doubt that Kay and Bernard had made a connection. Yet whether there would be time for it to develop into anything more, remained to be seen.

Chapter 46

Back in her room, Kay focused on getting ready for the afternoon festivities. Instead of her blouse and slacks, she now put on a pretty, short-sleeved, primrose swing dress, with a white collar and buttons. The dress revealed part of the soft, smooth skin on her neck, against which lay a delicate gold necklace. Brushing her hair up and back, she put on a yellow hair band, allowing the natural waves and curls to frame the sides of her face. Putting on her white heels, she made her way downstairs.

Entering the kitchen, Kay could see an elderly lady taking a tray out of the oven. Not wishing to startle her, Kay waited until she had placed it on the top before speaking.

"Hello, I'm Kay, a friend of Larry's. Do you need any help?"

The old lady gave a reassuring smile. She looked very homely with her grey hair wrapped neatly into a bun and her diminutive frame enveloped by a large, cooking apron.

"I've all but finished now dear and I wouldn't want you to risk messing up that lovely dress."

"Oh, I'm sure it'll be all right."

"Well, it's best not to take the chance now, is it?" asked the old lady, speaking with the wisdom of experience.

"I suppose not," replied Kay.

"Ah, you're ready Kay, that's good."

Turning round, Kay saw that Violet had entered the kitchen.

"I see you and Alice have already met."

"Yes, she's a very polite young lady. Knows her manners and wants to help," said Alice, approvingly. "She can come and visit us any time."

Violet laughed. Kay had just been given the final seal of approval.

"I'll be back in a few minutes Alice. I'll just take Kay out to meet Roger, Barbara and the boys."

As they made their way outside, Violet expressed her appreciation of Kay's appearance.

"You look lovely Kay. That dress is beautiful. You're so lucky. You can wear anything and it flatters you. I always feel the need to buy expensive outfits if we go anywhere. Otherwise, I'm not confident about how I look. It's not a problem that you'll ever have."

Kay was quiet. She wasn't used to being so warmly praised.

"Oh, I'm sorry," said Violet. "I wasn't meaning to embarrass you."

"No. That's all right," replied Kay.

"Come on then, I'll introduce you to the rest of the family."

Roger was the oldest of the three brothers. A partner in his father's firm of solicitors, he'd inherited Norman's aptitude for the legal profession. Today he was here to relax. Puffing happily on his pipe, he was taking a keen interest in a friendly game of cricket involving Larry, Robert and his young sons, George and William. His wife Barbara, seemed somewhat reserved and Kay found it hard to sustain a conversation with her. She was therefore thankful when Violet returned to tell them all to come to the table, where she would be sitting with Robert and Larry.

For the visitors, the spread of food was astonishing. Different meats and vegetables and side dishes totally alien to the average Mancunian palate. And then there was a selection of cakes and puddings on offer, all rounded off by a selection of strange cheeses and savoury biscuits. Wine too. It was more than a meal; it was nothing short of a banquet. Neither Kay nor Robert had experienced anything like it.

When they had finished eating and Violet poured out the coffee, attention turned inevitably towards the three undergraduates. Although Larry's brothers had attended King's, neither of them had chosen to go to university. Interested in student life, they hoped that Kay and Robert would be more forthcoming about it than their brother had been in the past. Roger came straight to the point.

"Do you think that university has benefitted you, Robert? Given you advantages that you wouldn't have had if you'd gone straight into work?"

"For Kay and I, definitely. It's opened our eyes to new ideas and we've mixed with people, like Larry, who we would never have met if we'd left school at eighteen. It's given us a different experience and a new perspective on the world around us. It might open up opportunities for us that would normally be reserved for those with public school, Oxbridge backgrounds."

"Spoken like a true Northerner," said Roger, approvingly. "No beating about the bush. Refreshing too. If you lived in the South Robert, you'd have to get used to rarely getting a straight answer."

"I'm sure it's the same for Larry," added Kay, "but in a different way. He's had a chance to see the realities of life in Manchester. I think you'd agree Larry, that in itself has been an education for you."

Larry nodded, yet seemed reluctant to speak. It appeared that he wanted to keep his life in Manchester separate from the one he shared with his family.

"Looking from the outside, Roger and I certainly agree with you," remarked Bernard. "We think that Larry made a brave choice going to Manchester. It would have been very easy for him to take the comfortable route of going to Cambridge. There, he would have been closeted in the fairy tale world of academia. He could have lost all his ambition to strike out in the world and instead have become one of those very eminent, but ultimately impractical academics, who are of little use to anyone."

"And especially after I got out of national service," noted Larry, rather petulantly.

"And so did I," said Robert. "And, no disrespect intended Bernard, but I have to say that I'm pleased I did."

Robert's remark brought a loud and hearty burst of laughter from Norman, who was soon joined by his two eldest sons.

"You certainly don't mind telling it how it is," spluttered Norman, finding it difficult to retain his composure.

"Norman, I think you've had a little too much wine."

It was Violet. Soft and insistent, her measured tones sought to bring back a semblance of order to the proceedings.

"Yes, dear," replied Norman, before once more bursting into laughter.

Kay noticed Barbara move uneasily on her seat. Unlike Kay she seemed uncomfortable in male company and didn't find the more boisterous elements of their conversation, agreeable. Mindful of her discomfort, Violet invited her into the house to look at some new clothes she'd bought for her grandsons. With their departure, the atmosphere became more relaxed and the conversation soon continued.

"I sympathise with you completely Robert. I hated my national service," continued Roger. "We were bullied through basic training, mainly because we'd all just missed out on the fighting at the end of the War. I couldn't wait to get out after that. If I'd had a choice, I would never have done it and I'm pleased that my boys won't be forced to."

"I agree," added Bernard. "We can't afford a large conscript army anymore and we can recruit men more easily now. Offer them proper trades and a chance to use their training in civvy street after they've served. It's so much better to have recruits who want to be with us. Men who are motivated. You and Larry would find it very difficult to accept the discipline, especially when you're both so independently minded. National Service would have brought you no benefits at all."

Later that night, as she settled down to sleep, Kay was tired but content. Going over the events of the day, she had to admit that spending time with Larry's family, she had been impressed. Most surprising was how open-minded they had been, given the reservations Larry had expressed before coming home to see them. His parents and brothers could not have been more welcoming of their guests and accepting of Robert's rather forthright comments.

More importantly, as the day had worn on, Bernard and Kay had spent an increasing amount of time together. They were quick to value one another's company. Their conversations were lively and it was apparent that they had a growing attraction to one another; one that was becoming difficult to ignore. When Kay had mentioned the possibility of visiting the coast, Bernard had acted decisively. He had suggested that if she were agreeable, they could drive to Whitstable together in the morning. Even though his invitation was for her alone, Kay had no hesitation in accepting. It meant that there was now an opportunity for their budding relationship to blossom into something lasting and substantial.

Chapter 47

Awake early, Kay was quickly washed and dressed and made her way downstairs. Alice, who'd stayed overnight, greeted her cheerily as she walked into the kitchen.

"You're up with the lark dear. I didn't expect anyone down until later."

"I thought you might like a hand with the breakfast."

"That's very kind, but I'm sure I can manage and Larry's mum will be along later."

"I'd still like to help; do my share."

"You're a breath of fresh air," replied Alice, smiling. "Don't take it the wrong way, but I knew as soon as we met, that you're one of us. Lots of young ladies have stayed here, but not one of them has mucked in like you have. Most can't even make their bed."

"Well, I've been brought up to do my fair share around the house. I learned early how to cook, clean and help with the washing. It's natural for me to do it and even if I could afford to have someone do it for me, I don't think that I ever would."

"Good for you. It's why I've stayed with Violet so long. I'm well paid, but she's never acted like a boss. She's always pitched in with everything; she's one in a million."

"Yes. She's made us very welcome, as have all the family."

"Have you anything nice planned for today?"

"Bernard's taking me in the car to the coast. I'm looking forward to it."

"He's a good lad, Bernard. I worried about him joining the Army at first, but he seems to have done well on it."

"Yes, he isn't really what I imagined an army officer would be like."

"And what would that be?" asked Alice, smiling mischievously.

Kay hesitated and then blushed. It seemed that there was a hint of romance in the air.

"Well, sensitive and considerate, I suppose," she finally ventured.

"Yes. I think you're right. Anyway, it won't be too much longer before everyone begins to stir, so we'll make a start on setting the table, shall we?"

Kay nodded, grateful that Alice had no intention of prying any further.

It was Bernard who was next into the kitchen. Alice noticed a broad smile on his face as he saw Kay laying the table in the breakfast room.

"I don't think that smile is for me, is it?" asked Alice.

"It's always nice to see you," replied Bernard. "Good morning, Alice."

"It's not because you've seen Kay then?"

Bernard blushed and shook his head. She was teasing him. Nevertheless, he was aware that she had known him long enough to have recognised that he had become quite attached to their visitor. Choosing to ignore her question, he quickly offered his assistance.

"Is there anything I can be doing?"

"Well, you can go and help Kay."

"Right you are," replied Bernard, with enthusiasm.

Bounding through to the breakfast room, Bernard watched as Kay carefully laid out the cutlery. Saying hello, she warmly returned his greeting. He could see that she was ready and dressed to go out in the car. It was a reassuring sight. All fears that she may change her mind, were gone.

"A very sensible choice of clothing, if you don't mind me saying," continued Bernard. "I forgot to mention that the MG can get a little chilly, especially if we get to the coast and the sun disappears. But bring a coat as well, just in case."

Kay was wearing her blouse, cardigan and slacks. They were perfect, she thought, for jumping in and out of Bernard's MG. She hadn't seen the car yet, but was sure that it was designed with the emphasis on speed rather than comfort.

"I thought we could get off around ten," suggested Bernard. "There's some lovely villages that we can drive through and we can pick up a spot of lunch after we get to Whitstable."

"Oh. That's the seaside, is it?"

"Yes. Whitstable's famous for oyster fishing, although the industry is considerably smaller now. It's a rather sedate little seaside town; nothing like the hustle and bustle of Margate. I'm sure you're going to enjoy it though."

"I'm sure she will, or you'll have me to answer to."

It was Alice. She had just entered the room and in her hands were two large plates, both of which contained a full English breakfast. Carefully, she placed them down on opposite sides of the table.

"Come on you two. Sit down and have your breakfast. It sounds like you're in for a long day and you'll need something substantial inside you."

Kay and Bernard sat at the table, looking fondly across at one another.

"And you don't need to be bothering about your lunch young man," continued Alice. "We've got plenty of food right here. Whilst you're having your breakfast, I can put together a nice hamper and you can have yourselves a picnic."

"Oh, you mustn't Alice," said Bernard. "We wouldn't dream of putting you out."

"Putting me out? Are you trying to say that it's too much bother for me? Do you think I'm past it?"

"No. No. Of course not. I just meant ..."

"You meant nothing," interrupted Alice, rather dismissively.

"Thanks Alice. We both think it's a lovely idea," said Kay, smiling.

"Well, there's an end to it," replied Alice, a self-satisfied look on her face. "Things soon get sorted out don't they dear, when we don't have men interfering in things that don't concern them?"

"Yes. That's right," replied Kay, laughing.

She looked across at Bernard. His head bowed, he appeared very contrite.

"He forgets that I've known him since he was a nipper. Out there, he may well get to order his soldiers around, but here, he still has to do as he's told."

"I'm sorry Alice," said Bernard, quietly. "I didn't mean to offend you."

"I should think so too."

Tutting and shaking her head, Alice retreated back into the kitchen.

"I'm afraid I made rather a mess of that, didn't I?"

Kay smiled. Bernard's reaction was touching. He'd shown a sensitivity towards Alice's feelings, that was appealing. She was continuing to discover facets to his character that belied the military stereotypes.

"No, I don't think so," replied Kay. "Alice is just letting you know who's boss. She could see that you were upset when you thought you'd offended her. We women have a habit of getting our own way when we put our foot down, especially with someone as generous minded as you."

They were kind words and she could see they had pleased him. Yet for a moment, Kay felt slightly embarrassed. She didn't want Bernard to think that she was praising him. Quickly, she changed the subject.

"So, I'm going to be impressed by your sports car, am I?"

"Well, I hope so. It's a lovely red, 1955 MGA."

"Oh."

"Yes, but I suppose that doesn't really mean very much to you, does it?"

"You could say that," replied Kay, laughing. "Hardly anyone on Bennett Street owns a car, so I'm not very knowledgeable about them."

"Well hopefully, you'll enjoy the ride. Find it an interesting experience. A car's more than useful Kay. You'd be stood there a very long time if you were waiting for a bus around here. It's not like in Manchester."

"No, that's for certain."

Finishing their breakfast, the pair took their plates and cutlery back into the kitchen. A wicker hamper was waiting for them on the side.

"Everything's ready for you," said Alice. "The weather's going to be beautiful, so you can make a full day of it and have a good time. There's no reason that you shouldn't get off now."

As yet, Kay and Bernard were the only two members of the household to put in an appearance.

"Shouldn't we wait for the others to come down?" asked Kay.

"No, you two get off," insisted Alice. "I'll let everyone know where you've gone."

Going to fetch her coat, Kay felt a little concerned. She would be out with Bernard for longer than she had anticipated. For a moment, she wondered how her friends would react, then reproached herself for being so silly. She had the opportunity to spend the day with Bernard. They would be alone. They could talk openly; find out so much more about one another. When Kay had left Manchester, the possibility of finding love was inconceivable. Yet, things were changing and Kay had no desire to return home with any regrets. By the end of the day, she would know whether her growing affection for Bernard was simply an infatuation, or something far more meaningful.

Chapter 48

When Kay left the house, the MGA was stood ready on the drive.

"Well, here she is!" exclaimed Bernard, proudly.

Kay had to admit that the car was pleasing on the eye. Low to the ground, with its sleek lines, its deep, red bodywork was embellished by the gleaming chrome of its grille, bumpers, mirrors and its spectacular wire wheels. She was pleased to see that Bernard had raised the hood over the windscreen. It would allow her the chance to get settled in the car, before being placed at the mercy of the elements.

Opening the passenger door, Bernard smiled.

"Madam, your carriage awaits."

Gracefully, Kay lowered herself into the seat, raising her legs, then carefully swinging them round and into the footwell. She was pleased that she was small. It meant that she could stretch out in relative comfort.

Carefully closing the door, Bernard walked around the bonnet and was soon settled in the seat beside her. She was surprised at how relaxed he appeared.

"Don't you find it cramped," she asked, "fitting those long legs in?"

"Not at all. I think it's rather snug. Don't you?"

"Well, that's one word for it I suppose," replied Kay, laughing.

She could certainly see his point. There was no room to move their seats back and space was further restricted by the gear stick placed between them. Sitting close together, there was an unavoidable sense of intimacy and Kay understood that this was part of the function of the car's design. In front of her the dashboard contained a number of glass and chrome displays, detailing speed, the revolutions of the engine, temperature and fuel. It looked very technical, just what she imagined it must be like in an aircraft's cockpit.

Bernard turned the key in the ignition and the engine roared into life. Releasing the hand brake, followed by the clutch, the car started to move slowly down the drive. Glancing at Kay, he noticed that her left hand was gripping the edge of the seat. It was the first time she'd ridden in a sports car and he could appreciate that she was feeling a little apprehensive.

"It's noisier than father's car, isn't it?"

"Yes. much," replied Kay, raising her voice to ensure that he could hear her.

"Well, we're closer to the ground and the top is obviously softer than the body of the Rover. It means that we can hear more of the outside noise. Don't worry though. You'll soon get used to it."

"I hope so."

As they made their way along the narrow lanes and on to the main road to Faversham, Kay began to feel more comfortable. Bernard was driving sensibly, just as he had done in the Rover and her nervousness had disappeared.

"I thought that you might want to put the car through its paces," said Kay. "I have to say that you're being very restrained."

"Of course," replied Bernard. "It's important that you enjoy yourself. It's also true that the car can do close to a hundred and there are those who buy them hoping to impress the ladies."

"But not you then?" asked Kay, smiling.

"No, not me," replied Bernard, laughing. "Anyway, I think I'm a bit old for that now. I enjoy the experience of the drive, especially in the summer. The shafts of sunlight streaming from the sky; the hood down and the warm wind rushing through your hair. There's nothing like it. It lets you know just how good it is to be alive."

Bernard was enthused and Kay found his words inspiring. If the MGA had been designed for affluent young men to impress their girlfriends with speed and power, Bernard was showing no such signs of immaturity.

By now, they had reached the Thanet Way and were driving on towards Whitstable. The traffic was starting to build up; after all it was a warm Sunday in July and they weren't the only ones heading for the coast.

"Most of these cars will be going to Margate," observed Bernard. "Whitstable doesn't have much in the way of glamour and popular entertainment, but it's beautiful and relaxing. I thought that given all the hustle, bustle and excitement you have in Manchester, it would provide you with something different."

Leaving the Thanet Way, Bernard drove down the long road into Whitstable. Just before they reached the High Street and the road started to narrow, he turned off and parked the car. Heading for the West Beach, Kay was fascinated by how tightly packed the narrow streets and alleys became. Many of the houses were faced with wooden boards and brightly painted. It seemed as if they had huddled themselves together so that they could shelter from the effects of the wind and waves, brought in by the winter storms. Walking along Island Wall and then up Marine Terrace, Kay could see a number of small sailing boats lined up beyond. Continuing on, they passed Wavecrest, where a long terrace of three storey houses, with wooden balconies and dormers, looked out impressively towards the sea. With the essence of salt in the air, the sun reflecting off the quietly lapping waves and the seagulls circling in a cloudless sky, it was calm and satisfying. Yet, as they stood on the beach, Kay couldn't hide her disappointment.

"Is this the only beach?"

"No," replied Bernard. "There are beaches extending through Seasalter to the west and eastwards to Tankerton and beyond."

"And are they proper beaches?"

Bernard looked confused.

"But this is a proper beach."

"No," replied Kay. "It's all pebbles. Where's the sand?"

"You don't need to have sand for a beach."

"Of course, you do. How can you make sandcastles, or walk into the sea in your bare feet? It's not like Blackpool, is it?"

Bernard looked at her. She had a face like a disappointed child's; her eyes half-closed, her bottom lip pushed out as if she were sulking. She looked so cute, but it didn't stop him from bursting out laughing.

"What's so funny?" she asked.

"Well, I suppose I'll have to round up a herd of donkeys and see if we can't build a mini tower, to make you feel more at home."

"Don't get cocky Bernard. You know I'm right."

Her comment brought further merriment. Bernard couldn't stop laughing and soon it became infectious as Kay was unable to resist joining in. Instinctively, he placed his arm around her shoulders and gave her a gentle hug. Realising that his demonstration of affection was somewhat premature and probably inappropriate, he quickly drew back. Yet for Kay, his sudden reticence was disappointing and smiling, she took his hand.

"Don't worry Bernard, it's fine. I don't mind."

"You're sure?"

"Of course."

Kay felt him take her hand and his fingers tighten around hers. It was clear that neither of them could deny the bond that existed between them. They had been completely natural with one another. There had been no hesitancy or formality; only openness and honesty. And now their relationship had suddenly become serious and here they were, hand-in-hand, so content in each other's company.

Breathing in the fresh, sea air, strolling along the beach and around the town and harbour, the young couple worked up quite an appetite. Bernard suggested that they drive up to Tankerton Heights, where they could enjoy their picnic hamper and Kay readily agreed. Once there, they found a table and benches where they could sit and eat. There was certainly no danger of them going hungry. Alice, as expected, had done them proud. Looking out across the sea, Kay could see land in the distance.

"Where's that?" she asked.

"It's the Isle of Sheppey."

"Oh. Being out there, it seems like another country."

"Yes, I suppose it does, but it's very much part of Kent."

"Larry told us that you've been posted abroad."

"Yes, I've been based in Germany and elsewhere too."

"Nowhere too dangerous, I hope."

"No, nothing out of the ordinary."

Kay liked his modesty. He had no intention of trying to impress her.

"I'm sure Larry told us that you were in Suez though, weren't you?"

"Yes, I was. That didn't end up being as dangerous as it could have been."

"I suppose we were on different sides in that campaign," suggested Kay.

"Oh. How's that then?" asked Bernard.

"Well, Robert and I went on a protest march against the invasion to Manchester Town Hall."

"That's good Kay. It showed that you cared and also had the courage to follow your convictions. When we ourselves got out there, it didn't take us long to realise that the situation wasn't as clear cut as we'd been led to believe. Many of us were pleased to pull out so quickly."

"Did any of you make your feelings known?"

"Well, we didn't have to. But to be honest, our job is to trust in the politicians and go where they tell us; accept that it's for the protection and good of the country. I'm persuaded that most of the time they get it right. Yet there could come a time when it might be awkward; then I'd have to resign. I think whatever careers we choose, there are always going to be difficult choices to make."

There was an inherent logic in his words and Kay appreciated his thoughtfulness. Before she had met Bernard, it would have astounded her to think that she could have been attracted to someone who had chosen the armed forces as his profession. Yet as the varied and surprising facets of his character had been revealed, he had made an indelible impression upon her. Kay was aware that he felt the same way too, a fact that was soon apparent.

"I hope you realise just how much I've enjoyed our time together," remarked Bernard. "I'd love to see you again Kay; explore how far our relationship could go. I know that it's important that you complete your degree and find a vocation. I may be a royal engineer now, but I've always been open about the future and I'm fully prepared to change direction, if it's the right thing to do."

"Of course, I want to see you again," said Kay, clearly perplexed. "Haven't we been holding hands along the beach and in the town, with everyone taking it for granted that we're quite the happy couple? You are puddled Bernard. I wouldn't do that if I didn't have feelings for you, would I?"

"I know," replied Bernard softly, "but I didn't want to appear presumptuous."

"You never will. You're too much of a gentleman to ever take a woman for granted. And I can say that with certainty, because there are so few of you around."

"I'm sure that can't be true," remarked Bernard, somewhat embarrassed by her praise.

"I can assure you it is. Anyway, we'll need to exchange addresses, so that we can write to one another," suggested Kay.

"And when I'm on leave, I'd love to be able to come to Manchester and spend some time with you. That is, of course, if you agree."

"I should think so! If not, how can we get to know one another?"

Kay shook her head and rolled her eyes.

"Honestly Bernard, for someone with responsibility for so many others, you aren't half gormless at times."

"Gormless?"

"Yes, gormless. You're going to have to learn some proper vocabulary. The 'Queen's English' just won't do when you come to Manchester."

"Yes, Miss. Whatever you say," replied Bernard, with a chuckle.

"Anyway," continued Kay, changing the subject. "We've been at the seaside all this time and I still haven't had an ice cream."

"Well," said Bernard, "we can take the hamper back to the car and then if we walk along the top, there's a little café and we can get one there."

Reaching the café, they went inside. Approaching the counter, Bernard was about to ask for a couple of cornets when he noticed that Kay was carefully studying the list of ice creams available. Satisfied, she turned to the proprietor.

"We'll have two 'ninety-nines', with some strawberry sauce on them as well please. That's all right for you, isn't it Bernard?"

Kay looked at him, followed by the proprietor.

"Yes, I'm sure it'll be fine."

"Good," replied Kay.

As the first 'ninety-nine' was ready, Kay indicated that it should be given to Bernard, who then watched as she took the second. About to hand the money over the counter, Kay put her hand on his arm.

"No, Bernard. You were good enough to bring me here and so this is my treat."

Hesitating, for just a moment, Bernard soon appreciated that her offer was unsurprising and he stepped back to allow Kay to complete the transaction. It seemed such a small thing for her to do, but it flew in the face of convention and underlined her independent streak. She would never be the little woman, cared for and supported by any man. It was her way of establishing the equality between them and something that Bernard cheerfully accepted.

Outside, the couple walked slowly back along the heights. Bernard knew that he was slowly falling under her spell. She was a young woman of many parts; complementary, yet contradictory too. Enjoying her ice cream, she seemed so carefree and happy, yet her intelligence, confidence and authority gave her a maturity at times, greater than his own. She could be both serious and amusing and had the resourcefulness to function confidently in the two very different worlds of Ardwick and Owens. And, of course, she was incredibly beautiful.

Stopping to point out some small boats on the horizon, Bernard turned towards her. Looking into her eyes, he took her in his arms and kissed her soft, inviting lips. It was the moment she'd longed for; a sign that his passion for her, matched her feelings for him. Responding eagerly to his advances, Kay snuggled tightly into his embrace. Casting aside her inhibitions, she kissed him with an ardour and intensity that shocked them both. Drawing apart, they were breathless; their bodies tingling with exhilaration. It was a defining moment. The lives of the lovers were now irrevocably entwined.

Chapter 49

Later that evening, Kay and Violet were together in the upstairs sitting room. It was an impressive space. A large room with white walls and French windows that opened out on to the balcony. The centrepiece however, was the large brick fire place, set between magnificent oak beams. In front of it was a large, square coffee table around which, on three sides, were identical white, two-seater, English rolled arm sofas. After her busy day out and the excited chatter of the dinner table, Kay found the atmosphere acceptably tranquil. Almost inevitably, Violet turned the conversation to Larry and his life in Manchester.

"We had Larry nearly ten years after Bernard. Norman and I didn't think that I'd ever be expecting again and when he came along, he was such a welcome surprise. Larry was a lovely little boy and I suppose, we could never be as firm with him as we had been with his brothers and with the age difference, they spoiled him too. He was always so happy, but after he passed for King's and got older, he became very serious and a little withdrawn. He's a sensitive soul Kay, as you've probably realised and he questions everything. It was a bit of a shock to us really. We had a hard time getting him to stay at King's when it was time to go into the sixth form. He was all for transferring to the local county grammar. Now, because I can see how well you and Robert have done, I think that perhaps we should have let him go. At the time however, we wanted to be sure that he'd have the best possible education and we knew he'd definitely get that if he stayed at King's."

"Yes, I understand," remarked Kay, sympathetically. "I'm sure my mam and dad would have done the same for me, if they were in your position. Parents should always want what's best for their children, but it isn't always obvious what that might be, is it?"

Violet nodded in agreement, impressed by Kay's maturity.

"I wanted this chat Kay, to let you know how grateful Norman and I are for everything that you and Robert have done for Larry."

"Larry's become a good friend to both of us. We've gained as much from knowing him, as hopefully he has from us."

"You're too modest Kay," remarked Violet, "Norman and I know that without you and Robert to guide him, it may have turned out very differently. We were so worried about him when he left here, but when his letters started to arrive, we could tell how happy he was. And the reason was obvious, because he told us that you'd taken him under your wing and that both you and Robert had introduced him to your families."

"It's really nothing special," replied Kay, feeling a little embarrassed. "It's just Mancunian hospitality. People look out for one another and Larry's our friend. I suppose, from what you mentioned when we first arrived, it isn't like that down here."

"No, I'm afraid that all too often, it's not. You'd find it very frustrating here Kay. Being generous and warm hearted, isn't as highly regarded as you might expect. All too often you would find your smiles falling on stony ground and at a loss to understand why."

"Well, I'm sure I'll be remaining around Manchester for the foreseeable future, so I don't expect to be given the opportunity to find out."

"Did you enjoy your time in Whitstable?" asked Violet, changing the subject.

"Yes. I love going to the seaside. Even when there's no sand!"

"You should have gone to Margate. There's a sandy beach there."

"Yes, but Bernard said that it would be packed."

"He could have taken you to Broadstairs. They have sandy beaches and it's nowhere near as popular as Margate, where all the amusements are."

"I'm happy enough. Whitstable was lovely; so very different to Blackpool. Until today, it's the only resort I've ever been to and then only on day trips organised by the local pub."

"Really?" asked Violet, surprised. "You've never had a family holiday?"

"No, most of my friends, including Robert, haven't."

"I think that those of us who are more fortunate, simply assume that everyone has. This weekend has certainly opened my eyes, Kay; made me realise just how lucky I am. I'm full of admiration for what you and Robert have achieved, without any of the advantages that our boys had."

"But that doesn't alter the fact that they've had to work hard too," replied Kay. "Robert and I know how clever Larry is. He's more than earned his place at Owens."

"Yes, I know, but I'm sure you understand the general point I'm making."

Kay was quiet. Violet knew that praise made her feel uncomfortable but, impressed as she was by her guest, it was hard to disguise her admiration.

"I suppose we'd best be getting back to Norman and the boys," continued Violet. "I'm sure you'll want to spend a little more time with Bernard. You seem to have made quite an impression on him."

Violet smiled, but had no intention of pushing Kay for a response. There was no need. She could see how close they had become and Kay was a young woman of whom Violet heartily approved.

"It's going to seem rather dull tomorrow, when you've all gone home," she continued. "It's been a very busy and enjoyable weekend."

"Yes," replied Kay, "one that Robert and I have thoroughly enjoyed."

"Well, hopefully we'll be able to see you again some time."

"Yes. That would be lovely."

Leaving the room, the two women made their way back downstairs to join Norman and the boys for the remainder of the evening.

Chapter 50

There was more than a tinge of sadness when, the following morning, it was time for Kay to say her farewells and leave for Faversham Station. Furthermore, she knew that once aboard the train, it would be some time before she would be able to see Bernard again. They had both risen early that morning, enabling them to spend more time together. They had kissed passionately. It was a reaffirmation, if it were needed, of their commitment to one another. As Bernard waved them off from the platform, Kay fought hard to control her emotions; determined that her friends wouldn't discern any hint of sentimentality. For the moment, her relationship with Bernard was intensely personal and she had no wish for her friends to pry into her affairs.

Reaching Victoria, they made their way to Euston and were soon sat on the train to Manchester. Leaving the station and embarking on their journey north, it wasn't long before Robert had fallen asleep.

"He can't stand the pace like us, can he?" asked Larry, laughing.

"No, clearly he can't."

"He's letting the side down," continued Larry. "Doesn't look the tough, hardy Northerner now, does he?"

Kay chuckled and shook her head.

"I don't know. You two. You've always got to be so competitive, haven't you?"

"Of course."

Settling down, Kay and Larry watched the scenery rushing past the window. The swaying of the train and the periodic rumbling of the wheels along the track, had a calming effect. Looking across at Larry, Kay expressed her appreciation of the time they had spent with his parents.

"I've really enjoyed this weekend, Larry. So different to being in Manchester. Robert and I were made to feel so welcome. I'm so glad that we came with you."

"I'm pleased that you did too. I told you that my parents would be more than happy to see you."

"Your mam's lovely and your dad too," continued Kay. "They might have more money and a completely different lifestyle than my parents, but essentially they aren't that different."

"How so?" asked Larry, looking slightly bemused.

"Well, they clearly want what's best for you, but not at the expense of seeing you unhappy. They didn't try to stop you coming to Manchester, when you could have gone to Cambridge. I suppose it might be said that they've indulged you, because you're the youngest. I don't agree. I've not seen any evidence of that. They just care about you, that's all."

"I don't think Roger and Bernard would agree with you," replied Larry. "Their lives were mapped out from the start. They were determined to do the sensible thing; 'responsibility, don't you know!' I'm sure they'd say our parents have spoiled me."

Kay found his comment surprising and rather disappointing. At times she detected a hint of bitterness when Larry talked about his brothers. Yet over the weekend Kay had seen no evidence to suggest that either of them was judgemental towards him. Furthermore, she was irritated by the fact that he had been disparaging towards Bernard.

"I don't understand why you're so critical of your brothers. They were the ones who chose the paths they wanted to follow, just as you have. Face it, Larry. Not everyone sees the world like you do."

"That may be so," replied Larry, rather grudgingly. "Nevertheless, I'm sure they believe that I lack direction; that I'm feckless even!"

"Now you're being childish," said Kay, sharply. "And in fact, completely gormless!"

Larry chuckled.

"I supposed I'm puddled too. Am I, *our kid?*"

Larry's attempt at a Mancunian accent was woefully inadequate and unappreciated by Kay.

"Grow up and don't get clever! I'm being serious Laurence!"

Kay was angry. Larry found it impossible to avoid her pretty, hard stare; to take his eyes off hers. He felt uncomfortable. He realised that he had badly misjudged the situation and that his comments had been inappropriate.

"I'm sorry Kay," he said quietly. "I didn't mean to upset you."

"You didn't upset me. I'm annoyed and I certainly don't like being condescended to!"

Kay knew that her last comment would unsettle him. She felt like taking hold of Larry and giving him a good shake to make him realise just how fortunate he was.

"You couldn't be more wrong about your brothers, but you're too stubborn to see it. You're so obsessed with rejecting everything about your life in Kent, that you fail to appreciate those closest to you. It's clear that both Roger and Bernard admire you for sticking to your guns. That you turned your back on Cambridge and ignored the pressure applied by your teachers to go there. And for wanting to come to Manchester and broaden your horizons."

There was an awkward silence as Larry considered her words. He was eager for reassurance that she had forgiven him for his ill-judged and flippant remarks.

"I suppose you and Bernard talked about me. That's what made you say he admired me."

As soon as he'd spoken, Larry realised that he'd compounded his problems. Kay was far from happy.

"I don't think that my personal conversations are any business of yours and you know me well enough to understand that I would never, ever allow anyone to criticise one of my friends behind their back."

"No. No," Larry hurriedly replied. "Of course, I don't think you would."

"Bernard was complimentary if you must know. I'm sure you don't want me to elaborate, do you?"

She stared at him fiercely, clearly not appeased. Larry began to feel frustrated, incapable of controlling what he was saying.

"Yes, I know," he replied. "Bernard's very nice. All the women say so."

Kay was shocked. Suddenly, their whole conversation made sense. Why had she been unable to see it? Larry was jealous of his brother, not for anything he had achieved, but for the fact that he had made such an obvious impression on her. She had been so naïve. For all the time that she had known Larry, she had failed to realise that he was in love with her. Determined that he would remain unaware of her discovery, Kay acted to defuse a potentially embarrassing situation.

"Come on Larry, let's forget it. We're both tired. It's been a long weekend and we're getting irritable. I don't want to fall out."

Immediately, Kay could see the relief on her friend's face. Her words were reassuring.

"Yes, Kay. I don't know what got into me. I'm really sorry."

Kay reached over and patted his arm.

"It's all right Larry. It's all forgotten."

Kay valued Larry as a dear and close friend. Notions of love could prove awkward and ultimately destructive of their relationship; even more so given her burgeoning romance with Bernard. Inevitably, Larry would become aware of the depth of that relationship and it would prove a tricky minefield for her to cross. Kay remained confident however, that she would be able to do so.

Chapter 51

Almost a year had passed. It was early July, 1961 and Bernard was in Manchester. It wasn't the first time he'd been to see Kay; in fact, he had been twice before. On his initial visit, just before Christmas, he'd met Kay's parents. When Ethel knew that her daughter intended to bring Bernard to Bennett Street, she had been particularly nervous about meeting him.

"Isn't it better that he doesn't come here, love?"

"Why?" asked Kay.

"Well, with what you've said about his family's home, he's not likely to think much of ours. Is he?"

"Do you think, I'm ashamed of where we live Mam?"

Her tone was a little harsher than she intended. Nevertheless, her words made Ernest proud.

"See love," he said to Ethel, "Our Kay'll never turn her back on family, or where she comes from. She might go to Owens and hobnob with the rich and favoured, but it won't ever change her."

"All I'm saying Ernest, is that we don't want to put the young man off. I'm only thinking of our Kay."

"Do you think our daughter would get mixed up with a posh 'un? I'm sure the lad's just like us. Except for the money of course," he added, laughing.

"He's right Mam. Bernard knew all about me, even before we met. He already knows what to expect when he gets here. And," she continued, turning to her dad, "he's not a lad either. He's a major in the Royal Engineers, with lots of men under his command."

"Is that right? I'm not going to have to salute him, am I?" he asked, laughing. "I don't want taking back to my old wartime days!"

"Get off with you. Don't be so silly," said Ethel, getting annoyed.

"He's only joking Mam. He's not serious."

"Trouble is love, you can't tell when he is."

Ethel looked sternly at her husband. Kay tried hard to stifle a chuckle, not wishing to invite any more criticism from her mam.

When Kay's fiancé had arrived, the visit had gone seamlessly. Bernard had pitched in, just as she had said he would. Ethel thus found herself apologising for their lack of space, which meant that he had to stay in a hotel. Bernard recognised that Ethel and Ernest were good people. In turn, they saw a considerate and upstanding young man, who was clearly in love with their daughter.

This time, on their first night together, the couple had arranged to meet with Robert and Larry in the College Arms. Although they harboured romantic notions about her, Kay's friends accepted that her relationship with Bernard stood on strong foundations and had accepted it accordingly. The reason for the get together was because the three students had been informed of their final results and were now looking forward to their upcoming graduation. Whilst Kay and Robert went to the bar to get some drinks, Bernard offered Larry his congratulations.

"You've done well Larry. A first I hear. But that's not surprising. You've always been the cleverest by far of the three of us."

"How did you know my result?"

"Kay told Mother and I in her letters. She's very proud of you, just like everyone in the family. Mother was pleased to hear. She wasn't expecting that you would be quick to tell her."

"Well, you know me. It all rather smacks of attention seeking and showing off," replied Larry. "You know that I don't set much store by that."

"Of course," said Bernard, "but I'm sure that you can appreciate just how pleased Mother and Father are."

"I've worked hard for it. I think I've earned it."

"You've certainly been vindicated. Coming to Manchester, was certainly the right decision."

"And for you."

Bernard looked surprised.

"Well," continued Larry, "if I hadn't, then you would have never met Kay, would you?"

"Of course."

The two of them smiled.

"Are you going to take some time now, to think about your options?" asked Bernard.

"No. Robert and I have really enjoyed the work we've put in to help produce the *News Bulletin*. We're hoping that our experience will help us to get taken on by the *Manchester Evening Chronicle*. We both have an interview with them in a couple of weeks."

Bernard was pleasantly surprised; pleased to see that his younger brother had found direction so quickly. He was sure that Larry's friendship with Kay and Robert, had helped him adopt their more pragmatic, working-class values.

Returning from the bar, Kay and Robert put down the drinks on the table. Taking his glass, Bernard raised it.

"Here's to the three of you. Congratulations."

Lifting their glasses, they clinked them against Bernard's.

"Well, we'd all better watch out, now that the three of you have been unleashed upon us!"

Bernard smiled. He could sense that they were relieved to put their student days behind them; eager to take up new and exciting challenges. With all three of them possessing such talent, drive and ambition, the World surely was their Oyster.

Chapter 52

The following day was one that the happy couple were determined to spend alone and Bernard arrived early in the MGA to pick up Kay and take her on a drive out to the Pennines and the Derbyshire countryside. It was a beautiful morning. The weather forecast was full of promise and so Bernard had arrived with the hood down.

"I thought that we could head out to Glossop and then over the Snake Pass towards Ladybower," explained Bernard, as they proceeded along Hyde Road, leaving the familiar sites of Ardwick, Belle Vue and Gorton behind them.

"What gave you that idea?" asked Kay.

"One of my chums in the regiment. He's from Chesterfield and told me about how beautiful the scenery is. He said that there isn't a better drive in England."

"It can be quite dangerous too."

"Oh?" replied Bernard, expressing concern. "We can go somewhere else if you prefer."

"Don't worry. It's fine. I trust you."

Bernard smiled, pleased with her response.

"I take it that you've been on the Snake Pass before then?"

"Actually, I haven't. It's what I've been told by friends who have and the accidents I've read about in the papers."

Reaching Glossop, the couple drove on. As they left the town, the road began to climb. They were now on the Snake Pass and in the Peak District National Park. Changing gear, Bernard slowed the car as they approached a tight right-hand bend, behind which was an attractive, but isolated stone cottage. A steep climb lay in front of them and as they ascended, Kay looked back towards Glossop and Manchester beyond. She was pleased that they weren't on the other side of the road. There, over the roadside barriers, she would see the sheer drops beyond. She had read about careless drivers who had plunged with their cars over the edge. She couldn't imagine that they would face anything other than certain death. Yet, with Bernard at the wheel, she began to relax. As their ascent continued, the scene appeared more desolate. Here was an absence of trees. Heathland and bogs where the dominant plant was heather, stretching as far as the eye could see. Reaching the summit, other cars were parked at the sides of the road, but with the boggy surface interspersed with pools of water and vegetation that bristled inhospitably, only those suitably attired in hiking gear could venture beyond the tarmac. Continuing, Bernard steered the MGA carefully around the descending twists and turns of the narrow road. Spotting a small parking area, adjacent to a stream that cascaded down between a series of large, exposed rocks, he pulled off the road.

Leaving the car, Kay and Bernard walked across to the side of the stream, filled with water tumbling down from the layers of Millstone grit above them. The water burbled happily along a course that had, over millions of years, been etched deep into the rock. Bernard, camera in hand, persuaded a passing hiker to take a photo of the pair of them against the magnificent background. It was one that both of them would treasure.

Back on the road, the terrain became more hospitable. There were trees now and green vegetation abounded. With the sun shining brightly in an almost cloudless sky, the bleakness of the summit seemed a distant memory. Spotting a sign announcing the presence of the famous 'Snake Inn' ahead of them, Bernard suggested that they pull in for refreshments. It was now past noon and Kay readily agreed.

Ordering tea and sandwiches, the couple took them outside to enjoy the sunshine and take the opportunity to discuss the future.

"I'm so pleased I was able to get leave; to actually see you at the time you've graduated. A letter just couldn't have expressed how happy I am for you."

"And I'm glad that you're here too," replied Kay. "I just wish that we could see more of one another."

"Yes, but we knew that there would be difficulties and we've both accepted that. We still have plenty of time to be together. Now Kay, you must take advantage of your degree and get started on that career in social services. Make use of your enthusiasm and develop your expertise."

Bernard's voice was earnest; his eyes full of love. Intuitively, Kay knew that only he could have captured her heart; so strong, yet so gentle and kind. Reaching out, he took Kay's hand. She felt a thrill of excitement; a deep desire. And it was the painful sacrifice that both of them had to make; longing to give themselves completely to one another, but unable to do so. Only marriage could see their lives fulfilled.

"It's just having you here, so close, that makes me wish that it could be like this all the time," said Kay, softly.

"It will be. I've less than four years to go now and my days as a royal engineer will be over."

Kay was surprised. Bernard's words should have pleased her, but instead they caused concern.

"You've not mentioned this before. Are you sure that you've thought it through?"

"Yes, of course and don't you remember that I talked about the possibility of leaving when we first met? I mentioned that I was keeping my options open."

"Well, yes. But I thought you were happy in the forces. I wouldn't want you leaving on my account."

Sensing Kay's concern, Bernard was quick to reassure her.

"When I joined up, I was told to regard the military as being only 'half a career.' Most officers are gone by their mid-forties and many in their thirties. We're expected to spend as much time, if not more, in a second career. The recent Grigg Report proposes to encourage officers to serve until they're fifty-five. Yet once you've reached the rank of major, the chances of promotion are slim. I made sure that I prepared myself for that eventuality. I've become well qualified; a chartered civil engineer. I'm registered with the Institution of Civil Engineers and that enables me to get a good job in 'civvy street'. There's a lot of opportunities out there. Companies are keen to take on ex-servicemen with my background and experience and there are a lot of them in the North-West."

"Yet if things are changing, shouldn't you reconsider?"

"No, because I don't want to. You and I, our relationship, are what matters. I love you Kay and our future together doesn't include me remaining longer in the forces. It's best for both of us."

"But I feel that you'll be making personal sacrifices, when I'm not."

"Finally, Kay Thompson, I've got the chance to say that you, are completely puddled."

Bernard smiled, pleased that he could bring one of her favourite words into the conversation.

"We'll be together and both of us will be doing the jobs that we want to. I wouldn't mislead you, Kay. It really is what I want."

Kay didn't doubt his sincerity. He was showing his commitment to her and she believed in him. Theirs was a relationship based on mutual respect and she was certain that it would stand the test of time.

"And now there's something I'd like to ask," continued Bernard.

Reaching towards his pocket he pulled out a small red box. Her heart fluttered as she took a deep intake of breath. Suspecting what was coming, Kay was surprised that there had been no indication from Bernard as to his intentions that morning. Opening the lid, Bernard removed a beautiful engagement ring.

"Would you please wear this as a symbol of our engagement to be married?"

Kay smiled. It was beautiful.

"Of course, I will."

"It should fit. I hope you don't mind, but I asked your mother what size I should buy. I didn't say it was an engagement ring; just a gift. And in any case, I didn't know if you might turn me down."

Seeing the look of uncertainty on his face, Kay began to laugh.

"Well, I don't think too many proposals get that type of reaction," remarked Bernard.

"But why should I turn you down?"

"Well, it's a woman's prerogative."

"But you know I love you. You're just being gormless."

"Yes, I suppose I am. Anyway," he continued, "if you're agreeable, I'd like us to be married before I've left the Army and we can buy a property together, to move straight into."

"It seems that you've got it all worked out."

"I've been thinking about it a lot. It'll be your decision where we choose to live. Don't worry, I'll be guided by you completely."

"We're going to need at least three bedrooms," replied Kay, "more if possible."

"Oh?"

"Well, there won't only be the two of us forever, will there?"

Bernard looked at her blankly. Kay shook her head.

"Honestly, you really are behind the door. You don't think we'll be having a family then?"

"I haven't been thinking that far ahead. I've just been taking matters one step at a time. The important thing was to have you agree to marry me."

"But raising a family is a natural outcome of marriage. Surely you recognise that?"

"Yes, of course. But it's your choice when that happens. You may want to wait until you've gained enough experience to establish your value at work. Then you can return in the future, when the children are older."

"Well," said Kay, smiling. "You seem content to let me make all the decisions. Is that because you're always having to make them for your men?"

Bernard chuckled, aware that she wasn't being serious. Still, he felt the need to explain.

"Let's just say that I want you to be entirely happy. You're wonderful, with so much to offer and I wouldn't be happy if you ever felt that you couldn't fulfil your ambitions because you were married to me."

"Don't worry, my most important wish is to have our children and when I do, the job can wait."

Bernard's words had touched her. Kay began to feel her eyes moisten, but was determined that there would be no tears.

"Come on then," she continued, "we'd best get weaving. We've still got lots to see. Let's take the cups back and get on towards Ladybower. I've always wanted to see it and we've got the rest of the day in front of us."

Leaving the Snake Inn behind them, the two lovers continued their journey. Today was proving to be a definitive point in their relationship. There had been a joint confirmation of their intentions. They had become engaged, formally committing themselves to one another. All that was now left, was the setting of the date for their marriage.

Chapter 53

As Robert and Larry's time at Owens was coming to an end, so too was their work on the *News Bulletin*. On the evening of Tuesday July 11th however, the two of them were waiting nervously in the journal's office, waiting for the phone call that would confirm that they were about to get their most important and spectacular story yet.

Just three months ago Russian cosmonaut, Yuri Gagarin, had orbited the Earth in Vostok 1 to become the first man in space and subsequently, an international hero. The Amalgamated Union of Foundry Workers, whose headquarters were in Manchester, had discovered that before training as a pilot, Yuri had worked as a foundryman. Consequently, the union's executive had invited him to Manchester to receive an honorary membership of the AUFW. With one of Robert's neighbours being a member of the union, he had found out that the invitation had been accepted and having told Larry, the latter had speculatively approached the Soviet Embassy, asking for an interview with the cosmonaut. To his surprise, the request was granted. To Robert however, the embassy's agreement seemed eminently logical.

"It's because we're a student paper. We represent youth and the Soviet authorities believe that our age group are far more sympathetic towards them. They believe we'll be positive towards the visit and remember, many of our students are potentially going to be key figures in the future running of the country."

"And there I was," said Larry, with a chuckle, "thinking that I'd won them over with a brilliant presentation of why we were deserving of their consideration."

"I'm not saying you didn't put forward a good case," replied Robert, "just that it suited them to use us. They know that young people are more open-minded and less cynical than the old. They've seen the support for CND and the Aldermaston marches and they assume that the idealism of socialism is more attractive to the young. And think about Yuri. He's still only twenty-seven and look at what he's achieved. The Soviets have allowed him here so that he can appeal to the country over the heads of the government. What a propaganda coup it could turn out to be, with all these problems rumbling on over Berlin and Cuba."

"Let's wait and see what Yuri has to say for himself. You might be surprised," suggested Larry, "perhaps he won't simply toe the party line."

Although the invitation had been accepted before the end of May, the timing of Yuri's visit wasn't confirmed until July 7th, when it was announced that he would attend the Soviet Trade Fair at Earls Court on July 11th and then remain in the country for a few days. Locally, the plans for the visit to Manchester were set in place for Wednesday, July 12th. The only problem was that the Soviet Embassy was yet to confirm the details and Larry and Robert were becoming more desperate with every passing minute. Finally, the Town Hall was in touch. The Soviet Embassy had telephoned the Lord Mayor and Yuri's visit was on.

Officially accredited members of the press contingent, Larry and Robert, the latter acting as photographer, were in place at Ringway Airport when the Vickers Viscount carrying Yuri Gagarin, landed at 10am on Wednesday morning. The sky was grey and the rain was tumbling down, but nothing could dampen the enthusiasm of the waiting crowds. Emerging from the aircraft Yuri, accompanied by AUFW President, Fred Hollingsworth, made his way towards the waiting dignitaries. Approaching the Rolls-Royce convertible that would be his transport for the day, Yuri insisted that the hood be taken down, so that he could stand up in the back and wave to those who had come to see him. The key features of the day were apparent almost immediately; the humility of the cosmonaut and the enthusiasm of the crowds who welcomed him so warmly to their city.

As Larry and Robert followed him on his drive into Manchester, they were astounded by the tens of thousands lining the streets waiting to catch sight of the cosmonaut. The rain hadn't abated but it had little effect on the spirits of the crowd. There were countless numbers of school children. Some with their teachers, whilst others had obviously taken a day off to see him with their parents. Standing in the car, waving and smiling, his green uniform covered inadequately by a loose-fitting cape, Yuri was soaking wet.

The first scheduled stop was at the AUFW offices at 164 Chorlton Road, Brookes Bar. Able to cram into the upstairs boardroom, Larry was able to see Yuri receive his honorary membership and a gold medal which bore the inscription: 'Together moulding a better World.' Proudly, Yuri attached it to the left lapel of his jacket. It provided symmetry to the 'Hero of the Soviet Union' award that he wore on the right. He declared that he would wear the medal with pride, as "a symbol of the ideal of a better world. A world of peace and friendship." Walking out on to the balcony, Yuri waved to the crowds who had gathered below, bringing the traffic to a standstill.

The entourage moved on to AEI'S Metropolitan Vickers Works in Trafford Park, the second stage of Yuri's visit. Here, Robert followed him on his tour of the factory, whilst Larry circulated among the crowds who had gathered in the car park, where a platform had been erected for Yuri to make a speech. The audience was varied. There were workers, young and old, from AEI and the surrounding factories, who had come during their dinner break. There were teenagers, many of them girls and mothers with their young children. Common to all was an admiration for the young cosmonaut who, despite his youth and slightness of frame, had achieved distinction in the face of danger. When Yuri emerged to speak, he talked of arms reduction, international peace and co-operation and was met by loud cheers and thunderous applause. Larry could clearly see that Mancunians had taken the young Russian to their hearts.

Heading off for the official reception at the Town Hall, Yuri stopped at the Cenotaph in St Peter's Square to lay a wreath. It was a symbolic acknowledgement of the days, not too distant, when Britain and the Soviets had been allies in the struggle against the Nazis. Then it was just a short distance to Albert Square, where the Town Hall was flying the 'Hammer and Sickle', a brass band played 'The State Anthem of the Soviet Union' before the Lord Mayor, Sir Lionel Biggs, welcomed Yuri inside. Even here, the cosmonaut caused a stir, as office staff came out and lined the entrance hall, warmly applauding him as he came in, resplendent in his green uniform. The official five course banquet followed, to which the Soviet Ambassador and other dignitaries had been invited. Once again, in his address, Yuri spread the message of peace and co-operation. It was now the moment that Larry and Robert had been waiting for, as they were taken to a private room to interview the guest of honour.

Entering, they saw Yuri sat relaxing in a seat behind a small table at the side of the room. Beside him was his interpreter, Boris Belitzky. The latter had long been a presenter on the 'Voice of Russia', Moscow's English language radio station. He'd also acted as an interpreter and translator during the espionage trial of the U2 pilot, Gary Powers, in August 1960. Belitzky's command of English was exceptional, meaning that the interview flowed smoothly. Importantly, no restrictions had been placed on the questions that Larry would be able to ask and Yuri was happy for Robert to take pictures of him as their meeting unfolded.

Larry had quickly appreciated the opportunity that he had been given. Only a student journalist, he had been provided access to Yuri, when renowned reporters from the national press had not. He was therefore determined to try and uncover something of the real man and his beliefs; to see if he could penetrate through the myths and propaganda. Straightaway, he threw out a challenge to the sincerity of the cosmonaut's words in the speeches that he had made whilst in Manchester.

"You stressed the need for a spirit of peaceful co-operation; to use science and technology to bring countries together, rather than for military advancement. It's something that young people in this country readily agree with, but with all the current tensions between East and West, do you really think that it's possible?"

He watched Yuri's face as the question was relayed to him. Seeing no obvious signs of discomfiture, Larry wondered if his question had been correctly translated. Perhaps Belitzky had modified it to protect Yuri from saying anything that could be deemed controversial. The cosmonaut's answer, indicated that he hadn't.

"Yes, I do. It's natural for people to want to work together, we see it all the time. To put me, just one man, into space, took the efforts of tens of thousands of people. They are the real heroes, not me. And today when I toured your factory I saw hundreds of workers, each with their own specific responsibilities, united together to achieve the common goal of production."

"Yet the people you refer to," replied Larry, "are all from one, specific country. How can we get them to forget their national differences so that they can co-operate together."

"When I was in Vostok 1, I looked out and could see the Earth, all blue, green and white. If you saw it as I did, then you would know that all of us, wherever we come from, are just a part of one world. One community."

"But do you think that the rest of us will ever feel the same way?" asked Larry.

"I believe that many people already do. Today, I was given the warmest of welcomes. I looked out along the streets and was met by happy, smiling faces. I felt the warm handshakes of my fellow workers and sensed their genuine affection. Today, people didn't see me as being Russian, they saw me as a human being, the same as every one of them. It's this spirit that can make us all appreciate our common humanity and bring forth a world where conflict no longer exists. That is why I can see a future where British and American scientists will work together with their Russian counterparts, in order to push forward the conquest of space."

Having delivered Yuri's response, Belitzky indicated that there was time for just one more question. Satisfied with the ground he'd covered, Larry felt that his final question should be one that Robert would appreciate.

"Yuri, it's very clear that Manchester is very impressed with you. What is your impression of our city?"

"I don't think I'll ever be able to forget my visit here. The real highlight for me has been the warmth and generosity of the people of this city. Manchester has proved the correctness of the words inscribed on the medal I received today. 'Together we shall mould a better world'.

Rising to his feet, Belitzky signalled that the interview was over. Yet there was still time for an aide to use Robert's camera to take a photograph of the two of them with Yuri, before they finally left the room.

That evening found the two of them sat together with Kay in the 'College Arms'. She was eager to hear about their impressions of the famous cosmonaut.

"You're so lucky to have met him. I wish I could have been there."

"Yes," said Robert. "Yuri certainly seems to have been a hit with the women. Young or old, they all seemed to be keen to get near him."

"Well, he does look handsome in that uniform," replied Kay. "You're not getting a little jealous, are you Robert?"

"Me, jealous? Why would I begrudge him the chance to get all that adulation as he jets around the world, staying in the best hotels and being wined and dined?"

The three of them laughed.

"Seriously though," said Larry. "I thought he was pretty decent. He wasn't at all arrogant and all the time he acted with real humility. It must be overwhelming coming to a country where you don't understand the language and yet everyone is talking at you all at once. He had time for everybody; shook their hands, took their flowers and even allowed some of the girls to kiss him. If he wasn't genuine, he could never have kept it up for so long."

"Yes, but the Kremlin knew their man," replied Robert. "They studied his character and could see that he'd be able to handle all the attention and create a good impression for the Soviet Union overseas."

"You're being too cynical," insisted Larry. "I agree that he certainly holds good propaganda value for the Soviets, but you're missing the point. Yuri's got far more about him than that. He possesses qualities that politicians on both sides fail to see, but ordinary men and women can."

"What do you mean?" asked Kay, surprised that such a seemingly uncontroversial figure could possibly be a focus for disagreement.

"Well," replied Larry, "people love him because he's so like them. He has the same aspirations as they do. He's young and dynamic and eminently human. He's nothing like the ageing figures who haunt the Politburo. Unlike them, he's no fraud, but a true worker and a hero to boot and that's why the working classes identify so strongly with him."

"Maybe so," said Robert, "but how does that alter my point. The Soviets are still using him to portray their country and system in the best possible light. You could say that he's just a dupe and he's too politically naïve to understand that."

"No, you're wrong," insisted Larry. "The people who saw Yuri today, are looking at a man, not a country. They can recognise that and what he brings to them, is hope. They see in him the common humanity he spoke to us about; a decent man who has the same dreams as ordinary people all over the world. That is the essential truth that penetrates through the veil of lies and misinformation created by both sides, East and West, against one another."

"But he's still the tool of Soviet propaganda," insisted Robert. "His human face undermines the West's argument that communism is essentially evil. How can it be, they ask, if Yuri is a product of the Soviet system? It's brilliant, because it makes it harder to justify the concerns about Soviet intentions towards Berlin and Cuba. Once we trust Yuri, then Khrushchev won't be seen as a threat either."

"I think you're just going to have to agree to disagree," said Kay, concerned that the discussion may become a little too intense.

"There are some things we agree on," said Larry, "especially how well the visit has reflected on Manchester."

"Yes," added Robert. "For once the Corporation is to be applauded. As soon as they knew about the AUFW plan to invite Yuri to Manchester, they were right behind it."

"Not like Macmillan's government," said Larry. "They dragged their heels over giving him any official recognition, when they knew he was attending the Soviet Trade Fair."

"Yes," noted Robert, "The Corporation had the banquet planned straight away."

"And they flew the 'Hammer and Sickle' from the Town Hall and had the brass band play 'The State Anthem of the Soviet Union'," concluded Larry.

Kay smiled, the two of them were now like a double act, happily agreeing with one another.

"You know," said Larry, quietly. "You experience a day like today and you dare to think that it could be done. People could actually get together and boot the politicians into touch. We'd be together, moulding a better world, just like they put on Yuri's medal."

"I wish it could be true," said Robert, "but this afternoon when he climbed those steps and waved to us all before entering his aircraft, the chance, if there ever was one, had gone. The idealism and hope you claim he's brought, will soon be forgotten. You're naïve if you believe anything different, Larry."

Kay looked at them. Their exchange summed up just how their characters were beginning to diverge. Idealistic and hopeful that a more peaceful and equitable world was possible, Larry remained optimistic. On the contrary, Robert had slowly become more cynical. If either of them was likely to champion the working-class cause, it was now far more likely to be the privileged young man from Kent.

Chapter 54

Manchester played the crucial role in newspapers becoming national. Full coverage of the United Kingdom, by daily titles published in London, was impossible due to the problems of time and distance. The daily reach of newspapers was dependent upon the speed of the railways.to deliver them. Ideally, the London dailies needed to be printed as late as possible, so that they contained the most up to date news. Yet publication had to be far earlier if copies were to reach areas of the country beyond the Midlands. The solution to the problem was found in the production of Northern editions of the national dailies in Manchester. The latter was ideally located, being within a couple of hours of most Northern cities. North and Mid-Wales, as well as Belfast and Dublin, could be accessed too. In all, twenty-six newspapers were written, edited and published within a couple of square miles of the city's four central railway stations. Manchester thus became, after Fleet Street, the home of the national newspaper industry. It wasn't one of the nationals that provided Larry and Robert with an opportunity in the business however, but a local, evening paper.

It was just before nine in the morning, on Monday, July 24th 1961. Robert and Larry were at the offices of the *Manchester Evening Chronicle* on Withy Grove. Only the *Chronicle* had shown any interest in the pair, after they had contacted numerous local and national newspapers seeking employment. Arriving for their meeting with the editor, they sensed that this may be their only chance to get their foot on the journalistic ladder. Furthermore, they didn't know how many junior reporters the *Chronicle* was considering taking on. Both knew it was possible that they were in direct competition for a position on the staff.

Before their interviews, the pair were shown around by George, the deputy to the chief-sub. In his fifties, George had thinning black hair, horn-rimmed glasses and was wearing a tired, tweed jacket over a crumpled shirt and tie. Puffing on his pipe, his eyes gave the pair a quick once-over. The contemptuous look on his face, suggested that he didn't think much of them.

Any newspaper is always a work in progress. News is non-stop; constantly coming in through the phones on the news desk or via the teleprinters in the telegraph room. With several editions of the paper put out throughout the day, the stories and page layouts were being constantly altered, as new and more significant stories emerged. Consequently, everywhere was a hive of activity; typists, telephonists, reporters, photographers, librarians and the various editorial teams, constantly engaged in updating the news. It was frenetic; organised chaos. For Larry and Robert, who were seeing it for the first time, it made the production of the *News Bulletin* seem amateurish. This was real journalism and on a grand scale. Regardless of the excellent articles they had produced for their student paper, they had never had to work under such intense pressure as this. Realising just how inadequate their experience was, Robert and Larry knew that they had much to learn before they could establish their credentials within the industry.

At the desks of the sub-editors, jackets had been discarded on the backs of chairs and shirt sleeves rolled up to the elbows, as men sat scribbling away. Cigarettes were stuck fast between their lips; the room filled with smoke. Altering, cutting and refining the efforts of journalists, the subs worked to meet the demands of the chief-sub and his deputy; stories tidied up to meet the constraints of column inches and the interest of the readers. Noting the fascinated expressions on the faces of the young hopefuls, George asked them a question.

"Do you lads think that you'd be able to keep up if we put you in here? You're always working against the clock. There's not much room to think."

"I suppose it takes a little time to get up to speed," suggested Larry.

"Oh no, lad. You've got to be able to do it straight away, or you'll never make a sub. It's a different set of skills to journalism. Condensing stories and writing headlines is what we do."

Larry nodded, feeling a little overwhelmed.

"What about you?" asked George, turning to Robert.

"I suppose we've had to do it with our own articles on the student paper but, I'll grant you, we don't have to do it against the clock and we're not constantly refining a succession of stories for several, different editions."

"I'll tell you what lads, sit down on the end there and I'll give you a story to edit. Let's see how good you are."

George pointed to the far desks in the subs room. These were the lower desks, where the less experienced, 'down table' subs worked. The 'top desks' were reserved for the best and most experienced subs, who were trusted to handle the pressure of delivering the biggest stories. George grinned as he noted Larry and Robert's surprise. It was clear that neither of them had been expecting to carry out any sort of practical test.

"You get shocks all the time in this business lads," he remarked. "You just have to get on with it."

To their credit, Larry and Robert quickly took off their jackets and sat down, whilst George placed copies of the story down before them.

"Right then lads, this is a story about the search for a missing child. There are ten folios off the teleprinter and you've got to cut it down to three paragraphs of no more than two to three sentences. Then, I want a headline of no more than twenty characters over two lines, with the first no longer than twelve. I'll be generous and give you fifteen minutes. Off you go!"

George watched, impressed as they got on smartly with the task. As he walked behind them, looking over their shoulders, he could see that they were working quickly and effectively. It seemed as if they were both enjoying the task. With time running out, both were struggling for a headline, given the strict limits imposed upon them. Finally, Larry settled on 'Relief as boy found', whilst Robert came up with 'Mother's relief'.

Reading through their submissions, George declared himself satisfied with the results.

"You've not done bad at all lads. I think that you might actually have something that we can work on."

Standing up and putting on their jackets, Robert and Larry smiled.

"Oh no, don't get excited," observed George. "I'm not the one who does the hiring around here. You'll still need to impress the editor and it's time we got to his office."

As they accompanied George, Robert was pleasantly surprised to see that there seemed to be a healthy number of pretty, young women working in the building. George didn't fail to notice his interest.

"You won't get too much time to chase after women if you're working here lad. You'll be far too busy for that and so are they. Anyway, a lot of them are married. I doubt that would stop you though, would it?"

Larry grinned. George had summed up Robert, who appeared slightly embarrassed, quickly and accurately. His observations however, weren't restricted to Robert alone. George turned to Larry.

"And with you not being inclined towards admiring the ladies," he continued, "I can only assume that you'll be obsessed with the job to the exclusion of all else."

Now it was Robert's turn to be amused. As far as he was concerned, George had got it spot on.

Arriving outside the editor's office, Larry and Robert were told to sit down by his secretary who, sat behind her desk, peered at them over the top of her spectacles. With tidy, short grey hair and a neat, brown two-piece suit, she was organised and efficient. Her remit was certainly not an easy one. Filing papers, typing letters, organising her boss's diary and with a constantly ringing phone to answer, she also had to review the readers' correspondence. Economical in her use of language, enquiries were quickly and smoothly dealt with. Meanwhile, George had gone in to see the editor and no doubt was relaying his own impressions of the two graduates to his boss. After a quarter of an hour, he re-emerged and wished them luck, before departing. Larry and Robert were again left waiting until finally, having answered her telephone once more, the secretary rose from her desk and indicated that the editor was now ready to see them.

Entering the room, they were immediately confronted by a large desk, its surface covered by a battery of telephones and piles of folders. Here was the nerve centre of the whole operation; every department and every detail within touching distance of the editor. He certainly didn't appear a fearsome man, however. He seemed calm, almost studious as he watched them coming into the room.

"Take a seat, boys," he said, indicating a couple of chairs to the side.

Waiting for them to settle down, he picked up a couple of folders from the desk and leaned back in his chair. Robert and Larry recognised them as the portfolios of work that they had sent to the *Chronicle*.

"When I looked through these, you awakened my curiosity. You've both written some good articles, but it wasn't the only detail that impressed. What's here tells me that the pair of you aren't afraid to use your initiative in order to chase a story. Getting a personal interview with Gagarin Larry, was amazing. We couldn't get one, neither could the *Evening News* or Granada Television, who had him booked into their studios. And you, Robert, why would Stanley Baker want to be interviewed by a student newspaper? I'm surprised you managed to pull that one off. You both have the potential to make good reporters and feature writers too."

The editor paused, giving his words chance to sink in. Robert and Larry felt pleased, the signs were looking hopeful for both of them.

"The industry is starting to change. Graduates are becoming more accepted, although there's still resistance. Most journalists and subs are like George and I. We started after leaving school at fourteen and worked our way up from being copy boys and junior reporters. We had to empty the ashtrays, clean the desks, sweep the floors, run errands and make the tea. You can understand it if there's more than a little resentment towards graduates who come straight in as reporters, without paying their dues. It doesn't bother me, for I know that you can only survive in the business if you're practical and can learn and adapt. It's why George gave you the subs test, to see if you could handle the pressure. He and I, have been impressed with the results. George seems to think you've got a chance, so turn up next Monday morning at eight and we'll take you on trial and see how you get on."

Unsure of what he meant by "on trial," both Larry and Robert looked confused. Quickly, the editor explained.

"That means that although you'll get paid, we won't be officially adding you to the pay roll for a couple of months. Do well boys and we'll take you on; fall short and you'll be on your way."

Larry and Robert nodded. They had wanted a chance and an important provincial newspaper had given them one. The precise nature of that opportunity, was nothing less than what they had expected. They were going to have to prove themselves to their new boss, but both of them were confident that they would be able to do so.

Chapter 55

With Robert and Larry's futures on the way to being resolved, it was now up to Kay to find employment. As part of her course in social administration, Kay had been given placements at Children's Services in Stockport and Bolton. Although the work proved challenging, Kay was convinced that she had found a potentially satisfying vocation. At the end of July, Manchester Children's Services advertised for child care officers. Kay applied and was invited for an interview on Thursday, August 3rd.

Kay's friends were pleased to hear the news and called round on Wednesday evening to offer their support. Welcoming them, Ethel soon indicated that Kay was taking the interview in her stride.

"Come in lads. She's in the kitchen, making a brew."

"Is she nervous?" asked Larry.

"Nervous? Our Kay?" replied Ethel, with a smile. "To see her, you'd never dream she had anything important on tomorrow."

"That seems about right," replied Robert, with a grin. "Nothing ever seems to bother her, does it?"

"Well, here she is," said Ethel, opening the kitchen door.

Walking in, they could see Kay filling the teapot with boiling water from the kettle she'd taken from the stove. Putting it down, Kay picked up a spoon and carefully stirred the contents of the teapot, before replacing the lid and covering it with a bright, striped cosy. Having finished, she turned to her friends and smiled.

"I suppose you two would like a drink as well."

Robert and Larry nodded.

"Well, sit at the table, whilst I get the cups."

"They'll want some biscuits as well love," said Ethel.

"Oh, yes please," remarked Robert, with enthusiasm. "Have you got any chocolate digestives?"

"There's some in the biscuit tin. McVities. We only buy them," noted Ethel, proudly.

"None better," insisted Robert. "The original and by far the best."

Larry smiled. Another Manchester favourite, he assumed. Noting his reaction, Kay enlightened him.

"McVities factory is on Wellington Road on the boundary between Manchester and Stockport. As you know, their chocolate digestives are popular nationwide, but we consider them ours."

Putting four cups down on the table, Kay poured out the tea and added the milk and sugar.

"Are you sitting with us Mam?"

"No, I'll take mine in the front room. Coronation Street's on in a few minutes. I don't want to miss it."

With Ethel's departure, Kay expressed surprise at her friends' visit.

"I didn't expect to see you two tonight. I hope you weren't wanting to go out. I hardly look the part, do I?"

"Oh, I don't know about that," replied Robert. "You're just a typical Ardwick lass; your hair in rollers, covered by a scarf, preparing for a night out. I bet you'd have your hair done in no time if we had somewhere to go."

"Well, that's where you're wrong, because I'm leaving them in all night."

Larry was quiet. He'd never seen her in a head scarf and rollers before, but he thought she looked wonderful. Her hair was taken up at the front and away from the sides of her cheeks, revealing more of her beautiful face. Like Robert, he thought that Kay looked gorgeous when she had her hair piled up, or placed it in a ponytail and he now felt a similar, pleasant sensation. But not for too long. Kay was his brother's girl and he couldn't allow his guilty pleasure to continue.

"We wanted to wish you luck for tomorrow," continued Robert.

"Yes," added Larry. "And we thought we could take your mind off the interview. Although it doesn't seem as if you need our help in that respect, do you?"

"There's no point worrying about interviews," replied Kay. "You just have to prepare well and try your best. You can't do any more than that."

"Don't you get at all worried?" asked Larry.

"What for? What can they do? They're only going to talk to me at the end of the day."

"Yes, but you must worry about the types of questions that they might ask. I know that you'd really like the job, so doesn't that put you under any pressure?"

"Why? If I'm not meant to get it, then it's something I have to accept. Other jobs will come along. This isn't the only opportunity out there."

"Yes," said Robert, "but it's in Manchester, which means you already know the city and you won't have to move and be away from friends and family. It'll be a lot better if you land this job tomorrow."

Having taken a sip of her tea Kay was forced to swallow it quickly, before exploding into laughter. Seeing her shaking body and flushed face, Robert and Larry looked at her with their mouths wide open.

"I don't know," said Kay, slowly, as she began to calm down. "You both said that you came round to take my mind off the interview and yet so far, you've spent most of your time trying to convince me that I should be getting worried about it! What are you like?"

Kay sighed and shook her head. Her friends looked rather sheepish.

"I'm sorry Kay. I suppose we weren't really thinking," suggested Robert.

"We didn't intend to upset you," added Larry.

"Yes, thinking isn't always a strong point with you two, is it?" she asked, with a chuckle. "You're lucky that I already know how gormless the pair of you can be and after all, you have given me a good laugh."

Robert and Larry smiled, pleased that they hadn't upset her. The subject of Kay's interview was forgotten and her two friends spent the rest of the evening talking about how they were settling in during their first days at the *Chronicle*. As they left, Robert and Larry wished Kay luck. Yet knowing how well prepared and calm she would be, they were sure that she wouldn't need it.

Chapter 56

Arriving at children's services, Kay was show into a large room that seemed crammed with desks and filing cabinets. There were several members of staff present, but none offered more than a cursory glance or half-hearted nod towards the new arrival. Asked to take a seat, Kay watched as her escort walked over to a connecting door and disappeared through it. Looking around, Kay observed several women busily writing reports, whilst others were reading through case files or putting paperwork into their bags, as they prepared to go out on visits. The scene was familiar; just like the field work offices in Stockport and Bolton.

It wasn't long before Kay was summoned in to see the Assistant Children's Officer. Once Kay had sat down, Anne Martin greeted her with a smile. In her mid-forties, she was small, stocky and had a pleasant, ruddy face. Her brown hair, which already contained signs of grey, was coiled up into a bun. Wearing a two-piece, green tweed suit, Anne looked very much a woman of the post-war era. Kay noticed too the absence of either an engagement or wedding ring on the third finger of her left hand. As the interview progressed and Anne talked about the expectations of someone entering a career in social services, it seemed clear that she was a woman whose life revolved around a total devotion to the job.

Straight away, Anne wanted to know why Kay had decided on a career in social work, when obtaining her degree had opened up a range of opportunities.

"I'm sure that by getting a first, most employers would be keen to take you on. You've had placements working in children's services, so you know how demanding the work can be. In truth, it can be a thankless task. You have to be physically and mentally durable and at times, almost impervious to hostility and criticism. I'm sure you're aware that some staff struggle to cope with the distress that the job can bring. Why then, have you decided to ignore other lines of work, when they can offer you a higher salary and a quicker chance to progress?"

"It's something I've spent a lot of time thinking about," said Kay. "When I entered the sixth form I became a volunteer, working with the youth club at St Paul's Church on Brunswick Street. I understand the children there and the problems they face, because I was raised in Bennett Street and I still live there. I know how difficult it is for children to make something of their lives if they lack a safe home, food on the table and caring parents. Families in Ardwick, Chorlton-on-Medlock and all the other working-class districts of Manchester, don't have very much. It's a demanding environment to grow up in and so, without guidance, it's easy for kids to go off the rails. I saw it happen to so many when I was growing up. There are no simple answers for bringing change, but we have to be able to intervene in children's lives and help them and their families as much as we can. I want to be a part of that and help children from communities like mine."

"It's not just working-class families who need our help," replied Anne. "Having money doesn't necessarily provide children with a safe, family environment."

"Of course," said Kay, "but you asked me why I wanted to become a child care officer and my starting point has always been a desire to help my own community. That's what motivates me."

Anne had listened intently to what Kay was saying. Her background was certainly authentic and sparked Anne's interest, but as yet, her words sounded too familiar; a conventional response to typical interview questions. Anne pushed her further.

"If we were to employ you and send you out into the field, what do you think would prove to be your greatest challenge when trying to work constructively with children and their families?"

"Gaining trust," replied Kay, without hesitation.

"Go on," said Anne.

"I'm not naïve. I know that families to whom child care officers are assigned, regard them as interfering outsiders and they never welcome them with open arms. With middle-class families, the hostility is because of the embarrassment they feel at being involved with social services. To the working-classes however, social services are regarded as just the same as the police and courts; hostile organisations who exist to punish, rather than help them. It's very difficult to build relationships and you have to accept that you'll always be seen as part of 'officialdom'. Nevertheless, a compromise can be reached and hopefully, progress made. I know that I'll never be totally trusted by the people I'm trying to help and that consequently, I'll have to constantly temper my expectations."

Anne nodded, impressed with what she'd heard. There was a strong sense of practicality evident in Kay's response. She had a mature head on her shoulders for someone so young. There was no danger that she would view her work through rose-tinted glasses.

"I'm sure you realise Kay, that as a graduate you would be very much in the minority in terms of the typical profile of our officers. Few of us have been to university and most haven't received any official training. We have learned the job through experience. Many of our staff go back to the days of the Public Assistance and Social Welfare Committees. All that is going to change. Training and professional qualifications will become an essential requirement for those employed in all areas of social work. In that sense, people like you will eventually become the norm. That's not to say that you won't experience some resentment from your more established colleagues. That's another area where you'll have to work hard on building relationships."

"Yes," agreed Kay. "I can see that anyone coming into the job straight from university will be regarded by some, as inexperienced and idealistic."

"Nevertheless Kay, you have an advantage over most here. Your background makes you an unusual applicant. You can empathise with the majority of the children and families we support and use it to your advantage. You talked about the lack of trust that many working-class families have towards us. I think it's because ours is a middle-class occupation and many of our officers display a smug, self-satisfied sense of superiority towards those they work with. Listen to conversations in the office and read through the case files and you'll notice condescending, even derogatory observations, about children and their families. Experienced as they are, so many child care officers are too judgemental and unable to avoid the assumption that we must necessarily know better than those we are trying to help. That isn't a trap that you are likely to fall into."

Anne paused, giving time for her words to sink in. Kay sensed that the interview was going well.

"Furthermore," Anne continued, "you strike me as being level-headed; well aware of the difficulties you'll have to face working in child care. As such, I don't see a risk that you'll quickly leave us, like some graduates whose idealism deserts them when they're faced with reality. I'm hoping Kay, that you won't let me down. That is, if you still want to accept a job with us."

There was a momentary silence as Anne looked expectantly at Kay who, still processing her words, was trying to make sure that she had actually been offered the job.

"Well?" asked Anne.

"I'm sorry," replied Kay, looking confused. "Have you just offered me a job?"

"Yes. You look surprised."

"I wasn't expecting you to come to a decision today."

"Well, are you going to give me an answer or not?" asked Anne, who was beginning to find the situation somewhat amusing.

"Yes, of course. I'd be delighted to accept," confirmed Kay, smiling.

The two women shook hands; the deal was done. Kay would now start her working life as a child care officer with Manchester Children's Services Department.

PART THREE

New Horizons

Chapter 57

It was July, 1962. A year had passed since Robert and Larry had taken their first steps in the newspaper industry. Both had impressed during their probationary period at the *Chronicle* and had been officially taken on as full-time members of staff. It had been a steep learning curve. Working under pressure, they were learning new skills; part of a team racing to deliver regular editions of the *Chronicle* throughout the day. It was quickly apparent that producing the news required them to be available around the clock. Often, they were active well into the night, chasing breaking stories, or back in the office working on those coming in over the wires. It may be that they were helping to lay out the next day's early edition, for reporting was but one aspect of the production of a newspaper.

Withy Grove, where the *Chronicle* was based, had grown to become the largest newspaper and printing house in Europe. It was officially named Thomson House, after the recent purchase of the Kemsley Newspapers Group by the Canadian media entrepreneur, Roy Thomson. The offices of six other Sunday and daily titles shared the site, where their newspapers were produced and printed. In the hustle and bustle that was Withy Grove, the presses never seemed to stop.

Working through the night, Larry and Robert learned that regardless of the licensing hours, nearby landlords would admit print workers for a drink during their breaks. This would be in the early hours of the morning and was the most secret of operations, given that policemen on the beat were regularly patrolling the area and on the lookout for anything amiss. Pub windows were blacked out, the interiors were dimly lit and the drinkers talked quietly, keeping noise to a minimum and reducing the chance of discovery. So too, did the pub entry codes; a series of knocks needed to gain admittance. The secret knock was changed nightly and was written in chalk on the inside of the printing staff's exit, by the publican, a few minutes before the bell for break time was sounded. It meant that only print workers and journalists too, could gain admittance and therefore landlords couldn't be caught out by the police, or potential informers who wanted to see them lose their licence.

At first, Robert and Larry had been attached to the news desk, sent out to the scene of potential stories that had come in over the telephone. Over time however, their roles began to develop and diverge. Larry was soon involved in the paper's coverage of local politics. Much of his work was routine, but it was also detailed and time consuming. His remit was wide. He had to attend council briefings and press conferences, as well as keeping contact with community groups and local health services. Building relationships with Manchester's members of parliament and its key councillors, was a crucial part of Larry's role and he was soon trusted by politicians of all persuasions, who found that he would never betray a confidence. It meant that Larry had his finger on the pulse of local political life and so was usually first to be aware of any important developments. After a relatively short time, Larry was already being trusted to produce features on local politicians and national issues.

Whereas Larry's role on the paper continued to be very much as a journalist, different opportunities were made available to Robert. When a temporary vacancy arose on the sports desk, Robert was given the position. His main task was to work on the production of the *Football Pink*. The *Pink* was Manchester's favourite Saturday evening sports paper, available in the newsagents with full reports of City's and United's matches, just an hour after the final whistle. It was far more popular than the *Football Green*, produced by its rival, the *Manchester Evening News*. During the week, Robert worked on local sports stories and features that would, with other articles, fill up the interior of the *Pink* prior to the addition of the match reports to make up the final edition on Saturday evening.

It was Saturday afternoon that was Robert's real challenge, for as a sub-editor, he was handed updates of the match action as it unfolded. At regular intervals, the details of the game were dictated over the phone, from the press box at the ground, to the copytakers. The reporter's words were then passed on to Robert who had to work rapidly, rewriting the action as new, key incidents occurred and goals flew in. Delays to the kick off and excessive injury time, could mean that it was almost impossible to meet the print deadlines, although last-minute goals and final results, could usually be placed in the stop press column. Robert would add a headline, that hopefully satisfied the editor and the match report went straight to the compositors, to become part of that Saturday's *Pink*. A fleet of delivery vans then shipped out copies to vendors and newsagents across the city. It was a challenging and demanding job, but an excellent grounding for those who had ambitions of climbing to the top. Robert was well aware that the renowned editor of the *Manchester Evening News*, Tom Henry, had himself started out as a sports-sub.

His temporary role on the *Pink* coming to an end, Robert found himself attached to the crime desk. As a journalist in this department, it was crucial that Robert established contacts within the Manchester City Police, trying hard to earn their trust so that they would give him inside information on any developing cases. Like those working in the field at rival publications, Robert frequented the Abercrombie Inn, the watering hole of officers who'd come off duty at nearby Bootle Street Police Station. On the back of the features that he'd written for the *News Bulletin*, Robert was also asked to carry out reviews of films and concerts for the entertainment section. Robert was paid extra for these assignments, but more important to him was the fact that he was proving his adaptability to his employer.

Unlike Larry, whose ambition was to build a reputation as a first-rate political correspondent, Robert's aspirations had already grown much wider. He was fascinated by all aspects of the newspaper industry and realised that by gaining successful experience in many departments, he would increase his chances of rising up through the management structures. Unlike Larry, he could never be satisfied with journalism alone. In short, Robert was determined that one day he would become the editor of a great provincial or national newspaper.

Chapter 58

In early September, Kay became involved in a new case involving a family on Higher Temple Street in Chorlton-on-Medlock. Concerns had been raised about the children. Her role was to make contact with the mother, Mary Cullen. Children's services could then begin to build a profile of the family, which would help them to develop a plan of intervention, should it be necessary.

On the day of her visit, Kay arrived at the front door at two-thirty. She knocked but received no answer. The time had been chosen carefully, as Mary was likely to be alone and would feel more inclined to discuss her family's situation. While she waited, Kay watched the next-door neighbour, who was down on her knees brown stoning her front step. In her late sixties, wearing a scarf over her head and a flowered dress covered by a pinny, her bottom swayed from side to side as she applied the finishing touches to her work. Satisfied, she stopped, then looked up at Kay.

"Hello love. You after Mary?"

"Yes," replied Kay, smiling.

"She'll be in the kitchen. Won't hear you in the back I wouldn't think."

"Yes, I thought so. I'll go down the ginnel and see if I can't catch her."

For a child care officer, neighbours were always one of their best sources of information. But that was if they could get it. For these were proud communities, where people were self-reliant and protective of one another. As such they tended to close ranks against officialdom, be it the police, council or children's services.

Getting to her feet, the old lady looked carefully at Mary's visitor. She noted that she was pretty and friendly too. Her accent, her reference to the ginnel and the absence of any hint of arrogance, was appealing to her. Carrying a large shoulder bag, with cardboard files peeping out of the opening, the old lady guessed that Kay was some kind of social worker. It seemed likely that she was checking up on Mary and the children.

"You've made a good job of that. It looks lovely," said Kay, admiring the step. "It's hard work. When I was a kid, I used to earn spends doing it for some of the neighbours."

The old lady gave her a look of approval.

"Where are you from love?"

"Bennett Street, off Hyde Road."

"I know it. You're not there now though, are you?"

"Yes. I still live at home with my mam and dad."

"You're not married then?"

"Not yet, but I'm engaged and hopefully, I will be soon."

"Well, your young man needs to get a move on. A pretty thing like you and still available. Aren't men gormless love?"

Kay blushed.

"It's true. There's no need to be embarrassed. But make sure you've got a good un. Make him appreciate what he's got."

Kay nodded.

"She always does her best with the kids," continued the old lady. "It's Charlie, her husband, you know."

"Oh?" replied Kay, surprised.

"Yes. He's the quietest, loveliest fella you could meet, but once it comes to the weekend, he's out drinking and when he comes back, the arguments start."

Kay nodded in acknowledgement.

"He's given her a real shiner a couple of times. I'm sure the kids can't sleep through what's going on."

"No, I doubt they can."

"Anyway love. I've got to get on. Nice to talk to you."

"And you."

Kay smiled as the old lady picked up her bucket and donkey stone and walked back into her front room, closing the door behind her.

Making her way to the back yard, Kay considered what she'd learned about the family. Although she had to remain objective, she'd certainly been given some useful indications of the problems they were facing.

Knocking on the back door, it opened quickly. A woman stood in the doorway clutching a small book and a pound note in her hand.

"Oh, I thought you were the rent man."

Kay smiled.

"Hello, its Mrs Cullen, isn't it? I'm Kay. Kay Thompson. I'm from children's services. Here's my card."

Kay held it out in her hand, but Mary Cullen showed no inclination to take it. Kay's arrival had taken her by surprise and an awkward silence followed. Nevertheless, she appeared neither hostile or threatening. Twenty-five years old, Mary had long black hair, left down in an attempt to hide the bruising on her face. She had the careworn appearance of a woman twice her age. Delicate and tired, her thin arms and hands at odds with a swelling tummy; her clothes were worn and frayed.

Left standing, Kay was rescued by the sound of whistling and the yard gate being opened behind her. It was the rent man. Facing the potential embarrassment of Kay's presence on the doorstep, Mary quickly stood to the side.

"Come in and sit down."

Kay quickly moved past her. Sitting by the table under the window, she placed her bag on the floor. Whilst her host chatted to the rent man, she took the opportunity to survey the room. To Kay's right, an old brown settee was pushed up against the wall. It looked perfectly serviceable with its attractive, home-made cushions. To the left was the sink and draining board, an 'Ascot' boiler for hot water and a gas cooker. The floor was laid with lino, upon which sat a large, flowered rug. On it, two toddlers were at play with a number of old, toy cars and building blocks. On the opposite wall was a small, rented television set, with a box for sixpences on its side. The room was clean and tidy; the children, both boys, were nicely dressed and content. It was clear that Mary was a devoted mother, prepared to sacrifice everything for the sake of her children.

Getting up, Kay crouched beside them. Absorbed in play, only now did they notice her.

"Hello."

Kay smiled. Curious, the boys turned towards her. They stared silently, unsure of how to respond.

"My name's Kay. What are yours?"

The boys were silent.

"There's no reason to be shy now, is there?" came a soft, Irish voice from behind.

It was Mary. Finished with the rent man, her attention had turned to Kay.

"They're not usually this quiet," she continued. "Come on Michael, Paul. Say hello to the lady."

Two faint "hellos" escaped reluctantly from the mouths of the boys.

"There. That didn't hurt. Did it now?"

Shaking their heads, the boys quietly returned to their toys, whilst the two women sat at the table. Kay hoped that she wouldn't be seen as a threat, yet it was apparent that Mary would take some convincing.

"You can see they're fine," said Mary, defensively. "Charlie would never lay a finger on them. He loves them as much as I do. Anyway, if he's had a wrong un and he starts, they're long in bed. They don't see or hear anything. I don't care what any of the neighbours say!"

Her words were insistent and defiant.

"Kids do see and hear," replied Kay, quietly. "It's the school that contacted us, not any of your neighbours. Barry was upset one morning and told his teacher that he'd heard Charlie shouting at you."

Mary was surprised, but irritated too.

"We're not the only couple that argue round here. Lots do. Are you going to take their kids away too?"

"No one's said anything about taking them away, Mary."

"Well then, why are you here?"

"Because when children are involved, we have to follow it up. We don't have a choice. But that doesn't mean we're going to find fault. We want to help if we can. That's if we think you might need us to."

Kay paused. She understood Mary's fear of failure; of not being able to protect her children and the good name of her family.

"I can see that Paul and Michael are healthy, clothed and fed," continued Kay. "The school say the same about Barry and

Geraldine and that they're well behaved. No one can fault how you're trying to bring them up."

"The kids want for nothing. My Mam makes sure of that. When they need new shoes or clothes, she'll take them to 'Stewarts.' I won't let her give me anything for myself though."

"Oh?"

"No. She and Dad don't like Charlie. Won't come round when he's here. He's my hubby, so I've got to be loyal. With the kids, it's different."

Kay nodded. She understood both Mary and her parents. It was hard for the latter to see the violence Charlie regularly inflicted on their daughter, yet know that she would never leave him. For Mary, it was all about saving face; not admitting to them that her married life had turned into a disaster.

"But are you okay Mary?"

"Yes. Of course. Don't look at my eye," she insisted. "I tripped down the stairs a while back. It's taken ages to go."

"I can see."

"Yes. I should have been more careful."

Mary was in denial and Kay knew it was pointless to press the matter any further.

"And how far on are you?"

"Seven months."

"So, not long now then?"

"No."

"And Charlie?"

"Oh, he's over the moon, although having another isn't going to make it any easier to manage."

Mary was finally starting to open up, more trusting of her visitor. Kay encouraged her to continue.

"I suppose you've got your mam to fall back on."

"Well, yes. But do you know, I was hoping that when Paul and Michael went to school, that I could get a part-time job. Earn some money of my own and not need Mam and Dad so much."

"After this baby you could ask your doctor for the contraceptive pill. I could come with you if you like. Insist that it's for the good of your health. You'd have five young kids and that's tough for anyone. And when this next one goes to school, you'll be free to work."

"Oh, I know. I've thought about it, but there'd be no use."

"Why?"

"Charlie wouldn't agree to it."

"But would he have to know? The doctor can't tell him."

"He'd find out. I'd forget to hide them; leave them lying around. Then there'd be hell to pay. We're Catholics and Father Boyle's always preaching against the pill. Perhaps he's right. Perhaps it's not what God wants."

The two women lapsed into silence. Kay had no right to question the family's religious beliefs and management wouldn't sanction her behaviour if she did. Yet she had consistently opposed the traditions that kept her gender subservient. Unable to avoid the risk of pregnancy and with the worst type of husband, many women were destined for a life of drudgery. Kay knew that religious rules had been made by men, for men and to maintain their control of women.

Without warning, the back door was flung open as Barry, followed by Geraldine, almost fell into the room.

"Mam, Mam," shouted Barry excitedly. "I've got you a picture."

As he flailed it around, Mary found it difficult to take it from his grasp. Successful, she stared at it curiously whilst her son waited eagerly for a response.

"Oh, it's lovely," she replied, as she slowly moved it away from her.

Peering over at it, Kay understood that Mary was trying to focus on the subject. But it was tough at any distance. With blobs of paint of varying colours placed above some rectangular blocks, what could it possibly be? Barry, growing impatient, was eager for Mary to tell him more. Surely his Mam could see what he had painted? Fortunately, it was Geraldine who came to the rescue.

"I think it's a really good picture of you, Dad and us kids. Don't you Mam?"

"Of course, it is. We can save it for Nanny, can't we?"

Barry and Geraldine nodded in agreement.

"Can I have a jam butty please Mam."

"All right Barry, but only one. You don't want to spoil your tea."

"Can you do it for me Geraldine" she continued, turning to her daughter. "And get one for yourself if you want."

"Right Mam. What about our Paul and Michael?"

"They're all right, they've had plenty."

Almost nine, Geraldine happily accepted her responsibilities as the family's eldest child. She shared the maturity of many girls her age, who in a sense assumed the role of surrogate mothers to their younger siblings. They would mind them when they played out in the streets and would help to clean and run the house. Kay had been told by Geraldine's school that she was an exceptionally bright girl and expected to pass the eleven plus. Yet it would be almost impossible for Geraldine to escape the limitations of her circumstances, especially as her parents were indifferent to any aspirations, beyond motherhood, that she may have.

Satisfied that the children were in no immediate danger, Kay picked up her bag and stood up ready to depart.

"Well Mary, I'd best let you get on. The kids are a real credit to you."

Mary smiled. She was reassured now; confident that her children were safe.

"I've left my card on the table. If you feel the need, you can contact me at any time."

Mary nodded, but Kay knew that it was highly unlikely that she would ever hear from her again. Descending the steps, Kay heard the back door shutting quickly behind her. It was a fact of life she'd learned to accept. Despite being a native of these streets, as a child care officer, she would never be accepted by the people she was here to help.

Chapter 59

Although Charlie's dark, drunken moods were of concern, his behaviour was similar to many husbands and fathers. In districts like Chorlton-on-Medlock, many children learned to cope with that reality. Kay appreciated that the courts were only concerned with a child's physical well-being; they would be expected to 'toughen up' when witnessing difficulties between their parents. And of course, judges and magistrates invariably acknowledged the right of a man to reasonably discipline a wayward wife or child. Kay would recommend that they continue to monitor Mary's family, but with so many demands on children's services, she wouldn't be surprised to see the case file closed.

Kay had learned that it invariably proved difficult to decide whether children should be taken away from their parents. Situations were rarely clear cut. There was always such a range of conflicting factors to consider and the concern that came with the knowledge that any mistake could lead to terrible consequences. She had seen how the pressure of decision making had overtaken many of her more senior colleagues. In her first days in the job, Anne Martin had advised her that if she wanted to survive, she had to try and reign in her emotions and as far as possible, develop a thick skin. If you can't do that, Anne had said, you would find it hard to make tough decisions and soon find yourself heading for burnout.

Having left Mary's, Kay walked toward Brunswick Street and the tall and imposing edifice of St Paul's Church. As she continued on to the corner, she looked across and noticed Artie's Barbers. It was where Robert had got his hair cut for as long as she could remember and where he'd taken Larry when he'd first come to Owens. She recalled how outraged Robert had been when the *Chronicle* had run an article about the inevitability of the three shillings haircut. No, Artie's would never do that, he had said. But he was wrong. It was strange, thought Kay, how the mind so readily entertains trivia at such stressful times.

Seeking respite, Kay approached the entrance to the church. Setting foot in the porchway and opening the heavy wooden door, she walked inside. She had often done this when she needed time to think. The church had been conveniently on the route to Oxford Road, during the three years she had been at Owens. Unlike Robert and Larry, Kay was a believer; in a divine will that guided the world. Although she wasn't one for regular church attendance, in St Paul's she always sensed something deeply spiritual. It provided a sense of inner peace to help confront any doubts and problems she faced.

The substantial stone work that faced the exterior of the building had long turned black, a victim of its century long exposure to Manchester's industrial atmosphere. To the uninitiated, the splendour of the interior therefore came as a welcome surprise. Built in the Gothic style of the Perpendicular period, so popular in the mid-Victorian age, the church consisted of a long nave, aisles and chancel. A magnificent wooden gallery, etched with exquisite carvings, ran around three sides of the building. On the fourth, was the stunning east window. Rising above the chancel, it was filled with stained glass, representing scenes from the life of the Apostle Paul. Designed to accommodate a thousand worshippers, congregations now rarely reached a hundred.

Walking down the nave, paved with its Minton floor tiles, Kay sat in the front pew across from the pulpit. Alone, she stared up at the east window, contemplating its bright colours and images. More relaxed in the welcoming silence, Kay could feel her mind drifting until the unmistakable sound of footsteps brought her back to her senses. Turning to the side, she saw a familiar figure approaching.

"Hello Kay. I've not seen you for a while."

Kay smiled. The shock of red hair and neatly trimmed beard, unmistakably announced the presence of Peter Jardine. A genial Scotsman in his mid-thirties, Peter was devoted to his family and an active member of the congregation. Kay had met him whilst working as a volunteer for the youth club he organised at St Paul's.

"No," replied Kay. "It's been quite a time, hasn't it? Not since I finished at Owens."

"I suppose you're busy working now. Are you?"

"Yes, for children's services."

"No doubt there are a few families around here that warrant your attention."

"Yes, unfortunately. It's why I'm here this afternoon."

Peter sensed her disappointment. Having a close commitment to the parish, he knew of the challenges that life brought for so many of the children here. He understood that charged with the responsibility for their welfare, it would prove emotionally challenging to one who had a kind and generous spirit like Kay.

"Would it help to talk about it?" asked Peter, sitting on the pew beside her.

"It's so difficult to know what's the right thing to do," sighed Kay. "It can't be good for kids to hear the arguing and see their mam's bruises and know it's their dad that hits her. Yet she would never leave him and would the kids ever be happy if they were taken away and put into care? I'm positive they wouldn't. Growing up, I knew that many of my friends were going through a lot worse than the kids I've seen today. We never really thought about it at the time. I suppose children have a resilience that we lose as we get older. Yet perhaps too, we develop an understanding that such things are wrong and that they have to change. You can see how it all becomes so confusing and so very frustrating."

"Yes. Yes, I can see that."

Peter spoke quietly, his voice almost soothing.

"I suppose we have to accept that we can't always do good," he continued, "no matter how hard we try. You've worked out what's true; that life's never simple. It seems to me that you're trying your best in the most difficult of circumstances. As long as you do that, then you have no reason to reproach yourself."

"That's a fair point," replied Kay, "but when I came into this job, even though I knew it would be difficult, I was still optimistic. I hate the thought of failing any child and I really want to be able to make a difference. Yet I sometimes feel that as child care officers, too often we're simply sticking plasters over problems that have causes way beyond our capacity to control."

"But Kay, we always accepted that it would take far more than good intentions and a couple of Labour governments to bring fundamental change for the poor of this city. We have to stay here, be the voice that these communities need, for who understands them better than us? You chose to care about the children here, at the youth club and now as a child care officer. You can still help them. You can do good."

Kay appreciated his sentiments. There was no questioning his commitment to the cause.

"We must keep our faith if we are to stick to the task," he continued. "Whether it be for religious, moral or altruistic reasons, we have to keep striving for change."

Falling silent, Peter waited whilst Kay considered his words. He didn't doubt her commitment. To question her role seemed natural and he suspected that her critical outlook only reinforced her desire to help the families she encountered.

"I think," said Kay eventually, "that sometimes we have to reflect on those things we find unpleasant. Always question ourselves; our motives and beliefs. I see too many colleagues just going through the motions. If they ever did truly care, they certainly don't now. I don't want to judge them, because this can be a very difficult job. What really scares me though, is that I too could find myself sliding into complacency. Then again, I'm sure that if I ever suspected that was happening, then I'd walk away."

Peter nodded.

"Well," continued Kay, "I'd best be making a move. I think I've taken up enough of your time."

"Certainly not. It's been good to see you again. And if you ever think that we at the church might be able to help out children's services, don't hesitate to get in touch with us."

Leaving St Paul's, Kay emerged into the welcoming late afternoon sunshine. It was rush hour now and she could hear the hum of the traffic, as a multitude of cars and buses made their way across the roundabout at the top of Brunswick Street. Out along Hyde Road, passengers were travelling to East Manchester and beyond, whilst others made their way down Stockport Road, for the south of the city and on into Cheshire. Closer to home, Kay was pleased that she could avoid the crush of public transport and take a more leisurely walk back to Bennett Street. It was a perfect remedy for the anxieties of the day.

Chapter 60

Bernard and Kay had continued to meet regularly, not only whilst he was on leave, but on any free weekends he happened to be given. They didn't just spend time in Manchester too. In fact, straight after telling Kay's parents of their engagement, they had driven to Kent to inform Norman and Violet about their news. Bernard's parents were delighted and as Kay talked with Violet for the first time as a future 'in-law,' the latter made clear what a positive impression she had made upon them.

"We're so pleased that Bernard's going to settle down. That he's met someone to care for. I did wonder if he ever would. I worried that his work in the Royal Engineers had become all-consuming; that he was losing the capacity to see that there were more important things in life. I understand now, that until you came into his life, he just hadn't met the right girl."

Kay looked away. Violet knew that she was embarrassed.

"It's true Kay," she insisted. "I wouldn't say it if it weren't."

"Well, I'm grateful that Larry didn't go to Cambridge," replied Kay. "I'd never have met Bernard otherwise."

"Yes, fate has been good to the pair of you. I'm certain that you'll be happy together; a perfect fit for one another."

As Christmas 1962 approached, Bernard was back in Manchester. Both he and Kay were finding the restrictions placed upon them by the conventions of courtship, increasingly frustrating. When alone, they struggled hard to contain their mutual desire. The couple were therefore keen to finalise a date for their wedding and decided that June 1963 would be ideal. By then they would have their own house for Kay to move into. Once married, Bernard could stay there too and eventually join her permanently when his commission ended.

As the couple discussed their plans, Kay realised that their wedding could create a tricky situation, as tradition dictated that the bride's family paid for the wedding.

"Our wedding won't be as grand as I assume Roger's was. Dad has been putting money aside for years to pay for mine and Joan's, but his budget will be limited. We'll have a local reception; nothing spectacular. I hope your mam and dad will understand."

"You are silly," replied Bernard, softly. "You've no need to ask. My parents will fully appreciate that. What matters is that we love one another. The fanciest, most expensive wedding, couldn't guarantee what we already have."

Kay smiled, relieved at his response.

"There's often much to say for custom and tradition," she continued, "but where weddings are concerned, I'm not so sure. I'd like the couple themselves to have the responsibility. After all, they are the ones getting married."

"My parents felt guilty when Roger got married. They wanted to contribute, but Barbara's family would have none of it."

"I know Dad would be the same. It's a matter of pride among the working classes. Parents have to give their daughters the best possible wedding that they can afford. Accepting help off the groom's family, would be seen as humiliating."

"Couldn't my parents put some money behind the bar?" asked Robert. "It would be separate to the ceremony and reception, but it would help to pay for the guests' drinks."

"Well, I can suggest it, but I don't think I'll get very far. The trouble is that when Joan got married last year, Mam and Dad felt denied. Her husband Colin works as an area manager at Boots. He's a widower and didn't want another church wedding. Joan didn't complain and they decided on the Register Office at All Saints. There was no reception afterwards either. They were in a taxi straight down to Ringway and flew to join the 'Jet Set' for a honeymoon in Paris. It didn't cost Mam and Dad anything."

"Didn't Joan realise that it might upset them?"

"I don't know. I assume she was just led by Colin," suggested Kay, rather generously.

As Kay had predicted, her dad was cool to the suggestion of any kind of contribution from Bernard's family. He was delighted that he and Ethel would now get the chance to put on a proper, white wedding, for at least one of their daughters.

"No love," he had said. "It's our responsibility; me and your mam. Bernard's folks are doing enough buying suits for the groom and best man. I'm sure they'll be paying for the honeymoon too. That's all that anyone can expect them to do."

Chapter 61

As Kay had indicated, in her conversation with Peter Jardine at St Paul's, she was becoming increasingly frustrated at the inability of her department to effect real change in the lives of many of the children they worked with. Kay recognised that there were issues of poverty, housing, education and health that led to an overwhelming sense of desperation, that could only be addressed through concerted political action. Dealing with these issues was outside the remit of children's services, yet Kay was convinced that she had a moral responsibility to engage with local politicians. With Anne Martin's support, she intended to lobby them to divert more resources into creating an environment for vulnerable children, which would improve the potential for change. At the start of 1963, with eighteen months in the job behind her, Kay felt that she had the experience for her views to be taken seriously by the local political establishment. Kay knew that she would have to choose her first contact carefully. Someone who was not only respected by their political peers and the Manchester public, but also likely to be sympathetic to her views. It wasn't surprising that the man she chose to approach, was Leslie Lever.

Leslie Lever had been Labour MP for Ardwick since 1950, but he had been a key figure within Manchester's legal and political communities for many years before that. From a wealthy family, Leslie had qualified as a solicitor at the onset of the Depression and gained a reputation for representing the poor and meeting their legal costs himself if he failed to win their cases. A councillor from 1932, Leslie was selected as the city's lord mayor in 1957 and became famous for attending a staggering 2700 official engagements, during his year in office. What appealed most to Kay was his reputation, even after being elected to Westminster, of putting local before national issues and defending the interests of the poor, rather than pursuing his own political advancement. If anyone could claim to be a man of the people, it was Leslie Lever. He may have been from a privileged background, but he mixed freely with his constituents. They regarded him as one of their own. Always available to offer help and advice, Leslie was in and out of people's homes, with friends and neighbours invited in to voice their concerns. He respected the people of Ardwick and they loved him in return.

Growing up in Bennett Street, Kay knew all about her local MP and the complimentary and often humorous stories told about him. She had seen him visit Armitage Street School and was aware of his regular attendance at the Whit Walks among the crowds in Albert Square. Her parents were enthusiastic supporters of the MP and Kay herself had been impressed by his concern for women's rights. He had criticised building societies for insisting that women applying for mortgages must have a male guarantor and he was constantly pushing for increases in widows' pensions. As one of Leslie's constituents, it was a relatively easy matter for Kay to contact the office of the Ardwick Labour Party and arrange an appointment. When she walked into his office, he came out from behind his desk and greeted her warmly.

"It's Miss Thompson, Kay, isn't it?" asked Leslie, with a smile

"Yes," replied Kay, shaking the hand that was thrust out towards her.

"I know your father, Ernest. He works for the Corporation, doesn't he? A driver at Hyde Road depot."

"Yes, that's right."

Kay was a little surprised. She knew that her father had met Leslie when he had visited the depot, but that was a long time ago and she was impressed that the MP could still recall meeting him. To those who knew him, Leslie was the consummate politician. He had a knack of remembering names and faces and the details of the matters he had dealt with for his constituents. It meant that he always brought a personal touch to his dealings with others. This naturally reinforced the perception of him as a politician who wasn't merely going through the motions. Leslie was seen as a man who really cared about the people he represented.

"He and your mother must be very proud of you. Brought up in Bennett Street, attending Armitage Street School, graduating from Owens and now you're working in children's services. You've come a long way Kay and no doubt you'll go much further."

"Well, I'm not sure about that."

"Now, don't be modest. It's good to see bright young women like yourself getting on. It's a welcome sign of progress."

Kay was quiet. It was clear to her that Leslie was well prepared for their meeting. His staff had obviously researched her background after she had been in touch with them. It was reassuring that he intended to take her seriously and she was further impressed when, realising that his praise had left her slightly embarrassed, he quickly changed the subject.

"Well, straight down to business," he continued, "what is it that I can do for you?"

Kay explained that all too frequently she felt that the work of her department was being hampered by a lack of a co-ordinated approach to the myriad of problems faced by poor families, of which the difficulties faced by children were symptomatic.

"You see Mr Lever..."

"Leslie, please."

"As child care officers, we work with families to identify the barriers to the well-being of the child. Yet our plans often only deal with the symptoms, not the underlying causes of the problems. We have no control over so many of them. We need action in terms of health, education and housing and we can't do that. The Corporation can. They could support us, but politically there's not enough will to do it. Even within social services, there's no co-ordination between the child care, mental health and welfare departments. I visit families where we're dealing with the children, whilst there are adults in the home that are under the care of mental health services. Yet although their work impacts on ours, there's no formal co-operation between us."

"I see," replied Leslie. "How do you think that I'm best able to support you?"

"Be a point of contact for us, working for that co-ordinated approach. A voice to be heard in the council chamber and in the committees. I know that it's difficult to change established processes, but with your personal standing, you can give prominence to the issue. It will take time, but we have to start somewhere."

"You're right in your assessment, Kay," Leslie agreed. "We need a far more co-ordinated approach to the care of our vulnerable children. It's the same in towns and cities across the country. I suspect that the answer lies in Westminster, for the kind of service you envisage will ultimately need to be established by legislation. That's not to say that I won't use my influence in the council to make members aware of the difficulties you face and if you think I can help in any individual cases, please get in touch."

Kay nodded in acknowledgement of his offer.

"Poverty," he continued. "It's poverty Kay, that's the biggest danger to our children. It's why I'm fighting the government to get an increase in widows' pensions and allowances for wives from poor families. Without that extra money, these women are forced to go out to work. It means that they can't be at home to sustain and encourage their children. I've argued in the Commons that this brings far-reaching social consequences. I'm convinced that the concerns over teenage crime are due to the fact that because they're out working to provide their children with material security, mothers can't offer them the emotional stability and moral guidance that they need."

"It's unfortunately the case," replied Kay, "that governments think that by saving money in one area, it won't end up potentially costing them more in another. Yet in terms of teenage crime, I don't think the present government is too concerned. It's more likely to be working-class districts that are affected. That won't bother Macmillan and others of his kind too much, will it?"

Leslie laughed, delighted by her comment.

"So, you're on our side then Kay."

"At the moment. I hope that if Labour can win power, the party will deliver on its promises. We're still living in an unequal society and it needs more than mere platitudes to put things right."

"I can see that you're a shrewd young lady, Kay. There'll be no fooling you."

The affable and popular MP had been highly impressed by the confident and intelligent young woman from children's services. Her upbringing in Ardwick had certainly helped provide her with a no-nonsense approach to getting things done. Henceforth, Leslie would keep a keen eye on her progress. He was sure that Kay, just like himself, would be engaged in serving the young people of Manchester, well into the future.

Chapter 62

After acquiring the Kemsley Newspapers Group in 1959, Roy Thomson had identified the *Chronicle* as one of its weaker assets. It had a steady circulation of over 250,000, strongest in Manchester's Lancashire hinterland, but it was losing £100,000 a year. It was regarded by many as a better paper than its rival, the *Manchester Evening News* and by no means a lost cause. Nevertheless, it lagged well behind its competitor in securing the highly lucrative classified ads market. Thomson referred to the paper as the "rotten apple in the barrel" and had no interest in trying to reorganise its advertising department, in an attempt to save the paper by making it profitable. Instead, always looking for opportunities to wheel and deal, in 1963 he agreed that he would merge the *Chronicle* with the *Evening News*, gaining a twenty per cent stake in the latter. A year earlier, Thomson had shut down the *Empire News*, another paper purchased from Kemsley, merging it with the *News of the World*. Without the production of the two publications, Thomson had freed up capacity on the Withy Grove presses. This meant that he could focus on contract printing, which he believed to be a more lucrative and far less risky venture.

Like others who worked at the *Chronicle*, Robert and Larry had been aware of the rumours surrounding Thomson's intentions for some time. They had been preparing to look for alternative employment, but at Easter they were offered the chance to transfer to the *Evening News*, whose circulation and content would be expanded when the *Chronicle* finally closed in July. Already long established as the largest provincial newspaper in the country, the amalgamation with the *Chronicle* further enhanced the position of the *Evening News*. The opportunity to work for the paper was one that neither man was prepared to turn down.

It seemed just like the first day at school when the pair of them entered the Guardian Building on Cross Street, the location of the offices of the *Evening News*. Although they had already gained significant experience working at the *Chronicle*, where they were well thought of, Robert and Larry knew that they would have to quickly prove their credentials to their new colleagues. In that respect, both were helped by the fact that their roles at the *Evening News* were going to be similar to those at the *Chronicle*. Robert would be working on the crime desk, whilst Larry would function as a political reporter. For Robert, willing to expand his breadth of experience, the decision wasn't too important, yet for Larry it certainly was. Unlike his friend, he had retained his socialist ardour and had lost none of his belief that journalism could be a force for good. Only as a political correspondent would he have the chance to pursue that ambition.

The Guardian, as it was now styled, having dropped Manchester from its title in 1959 and the *Evening News*, were both owned by the Scott Trust and had shared the building on Cross Street for eighty years. Their offices were on different floors and they had separate composing rooms, but they shared the presses and cafeteria. In the latter, the atmosphere was not always harmonious, given the perceived arrogance of some writers on the national broadsheet towards their provincial counterparts. Attitudes weren't helped by the fact that for decades the revenues and profits generated by the *Evening News*, were subsidising the loss-making *Guardian*.

The driving force behind the *Evening News* was undoubtedly Tom Henry, the paper's editor-in-chief. Stocky, with glasses, a razored moustache, a spotted bow tie and wearing a white shirt, with his sleeves usually rolled up to the elbows, 'Big Tom' would prowl through the offices, chomping on a cigar, unrelenting in his insistence that the paper went out on time. He was hands on; rewriting headlines, chivvying his subs and taking his reporters to task. Even the most experienced could tremble when hearing his gruff voice barking out instructions over the intercom. Yet none of them could question his dedication and both subs and journalists knew that there was no one who could write a story with such speed and skill as Big Tom. Although he was a hard taskmaster, many who had worked for him had cause to be grateful. It was said that half of Fleet Street had passed through Tom Henry's door.

It wasn't long before Robert became another young reporter whose potential was identified by the great man. Receiving a note expressing satisfaction at his recent efforts and an award of a bonus payment, Robert was told to report to the editor's office. Big Tom's reputation was such however, that when he received the news, Robert couldn't help but experience a sense of trepidation.

"Ah, Wilson, take a seat," said Big Tom, as Robert entered the impressive wood panelled room.

The editor-in-chief was sat behind a large desk in front of a window that let little light into the room, given that the leaf print curtains had been left partially closed. That was of little consequence however, given the bright glare of the humming, electric lights. To Robert's far left he could see a large framed map of the world, which to his surprise was physical and not political. Just before it, resting against the side of the wall, were the 'spikes'; collections of recent copies of the *Evening News*, secured together for Big Tom's perusal. On the left side of the desk were placed a number of telephones, whilst piles of letters covered most of the surface on the right. It seemed that Robert had arrived as Big Tom was about to go through the daily correspondence.

"Do you see these, Wilson?" he asked, picking up a handful of letters. "These are all from our readers. You don't ever ignore them, because it keeps you in touch. You're damned as an editor if you do, for it's a sure way to help run your paper into the ground. Do you know why that is?"

Big Tom looked intently at Robert who, feeling increasingly nervous, found it hard to respond.

"It's because these letters tell us all about the concerns of our readers, Wilson. Knowing what they are, we at the *Evening News* can address them and if necessary, take up issues on their behalf. It's the reason I've called you in today, because I'm concerned that we're not listening to young people and you're the man who can help us."

He paused and looked at Robert who, hearing his positive words, was now feeling more at ease.

"You've written some entertainment reviews for the *Chronicle*, haven't you?"

"Yes, that's right," replied Robert.

"And I believe you interviewed various celebrities, actors and pop stars, for your student newspaper."

Robert nodded, unsure as to where the conversation was leading.

"So, I think it's safe to say, that all-in-all, you're knowledgeable about this strange youth culture that suddenly seems to have erupted all around us."

"Well, I suppose you could say that."

Big Tom scowled.

"Well, you're no use to me lad, if not," he growled. "I'm not after maybe's or suppose so's."

"Oh, I definitely am, Mr Henry. You can depend on me," insisted Robert, worried that his indecision had just cost him an opportunity.

"That's more like it! You can't afford any hesitancy if you're going to be a success as a newspaper man."

Robert looked suitably contrite and nodded his head in acknowledgement.

"In this business Wilson," continued Big Tom, "you have to be looking to the future and who are the readers of the future?" he asked.

"The teenagers of today," replied Robert, with confidence.

"That's right," replied Big Tom. "The fact is that we have to concentrate on getting those readers now and that's where you come in. At the *Evening News* we've been getting it all wrong. We've treated rock 'n' roll and pop music as we would any other type of entertainment. We've sent out our usual reporters to cover these artists' concerts, but the truth is that our reviewers are too old and they don't understand the appeal of the music to the teenage audience. You're young Wilson and so you do. Your reviews will be sympathetic. They won't be shrouded in the dismissive disapproval of curmudgeonly old reviewers, longing for times past. But I still want you to be honest; criticise acts if you feel you need to. Respect our young readers, for they aren't stupid. Your honesty will bring them to trust you and so they'll take our entertainment sections far more seriously. Local teenagers need to know that what they care about, we do too. As you said Wilson, these youngsters are the adults and readers of tomorrow. Let's get them into the habit of looking at the *Evening News* as soon as possible."

"Yes. There's no reason why we can't do that," said Robert, enthusiastically.

"Of course, you'll still be fulfilling your duties for the crime desk," continued Big Tom, "but you'll be paid extra for any reviews or interviews we use. You could say that it's a kind of promotion. Do well and I'll have other openings for you in the future."

"Thank you. I won't let you down."

There was the briefest of smiles from Big Tom before, rather curtly, he dismissed his young reporter.

"Well, that's all. I'm sure you've lots of things to get on with."

Before Robert had got to his feet, his editor had already turned his attention to the letters in front of him. There was no farewell as he made his way out of the room. Big Tom was a busy man. The meeting had provided Robert with an important opportunity; one that he was determined to make the best of.

Chapter 63

On Saturday June 1st 1963, Kay was sat with her dad in the back of the wedding car, resplendent in her beautiful white, lacy wedding dress. It was almost two o'clock and they were parked alongside the pavement outside St Paul's Church, waiting a few minutes so as to uphold the tradition of the groom being left waiting nervously for the appearance of his intended. Whilst Kay was calm and confident about the upcoming ceremony, Ernest was becoming emotional and finding it difficult to retain his composure.

"I'm so proud of you love. I always have been. You've always stood up for yourself; stood up for what's right. You're decent and good and I can't understand how someone as clever as you, could be a daughter of mine."

Noticing that his eyes were starting to mist over, Kay reached for his hand and squeezed it softly.

"Come on Dad. You're being daft. If I'm clever, I've definitely got it from you. You don't need pieces of paper, qualifications, to be intelligent. I was lucky. You and Mam always encouraged me. You let me stay on at school and gave me the chance that you could never have. You didn't want me out working at the first opportunity. Everything I've achieved, is because of you."

"We'll still see you regular, won't we love? It won't be like our Joan, will it?"

"We're not far away. Only in Urmston."

"But she's only in Whalley Range and we rarely see her."

"Well, you just try to keep us away. You won't have a hope. And don't forget, I'll be expecting you and Mam to visit us too. We're only a bus ride away."

Ernest shook his head.

"I don't know, as usual telling your dad what's what. And here I was, thinking I didn't want to give you away. It's the only chance I've got of getting some peace!"

"Well, of all the cheek," replied Kay, trying to sound offended.

The pair of them laughed.

"You know love, he's a good lad Bernard, isn't he? And his mam and dad. Down to earth. You'd never think they'd all that brass, would you?"

"No, you wouldn't."

"And my daughter, living in a big detached in Urmston. You couldn't make it up, could you?"

Kay smiled.

"Are we ready then Dad?"

"Yes, come on," he replied, feeling more relaxed. "Let me have the privilege of walking my little girl down the aisle."

Leaving the car, the two of them took the short number of steps to the open church door. Hesitating for just a moment, Ernest focused, determined that he would take in every detail. It was one of the proudest days of his life. The culmination of all his years of care for his daughter and now she would start a family of her own, with a young man he liked and admired.

Taking Kay's arm in his, Ernest walked her slowly down the aisle, as the church organ began playing the familiar strains of the wedding march. Ernest had sat through many church weddings and the music had never affected him. Now, he found it enthralling; his emotions heightened by the recognition that it was a tribute to Kay. And so were the gasps and the whispered compliments that he could hear from the guests, their faces turned towards them. Wearing a striking white, tea length wedding dress, with lacy three-quarter sleeves and a short headdress, Kay looked sublime. Staring towards the altar, Ernest saw that Bernard had noticed too, a broad smile signalling his undoubted admiration for his intended. As they reached the altar, Ernest could see Norman and Violet sat to the right of them. Smiling, they both nodded towards him. With them were Roger, Barbara and the boys. They had all accepted his daughter with open arms and justified her conviction that the social differences between the families, would have no bearing on her marriage.

Reaching the altar, they were joined by Larry as best man and Joan as maid of honour. The wedding service was now ready to begin. Ernest gave Kay a kiss. His job was done and he joined Ethel on the front pew.

Outside, Ernest watched as confetti rained down on the happy couple, following photographs at the church door. As the newlyweds got into the wedding car, he was pleased to see the smile on Ethel's face and hear the laughter that came from her lips. His abiding memory of the service would be the tears she had shed, as Kay and Bernard made their vows. He understood that it wasn't simply tears of joy; there were tears of sadness too. The sadness that his darling wife had 'lost' her little girl. Although he tried to tell her not to be silly, his words were half-hearted. Ernest knew that he had experienced similar emotions himself, when he'd sat with Kay in the wedding car.

Moving on to the reception, Ethel directed Ernest to greet the guests, whilst she made sure that the catering was on track.

"We've paid a pretty penny for it," remarked Ethel, quietly.

"I know love. But, God forbid, you'll have the caterers thinking I'm as tight as a Yorkshireman."

"Just get on and do as you're told and leave me to it!"

Ernest knew better than to question his wife, especially on a day such as this and ultimately, he was grateful that she had directed his time so specifically. As a result, he had no chance to become nervous about delivering his speech and after they had eaten, he got through it with little difficulty. It had been good to see Joan too, but Ernest suspected that the attention she'd received from so many of the male guests, had proved difficult for her husband Colin. He and Ethel had certainly been blessed with two very beautiful daughters but Kay, with her wonderful heart, would always be Ernest's favourite.

Just after nine, Bernard and Kay departed. They were returning to their new home in Urmston to spend their first night together. Tomorrow they would be making the long drive down to Cornwall for their honeymoon. Kay had no desire to fly to an exotic location. All she wanted was for her and Bernard to be together, a feeling that he shared. Norman and Violet thus found, that when it came to the second of their sons' marriages, once again, their finances had been barely tested.

Chapter 64

It wasn't surprising that there was a clamour of young men paying attention to Joan at the reception. Sultry and sophisticated, classy and stylish, she exerted a powerful allure that was difficult to resist. Joan knew that men desired her and would trifle with their affections, revelling in the control that she had over them.

Joan had been married at nineteen. It had been a whirlwind romance; if romance is what it was. When Colin Taylor, area manager, visited the Market Street store, he couldn't miss the pretty young woman on the cosmetics counter. Stopping to chat, he had tried to be professional, but Joan had seen his nervous smile and how he'd blushed as their eyes had met. A flutter of her lashes, a pout of her lips, her soft, hazel eyes looking deeply into his and Colin was lost. Often returning, he would seek out Joan, who always appeared more ravishing than before. Aware of his interest, Joan's ambition took over. She had learned that head office believed that Colin was destined for great things. It was what she wanted; the opportunity for a comfortable life of leisure and she ruthlessly set about getting it. A widower, Colin was in his late thirties and flattered that such a beautiful young woman had responded so warmly to his attentions. They had dated and were soon engaged and married.

She had moved into his detached home in Whalley Range and was quite the lady of leisure. Domestic help took away the perceived drudgery of the household chores she hated and days could be filled with shopping in town. The price tags in Lewis's and Kendal, Milne were of no concern to her now and Colin was happy to indulge her in the buying of stylish new outfits. Always glamorous, Joan looked just like a film star. Colin had a trophy wife and he was the envy of his colleagues. He thus didn't press her for children. Joan was grateful; pregnancy was anathema to her. She had no intention of losing her stunning figure, or having a young child around to impinge upon her lifestyle. Colin already had two boys from his first marriage. Boarding school and doting grandparents, meant that they were rarely around. Without any real responsibilities, it was almost a perfect life for Joan. Except for just one thing.

Colin had been right to have concerns about the attraction that his wife was drawing at the wedding reception. Joan was a sensual young woman with needs that Colin was unable to satisfy. Understanding that he must never know, when the two of them made love, Joan would feign satisfaction, sighing and moaning; convincing him of his sexual prowess and boosting his ego. Often away on business and frequently tired from long hours at work, it was a performance that thankfully, she didn't have to deliver too often. Real satisfaction she found with others. Joan was always careful. She never cheated with anyone remotely connected to colleagues, friends and family. It was usually a chance acquaintance; someone she'd meet whilst she was out and then an afternoon liaison in an outlying hotel. There were no prying eyes and no reason for Colin to suspect her. Nevertheless, almost twice her age, it didn't stop him feeling vulnerable. Although she'd never given him any cause for concern, he still feared that a younger man would steal her away and then she'd be lost to him for ever.

Joan had never broken her rules on adultery for anyone before, but when she saw Robert at the reception, she sensed an opportunity that she wasn't prepared to miss. After all, he was the only man who had ever turned her down and now, she had a chance to set the record straight. What's more, unlike so many other of the male guests, he hadn't shown any inclination to approach her. For Joan this posed a challenge that was hard to ignore, but she remembered how eager he had been that past Christmas and she was positive that he would be so again. Confidently, she walked across the room to greet him.

"Hello Robert, how are you?"

Robert returned her smile. When Joan had stood by Kay at the altar, she had been a satisfying sight to behold and it had immediately triggered his memories of how she had tried to seduce him. Like her sister, she seemed prettier every time he saw her. Yet it still hadn't been Robert's intention to approach her. His initial thought was that he should leave what had happened between them, well in the past.

"I'm fine," replied Robert. "It's a long time since I've seen you."

"It must be."

"I hear that you've done very well for yourself," continued Robert. "Your husband has quite an important job, doesn't he?

"Yes, Boots have just promoted him to regional manager."

"A successful husband and a big detached in Whalley Range," observed Robert. "That can't be bad."

"Yes, that's right. I certainly can't complain," replied Joan, smiling. "But at this point aren't you supposed to ask me whether being wealthy makes me truly happy?"

Joan's eyes lit up and she smiled mischievously. Robert laughed. He was impressed with her repartee. She had a presence and maturity that pleased and surprised him.

"No, not at all," he replied. "There's nothing wrong in leaving Bennett Street behind. Good luck to you."

"Well, you've surprised me, Robert. You and our Kay always seemed to be fighting for some cause or other and you were always so proud of your working-class background."

"Yes. I still am, as is Kay, but it doesn't mean that you can't aspire to move on when the opportunity comes along."

Joan nodded approvingly. She sensed that the two of them had more in common than before and importantly, that Robert's deep affection for Kay, was now unlikely to prove a barrier between them.

"I fancy some fresh air, Robert. It's a little stuffy in here. Would you come outside with me for a minute?"

"Yes, of course."

The two of them walked through the hall, making their way carefully around the multitude of wheeling bodies, cavorting across the dance floor. A few other guests had ventured outside too, so Joan led Robert to a more distant spot, where they couldn't be overheard.

"Well then," asked Joan. "What do you feel about today?"

Joan tipped her head slightly to one side and fixed him with her soft, hazel eyes.

"What do you mean?"

"Our Kay, married."

"I like him. Bernard's a decent guy. He'll make Kay happy."

"But you must be disappointed," insisted Joan. "You idolised her. I know that night, you were holding back because of your feelings for Kay."

It was out in the open, the first signal from Joan that perhaps there was some unfinished business that later, the two of them may want to address.

"Well, I had to learn to accept that although I care for Kay, I probably couldn't have guaranteed her the complete commitment that she wants and deserves. She still means the world to me Joan and she knows that if she ever needs me, I'll always be there for her."

"Isn't there anyone else?" asked Joan

"No. I'm not ready for any kind of commitment just yet."

"Love them and leave them. Always the happy bachelor then?"

"You could say that."

The two of them exchanged glances, Joan's moist, soft lips parting into a deliciously wicked smile. She laid her hand softly on Robert's. He felt the gentle caress of her fingers; a sensation all too brief, as she quickly withdrew them. But it was enough to send a powerful tingle of expectation coursing through his body and he let out a quiet, involuntary sigh in response. Robert was excited and try as he might, he couldn't avert his eyes from hers. Joan knew, that if she wanted, he would be hers.

"When you ran off and left me," continued Joan, "I knew it was only because you were in love with Kay. Do you ever think about that night, Robert? If you had the chance again, knowing what you do now, that it wouldn't work out for you and Kay, would you have made love to me?"

She spoke softly and intimately. Her soothing voice and enchanting eyes were drawing him in. Robert had no chance of escaping her, but he didn't want to. He was happy for Joan to think that he was falling under her spell. Her question made perfect sense. The chance to share his life with Kay had gone. In fact, it had never really existed. Yes, his feelings for Kay had stopped him then but, as Joan had suggested, would it now?

Feeling confident that Robert would give it due consideration, Joan put forward a proposition.

"I believe that we have one life Robert and we owe it to ourselves to enjoy it. When we were lay together on the settee, I wanted you and I know that you wanted me…"

Her words took Robert by surprise and he stepped back. Joan followed him and took his hand.

"It's no good trying to deny it," she continued. "You know it's true and that you want it to happen now."

Joan paused, but there was no reply. His silence only encouraged her to continue.

"Why not take the chance and no longer have to think about what might have been. We can share an afternoon together and then go our separate ways. No commitment for either of us. The kind of freedom that both of us appreciate."

"But what about your husband? Aren't you concerned that he might find out."

Joan shook her head and smiled.

"That won't happen. I'm not daft. I wouldn't ever risk my marriage and lose everything I've got. I'm always discreet."

"Well, what about now? He probably noticed us leaving the hall."

"Oh, he won't be bothered about that. He knows that you're just like one of the family. He'd never think anything of us being out here together."

Robert laughed.

"I don't know. You've got it all worked out, haven't you?"

"Of course. When a woman has needs, she can be very resourceful."

"Obviously."

"Well, it's up to you, Robert. Give me a call. The number's in the phone book. There's only one C. Wilson in Whalley Range. You can reach me most mornings after nine."

The following day, looking back on their conversation, Robert was surprised by just how much Joan had changed. It was as if she was an actress who'd grown effortlessly into a new role. She had real maturity now, no longer just the gorgeous teenager whose appeal was raw and sexual. Marriage had brought Joan into contact with a different social circle where, in order to impress, she realised that she needed to possess qualities in addition to those of being a stunning and beautiful wife. As a result, she'd watched and learned. Her vocabulary and deportment suggested a developed intelligence and she had an ability to converse on a variety of subjects. She had a real sophistication about her. Of course, Joan was still incredibly pretty and much as Robert tried to maintain his cool persona, it had been a struggle, for she simply oozed sex appeal and when his mind had gone back to the missed opportunity of their past, he found it hard not to become aroused. In fact, if there had been a concealed room or corner close by and they wouldn't have been missed, if she had let him, he would have made love to her there and then.

Robert had accepted for some time, that there was little chance that he and Kay would ever be romantically entwined. Her marriage to Bernard had finally put an end to even the faintest of hopes that had continued to linger. In his mind there was nothing now to stand in the way of an afternoon of passion with Joan. They would be discreet. Both wanted the excitement of a secret liaison, without the trappings of commitment. It was sex, not love. Perfect for the two of them. Yet Robert had not telephoned her on Monday morning, for he never allowed himself to appear too eager for any woman. Not that it could have affected Joan, for she had purposely gone out that morning, to avoid giving him the same impression. Early on Tuesday however, Robert made the call and it was duly answered. They agreed to meet at noon on Friday at the Grosvenor Hotel.

Chapter 65

The Grosvenor Hotel was located at the end of Deansgate on the corner of Victoria Bridge Street, down which it was just a short distance to the River Irwell and Exchange Station. Walking past the hotel and into Victoria Street, could be seen the Cathedral, Chetham's Hospital and Library and Victoria Station. The attractive Victoria gardens lay opposite, a small park where the Victoria Hotel had stood until blitzed by the Luftwaffe and Cromwell's Statue sat proudly in an island in the middle of the busy road. Manchester had declared itself strongly for Parliament during the civil war and the monument was a tribute to one of Robert's old heroes. When he had secured his place at Owens, Robert imagined that he was just like one of Cromwell's 'plain russet-coated captains' who was striking a blow for meritocracy, against 'that which you call a gentleman and is nothing else'.

When it had opened in 1880, the *Grosvenor* was the most luxurious hotel in the city, but that accolade had long been lost to the *Midland* and from the exterior, the building was certainly looking very tired. Covered in black sooty deposits, the green tile cladding on the higher reaches of the building had been almost obscured, in complete contrast to those that were brighter and more colourful around the ground floor and the canopied entrance. Here, on the steps leading into the hotel's reception, a newspaper vendor would stand selling copies of the *Evening News*.

Joan had told him to book the room before she arrived and that she would meet him in the lounge at one. Robert was to go up to the room first and she would follow him ten minutes later. Although the *Grosvenor* wasn't a location that Colin or any of their acquaintances visited for business or pleasure, Joan wanted to be certain. It seemed very much like a cloak and dagger operation, yet Robert didn't mind. The fear of discovery only heightened the sense of guilt and excitement.

When Joan walked into the lounge, Robert was stunned. She looked breathtakingly beautiful. Wearing a pale yellow, two-piece pencil dress, Joan had a matching set of white hat and heels, handbag and gloves. Yet Joan's head turning appearance, seemed to contradict her intention to remain anonymous. As she walked over to his table, Robert wore an amused smile, as several pairs of eyes followed her every step of the way.

"You look lovely," said Robert, as she sat down gracefully beside him.

"Do you think so?"

"Yes, I most certainly do."

"That's good," noted Joan, approvingly. "Have you sorted out the room?"

"Yes, 317 on the third floor."

Ordering drinks, Robert finished his quickly and made his way up to the room. It wasn't long before a knock on the door indicated Joan's arrival. Entering, she seemed in a playful mood.

"I suppose this afternoon I'm Mrs Smith, am I?"

"No," replied Robert, smiling. "I went for Greene with an e. I thought that Smith was a bit too obvious, just like Brown, so I picked another colour and thought of Robin Hood."

"Of course," said Joan, "Richard Greene the actor. You think that you're acting like a bit of an outlaw, don't you?"

The two of them laughed. Both had been parties to adultery before and were at ease with the situation they found themselves in. And now that they were alone, Robert could fully appreciate the captivating woman with whom he was about to make love.

It was clear from the start, that Joan intended to take the lead. Removing her hat, she laid it on the table and turned to face Robert. Slowly, she took off her white gloves, pulling at each finger in turn to reveal her soft, delicate hands and then removed the short, fitted jacket that tapered sympathetically towards her waist. As she placed it carefully on a hanger, Robert had every chance to admire her splendid figure. It was suitably displayed in an elegant, knee length, yellow pencil dress, that hugged every curve of her wonderful body, before revealing her smooth, supple calves and slim, exquisite ankles, highlighted by a pair of white stilettos.

Robert breathed in deeply. She looked stunning. He was almost lost for words. Joan gave him a playful smile, well aware that he was impressed. Robert was already aroused, aware that she was starting to take control. It was a situation to which he was unaccustomed. Trying to appear calm and collected, he said the first words that popped into his head.

"Your dress. It's very nice."

"Yes, it is. Isn't it?" she asked, twirling around gracefully so that Robert could see how it hugged every inch of her curvaceous body. "It's a gorgeous colour, light and comfortable. Very summery in fact."

"Oh, yes," he mumbled. "Very summery."

"Would you like to help me off with it, Robert?"

Moving her head slightly to the side, Joan gave him an enquiring look. Her eye lashes fluttered and she slowly ran her tongue across the bottom of her slightly parted lips. Robert's heart was pounding. He wanted nothing more. Turning her back towards him, she issued her instructions.

"Take the zip with one hand and keep hold of the material at the top, with the other."

Robert did as she asked.

"Right, now pull it down carefully to the waist."

Joan needn't have told him what to do, for he'd been in this situation so many times before. But this time it was different. He'd waited patiently for her permission and he'd done as he'd been told. Joan was in charge and it was a different and exciting dynamic.

The task completed, Joan moved away and turned around. Taking her arms from the sleeves, she let her dress slip slowly to the floor, revealing her brilliant white underwear and stockings beneath. Stepping forward, she picked up the dress and placed it over a chair, all the while Robert was still and silent, spellbound by the satisfying sight before him.

Joan understood what pretty underwear could do for a man and she knew that Robert was no different to any other. She had chosen to wear an expensive, white lacy Basque, that emphasised her ample breasts and attractive, slender waist. Robert couldn't help his eyes being drawn lower, to where her suspenders revealed the promise of the smooth, soft skin that lay above the top of her tan, nylon stockings. Seeing his reaction, Joan smiled impishly.

"You approve of my underwear then?"

Robert nodded, far too desperate and aroused to answer.

"But, we're not here to talk about fashion, are we Robert?"

Her eyes opened wide, she looked knowingly at Robert, effortlessly beguiling him with her soft and seductive tones. Moving enticingly towards him, Joan raised her arm. Putting her hand on his chest, she moved him gently back to the edge of the bed.

"Sit down," she whispered in a soft, sultry voice.

Sat on the bed, Robert watched as Joan took off her stilettos. Then, one at a time, she placed her feet on the bed, bending forward to unfasten each of the suspenders before slowly removing the stocking from her leg. Unable to contain himself, Robert reached out to touch her, only to feel Joan playfully slap his hand.

"Not yet. Wait!"

Robert took a sharp intake of breath. Stinging his hand, she had caused a thrill of expectation. She was teasing him too much; making him wait too long. Robert wanted her desperately and it was starting to hurt. Putting her hands behind her back, Joan began to undo her Basque and looked straight at Robert.

"Aren't you getting undressed?" she asked, with a cheeky smile.

Needing no second invitation, Robert almost ripped off his clothes, flinging them to the floor in an effort to dispel his mounting frustration.

"Well, well," remarked Joan, shaking her head. "You are an eager boy, aren't you, Robert?"

Reaching out, Robert pulled Joan towards the bed. There was no resistance. He was desperate for her, just as Joan wanted. A young woman of passion and desire, she needed a virile man who would make love to her completely, so that for a time she could forget the frustration of being married to a husband who could never satisfy her voracious sexual appetite.

Lying on the bed, their thrusting bodies entwined, their kisses urgent, deep and probing, they made love with an intensity that neither had experienced before. In their wildest imagination neither had believed that it would be like this. The two were insatiable; they couldn't stop. Robert had never been so aroused. She teased and pleased him, gave him feelings so intense that he was desperate for more. He simply couldn't deny her, driven on to satisfy her every desire and finally, when they lay back exhausted, they were hot and satisfied, moist and sticky.

Lying on their backs, staring at the ceiling, the couple breathed in deeply. Their bodies were still tingling with pleasure, yet they felt calm and serene. Their lovemaking had been explosive and it had shocked them both. It was some time before Joan finally broke the silence.

"That was good," she said, softly.

"Yes," replied Robert. "I think we've broken the bed."

The two of them began to laugh, then getting out of bed, they were quickly washed and dressed. It had been a brief and exciting adventure, but for all that it had proved an exceptional experience, they knew that it would never happen again. Ready to leave, their parting words clearly acknowledged the fact.

"Perhaps we'll see one another again. Maybe at a family function," said Joan

"Possibly," replied Robert. "I'll let you go first, Joan. I'll wait ten or fifteen minutes and then I'll hand the key in at reception."

There was no farewell kiss or fond embrace before Joan closed the door behind her. Alone, Robert had the chance to consider the significance of their afternoon together. There was no doubt that the experience had been good. Joan was a great lover and together they'd reached the heights of sexual satisfaction. Yet for all the physical pleasure that she'd given him, conspicuous by its absence was that spiritual connection of the soul, without which true love could never be achieved. Now that he'd lost his darling Kay, Robert would have the challenging task of finding someone else in whom he could believe. He had to be honest. Love was the missing ingredient in his life and one that he seemed destined to be denied.

Chapter 66

Having been made responsible for the 'youth scene' section of the *Evening News*, Robert planned to write a special feature on the Beatles. He had been monitoring the group's progress since seeing them at the Oasis Club back in September. It was before they had released their debut single, 'Love Me Do' and he'd been impressed. Subsequently, Robert had promoted their appearances around Manchester and they'd now had three hits. On June 13th they would play at the Offerton Palace in Stockport, before appearing at the Southern Sporting Club in Manchester. 'From Me to You' was riding high in the charts. It was an ideal time to interview them.

Having already written some complimentary articles, Robert was hopeful that he would be given access to the group. Telephoning the Beatle's Press Office in London, he was soon making his case to Tony Barrow, the group's press officer.

"I'd like to spend some time with the boys when they come over to us on the thirteenth," said Robert. "I'd love to interview them for a feature in the *Evening News*. See how they're coping with their success. Give our readers an idea of what a day in the life of the Beatles is like. It'll be good publicity for the group. I can guarantee that the article will run in all our editions. As you probably know Tony, we have the biggest circulation of any regional, evening newspaper."

Barrow laughed, quietly.

"You certainly sell yourself well, but there's no need to. I've written for the *Liverpool Echo*, so I'm well aware of the coverage of the provincial press. I know what you've done for us Robert. I've seen your reports in the past. Of course, we can accommodate you. It's good for you and for us too. My office will be in touch to finalise the times and details."

"That's great. There's just another thing I'd like to ask though, if you don't mind."

"Oh, what's that?"

"I've spoken to Sid Elgar who owns both the Palace and the Southern Sporting Club. He told me that Brian Epstein was still prepared to honour the contract that he signed with him, even though it was made some time ago. He was surprised and very grateful. He said that as the group have now had three hits and 'From Me to You' has been number one for five weeks, that he expected Brian to have demanded a bigger appearance fee, or that the bookings would have been cancelled altogether. He told me that most other managers and agents would have done that. Are you able to comment on why Brian was so generous?"

Barrow took a deep breath, before replying.

"It's a shame that the business has operators like that and disappointing that you feel the need to comment on it. But I suppose that's the reality of it. Brian would never do that. He's a man of his word and I'd like to think, honourable. The deal he made, was acceptable at the time. Brian wouldn't exploit our surge in popularity with those who were prepared to support us before that. He has a sense of loyalty to those who have treated the boys well."

On the thirteenth Robert, together with a photographer, arrived at the Offerton Palace well over an hour before the show began. As expected, there were considerable numbers of teenage girls already waiting. Whilst some were queueing from the main doors, more were hanging around in large groups. Circulating among them, Robert introduced himself as being from the *Evening News*. The girls were giddy and excited; eager for their photos to be in the paper. Their love for the group bordered on obsession. Few had tickets, but were desperate to get a glimpse of their heroes when they arrived. By then, the crowds had swelled considerably and it was only with difficulty that the boys were able to get to the sanctity of their dressing room.

Let inside, the audience reluctantly waited whilst the supporting artists were put through their paces. It wasn't a night where the latter were likely to be given a chance. All were here for the Beatles and desperate for them to be on stage. As each act's performance ended, expectations were raised even higher. Finally, the group's appearance led to an explosion of noise and unbridled emotion; girls screaming uncontrollably at the top of their voices. Robert wondered just how the group coped. Yet they did, smiling at their adoring fans whilst concentrating hard on keeping their performance as tight as possible. Not that it mattered. The music was the least of it. Their concert was an event. A promise of something much greater; an almost religious experience that was fuelled by the wild abandon of three hundred hysterical young females. All told, the group were on stage for just thirty minutes. But it was enough. Their adoring fans, now weak and limp, were wrung dry of emotion.

Off stage, it was quickly on to the next performance in Manchester. Barrow had arranged for Robert to travel with the group and they welcomed him warmly into their midst. They were confident, charismatic and witty; theirs a dry, typically working-class humour. Robert readily identified with them. They too were intent on using their talents to break free from the social constraints imposed upon their parents' generation.

The Southern Sporting Club was on Birch Street in West Gorton, close to the junction with Hyde Road and not far from Robert's childhood home in Armitage Street. Previously the old Corona Cinema, its white tiled façade had deteriorated somewhat from its original splendour. Flanked by Malpas Street and its engineering works on one side, on the other was the long row of terraces of Great Nelson Street. It was a location and environment reminiscent of those the Beatles were familiar with back home in Liverpool. Not that the streets needed to make them welcome, for just like at the 'Palace', the group were met by throngs of excited, cheering fans, who hammered on the top and sides of their vehicle, eager to lay hands on their idols. Surrounded, Robert felt more than a little intimidated, even afraid. Yet it seemed to have little effect on his fellow passengers who, seemingly relaxed, waited for a passage to be secured for them into the venue.

Safely ensconced in their dressing room, some sandwiches and soft drinks laid on for them, John and Paul played on a couple of acoustics, working through ideas for a new song. Ringo read some magazines, leaving George to handle the interview duties. Friendly and cooperative, he was happy to answer Robert's questions, emphasising the group's debt of gratitude to their fans. There was no hint of arrogance; no getting carried away with the acclaim. George hoped that their musical careers would continue to prosper, but they all recognised how fickle the business could be. Back on stage, there was pandemonium; the audience whipped up into a frenzy. The group's energy was incredible and Robert wondered how John's voice could possibly survive a second, all out, thunderous delivery of 'Twist and Shout'. Yet it did. It was an incredible performance. The day had provided a revealing insight into the extraordinary working lives of these talented, young musicians.

The next morning Robert was at his desk early, writing up his article ready for the day's first edition, before sending it to the subs. When the paper came off the presses, Robert opened a copy eagerly, only to find that that his piece had been cut significantly. He was surprised, having understood that it was going to be given more prominence. Approaching the features editor, Robert politely asked whether his article had been deemed in any way inadequate. The answer surprised him.

"Not at all. It was well written. But we're tight for space and I asked the subs to cut it. You know how it works. Can't get disappointed in this game."

Yes, I understand," said Robert, with a sigh. "These boys though, they're a real phenomenon. Cutting down the piece, our young readers have been left waiting for more."

"They'll soon get over it. These Beatles are just another teenage fad. It'll be someone else in a couple of weeks. We can't justify the column inches."

"No. You're wrong," insisted Robert. "They're going to be around for some time. They're talented; they write their own songs. Both boys and girls like them. They're witty, clever and fashionable. The mams and grandma's love them too; they remind them of the nice lad next door. There's an exciting youth culture that's really taking hold of the country and the Beatles are going to be right at the heart of it. The near hysteria I witnessed last night, is only going to get bigger. If we don't recognise it, we risk being left behind by the nationals. They'll be quick to jump on the bandwagon."

As they were talking, Tom Henry had been hovering in the distance. On one of his periodic sweeps of the building, he had heard their every word. Announcing his presence, he nodded at Robert and told him to leave them.

Disappointed, when the late edition came out, Robert was shocked to see that his piece had been reproduced in its entirety, with two additional photographs. Grateful, he immediately went to thank the features editor.

"Nothing to do with me," he said, grinning. "Thank Big Tom. He heard our conversation and thought your views had merit. I do hope for your sake, that you're proved right."

Robert thought so too. He realised how significant Big Tom's backing was. If Robert's judgement about the Beatles proved correct, then his future at the *Evening News* would be on an upward trajectory. Yet if wrong, he had no wish to consider the consequences.

His vindication with the *Evening News* had to wait until November, but during the previous month the nationals had already begun to use the term 'Beatlemania.' There had been half a million advanced sales for the release of 'She Loves You', even though fans hadn't heard it. The song was dominating the charts when the Beatles rolled into town to play two shows at the ABC Ardwick on the twentieth. The impact of their visit was huge. The scenes of devotion of young female fans that Robert had witnessed back in June, had now reached staggering new levels. Nothing less than mass hysteria was expected and the civic authorities were determined to be prepared. Police rosters were torn up as officers were redeployed to the ABC, with operations directed from the mobile HQ stationed outside the theatre. To cope with the expected cases of emotional trauma and personal injuries, first aiders from the Red Cross and St John's Ambulance came to offer their services. Even the fab four themselves had to be protected from the overexuberance of their fans, much to the chagrin of MPs at Westminster. It was a huge event for the city and the *Evening News* was there to report on all its aspects. In Robert too, they had a journalist who'd long established his credentials with the group and its manager, giving the paper closer access to them than many other publications.

The following day, Big Tom called Robert into his office to congratulate him for originally seeing the potential in featuring the Beatles.

"You've got a good nose for a story and have shown an understanding of our readers. It was smart thinking that those lads would attract interest from older, as well as younger readers; especially the mums and grandmas. You've grasped the importance of knowing the market. If we lose touch with our readers Robert, our sales will soon drop. It's why I never ignore the letters I receive, whoever the writer may be. Ordinary folks and their concerns are every bit as important as the views of the rich and powerful. Never forget that. They are the people a newspaper should represent and on whose patronage we depend. There are many editors who delegate their correspondence to others. It may save time, but they lose touch with real opinions. Then they're left standing at the top of a slippery slope. Make sure you remember that, for you've got potential Robert. Keep working hard, gathering experience and you never know where it might take you."

Chapter 67

The following year, 1964, saw significant change at Cross Street. *The Guardian* finally completed the process of transforming itself into a national daily newspaper. The editor's office, along with all the major editorial departments, were relocated to London, where they joined their existing staff at their premises on Grays Inn Road. Only a small team were left behind in Manchester, tasked with covering any developing stories in the North.

There were developments in Robert's career too. When Big Tom had given him the chance to produce articles and reviews on the local music scene, he'd certainly been fortunate. He happened to be in the right place at the right time, as the emerging teenage culture not only began to have a massive effect on entertainment, but also on wider society. These changes began to have an impact on sport too and with the emergence of young footballers like George Best and David Sadler at United and Glyn Pardoe and Alf Wood at City, it was another area in which Robert could contribute. The senior editorial staff were impressed by Robert's adaptability and the incisiveness of his writing. It was therefore unsurprising that he acted as cover on the subs desk for a short period before resuming his duties on the crime desk. Content to learn so many aspects of the business, colleagues commented that it would only be a matter of time before he would aspire to a move to Fleet Street, for Manchester was known to be the recruiting ground for talent for the nationals.

Meanwhile, Larry's focus hadn't shifted. He was a political correspondent and his ambition to excel in that field, had never wavered. On Friday, December 4th, an exciting opportunity was presented to him, when he was sent to cover Malcolm X's visit to the University. The leader of the Organisation of Afro-American Unity was to deliver a speech at the Student's Union, following his appearance in Oxford the previous evening. Fearing disorder, student officials at Owens were initially reluctant to host the controversial figure, but finally agreed to because the university unions at Oxford and Sheffield had openly welcomed him. Following his departure from the Nation of Islam, Malcolm had been on a pilgrimage to Mecca. On his return, he had publicly renounced the sweeping indictments of all white people, that he'd made whilst a member of the Nation. Despite that, many still regarded him as a firebrand and the political establishment was suspicious of his intentions. Malcolm had been invited to speak in Manchester by the Federation of Students' Islamic Societies, who were eager for him to clear up the misconceptions that the media still had of him. Sympathetic to the Black American leader, it was Larry's intention to produce a balanced and detailed account of the speech.

Amongst the students, there was an unusually high level of interest in Malcolm's visit. The debating hall was packed, the doors being shut an hour before he was due to speak. Malcolm was addressing a predominantly white audience with few Muslims among them. The audience of young men and women responded well to the charismatic speaker, applauding him warmly and on occasions, acknowledging his humour. Malcolm's views were clear and forthright. He confirmed his support for the right of Black Americans to defend themselves against violence and intimidation and his belief that the US Government was not committed to real change in the field of civil rights. Linking the latter to the fight against colonialism in the Congo, Malcolm asserted that the struggle for equality, should be dealt with as a human rights issue at the United Nations. When the speech was over and the audience had departed, Malcolm was interviewed by members of the local and national media.

Rushing back to Cross Street, Larry quickly wrote up his report. He was confident that he'd produced a balanced representation of Malcolm's views and he waited eagerly for the next edition of the paper to come off the presses. When it did and Larry found his article, attributed to a 'staff reporter', he was disappointed. The visit had not been regarded as important enough to make the front page and Larry's words had been almost totally re-written. Instead of balance, the portrayal of Malcolm was extremely negative, with the emphasis on sensational and emotive language. Certainly, the sub-editor designated to deal with the report, had portrayed the Black leader as violent and radical. The headline, 'Black Muslim chief lashes out', set the tone and the opening sentence, reinforced it further:

"Malcolm X, known as 'the angriest man in America', defended his extremist - 'bloodshed if necessary' - racial policies in Manchester today."

Larry was shocked. Where was the balance that good journalism demanded?

Once the final edition had gone to the presses, Larry sought out the sub-editor responsible for the changes and questioned the complete lack of impartiality in the report.

"It is impartial," came the reply. "We've only used the quotations that you provided in the piece you submitted. Everything we attributed to Malcolm X are his own words. I don't see anything wrong with that and I can't understand why you have a problem."

"Because you've ignored all his positive comments about opposing racism and colonialism, working with the United Nations and being prepared to co-operate with sympathetic white Americans. Those were in my article too, but you cut them."

"Not entirely. We included his assertion that he believed all men should be free."

"Oh, yes. Such balance," remarked Larry, sarcastically. "It was the final sentence," he continued, "the damage had already been done by then."

The sub-editor shook his head. He was becoming a little irritated.

"You need to look at yourself, Larry. If anything, you're the one who's lost their balance and perspective. The trouble is that you admire the guy; you're emotionally invested in what he has to say. That's not good for a reporter. Your job is to see in the story that which is of concern to our readers and you've missed it. That's why we had to change it."

"And what concern is that?" asked Larry.

"About the racial tension and murders that are taking place in the States, coming to the streets around here. We've had letters. Readers are concerned about it. We have a responsibility to go hard against anyone who advocates violence as being acceptable to achieve political ends. You quoted him yourself. He said, "you don't get action until you get mad." To the readers, such individuals are just troublemakers. The *Evening News* can never condone such sentiments."

"So, are you saying that the article has effectively fallen victim to editorial policy?"

"In a way, yes."

"But the article's politically biased. That's something the *Evening News* has always tried to avoid," insisted Larry.

"Look Larry, you know the score; you're a journalist and an employee. When you work on a newspaper, it's your role to write what the proprietors, through the editor-in-chief, want you to. If you have ambitions to remain a political correspondent, you have to learn that it's not your place to question the editorial policy of the paper. You have to be mindful of it at all times."

There was no more to be said. The sub-editor had given him good advice and Larry appreciated that he was only trying to help. Nevertheless, he still felt frustrated. Larry was pleased with his article and he'd been keen to give a more sympathetic treatment of Malcolm in the paper. Perhaps the sub-editor was right. At times he did care too much about the truth and if he wanted to make progress in the business, he would have to be more prepared to compromise his ideals. For Larry, who had always been so independently minded, this was going to prove a difficult challenge.

Chapter 68

On the same day that Malcolm X had been addressing the students at Owens, Paul Rose, Labour MP for Manchester's Blackley constituency, was addressing the House of Commons. Rose expressed his concern that there was a danger of the young generation becoming detached from their social responsibilities. He was convinced that teenagers, growing up in more affluent times, didn't face the urgency of addressing their futures, unlike their parents' generation who'd experienced the War and Great Depression that preceded it. Furthermore, many adolescent males, no longer facing the experience of national service, lacked guidance and direction. Yet Rose believed that young people could be kept on a responsible and productive path. One way this could be achieved was by increasing the number of youth clubs, the best of which had already been successful in engaging with teenagers. Furthermore, he advocated the funding of a training programme to produce more qualified youth leaders. These, he believed, would prove inspirational to their young charges. Rose's main focus for change was in the field of recreation. He argued that young people weren't being given enough opportunity to play sports, or to engage in pursuits such as art, drama and music. These activities would help teenagers learn how to work together and it would provide them with a sense of purpose and pride in their achievements. This, Rose argued, would help produce well-rounded adults who would make a positive contribution to society.

The concerns about the nation's teenagers had been a matter of public concern for some time. It had become prominent in the media with the broadcasting, four years ago, of the ITV documentary, *'Living for Kicks'*. Although the programme had noted that most teenagers were perfectly respectable, it warned that there was a significant minority of young people that had become "lost" and "lived in a world apart." The programme claimed to be an objective analysis of the lifestyles of typical 'lost' teenagers, yet its impact was sensational, causing shock and outrage to the majority of adult viewers. Teenagers were portrayed as earning far too much money and spending lavishly on frivolous items like records, clothes and cosmetics. Church and authority had been rejected and moral values too. "We don't ride with religion" asserted one young man, whilst girls who were 'going steady', were prepared to have sex with their boyfriends. One teenager claimed that it was a "natural development of their friendship." With relationships based on such unsure foundations, it was no wonder that "the divorce rate is highest amongst those married in their teens," proclaimed the programme's presenter.   And now Paul Rose's speech in the Commons had provided the editorial team at the *Evening News* with the opportunity to revisit a subject that they knew would hold the attention of their readers.

The obvious members of staff to turn to, for a feature on the city's teenagers, were Robert and Larry. Through his reviews and features for the entertainments section, Robert had already proved that he had his finger on the teenage pulse and Larry would be the ideal choice to interview Paul Rose and examine the political aspects of the teenage 'problem'. The following morning, they were called in to see the features editor, who was very clear about how he expected their submission to look.

"There's a real concern about the problem of teenagers in this city. Big Tom receives letters all the time about wayward youths and juvenile delinquency. People are clamouring out for something to be done about it and the honourable member for Blackley has brought the matter fully into focus."

"Yes, he certainly has," agreed Robert.

"We intend to produce a couple of articles, to go in the paper a week next Tuesday and Wednesday. The first dealing with the teenage problem and the second, the various solutions. We've decided to give you two the task of putting it together. Larry, you're best placed to interview Paul Rose and you should also get the views of other local politicians."

"Yes," agreed Larry. "I know that giving youngsters more access to sport, is an issue that Leslie Lever's concerned about too."

"Good," replied the editor, nodding with approval. "Now, it's important that you treat the assignment as an exposé," he continued. "Whatever dirt and degradation you happen to find, we want it revealed. Make sure there's no holding back. There's a seething morass of moral degradation out there and our readers demand to know about it."

"Of course," said Robert. "We understand."

By handing them the assignment, the editorial team had shown a great deal of faith in the ability of their young journalists. It was a fact that Robert immediately recognised and he appreciated that if they delivered the feature successfully, it could only lead on to further opportunities. Larry understood it too, but he felt uncomfortable with the topic that they were being asked to address. Taking a break in the cafeteria before embarking on their task, his misgivings were soon evident.

"Well, it's clear what they want," observed Robert. "We're going to have to spice it up a bit. That shouldn't be too difficult and if we get it right and scare the living daylights out of our concerned parents and grandparents, then we'll have earned ourselves the chance to do any follow-up articles."

Robert grinned. It was obvious that he was enthusiastic to get on with the task within the narrow parameters they'd been set. Larry however, expressed his unease.

"I don't like the approach, Robert. We're just going to be producing a cheap imitation of the shoddy sensationalism of 'Living for Kicks'. You saw the programme back then. Where were all the 'moral degenerates' that they went on about? Nowhere! It was complete rubbish. It's no different today and they know it. We're just being asked to shock and titillate. There's no concern for morality; only sales."

Larry's response took Robert by surprise. He'd assumed that like himself, his friend would be eager to take on the assignment. He was now a little concerned, for he knew that Larry would have to be working at his best, if the feature were to meet the standards required. Robert realised that he was going to have to use his powers of persuasion, in order to make Larry understand the importance of the task to both of their futures.

"Look Larry, we're in the newspaper business. A business," he emphasised. "It's our job to sell newspapers and to do that, we tell the readers about young couples prepared to have sex before marriage. Teenagers with too much money burning a hole in their pockets, which they waste on outlandish fashions and music. Lads in gangs, fighting and out of control. All the privileges that youngsters these days have, without any sense of responsibility. How different to the older generation who sacrificed so much through the War."

"But …"

"There can be no buts," continued Robert. "Don't you see? When they read about the teenage problem, the old grannies, the mams and dads, will be quivering with rage and desire. Oh, they'll rail against the dissolute behaviour of youth, yet at the same time they'll wish that it could have been the same for them. They love all the sordid little details. It brightens up their dreary little lives."

"But it's still nonsense," said Larry, dismissively.

"Yes, but nonsense, when it's good, sells papers."

"Surely," insisted Larry, "we have a responsibility to tell the truth. We shouldn't inflame opinions and sow dissension between young and old."

"Come on Larry. It's nothing like that. It's your middle-class susceptibilities coming out again. You've had it easy growing up. Life's always been too comfortable for you and so everything has to be bathed in moral sunshine; it's all black and white. Well, it'll never be that way for me. Life's been tough and I'm not about to have any doubts when it comes to securing good copy. Look, we can't afford to do this half-heartedly. We've got the boss to satisfy and neither of us have enough credit in the bank, to entertain any second thoughts about what we've been asked to do."

Larry was quiet. Robert could see that he still didn't feel comfortable about the assignment. Nevertheless, Robert sensed that his words had made an impression on his friend. At the very least, he had made Larry understand that if he didn't commit himself to the task, it would have negative repercussions for both of them. He was sure that in such circumstances, Larry wouldn't let him down.

"Look Larry, I think this is how we can make it work. You focus entirely on interviewing Paul Rose, Leslie Lever and anyone else that you think is important and research all the historical background. Effectively you'll be covering the political angle, whilst I'll concentrate on the degeneration of youth. That way, you get to write the serious material and I'll be the one producing the shocks and thrills. Your reputation will be intact. When we've finished and you've had the chance to think about it, you'll thank me. If we do this, it's going to keep both of our careers on an upwards trajectory."

Larry nodded. Robert's proposal made sense and his friend had guessed correctly, for Larry had no intention of letting him down.

"Yes. That's fine. Thanks, Robert."

Patting his friend on the shoulder, Robert smiled and got to his feet.

"Come on. 'Let's get weaving'. We've got a lot to get on with."

Larry smiled, appreciating his friend's reference to one of Kay's favourite sayings.

"Yes, if Kay was here, she'd already be telling us off for being behind schedule."

Getting to his feet, Larry followed Robert out of the cafeteria.

Chapter 69

Paul Rose had taken the Blackley seat off the Tories in the recent general election in October. At twenty-eight, he was one of the youngest members of the new House of Commons, although he had been active in local politics for many years. As a student at Owens, he had been Chairman of the Manchester Federation of Young Socialists and was one of the main organisers of the anti-Suez march that Kay and Robert had attended back in 1956. Settling into his new role, the MP was keen to meet with Larry to discuss his speech and he arranged to do so after he'd held a surgery for his constituents at the weekend.

Prior to the meeting, Larry had been given the opportunity to speak to Leslie Lever about the issues that Rose had raised. The Ardwick MP had shown appreciation of his young colleague's stance on the issue.

"From my early days as a councillor Larry, I've always been concerned that youngsters don't have enough access to playing fields and sporting facilities. It isn't so bad when children are at school, but at weekends and during the holidays, those facilities aren't being used. It seems obvious that the wider community should be allowed access to them at such times."

"I suppose that schools may resent any interference with the right to control their facilities," suggested Larry.

"No doubt," replied Leslie, "but there must be a greater co-ordination of policies concerning health and leisure, especially for the young. Far too many decisions are being made without any reference to them."

"To increase access to sports and leisure, it's obviously going to require significant funding," noted Larry. "How can that be achieved, when there are so many other demands on the public purse?"

"By making governments realise that money spent on facilities to promote the good health of the nation's youth, is outweighed by the savings provided by having fewer unhealthy citizens to treat in the future."

"What you say seems logical," noted Larry, "but I'm not sure that the government will see it that way."

"Well, the first thing I'd like us to do, now that we've taken power, is announce a remission of taxes for sports clubs and those voluntary organisations that provide activities for children. That would certainly be a good start towards dealing with the issue."

Larry knew from Leslie's distinguished record as a councillor, that his sentiments were sincere. Time and again he'd helped in the provision of local amenities for the children of his city. Paul Rose had just started in public office, but his ideas went beyond those of his colleague from Ardwick and so provided Larry with some thought-provoking points for his article.

"We live at a time," Rose insisted, "when many young people find leisure a burden, rather than an enriched source of experience. This is mainly because we need improved recreational facilities with a wider choice of activities. We must encourage the constructive use of leisure, for it's the only way of ensuring that teenagers stay on a responsible and productive path and don't fall victim to delinquency."

"Isn't that rather a simplistic analysis," suggested Larry. "If these facilities are so important, why didn't the lack of them have a similar effect on past generations? If this problem of disaffected youth does in fact exist, then surely, it has to be the result of other factors too? It could be argued that the key one is the emergence of a distinct teenage culture, that is prepared to challenge existing values. Perhaps disengagement from society, is a way by which some teenagers express that idea."

"But," replied the MP, "disengagement from society isn't being challenging or rebellious. Young people should exercise their right to express their views, but if they turn their back on the rest of the community, how can that bring change? We need constructive criticism, where alternatives are being put forward to challenge the values of the Establishment. There can be no better example than all those young people attending the Aldermaston marches. I firmly believe that if we can engage all the nation's youth in sporting and artistic pursuits, we can produce healthy, creative and thoughtful children, who will make an active contribution to society throughout their lives."

"What are you proposing that the government should do?" asked Larry.

"They have to provide the funding to ensure that the arts and sporting activities will be freely available to all young people. And there has to be an ongoing commitment from all future governments to do the same, so that it becomes an essential feature of our national way of life. Furthermore, we must back the continued growth of youth clubs and train more youth leaders who can engage with young people and help them towards becoming responsible and productive adults."

"The state already controls much of what teenagers do," replied Larry. "Schools try to instil moral values through the curriculum and during assemblies. Outside school hours, don't kids have the right to be free to do what they want? If that's moving away from more traditional activities, then don't we have to accept that? Voices are bound to be raised against the prospect of state involvement in too many aspects of our children's lives. It's something that is completely against the customs and values of this country."

"In my speech," insisted Rose, "I made it clear that no government should ever prescribe how we spend our leisure time. Yet we must still ensure that teenagers have access to all types of leisure activities and at the moment, under-resourcing of facilities means that they don't."

"Yet all the references to sport, camping and hiking can be quite concerning. It does bring to mind Germany in the thirties."

It was a rather mischievous comment and Larry was sure that the MP didn't appreciate it. Nevertheless, he felt that many of his readers would want the question to be asked.

"I don't think that's fair or relevant," replied the MP, sharply. "It was Baden-Powell who started the scouting movement and it was only evil regimes like the Nazis, that twisted his original ideas. I'm sure that most of your readers understand that and it's a matter of public record that I've been a staunch opponent of fascism for many years. My concern is that significant numbers of youngsters seem to have lost their way and perhaps, we can put some purpose back into their lives. And yes, enjoyable activities like hiking and camping, can help to do that. I just want the facilities there for teenagers to take advantage of, should they wish to do so. I'm not the only one who believes this. You'll find cross party support for my proposals at Westminster."

Meeting with Robert to review their findings, Larry expressed some regrets about how he had conducted his interview with Paul Rose. In particular, he felt guilty about the links he had drawn between the MPs ideas and the Hitler Youth. After all, Rose did have a track record, going back to his student days, of being a committed anti-fascist.

"I'm not sure," said Larry, "that I'd like to keep the question about the Hitler Youth and Rose's response, in the second article."

"Nonsense," said Robert. "It was a legitimate question and there are those who believe that these proposed programmes of sport and leisure, are just a device for controlling the nation's youth."

"But I'm sure that's not Rose's intention. I was too harsh on him."

"Rather than having doubts, you should be pleased with yourself," insisted Robert. "Whether you like it or not, you showed that you have a good nose for the sensational. Your question brought a dimension to the issue that you knew would bring an emotive response from our older generation of readers."

"Yes, but I was unfair to him because I didn't ask the same question when I interviewed Leslie Lever. He's also a big advocate of the advantages of rambling and camping for building up the character of the nation's youth."

"Of course, you didn't and neither would I, because he's Jewish. You simply couldn't have asked him. You would have appeared to be disrespectful and devoid of any kind of empathy for his situation. Not only would you have been overstepping the mark, but the idea that a British Jew would be sympathetic to Nazi ideas of indoctrination, are ridiculous. In Paul Rose's case, it's different."

"Oh, so you do actually have boundaries then?" asked Larry, feigning surprise.

"Yes," replied Robert, "even I do. But," he continued, "I would never have asked Leslie that question, even if he hadn't been Jewish. That's because I've seen the help that he's given to so many families that I've grown up with. The man's well thought of in Ardwick and I'd never do anything to betray him. For all that he's well-off, there's no doubting that he's one of us."

Robert's words were a reminder to Larry of the sense of loyalty instilled in his friend by his upbringing. As Larry observed Robert's progress at the *Evening News*, it seemed evident that he was moving away from many of the values that he had held when they had first met at Owens. Robert's ambition seemed unbounded and was leading him to the inevitable point where he would leave for pastures new. Still, Larry had no doubt that however much Robert changed, there would always be a part of him that was Ardwick.

Chapter 70

It was a Saturday morning in February 1965 and Kay was taking Barbara, a girl in care, to visit her family who lived off Brunswick Street. The area was going through a period of rapid change and the streets of terraced houses, stretching back towards Rusholme Road, were in the process of demolition. It was a blighted landscape. The life had been sucked out of the once vibrant streets and only dust and rubble remained. As yet, the vision of new housing had still to be realised and a more unpleasant reminder of the past continued to haunt and terrify Kay. Approaching the end of Higher Temple Street, they passed the remains of two houses and as Kay looked in through their open front doors, she suddenly let out a scream. Shocked, Barbara grabbed her hand.

"Run. Run!"

Alarmed, Barbara raced after Kay to the corner of Brunswick Street. The latter's actions were confusing, given the fact that Kay had always remained unperturbed in the face of difficult or unpleasant situations. Now, she was almost hysterical.

"Eughh! Disgusting!"

Barbara watched as Kay bent her head and shoulders and shook involuntarily. Taking some deep breaths, she eventually regained her composure and straightened up.

"Oh, that was horrible."

"What? What was?"

"The house back there," replied Kay, slowly. "It was absolutely crawling with cockroaches. I can't stand them. They make my skin crawl."

Kay's expression was a mixture of fear and disgust. Once again, she hunched up her shoulders and shook, this time causing her young companion to chuckle.

"They're not that bad. Everyone's seen them at one time or another. You're being mard. They don't bother me," said Barbara, somewhat dismissively.

"Well, you're unusual," replied Kay. "None of my friends like them. Horrible, creepy, crawly, filthy things! They always get into the odd, dirty or empty house and then they can spread, under the floorboards, no matter how clean everyone else is. When I was young, I stayed at a friend's house. In the middle of the night, I wanted a drink of water and when I got to the bottom of the stairs and turned the light on, the whole kitchen floor moved. It was covered in cockroaches and they ran up my legs and I was hysterical. The next day, my friend's dad got some creosote and poured it round the edges of the floors. It never dried and they used to get trapped on it, until they were able to rid the street of them."

Barbara Perkins, now fourteen, had been placed under a care order over twelve months ago. She was a pretty girl and had been doing well at school. Her parents however, both working, took little interest in any of their children. Their rules were arbitrary, but not effectively enforced and merely encouraged a sullen resistance; an air of rebellion, in their offspring. Barbara had thus rejected her chance of educational success and gravitated towards the behaviour of her older brother and sister. Both had run away from home and had been committed to care. The former had since been caught breaking and entering and was now in a detention centre. Barbara had fallen in with a local gang of similarly disaffected youths and had been picked up by the police on a couple of occasions. At that point, with her parents unwilling to engage in discussions about her future, the authorities had no option but to take her into care.

Kay was concerned that Barbara's parents may not be in and if they were, wouldn't be enthusiastic about seeing their daughter. Yet the machinery of regular visits was important in order for her rehabilitation to progress. No matter how irresponsible the parents may be and the Perkins were unlikely to pass the 'unfit persons' test, even the most badly treated child would still, in Kay's experience, want to remain in contact with them. Barbara, although she tried to pretend otherwise, was desperate for any kind of recognition from her parents. She needed to know that there was still a spark of love left for her. It's what made the job of a child care officer so difficult. Concerned for the damage that could be inflicted on children in adverse family circumstances, they also had to recognise the potentially negative consequences of taking them into care. It was a balancing act of extreme difficulty and unsurprisingly, children's departments would sometimes get it wrong.

Reaching the front door to the Perkins' home, Kay's subsequent knocks went unanswered. Barbara, becoming increasingly frustrated, looked dismissively at Kay.

"They're not going to hear you, are they? It's stupid coming to the front door. They'll be in the kitchen."

"I know Barbara," replied Kay, calmly. "It's just that I'm supposed to come to the front door first. Now that we've tried that, we can go round to the back."

"I should think so. We've wasted enough time already!"

As they walked round to the ginnel and on to the gate to the back yard, Kay knew that there was nothing she could say to remove the sullen expression from Barbara's face. Whenever she came here, Barbara would become overly sensitive and disagreeable. It was symptomatic of the hurt of rejection and Kay was the only legitimate figure on whom Barbara could take out her deep-seated frustrations. Knocking on the door, they heard the muffled sounds of voices from within. Barbara had no intention of allowing her parents the chance to avoid seeing her. Almost knocking Kay off the back door step, she lurched forward and turned the door knob. It didn't open.

"Mam! Dad!" she shouted. "It's me, Barbara!"

Faced with the impossibility of denying their discovery, her parents had no alternative but to open the door.

It was mother who greeted them, a wry smile on her face that was intended to remove any signs of embarrassment. As Barbara made her way inside, there was no attempt from either mother or daughter to embrace. Mr Perkins, sat on the settee at the side of the room, grunted a half-hearted hello and then turned back to his newspaper. A powerful, ruddy faced man in his late forties, he'd told all and sundry that 'he'd washed his hands of her,' after Barbara's trouble with the law and now he had no intention of allowing the visit to interfere with selecting his horses for the afternoon's racing.

At least his wife didn't forget the conventions of hospitality. Asking Kay to sit at the table by the window, she proceeded to make them all a cup of tea.

"Have you got any biscuits Mam?"

"Yes."

Mrs Perkins went to the cupboard and brought out a tin. Opening it, she invited Kay and her daughter to take what they wanted. Peering in, Barbara appeared disappointed.

"Haven't you got any chocolate ones?"

"No, sorry. I've not had a chance to get to the shops."

Her response was clearly untrue. She'd known that Barbara would be coming for several weeks now. Mrs Perkins simply couldn't be bothered to make a good impression. Like her husband, she saw no real value in any time the family could spend together.

"Chocolate! They're spoiling you at that home," barked Mr Perkins. "Be thankful for what's there. There's many a kid round here that'd be glad of it."

Barbara winced. His stinging words had hurt her, but she made no response. Quickly, she brushed off his criticism. Turning to her mam, she was determined to give her some positive news.

"I've been getting on well at the new school Mam. They want me to stay on to take 'O' Levels. That's right, isn't it Mrs Foster?" she asked, turning to Kay.

"Yes, it certainly is. You have a very clever daughter," said Kay, smiling.

"Huh!"

Before her husband could continue, Mrs Perkins jumped back into the conversation. His negativity in front of Kay was starting to embarrass her.

"Well, you were doing fine at school when you were younger," she remarked, looking at her daughter. "So, you can do it now, can't you?"

It was the first encouraging words that Barbara had heard from either of her parents that morning and she smiled accordingly.

"Yes Mam. I'm really going to try. You can be sure of it."

She looked over to her dad, but his head was buried in his newspaper. He had lost all interest in her. Hard as that was for Barbara to accept, it came as no surprise to Kay. She had found it exceptionally difficult to arrange a meeting with him to talk about his daughter. When she eventually had, Perkins showed no interest in pursuing his right to challenge the care order and demonstrate his suitability, along with his wife, to resume their responsibility for Barbara.

After they had left the house, it was clear that Barbara was feeling a strong sense of betrayal. At times like these, Kay wondered if their visits had any real merit in them. Hope couldn't be sustained indefinitely and Barbara's anxieties only seemed to increase further, the more she had contact with her parents. As they made their way to the bus stop, Barbara suddenly stopped dead and launched into a verbal assault on all adults in general and then Kay in particular.

"You're all the same. Aren't you?"

"Who are?"

"You. My teachers, the people at the home. My mam and dad. None of you care less about me. Do you?"

Her words weren't shocking. Kay had been waiting for them. She knew that there was going to be a reaction. A visit home would never go as Barbara wanted and then she would be looking around for someone to blame. Regardless of the fact that she was the one who had chosen to join a gang and engage in delinquent behaviour, Barbara would never consider her own responsibility for her current situation. It could be so frustrating for Kay. In an ideal world she would like to sit down with her charges and their families and work through the difficulties that had brought about their situation. She could then calmly plan a programme of rehabilitation. But the real world was nothing like that. Social work inevitably ended up as a series of ineffective, crisis interventions that brought only momentary relief and a myriad of problems in the future.

Kay would have preferred not to respond to her charge, but that was impossible. Barbara was angry and she not only expected, but demanded an answer. Yet, it was clear that nothing Kay could say was going to satisfy her.

"That's not entirely true Barbara. You know that."

"Yes, it is. You know it is."

"No," replied Kay, calmly. "Several people have tried to help you."

"Oh yes, just like you I suppose?"

Kay was quiet. She felt it was better not to answer, but her silence merely encouraged Barbara's belligerence.

"You don't care. You're only with me now because you're paid to be. Just like those who work at the home."

"That's true. I am here because it's my job and I'm paid to do it."

Kay paused, believing that her honesty would prove disarming. She was correct. A startled expression settled on Barbara's face.

"I wouldn't lie to you about that," she continued, "but tell me, why does the fact that someone is being paid to work with you, mean that they don't care?"

She looked closely at Barbara, waiting for an answer. The situation was hanging in the balance. There had been times when Kay had feared that a child she was escorting, would make a dash for it. She had been lucky; it hadn't happened yet. She recalled Anne's advice the first time she'd carried out the task:

"If they run, just let them go. It's unlikely you'll be able to catch them anyway. You'll just humiliate yourself and become a figure of ridicule, because you can be sure that the child will tell all their friends what they did to you. We also had a case where a child, chased by an officer, ran across the road and was knocked down. The press were all for blaming the member of staff of course and you wouldn't want to have to suffer the perils of being tried by the media."

Barbara, wasn't about to run however. She'd made her point and was calming down. Prepared to push at the boundaries, Barbara had learned just how far she could go. In reality, she liked Kay, who treated her with patience and respect and who turned a blind eye to her having a crafty ciggy when they were out together. The two had known one another for almost a year now and Kay was one of the few stable points of reference in her life; someone she saw regularly and who would invariably stick up for her when she found herself in trouble.

"Are we getting the bus then?" asked Barbara.

Kay's question to her had been forgotten, or perhaps she didn't want to answer it. Either way, the situation had returned to some kind of normality.

"No, not yet," replied Kay, "I thought we could go and get something from the 'Wimpy', before we go back."

Barbara's eyes lit up; a faint smile flickered across her face.

Walking to the top of Brunswick Street, they reached the roundabout and walked over the zebra crossing on Stockport Road. There, by the side of the ABC, was the 'Wimpy'. It was just one of many treats that Kay had laid on and at her own expense. There was never any question that Kay didn't care for the children she looked after and Barbara certainly knew it.

Chapter 71

On Good Friday, the sixteenth of April, Kay was up early, eagerly anticipating her husband's arrival at their home in Urmston. The significance of the occasion was made more notable by the fact that it marked Bernard's final period of leave. In July, he would be relinquishing his commission. Bernard had never wavered from his decision not to re-enlist, an intention Kay had learned of when accepting his proposal on the Snake Pass. Yet Kay had continued to question the wisdom of that decision. After all, she knew that he was proud to be an officer in the Royal Engineers and she didn't want a husband unhappy with his lot in 'civvy street.' Bernard however, was adamant that it was time for a new challenge and just like Kay, was tired of the long periods of separation. He was determined that they would live like an ordinary married couple and had secured a job as a civil engineer with a large national construction company based in Manchester. Bernard would be starting with them in early August.

For two, long weeks, the couple enjoyed their opportunity to be together. Kay had booked the time off work as part of her annual holiday allowance. It had been at short notice, but regardless of the difficulties that it could create for the department, Anne Martin was insistent that Kay's request was accepted. The couple enjoyed visits to the theatre and the cinema, drives into the country and on Kay's insistence, an Easter Monday visit to Blackpool. In between, there was time for Bernard to help complete the re-decoration of one of the bedrooms, a task that Kay had been working on during his absence.

When Kay first moved in to her new married home, she felt as if she were living in a dream. It was an environment so far removed from that she had experienced growing up at Heywood House. Compared to her parent's compact flat, Kay's home was large and spacious, with five bedrooms and three downstairs receptions. It was detached and had large gardens; the latter a luxury possessed by none of the properties around Bennett Street.

Kay was grateful and determined that she would never take her good fortune for granted. She was conscious too that it took more than bricks and mortar to create a home. With limited resources and despite its shortcomings, Kay's parents had turned their rented, council property into a loving, family home and she was determined to do the same. Over the last couple of years, Kay had transformed most of the rooms in their house on Church Road, making it bright and welcoming. She and Bernard had wanted the five bedrooms so that it would be easy for friends and family to stay. Kay desired to live in a house full of life, laughter and colour. There was another reason why Kay was eager to complete the work on their home however; one which she made apparent to Bernard as they relaxed in the lounge on the evening of his arrival.

Lay across the settee, resting against her husband's chest, Kay was enjoying the soft, delicate touch of his fingers, as he teased back her hair and tenderly caressed her cheeks. Looking up, she stared dreamily into his eyes and smiled.

"I'm so pleased to have you home," said Kay, softly. "I've missed you."

"And I've missed you too. But we won't be apart for too much longer."

"Yes, and that's what I need to talk about."

"Oh?"

Bernard looked surprised and just a little bit concerned. Kay smiled reassuringly.

"It's nothing to worry about."

Kay raised her head and moved back on the settee. Bernard looked at her closely. He knew that she was about to say something significant.

"Well, what is it?" he asked, encouragingly.

"I'm twenty-five and like you said, I'll soon have you at home. I don't want to wait any longer. I think it's the right time for us to start a family and I want us to start trying right away."

Bernard looked at her thoughtfully. There was nothing he wanted more, but he had always appreciated that Kay enjoyed her job and so had never raised the issue of them having children.

"Are you sure that you don't want to wait longer? You're doing well at work. You could miss out on promotion. You know how much Anne thinks of you and for all the pressures, I know that you love your job."

"Yes, that's true, but I want our children. I want a little Bernard. A 'chip off the old block', just like you."

Bernard shook his head and sighed.

"Well, I'm not sure about that."

"No. I mean it Bernard. Although if there were two of you, it could prove to be a bit much!"

The pair of them began to laugh. It seemed clear to Bernard that Kay's mind was made up, but he still wanted to make absolutely sure that it really was what she wanted.

"But seriously Kay," insisted Bernard, "you have thought it through fully, haven't you?"

"Of course. I've gained enough experience now to hold me in good stead if I feel like returning to the job when the children are older. And we really shouldn't wait any longer, because we're going to need a lot of energy to look after them. Neither of us are getting any younger."

"Yes, that's true," said Bernard, laughing. "You shouldn't have married an old timer like me."

"No, you're not." insisted Kay. "You're handsome and very distinguished."

Kay moved forward and kissed Bernard softly on the cheek.

"And I wouldn't swap you for anyone."

Bernard looked into her soft, green eyes. They were filled with love. How grateful he was that the fates had conspired to bring the two of them together.

"I've not been for any tablets since the last time you were home," noted Kay. Hopefully, it won't be long before I'm expecting."

When Kay and Bernard were alone together, there was no denying the ardent desire they had for one another. Those feelings were heightened by the lack of physical intimacy that was a result of their prolonged periods of separation. Over the following days, the couple made love with passion and intensity, completing that essential spiritual union, without which, true love can never be achieved. There was no doubt that should Kay conceive, it would be as the result of the couple's deep feelings of love and devotion.

Chapter 72

On Saturday May 1st, the day before he was to return to his barracks, Bernard drove Kay down to Alderley Edge. Parking the car, they walked to the famous viewing point. Sitting on an exposed rock, they looked over the green trees and fields spread out before them on the flat Cheshire Plain, extending north towards Manchester. The smattering of houses and hamlets provided a stark, but appealing contrast, to the urban sprawl in the distance. It was quiet and peaceful. The sun was out, with just a few, fluffy white clouds, barely moving across the sky in the gentlest of winds. Sat with his arm around Kay's shoulder, his wife snuggled in beside him, Bernard squeezed her ever so softly.

"It's certainly an impressive view."

"Yes, it's beautiful," replied Kay. "All this wonderful countryside."

"We're blessed to have so much of it around us," continued Bernard. "It's something I'm always telling friends and colleagues about. The rolling countryside of Cheshire, right here to the south of the city and the rugged splendour of the Pennines to the north and east. I'm afraid that most Southerners are convinced that all you'll find around Manchester, are smoking factory chimneys and mile upon mile of crammed, terraced houses. Of course, they're shocked if they come here and find out it's different."

"So, you've been defending the city. I'm impressed. We'll make a real Mancunian out of you yet," said Kay, smiling.

"You never know. I can't ever see us living anywhere else," replied Bernard. "And why would we want to?"

"Do you know Bernard, from being a kid, I'd always felt the same way. Yet now, I can honestly say that you're far more important to me than any place could ever be. If it became necessary, I'd be happy to follow you anywhere and I never believed that I would say that to any man."

Bernard was quiet. He appreciated her sentiments but felt a little embarrassed by the praise she had given him. Quickly, Kay lightened the mood.

"Of course," she observed, "just because I've given you a compliment, don't think that I've gone soft. I'm still the boss, as you very well know, Bernard Foster."

Bernard laughed

"Yes, of course."

Bernard cuddled her gently and kissed her softly on the cheek. Kay nestled contentedly in the warmth of his embrace. Her words had been light-hearted. Theirs was a relationship of equals and Kay trusted his judgement in matters where she acknowledged his greater experience. Kay could do this, because she loved him unconditionally.

"Where is it that you're going to in Germany?" asked Kay.

"The Soltau-Lüneburg Training Area in Lower Saxony. It's south of Hamburg and the river Elbe."

"Is it like here?"

"Well, yes in the sense that it's countryside, but this part of Cheshire is lush and green. Luneburg is sandy heathland and woods and streams. It's a harsher environment than here. The population is small, there's an extensive area that we can use and so it's an ideal training environment for tanks and armoured vehicles."

"Oh. It doesn't sound that nice," observed Kay.

"Actually, parts of it are very beautiful, but then we're not going there to enjoy the scenery," replied Bernard, laughing.

"No, I suppose not."

For a moment, the two of them sat quietly, before Kay returned to the matter of the upcoming exercises.

"As you're so close to leaving, I wouldn't have thought that there was much point in you taking part in these manoeuvres. Wouldn't it make sense for the new officer to take over now? It would give him an early opportunity to lead the men."

"Well, I suppose they could do that, but you have to remember that even after I leave, I'll still be on the reserve list. That means I'm liable to get called up if there's an emergency. It won't do me any harm to take part in the training. It helps me to stay sharp, in case I'm needed in the future."

"But you will be careful, won't you?" asked Kay.

"Yes, of course. There's no need to worry."

Bernard was surprised by Kay's concern. He had been on exercises in the past and his wife had always taken the knowledge of his participation very much in her stride. Perhaps, he thought, it was the fact that he was so close to coming home for good, that had made Kay feel a little nervous.

Next morning, Bernard had to be up bright and early to report back to the barracks. Packed and ready, he and Kay stood at the side of his MGB Roadster, the sports car looking resplendent in racing green and with its sparkling chrome finish. Bernard patted the bonnet and spoke affectionately to the vehicle.

"It's nearing the end for you, old girl. It won't be long before it's time to trade you in for a sensible saloon."

Kay shook her head and sighed.

"I don't know. You treat that car as if it's a living thing."

"Well, along with the MGA, she's been a big part of our lives. We've been all over in her."

"Yes, that's true," said Kay, "but why do you need to trade her in?"

"Well, she's not much use for when the baby comes along. There's not enough room in her. I've to change now. It's all about having everything in place for when 'little Bernard', or 'little Kay' comes along."

Kay laughed, but she was delighted at his sentiments and pulled him towards her. Putting her arms around his waist she hugged him tightly.

"You're puddled, Bernard Foster. You, changing? You've always been Mr Sensible. I've never known anyone more responsible than you."

"Well, I'm just pointing out that I'm ready to take on the challenge of fatherhood. I'm really looking forward to it Kay and I'll devote all my energies to making sure that you and our children want for nothing."

"I know you will," replied Kay. "I'd never have married you if I wasn't certain that you'd always love and care for me. But you can keep hold of the 'old girl' until we find out that I'm expecting."

"Oh, I'm sure you soon will be."

"Yes, no doubt, given the way you've been carrying on for the last few days."

Bernard turned away and Kay chuckled.

"Are you alright?" she asked. "You seem a little flushed."

"Yes, I'm fine."

"Well, you don't look it. Your face is all beetroot. Whatever's the matter?"

"You know what the matter is," replied Bernard, quietly.

"Oh dear. Is Bernard all embarrassed?"

"No."

"I think you are."

"I'm not," insisted Bernard.

"Well, it's not my fault that you're insatiable, is it?" asked Kay, with a cheeky smile.

She was teasing him mercilessly, knowing that he was naturally reticent when it came to discussing their most intimate moments. Yet, as he saw the fun and laughter in her eyes, his inhibitions melted away and he began to smile.

"It's only because, you're so beautiful."

Bernard reached out and drew his wife gently towards him, kissing her softly on the lips. Parting, Bernard indicated that it was time for him to leave.

"I wish you didn't have to go," said Kay, tenderly.

"So do I, but it won't be for very long."

"I know."

"I'll telephone you as soon as I'm back at the base."

Kay nodded.

"Just you make sure you look after yourself."

"Don't worry, Kay. I will."

There was time for one final embrace and then Bernard opened the car door, eased himself into the driving seat and the MGB's engine roared into life. Kay waved frantically as the vehicle moved away, determined that Bernard would see her in his rear-view mirror for as long as possible. Just before the road bent away, Bernard put his arm through the open window and waved to acknowledge her. After that, he was gone. Walking back through the gate and towards the front door, Kay experienced a fleeting sense of unease. Shaking it off, she focused firmly on the fact that in just a couple of months, her husband would be back home for good.

Chapter 73

Before leaving for the Continent, Bernard had phoned Kay regularly and they had exchanged letters when he was at his base in Germany. Once he was on manoeuvres however, communication was impossible. It wasn't the first time that Kay had experienced such periods of isolation and she waited patiently for Bernard to contact her again. As July approached, Kay spent her evenings close to the phone, ready to answer it at a moment's notice. She was beginning to feel a sense of anticipation at Bernard's return. Soon, everything in her life would be complete.

The doorbell rang at eight on Monday evening. It was the twenty eighth of June and Kay was sat chatting with Larry and Robert in the lounge. As her friends worked long hours, Kay hadn't seen either of them for quite a while. Having finished the meal that Kay had prepared for them, Robert and Larry were eager to find out how she had been getting on. Expressing surprise that someone would be calling so late, Kay made her way to the front door. Opening it, she saw a young man standing before her with an envelope in his hand.

"Hello. Is it Mrs Foster?"

"Yes," said Kay.

"I've a telegram for you."

"Oh," replied Kay, surprised.

Taking the telegram from his outstretched hand, Kay watched as he walked back down the path, through the gate and out of sight. Closing the door, Kay made her way back to the lounge. Stopping just inside the room, she looked down at the envelope. Turning it over, she began to feel uneasy, fearful of what it contained. Quiet and hesitant, Kay seemed rooted to the spot.

"Are you all right Kay?" asked Robert.

There was no answer. Kay's eyes were still fixed on the envelope. Its arrival had induced a growing sense of anxiety in its recipient. Getting up from his chair, Larry walked over to Kay and put a hand gently on her shoulder.

"Kay, you need to open it."

"I don't want to."

Her words were said with an air of resignation that suggested the futility of resistance. Sooner or later, she knew that its contents would have to be revealed.

Larry felt uneasy. He was aware that Kay was afraid; concerned that the telegram may contain bad news about Bernard. Yet unless she opened it, there was no chance of putting her mind at rest. But what if it were bad news? Larry hated the thought of being the one responsible for persuading her to confront such a painful situation.

The deep-rooted affection of the three close friends wasn't to be denied. Robert sensed Larry's dilemma and quickly came to his aid. He had lost his father in the War and his mam had told him of the terrible day she had received the telegram informing her of his death. Like Larry, he understood Kay's reluctance to act, but he also knew that she had no alternative other than to open the telegram. Robert would share Larry's burden in convincing Kay to face her fears.

"Yes, come on Kay," said Robert, softly. "You need to find out what's in there."

Slowly, Kay opened the envelope. Reluctantly, she took out the message and started to read. As soon as she did, Kay's heart sank and the tortured words came tumbling from her lips.

"Oh no. Please, no. Please," she begged. "It's not true. It isn't. It can't be."

Kay slumped to the floor. A searing pain shot through her head; her chest heaved in despair. She seemed unable to take in the air, her words choked by the uncontrollable sobbing that rose from the depths of her tortured soul. Her whole world had come to a shattering end. Bernard, the rock upon which her life depended, was no more.

Kay was inconsolable, but somehow Larry was able to get her back on her feet. Slowly and carefully, he guided Kay to the settee and sat down beside her. Meanwhile, Robert had recovered the telegram that had been dropped on the floor. With 'deep regret', it informed Kay that her husband had died from injuries he'd received whilst on manoeuvres at Soltau-Lüneburg.

As she sat quietly on the settee, Robert and Larry assumed that Kay was spent of all energy and emotion, but it proved to be but a short period of respite, as Kay began to question the accuracy of the telegram.

"They must have got it wrong. They have. They must have," she muttered. "They've mixed up Bernard with someone else. You'll see," she continued, lifting her bowed head and turning towards Larry.

He and Robert looked despairingly at one another. They knew that the possibility of such an error was practically non-existent and they had no desire to raise any further, the false hopes that she was desperately clinging on to.

"I'm afraid Kay, that it's not very likely," replied Larry, as sympathetically as he could.

"That's right," observed Robert. "The telegram says that you'll soon receive a letter that will explain matters further."

"But they must be wrong. I know that Bernard would never leave me."

Once again, Kay began to sob, but softer and more laboured this time. Putting a reassuring arm around Kay's shoulders, Larry held on to her in silence. Eventually, it appeared as if Kay had, albeit reluctantly, acknowledged the reality of her loss.

"I want to tell Bernard I love him. I want to be able to say good bye. And I can't."

Hearing the mournful and grief-stricken note in her voice, it was almost impossible for her friends to keep control of their emotions. Her desperate pleas tore at their very hearts and souls. She had always been so determined; the voice of reason that they frequently turned to for advice. Kay had always been there to help them but now, in their turn, they felt inadequate; powerless to stop her being drawn into the very depths of despair. They were desperate to give her some form of reassurance; to tell her that someday in the future, everything would be all right. Yet only the passage of time would allow for such an adjustment of perspective. Anything they attempted to say now, would only appear as meaningless platitudes. Robert and Larry thus focused on securing more practical avenues of support for their vulnerable charge.

"I think I should go and fetch your Mam," observed Robert. "She and your dad will want to know about Bernard and your Mam will want to be here, with us, to help you."

Kay nodded her agreement.

"What about Violet and Norman?" asked Kay, weakly. "They'll be heart broken. I don't know how I'll be able to tell them."

Distressed, Kay struggled to hold back the tears. She was trying hard now to control her emotions. She wanted to put on a brave face for Bernard and show care and consideration for his parents. But this was too stressful a task and putting his arm around her, Larry insisted that he would take care of informing his family.

"Don't worry, Kay. Leave that to me. I'll telephone Roger now and he can go and tell my parents."

"But I should tell them," Kay insisted. "It's my responsibility."

"No, it's fine Kay. My parents will understand and Bernard's my brother. I have a responsibility, too."

"Yes," added Robert, "and it's not wise for you or Larry to tell Violet over the phone. Roger needs to be there to support them when he gives them the news."

Kay nodded. Going out into the hallway, Larry closed the lounge door behind him, before using the telephone to call his brother. Returning, he confirmed that he'd spoken to Roger, who had sent Kay his condolences and was on his way to inform his parents. With Larry free to sit with Kay, Robert was able to drive to Bennett Street, in order to collect Ethel and Ernest. Whilst waiting for them to arrive, Kay sought solace in talking to her brother-in-law about his relationship with Bernard.

"I'm sorry Larry."

"What for?"

"That I didn't think about how upset you must be."

"That's nothing to be sorry for. I understand."

Larry patted her hand reassuringly.

"Do you know, Larry. You couldn't fool me that first time we went to Kent."

"Oh?"

"Yes, when you said that Bernard and Roger didn't approve of your lack of direction. You were so pleased to see Bernard when he picked us up at the station and you chatted away to him like a long, lost friend."

Yes, I did, didn't I?"

"It was so obvious that you were really close to him."

Larry smiled. He noticed the hint of a sparkle returning to Kay's eyes, as she fondly recalled a memory of her husband.

"Bernard was so proud of you Larry. He admired you for doing what you believed in."

"I know Kay. I was silly and immature in those days, wasn't I?"

"Yes, you were. Completely gormless."

The faint flicker of a smile crossed her lips.

"Well, that goes without saying," agreed Larry.

Just over an hour after Robert had left, the doorbell rang. Grabbing Larry's arm, Kay held on tightly. He could feel her trembling beside him.

"It's all right." said Larry. "I'm sure that's Robert. It's about time that he was back."

Kay needed his reassurance, for the sound of the doorbell had reminded her of the arrival of the telegram. Understandably, she was still feeling raw and vulnerable.

"Do you want to wait here, whilst I open the door?"

Kay nodded.

Moments later, Kay rose from the settee and moved quickly to greet her mam. As she snuggled into the welcoming protection of Ethel's warm embrace, for a while, Kay felt safe like a child. Yet a long road lay ahead and whatever temporary respite her friends and family could provide for her, Kay knew that she would have to continue to confront the awful consequences of her loss.

Chapter 74

The following day, Kay awoke at nine. Even though she was physically and mentally exhausted, she had only finally fallen asleep in the small hours of the morning. Quickly getting washed and changed, Kay made her way downstairs where Robert, Larry and her mam were sat in the lounge. It was clear that they had been up for some time. Ethel had already provided a cooked breakfast for the 'boys' and suggested to her daughter that perhaps she would benefit from having something to eat.

"No thanks. I'm fine Mam."

"Well, let me get you a hot drink."

Kay nodded and followed her into the kitchen.

"I'll make another for the boys as well."

Kay watched as Ethel set about making the tea. It was her mam's way of coping with crisis and tragedy. Keeping busy and getting on with it; for what could be gained by doing nothing? There were still jobs to be done and by attending to them, emotions could be held in check.

"Your dad will be here at dinner," said Ethel. "When Robert came last night, he'd already gone to work and I had to leave a message for him at the depot to phone me here when his shift was over. He was going to come right away, but I said that you'd want him to get some rest first."

"Yes, he should," agreed Kay.

Ethel thought of asking her daughter how she was, but it seemed such a ridiculous question. She therefore decided to watch and wait, ready to step in if Kay needed her support. Calling through to Robert and Larry, Ethel placed the mugs of tea on the kitchen table. With the four of them sat together, it soon became apparent that Kay was determined to bring her husband home.

"I want Bernard to be buried in Urmston cemetery. He's not staying in Germany. I want him here, where I can visit him."

"I'm sure you'll be able to do that," said Larry. "We can ring his regiment or the Ministry of Defence, to find out what the procedures are."

"And I also want to know exactly what happened to Bernard."

"The telegram said that a senior officer from the regiment would contact you shortly," said Robert.

"No, I'm not waiting. I'm going to telephone his commanding officer this morning."

Robert and Larry looked at one another. They were pleased to see Kay's strong sense of determination. It was clearly driven by her desire to do the best she possibly could for her husband. Yet they worried about the inherent danger that lay in delving too much into what had happened to Bernard. They knew that under her brave exterior, Kay was struggling to contain her intense feelings of anguish. The revelation of facts and details that may cast Bernard's accident in a contentious and difficult light, could only have the effect of putting her into a situation of utter despair.

"Thank you for staying and helping me," continued Kay, "but you can see that I'm all right and I'm sure that I'll be able to get on with things today."

She reached over the table, patting first Robert's and then Larry's hand.

"No, it's fine Kay, we can both stay and help out if needed," said Robert.

"Yes, of course we can," agreed Larry

"But you need to go to work. Please, I insist."

"No," replied Robert, quietly, but firmly. "At least one of us needs to be here. You've had a huge shock Kay and you shouldn't underestimate it. What you have to do is going to be difficult and tiring and you may well need our support to help you through it."

"Look," said Larry, "if it makes you feel any better, Robert can go in and I'll stay here. I'm Bernard's brother. They'll understand that at work and expect me to need some time to support you. I'm owed lots of holiday time, anyway."

"Yes, they're right love," said Ethel. "It's all well and good being very brave, but think on, Bernard would say that you were just being stubborn and you know that he'd insist on Larry giving you some help. You wouldn't disagree with him now, would you?"

Until now, Ethel had held her peace and her words had a sobering effect. The wise voice of maternal experience bringing Kay to an acceptance of her vulnerability, when her friends could not.

"Okay, Mam. Perhaps you're right."

After Robert had left for work, Kay and Larry agreed that first, they should find out about how they went about the arrangements for Bernard's return. Larry was grateful that Kay was prepared to allow him to make the necessary phone calls, for it proved frustrating trying to track down the information. Furthermore, the off-hand attitude of many of the officials he spoke to, showed little in the way of sympathy for his family's loss. Larry felt sure that Kay would have found the whole process upsetting. It was far better that he supplied her with regular progress reports and made no reference to the callous attitudes of some of the petty officials he encountered.

To be given a definitive answer to his enquiries, Larry was finally directed to the Headquarters of the British Army of the Rhine. He was told that the repatriation of British soldiers who died abroad, wasn't the financial responsibility of the armed forces. This was because there were well maintained military cemeteries in Germany, where army personnel would be interred free of charge. Declining the offer, Larry was informed of the general order that governed repatriation. A number of documents had to be obtained to accompany the coffin on its flight home, as well as a customs certificate. Larry was told to secure the services of an experienced undertaker, who would then liaise with the military authorities in Germany, in order to bring Bernard home.

Larry found it difficult to find many local undertakers with the experience of arranging funerals in such circumstances. Eventually, after many fruitless enquiries, he was successful. As he'd been warned, the costs were high, but Larry was sure that Bernard had left Kay well provided for and in any case, if it were necessary, his parents would step in to meet the costs. The funeral director assured Larry that he would, through his contacts in Germany, get on to the collation of the necessary documents and arrange to have Bernard flown home. As Kay desired, a date and time for the funeral would be secured at Urmston Cemetery.

It had been a long and difficult task to fulfil Kay's desire for her husband's return. It meant that finding out further details about the circumstances surrounding Bernard's accident would have to wait until the following day. Nevertheless, Kay could see that progress had been made on putting Bernard to rest and it helped reinforce her sense of purpose. Bernard had always told Kay about how much he loved her confident and independent nature and it now seemed natural to her that she must continue to fight against her adversity, in order to honour his memory. At tea, Ethel was finally able to persuade her daughter to eat something; an acknowledgement by Kay that she needed to stay strong physically, as well as mentally, if she were to get through the difficult days ahead.

The support of Kay's friends and family was crucial in maintaining her ability to cope. There were emotional scenes when Ernest had arrived in the early afternoon and after tea, when Robert had returned with Anne. Seeing the latter, Kay had thrown her arms around her and squeezed her tightly. Before she left, Anne insisted that Kay must take as long off work as she needed. With her mam, Larry and Robert staying to support her, Kay was grateful that she and Bernard had bought the house on Church Road. Bernard had known how important Kay's friends and family were to her and the extra bedrooms always meant that they would have a place to stay.

Early the next morning, Kay was on the telephone seeking further information about Bernard's accident. Calls to his regiment, the Ministry of Defence and the headquarters of the British Army of the Rhine, proved unproductive. Kay was again advised that a senior officer would be writing to her shortly; that there was no one else available who had any detailed knowledge about the incident. Frustrating as it was, Kay had simply to wait, until a letter arrived for her the day before the funeral. It stated that Bernard and the driver of the Land Rover he had been travelling in, had been killed in a collision with a Centurion tank whilst on active manoeuvres in the Soltau-Lüneburg Training Area. It explained that exercises had to provide a meaningful experience, so were carried out in an environment as close to real combat as possible. As a result, this could occasionally lead to fatal incidents. Unsurprisingly, given that there was no reference to the specific circumstances surrounding Bernard's accident, Kay was far from happy with the response. For the moment however, her concentration would be focused on her husband's funeral.

Chapter 75

Bernard's funeral was arranged to take place at one o'clock on Friday, July 9th and as Kay had wished, her husband would be buried at Urmston Cemetery.

Located at the bottom of Queen's Road, the cemetery was only a short distance from Kay's home. It was a pleasant site and considerably smaller than Manchester's Southern Cemetery, which had become the final destination for most Ardwick residents after their own cemetery had closed in 1950. Unlike Southern Cemetery, the grounds at Queen's Road had none of the ostentatious monuments favoured by the rich, desperate to deny the Christian belief that all are equal in life and death. Kay valued the more intimate surroundings and felt it apt that Urmston was the resting place for other men who, like Bernard, had lost their lives in the service of their country. The majority of them during the two world wars.

When the funeral cars arrived, Kay, Violet, Norman, Larry and Robert sat together in the first. In the second car were Roger, Barbara, Kay's nephews, George and William, Ethel and Ernest. Kay's sister Joan, her husband Colin, Irene, Edna and Anne, made their own way to the service, whilst the soldiers from the Regiment were already waiting at the chapel.

Led by the hearse, the funeral cortège travelled a short distance along Church Road before turning right into Queens Road. Reaching the bottom, the vehicles passed through the entrance to the cemetery, with its two stone pillars. Proceeding slowly along the driveway, they turned sharply to the left. Around fifty yards ahead, through the trees on either side of them, was an imposing stone tower. Topped with a red tiled roof, it rose above an archway through which could be seen the rest of the cemetery beyond. Passing through the trees, the mourners could see that the tower was attached to two symmetrical chapels. The latter had large, arched windows and steep, red tiled roofs. There was a prominent stone crucifix attached to the far, gable end. Approaching the archway, the hearse turned left and came to a halt; the two funeral cars pulling in behind.

Waiting to receive the hearse were members of Bernard's regiment. They looked sombre and respectful in their number two, service dress uniforms. Sliding the coffin, draped in the union flag, out from the vehicle, four of Bernard's comrades raised it on to their shoulders. Followed by Kay and Larry at the head of the mourners, the men carried Bernard through the entrance to the chapel, placing him next to the altar. Holding back the tears, Kay held on tightly to Larry's arm. For days, she had been focused on the arrangements for the funeral, but now that the moment to say farewell to Bernard had finally arrived, the awful reality of life without him could no longer be ignored. Yet Kay's spirit didn't falter, for it was incumbent on her to thank all those who had come to say farewell to her wonderful husband.

There was no doubt that through all her difficulties, Kay had been sustained by the conviction of her faith and the belief that in the future, she and Bernard would be reunited. She thus took great solace from the service: the prayers; the readings and the singing of two of her favourite hymns, 'Abide with Me' and 'Amazing Grace.' Touching too was the minister's eulogy and the heartfelt tributes delivered by Larry and Sergeant McPherson on behalf of the regiment. As she stood at the graveside, Kay knew that this was no farewell. Bernard would remain in her heart and mind, his wisdom and experience, guiding her through the testing times ahead.

Back home for the reception, Kay was overwhelmed by the affection for Bernard that was evident from the men in his unit. It was a fine summer's day and Kay had opened up the back garden, accessible through the French doors of the dining room. Gathering his comrades, Sergeant McPherson had asked Kay to accompany him outside, where he presented her with a small bronze figure of a sapper and on its base was an inscription to Bernard from the men of his unit. Kay tried to respond, but with the tears beginning to flow, her words of gratitude, simply wouldn't come.

"That's all right, Mrs Foster. We understand. You take your time. There's no hurry."

The sergeant's gentle Scottish burr felt comforting to Kay. Sandy McPherson was in his late twenties. Able and experienced, he had served with Bernard for several years and Kay was aware of the trust that her husband had placed in his loyalty and judgement. The soft red hue of his hair and moustache, were in contrast to his alert, blue eyes and the fading scar that still lingered on the side of his face.

Slowly recovering her composure, Kay was finally able to express her gratitude for their gift. Spending time speaking to Bernard's men, Kay was touched by their heart-warming recollections of serving under him. It gave her access to the part of her husband's life that she had not been privy to. The positive portrait they painted of him, increased further the intense pride she felt in being married to him.

"Your husband was very popular, Mrs Foster," declared Sandy McPherson. "All the boys liked him."

"Yes, they've been very kind in telling me so. But please Sandy, call me Kay."

Sandy nodded. It was clear to him that Kay was no typical officer's wife. She didn't stand on ceremony and had genuinely welcomed his men into her home, grateful for their presence. Friendly, considerate and exceptionally pretty, Sandy understood why her husband had been prepared to give up his life in the regiment for her.

"Not all officers are as well liked as the Major," continued Sandy.

"Yes, I assume so."

"Your husband was firm Kay, but always fair. He was prepared to stand up for the boys if he felt they were being treated unfairly and they knew that he'd listen to their problems and try to help them if he could. You don't get too many officers like that. They'll miss him."

As Kay began to circulate among the other mourners, Sandy approached Larry.

"You're Major Foster's brother, aren't you?"

"Yes, that's right."

"I'm Sergeant McPherson. Sandy."

Sandy offered his hand and Larry shook it firmly.

"You served with Bernard then?" asked Larry.

"Yes. We were together for quite a time."

"Then I assume you took part in the manoeuvres on Soltau?"

"Yes, that's right," replied Sandy.

"Do you know what happened to Bernard? We've been told it was an accident and were promised further details. As yet, we haven't heard a thing."

Sandy averted his eyes, his feet shifting on the spot. It seemed clear to Larry that his request had made the sergeant feel a little anxious.

"Well, I'm not sure what I can tell you. I wasn't with your brother when it happened."

"But you must be aware of some of the details."

Sandy hesitated, clearly uncertain as to whether he should speak further about the incident.

"I understand, if you're reluctant to talk," continued Larry. "But we'll treat whatever you tell us in confidence. We don't want you to get into any trouble. We just want clarity."

Sandy looked closely at Larry. He was sure that if he was anything like his brother, then Larry would be a man of his word. Sandy nodded his head and breathed in deeply.

"Okay. But remember, whatever I'm going to say, you didn't hear it from me."

"Yes, of course," confirmed Larry.

"We were on night time exercises. Your brother was travelling in a Land Rover that collided with a Centurion tank. He died of his injuries, as did the driver. A couple of sappers were thrown clear, but were still badly injured."

"But how's that possible? Surely the driver couldn't have missed a Centurion?"

"It happens all the time because they make the exercises as tough and realistic as possible. They deprive us of sleep so that we learn to do without it, but it means that there are cases where drivers simply fall asleep at the wheel and accidents follow. Tanks and vehicles also have to operate without their lights on, to make them less visible to the enemy at night. It's very likely that's the reason the driver hit the tank. He couldn't see it."

Sandy paused. He could see that Larry was shocked. Most soldiers' relatives would be too, if they knew how dangerous going on manoeuvres could be.

"But surely, it's stupid to put men in so much danger. It is peacetime after all."

"There are complaints, from MPs for example, but they insist that if they don't prepare us properly, we'll have no chance when the Russians attack. We're told that it's being done for our benefit and the Army, of course, doesn't encourage you to question anything. They sweep as many of the incidents and accidents under the carpet, as they can. The Army of the Rhine and the MoD reveal few details about those that do emerge. I doubt that you'll be told very much at all."

"What you're saying, is that fatalities and serious injuries are happening all the time."

"Yes. I know of three other fatal accidents involving Centurions. Some TAs were crushed by one when they were sleeping. The crew of another were electrocuted when they brought down some high voltage cables and a radio operator was trapped and killed when his tank fell into a river."

"It sounds like going on manoeuvres is as dangerous as going to war."

"Well, it's not quite that bad, but you do need to have your wits about you. Even then, things happen that are out of your control."

"Yes. Clearly," replied Larry.

"There's just one thing," said Sandy. "I've told you what I know, but perhaps you need to think about how much of it, should be passed on to Kay. Losing her husband is bad enough. Thinking that it could have been avoided and not being able to do anything about it, could really hurt her. I'd hate to see that."

Larry understood Sandy's warning, but armed with the information he had been given and his personal belief in the pursuit of the truth, he was facing a difficult dilemma. Later that evening when Kay and her mam had gone to bed, Larry sat down with Robert and related to him the details of his conversation with Sandy.

"What he's told you about the attitude of the Army and MoD Larry, is spot on. You know that yourself. Uncovering the truth about incidents that happen on manoeuvres is almost impossible. MPs don't get very far making enquiries on behalf of their constituents, so I don't see how we could help Kay get any further. Besides, even if you could uncover evidence of culpability, there won't be any action taken. You've got the little matter of Section 10 of the Crown Proceedings Act to deal with. That prevents military personnel, or their relatives, from bringing claims against the Crown for personal injury or death, caused by other members of the British Armed Forces. So, whoever was responsible for the accident, you can't sue the MoD."

"You seem to know rather a lot about this," said Larry, surprised.

"That's because I looked into it as soon as Kay said she wanted to find out more about what had happened. I also came across suggestions that there's actually a higher rate of injury and fatalities for soldiers on training exercises, than in combat. The Army doesn't actively report or record accidents on manoeuvres however, so it's not official."

"Well then, we surely have an obligation to force them to acknowledge the truth of what's happened to Bernard. Even if training has to be as realistic as possible, that doesn't mean that it should result in someone's death. This is about a blatant disregard for life and the MoD needs to be held accountable. We should be supporting the removal of crown immunity from prosecution where the Army's concerned. It's the way the MoD will be forced to improve its standards and ultimately save lives. The MoD's insistence on policing itself, is completely unacceptable."

"Yet we still don't have any comprehensive legislation to ensure safety at work in civilian occupations," replied Robert. "In that case Larry, how far do you think you're going to get?"

"But surely, Kay has a right to ask for answers and also to expect that any issues will be addressed. What's happened to Bernard, shouldn't happen to anyone else."

"And going through that whole process, just how is that going to make Kay feel any better? It's just going to extend the pain and the upset. She really doesn't need that. Come on, Larry. Think about it. We can get Kay to pursue it, in order to do what you think is right, or we can do what we both know is best for her. And that's allowing Kay to put this unfortunate business behind her, so that she can start to move forward with her life. She mustn't know about what Sandy told you. We can't be responsible for allowing her to carry that burden. Let's keep it to ourselves."

"I suppose so," replied Larry with a sigh. "Of course, it's easier for you to do."

"Yes, it is."

Robert wasn't annoyed by Larry's claim. His comment had been made without any hint of censure and Robert couldn't deny that it was true.

"I accepted a long time ago," continued Robert, "that there are times in life when you have to forget all about your moral conscience. With matters like this, it really is for the greater good."

Chapter 76

Next morning, Kay came downstairs to find her mam sat in the kitchen nursing a cup of tea. Ethel was quiet, reflecting on the events of the last two weeks. She had proved a tower of strength for her daughter, freeing her from the routine of domestic responsibilities. She had also provided the crucial emotional support that Kay could turn to in her darker moments.

"Oh, hello love. You're awake then?"

"Yes."

"Sit down, I'll make you a brew."

As Kay sat at the table, her mam filled the kettle and emptied the teapot, disposing of the old tea leaves before going to the cupboard to take out the mugs, tea and sugar. Walking over to the fridge, she took out a bottle of milk and turned to her daughter.

"I have to say that before staying here, I didn't see the use of having a fridge, but they come in handy at times, don't they?"

"Yes. You should get one Mam."

"No. I'm not like you love. I shop every day, so I wouldn't have any use for it."

"And you're sure that's not the only reason?"

"What do you mean?"

"Dad. He wouldn't like spending money on fancy 'mod-cons' now, would he?"

"Well, you're not wrong there. But you know as well as me, that if I put my foot down, he'd have no choice."

Ethel was pleased to see the trace of a smile on her daughter's face. It was the one thing that worried her; the fear that having lost Bernard, Kay would never again experience any happiness in her life.

"I made the boys some breakfast before they went to work. They wanted to wait until you got up, but I told them that you'd want them to get off."

"You should have woken me up Mam. I can't be staying in bed until nine o'clock."

"And why not? You've been through a lot and you must have found yesterday tiring. You can't be doing too much, too soon love."

Kay nodded. She accepted that for the moment, her mam was right. Yet Kay also felt that before too long, she needed to get back to the regular routine of work, for if she didn't, she may lose all sense of purpose in her life.

"I've been thinking love. When Bernard's mam and dad come this afternoon, you should invite them to stay for a weekend."

"Yes, I asked Violet and Norman to stay here before the funeral, but they insisted that I had enough to worry about besides looking after them. That's why they booked into a hotel."

"Like you Kay, they've had a terrible loss and now you're the closest person to Bernard that they have. I know that you already do, but it's important that you continue to keep in touch with them. Seeing you, will help keep their memories of Bernard alive."

"I know Mam. I intend to. It's helpful for me as well, because it's a reminder of Bernard's life before he met me."

"When they get here," continued Ethel, "I'll nip out and run a few errands. It'll give you and Violet the chance to spend some time together on your own."

When Bernard's parents arrived, Ethel welcomed them with tea, sandwiches, biscuits and cakes. Even at such trying times, it was a point of honour that Bernard's parents would return home with their appreciation of good Northern hospitality intact. After engaging in some polite, but restrained conversation, apposite for the circumstances, Ethel duly made her excuses and left. Shortly after, Norman indicated that he needed to take the car to be checked at a local garage, before their long journey home. Just like Ethel, Norman realised that Kay and Violet needed some time on their own.

At the funeral, the solemnity of the occasion had denied the two women any real opportunity to share their grief with one another. Now, alone in Kay's lounge, the two women hugged each other tightly. Feeling the genuine warmth of Violet's affection, Kay found it difficult to hold back the tears. Breathing deeply, she tried hard to control her emotions.

"It's all right. Have a good cry."

Violet's voice was soft and soothing. Leading Kay over to the settee, she sat down beside her, waiting patiently for Kay to settle.

"I'm sorry," whispered Kay.

"Why?" asked Violet, surprised.

"Because I'm only thinking of myself. You've lost your son. Your grief is as great as mine."

"Oh, Kay. You are silly. There's no one less selfish than you."

Violet put her arm around Kay's shoulder and gave her a gentle squeeze.

"Norman and I both feel that when you married Bernard, we gained a daughter. That's not just some fanciful comment. It's the truth. For us, we can still be here for our son, by always being here for you."

Kay was quiet, overwhelmed by Violet's heartfelt words.

"You do understand what I'm trying to say. Don't you, Kay?"

"Yes, I think so."

"When I first met you," Violet continued, "I was so grateful for the kindness you had shown towards Larry and as I watched you that weekend, it didn't surprise me that you made such an impression on Bernard. Meeting you, gave him a chance of happiness that he could never have had if he'd simply stayed in the Army. I'm so grateful to you for that."

Since their conversations together during that first visit to Kent, Kay and Violet had struck up a rapport unusual for women so different in age and experience. In the period that followed, their relationship had grown closer and after Kay's marriage to Bernard, they spoke on the telephone at least once a week. It thus made it easier for Violet to broach a subject that could have been potentially embarrassing for her daughter-in-law.

"I hope you don't mind me asking Kay, but without Bernard, are you going to be able to manage everything financially?"

"Yes, I'm fine."

"Are you sure?" asked Violet.

Knowing how proud and independent Kay was, her mother-in-law was determined to seek some reassurance.

"Yes," Kay replied. "Larry helped me to look into what my entitlements are and I'm to receive a gratuity from the Army for Bernard's accident and I'll receive a war widow's pension too.

I'll also have my salary from work and Bernard had substantial savings and investments too. We put a large deposit down on the house, which means that the mortgage is relatively small. I won't have any problem being able to pay it off."

"It's a big house," observed Violet. "You don't think that it might prove to be a struggle trying to maintain it?"

"Don't worry, I'm sure I won't have a problem being able to manage. We wanted a large property. Plenty of room for a family. We'd looked at lots of houses and none of them took our fancy and then we saw this one and loved it. Bernard and I lived here together. It's our house. I couldn't envisage living anywhere else."

"I'm sorry Kay," said Violet, concerned that she may have upset her. "I didn't mean to suggest that you should consider moving. It's just, that if it did prove difficult to manage, Norman and I would be more than happy to help you with any unforeseen expenses."

"It's all right. I know you didn't mean anything by it."

Kay reached over to Violet and held her hand, eager to reassure her that the offers of assistance were appreciated.

"Bernard has left me very well provided for and with my job too, money isn't going to be a problem. There's no need for you and Norman to worry and I wouldn't hesitate in coming to you for help and advice, if I felt I needed it."

"Thank you, Kay. That's all we need to know. I don't want you thinking that we're interfering. We're just concerned. That's all."

"I understand and I hope that it's not too long before you come back for a visit."

"It won't be. Bernard was always telling us that there's no better place to take a break than Manchester. He was becoming a real Northerner and for that matter, Larry's not far behind either. You've had quite an effect on the family, haven't you, young lady?"

Violet's comments were light-hearted, but warm and generous.

"You must come and stay with us too," Violet continued.

"Yes, I'd love to."

When Norman and Ethel had both returned, the conversation reverted to more conventional matters, but as the two women stood by the garden gate, waiting for Norman to start the car, Violet gave Kay a final piece of advice.

"You must look after yourself. You're still young and you've so much to offer. I know that Bernard would be upset to think of you hiding yourself away and not getting on with your life and work. He was so proud of you. He didn't think twice about leaving the Army, because he wanted to be beside you, giving his support to everything you wanted to do. Now isn't the time to hold back. That's not what the woman he married, would do."

Chapter 77

By Monday morning, Kay was keen to get back to work and contacted Anne to say that she would like to return the following morning. Although Anne tried to persuade her to leave it for another week, Kay was insistent and so reluctantly she agreed, with the proviso that she stayed in the office for the next few days. Ethel also feared that her daughter was too eager to return and insisted on staying on for a further few days, in order to ensure that Kay was eating properly and coping with being out of the house. By the end of the week, Ethel felt confident enough to return to Bennett Street, where Ernest had surprised her by proving quite competent in taking care of himself in her absence.

As August arrived, Kay was faced with a situation where she had gone without a period for the past three months. At first, she had thought it probable that her metabolism had been affected by the trauma of losing Bernard. Recently however, she had been suffering from bouts of morning sickness. Kay could only conclude that she was expecting and therefore went to her surgery to request a pregnancy test.

Entering the consulting room, Kay was disappointed to see the figure of Dr Scott. Sat behind his desk, he was peering at some papers, indicating that they were of far more importance than affording his patient the common courtesy of acknowledging her presence. Kay had specifically asked to see one of his colleagues, but it seemed as if her request had been ignored.

Scott was a rather shabby man in his late fifties. His jacket looked rumpled, his tie was slightly askew and his shirt was frayed around the collar. His lank, grey hair was swept over the top of his head, in an unsuccessful attempt to disguise his baldness. With his wild, bushy eyebrows and moustache, he reminded Kay of Groucho Marx. When she'd met him before, Kay hadn't been impressed by his demeanour. He had been in private practice, but now in the NHS, he assumed an attitude of superiority, even arrogance, towards his patients. This was hardly surprising, given their obvious gratitude for the free medical services that they could now access through him.

"Take a seat," said Scott, rather gruffly.

Kay moved the chair to the side before sitting down. It was a small gesture, but significant in indicating that she wasn't daunted by her environment. Finally, looking up, Scott noted the pretty young woman in front of him.

"What can I do for you?" he asked.

"I was expecting to see Dr Brown. Isn't he available?"

"He's been called away. If you're ill, you won't mind seeing me. Will you?" he asked brusquely.

Scott looked at her closely. Kay would prefer not to discuss the matter with him, but this would confirm to Scott his suspicions that she was here to waste the surgery's time; a malingerer in fact. Consequently, Kay proceeded to tell him about her symptoms and explained her situation and asked if he would arrange a pregnancy test for her.

"Don't you realise the expense and the strain on the NHS young lady, if I agreed to every such request? To every fanciful notion that some giddy female has got into her head. Besides, you're obviously fit and healthy, so we wouldn't want to test you anyway. We don't need to send you any sooner to the ante-natal clinic. It isn't likely there would be any problems, even if you were pregnant."

Dismissive and indifferent, Scott's attitude only stiffened Kay's resolve.

"You say 'if I were.' You think I'm imagining all this, don't you? Well, my body is telling me that I am pregnant and as I've explained, I need to know, sooner rather than later. I can assure you that I'm not 'some giddy female' and I find your remark insulting. If my husband had been here, you would have never dared say such a thing and I won't stand for it either."

Kay stared at him fiercely. Just for a moment she saw a look of uncertainty flicker across his face. Yet sat behind the security of his desk and armed with a deluded belief in the infallibility of his professional expertise, his confidence in the utter certainty of his conduct and opinion, held firm. Staring straight back at her, he was silent. No apology would be forthcoming.

"If necessary, I'll pay for you to arrange a private test."

Scott smiled.

"My dear," he replied, condescendingly. "You're just wishing that you're pregnant. You've lost your husband and you're desperate for a child to help you hold on to his memory. It's a classic case. You might desperately want it to be true, but I can assure you that it won't be."

His words were brutal; uttered without tact or diplomacy. There was a bitterness in his voice; a barely disguised anger that she had continued to question his professional opinion.

"Well, regardless of what you say," replied Kay, "I insist that you arrange a private test. Then we can see which one of us is right. If you're so certain it's you, then you won't mind refunding the money if you're wrong, will you?"

Now, it was Kay's turn to smile.

"Huh! I can assure you that I am right. You'll just be wasting your money. My advice to you, young lady, is to get on with your life and forget these fantasies."

Hurriedly writing out a form, Scott handed it to Kay.

"Take this with your sample to the receptionist. She'll tell you what the fee is, which I'll expect you to pay when you come back to see me in three days for the result."

"Of course. If you're right."

"Oh, don't worry about that. I will be."

Returning as directed, Kay was surprised to find that it was Dr Brown who was waiting for her.

"I'm afraid that Dr Scott's had to attend an emergency, so he's asked me to see you."

Kay smiled in the knowledge that she had been vindicated. Scott would never have given up the chance to gloat at her expense.

"I'm pregnant, aren't I?"

"Yes, Mrs Foster. I'm delighted to tell you that you are."

"Well, it's nice to know that I'm not just an over imaginative, highly-strung female. Not that I ever thought I was."

Brown looked at her confused, obviously unaware of the heated exchange between Kay and his colleague.

"I see that you had a private test. Why was that?" asked Brown. "We normally offer them on the NHS."

Kay briefly explained what had happened, adding that it was her understanding that should he be wrong, Scott had accepted that he would meet the costs.

"Don't worry, Mrs Foster. I'll try to make sure that you don't receive a bill. If by chance you do, bring it to me at the surgery."

"You can count on that," replied Kay, with a smile.

"I've already written a letter of referral to the ante-natal clinic at Park Hospital," continued Brown. "You should receive an appointment from them in the next few days. You seem to be coping with your loss and are looking after yourself. Hopefully, things will run fairly smoothly."

The following week, Kay duly received an appointment with the hospital. On the same day however, she also received a letter from the surgery. Sent out under the authority of Dr Scott, it informed her that she was no longer on the list of practice patients and would have to find a new GP. She had been 'struck off'.

Chapter 78

Although delighted to receive confirmation that she would be having Bernard's child, Kay immediately realised that it had brought about a change in her circumstances and had therefore left her with a decision to make. The savings and investments that Bernard had left her, would be heavily drawn upon if she were to give up work for any prolonged period of time. Kay was mindful of the help that would be available from Bernard's parents, but as Violet had suspected, her daughter-in-law was far too independently minded to take advantage of their offer. Kay thus decided that she would remain in her post until the baby was due. She would then give up work for the following year. After that, if Ethel agreed to help look after her grandchild, she would seek further employment.

Informed of Kay's news, Ethel and Ernest were delighted. The baby would be their first and probably, only grandchild. The couple knew that Joan and Colin had decided against having any children and after Bernard's death, it seemed that the chance of being grandparents, had passed them by. When Kay told them about her plan to take a year off after the birth and then return to work, Ethel was quick to offer her support.

"I hope you'll be leaving him with me."

"Of course, Mam. That's if you're sure you don't mind."

"Mind! You cheeky mare! Who is it that's looked after you all these years and still does? And you've turned out all right, haven't you?"

Ernest burst out laughing.

"Steady on love. Calm down. You'll do yourself some damage if you're not careful."

"Calm down? I've never been so insulted."

"I'm sorry Mam."

Kay looked suitably contrite, but was having to work hard at trying not to laugh. Her dad, who was still chuckling away, wasn't making it any easier.

"You make out that what you're asking me to do, is something special," continued Ethel. "You know very well that round here grans always look after the kids so their mams can go out to work."

"Yes, I do Mam, but I didn't want you to think that I was taking you for granted."

Kay's words had an immediate and soothing effect on her mam.

"As if I could think that of you love," she said softly. "Don't be so daft."

Throwing her arms around her daughter, Ethel gave her a big squeeze.

"Careful love," said Ernest. "She's pregnant."

"Don't be so gormless!" replied Ethel, her ire rising once more following the ill-considered words of her husband. "She's not a China doll. She won't break! And anyway, I don't recall you being bothered when I was pregnant on Kay and our Joan."

"That's because I wasn't here. I was away doing my bit for King and Country."

"But you were here all right to enjoy yourself and leave me expecting. Weren't you?"

Ethel looked intently at Ernest who rather sheepishly, looked down at the floor. Unable to contain herself, Kay broke out into laughter.

"See love," said Ernest, his face still red from embarrassment after Ethel's comment. "Your news has put me in the doghouse now."

Kay shook her head; her sides were hurting. She was desperate to stop laughing.

"Come on love. Settle down."

Kay felt her mam's arm around her shoulders. Her soothing voice and her warm embrace, eventually quieting her.

Secure in the knowledge of her parents' support, the following morning Kay told Anne her news. The latter was delighted, but also expressed her concern when Kay indicated that she intended to work right up until the baby was due.

"As you're nearing the end, surely it's going to be harder for you to get out and about."

"No, I'm sure I'll be fine. Most women are."

"Well, I'm going to make sure of it," insisted Anne. "You'll only be working in the office, once I think you need to take it easy."

"You mustn't do that," replied Kay. "I don't want to be given any special treatment. It wouldn't be fair to expect someone else to have to take over any of my case load."

"Well, I'm afraid I'm the one in charge and you're just going to have to do as you're told. Besides, I've lost count of the number of times that you've covered for others in the department and without ever a word of complaint."

"I suppose so," said Kay, with an air of resignation.

It was clear that Anne wasn't going to change her mind. Just like Ethel, she was determined that Kay would be well looked after in the weeks and months ahead.

"You don't have to be so stubbornly independent. Sometimes you need to take the help that's on offer. It's not a sign of weakness to do so."

Anne paused and looked intently at Kay, determined to reinforce her message.

"I hope you don't mind me asking," she continued, "but I assume that Bernard's parents will be wanting to help."

"I haven't told them that I'm pregnant yet, but I know they will," replied Kay. "They've already offered to help me, so I'm sure that they'll be even more prepared to do so now. But I've thought it through. If Bernard was still here, I'd have taken a long break from work, but without him, everything has changed. I'm determined to support our child myself. I want him or her to be proud of me; to know that I can protect them and that they can always depend on me. I'm not daft; I know that being a parent brings more financial commitments and I've worked out how I can manage. I'll get my maternity allowance for eighteen weeks and Bernard's savings and my widow's pension will see me through the first year. I've talked with my Mam and she's eager to look after her grandchild as soon as I want to go back to work. From then on, my wages will enable me not to use up any more of Bernard's savings."

"Well, I'm sure that you won't be short of opportunities to get another post. You know yourself how difficult it can be for us to retain staff. I'd be very surprised if we didn't have an opening here when you decide to come back."

Anne was right and even if Manchester had no vacancies, others would surely be available in one of the many surrounding authorities. Kay knew that when she left work, she would have to stick rigidly to her financial plan, but she felt confident that she could do so. Growing up, she had experienced the care with which her mam had managed the tight family budget and she had learned the value of frugality and prudence. When it came to the question of money and possessions, Kay was a firm believer in traditional values. These held that you could only have what you could afford to pay for and firmly rejected the rise of consumerism, funded as it was by the explosion of needless credit. Grateful for what she had, Kay would have little difficulty in providing a secure home for her child.

Chapter 79

With her intended course of action set firmly in her mind, that evening Kay prepared to telephone Violet. She couldn't help feeling more than a little nervous. Her mother-in-law had always shown her understanding. Theirs was a friendly, open and honest relationship; a fact reinforced by their conversation after the funeral. Nevertheless, Kay's pregnancy had changed the situation and she worried that Violet may disagree with her intention to return to work so soon. Kay was concerned that any expression of disapproval could drive a wedge between them. As Kay picked up the receiver, she hesitated. For a moment she considered whether it would be better if she waited. Perhaps by telling Bernard's parents her news in person, there would be less chance of any misunderstandings. Yet, by delaying too long, would Norman and Violet gain the impression that she didn't see them as being an important part in their grandchild's life? That certainly wasn't true. Through them, Kay knew that her child could learn everything about their father in the years before she and Bernard had met. All things considered, Kay took a deep breath, composed herself and dialled the number.

It was Violet who answered, unable to hide her delight at hearing Kay's voice.

"Kay! It's good to hear from you. Are you well?"

"Yes, I'm fine."

"Good."

Kay paused slightly before continuing.

"I've something to tell you."

"Oh?"

"Yes. I'm pregnant."

The words were unexpected. Violet had to check that she had heard Kay correctly.

"You're pregnant?" she asked, quietly.

"Yes."

"Oh Kay, that's wonderful, I'm so, so pleased …"

Violet's voice tailed off. Waiting for her to continue, Kay heard the sound of quiet sobbing at the end of the line.

"Is everything alright?" asked Kay, concerned.

"I'm sorry Kay. I ..."

Violet's voice faltered once more and the tears returned.

"Don't worry. Take your time. My news must have come as quite a surprise."

Kay waited. She heard a cough and then a sharp intake of breath.

"It's the thought that Bernard's not gone completely. You're having a child Kay. Bernard will always be with us. We haven't lost him."

"I know," replied Kay.

"You do. You understand?"

"Of course. Although I know that Bernard's spirit is always with me, our child will be an ever present, physical reminder of him."

"That's right. Your parents must be delighted," continued Violet. "Their first grandchild."

"Yes. My Mam especially."

"Kay?"

Violet paused.

"Yes?"

"I hope you don't mind me asking and you can tell me to mind my own business, but are you going to be able to manage when you stop work? Norman and I can help. You're going to have a lot of expense. I know you made it clear to us that you were fine after we lost Bernard, but this has changed matters. Hasn't it?"

Although Kay had felt anxious before making the call, her concern for Violet when she had become upset, had dispelled her nerves. She now felt confident in relaying her plans for her pregnancy and beyond. Whilst she spoke, Violet listened quietly and patiently, without interruption. When she had finished speaking, Kay sensed that her mother-in-law was prepared to accept her decision.

"There's no denying it will be tough for you," commented Violet. "Norman and I understand that you want to retain your independence and we both admire you for that. But do look on us as a kind of safety net. If you ever need us to help out, as we've told you before, you mustn't hesitate to ask."

"I want you to be proper grandparents," explained Kay. "If you want to buy anything for the baby, such as clothes or toys, please do. It's just the bills and everyday expenses. I need to deal with those myself. I appreciate it's difficult that we live so far away from one another, but I hope you'll come to see the baby regularly and stay with us. When he or she's older, I'd love to be able to bring them to come and stay with you."

"Of course, you can. You know that you don't need to ask."

In the remainder of their conversation, Kay reassured Violet that she would look after herself and pointed out that she had Ethel, Ernest, Larry and Robert keeping an eye on her, as well as Anne at work. Finally, Violet realised that she had yet to inform Norman of the news and so in order to do so, the two women said their farewells.

Kay was delighted that the telephone call had passed off so successfully. Her relationship with Bernard's parents remained intact. She had made it clear that she had no intention of excluding Norman and Violet from their grandchild's life. Furthermore, Kay knew that if she did ever find herself in real need of financial help, she had been given further reassurance that Bernard's parents would be there to give it.

Chapter 80

On Thursday, November 18th 1965, the Labour MP for Wythenshawe, Alf Morris, took advantage of prime minister's questions in the Commons, to ask Harold Wilson about the government's attitude towards the reform of the House of Lords. The second chamber was dominated by the Tories and as such, it was proving obstructive to the passage of much of the Labour Government's proposed legislation. Traditionally, the Conservatives had dominated the Lords and as Morris had correctly identified, this was due to the fact that well over half of the members were hereditary peers. As the latter were unelected and naturally drawn towards the Conservative Party, there had long been calls for their removal. Morris asked Wilson if he would introduce legislation to exclude hereditary peers from the second chamber. In reply, the prime minister had expressed his disappointment at the opposition his government had encountered in the Lords, but he refused to support Alf's proposal.

Early next morning, whilst working at his desk, Larry was approached by the paper's political editor, Bill Young. A popular figure in the office, Bill's receding hairline, ruddy cheeks and rather prominent nose, belied the fact that he was a hero of the Normandy beaches. His affable personality and desire to encourage, rather than reprimand, made him different to most senior figures at the *Evening News* and as such, he had the genuine loyalty of those who worked under him. Just having arrived, Bill asked Larry into his office and told him to take a seat. Taking off a rather smart tweed jacket, he removed his pipe from the right-hand pocket, before hanging it carefully on the back of the chair behind his desk. Striding back towards the door he asked one of the juniors to fetch him a cup of tea, then rolling up his shirtsleeves, a sign that he was ready to get down to work, he settled into his chair.

"This exchange between Alf Morris and Wilson in the Commons yesterday, it's an issue that won't go away."

"Yes," replied Larry. "Alf's questions were hardly unique."

There was a pause as Bill opened a drawer in his desk, pulled out a tin and placed it down before him. Taking off the lid he took a pinch of tobacco from inside and started to press it carefully into the bowl of his pipe. Satisfied, he took a couple of puffs before applying a match. As he drew on the stem once more, the tobacco began to burn. As the smoky aroma began to fill the room, Bill settled back contentedly into the conversation.

"It's time for us to review just where we are with the second chamber," Bill continued. "Big Tom wants us to produce a special feature and I don't see any reason why you can't handle it."

By now, Larry was well established as a political correspondent at the *Evening News*, but he was still surprised that the paper's political editor had trusted him with the assignment. Given that the reform of the Lords had become such a pressing and contentious issue, Larry had expected that the task would have been taken on by a more senior figure.

"What are your initial thoughts?" asked Bill.

"Wilson acknowledged the fact that in the past session, the government's social legislation had been 'mauled'," replied Larry. "That's a strong word to use, yet he expressed no interest in Alf's proposals. He insisted that it wasn't the right way to deal with the issue. I think it's important that he tells us just what he thinks the right way is."

"You know Harold. He never likes giving anything away."

"I'm not surprised, because he's obviously well aware of the dangers that there are in raising the issue. It's one of several that could cause a potential split in the party. The left has always been hostile towards the Lords. With only a four seats majority, Wilson can't afford that."

"Yes, indeed. It gives you a good opportunity to examine the attitudes of the Tribune Group."

"And it shouldn't be too difficult to dig out something substantial to use on the attitudes of Harold and other members of the cabinet, towards the second chamber. We mustn't forget that he was once a Bevanite, just like Richard Crossman and Barbara Castle."

"They've re-invented themselves a bit since then," replied the editor, with a chuckle.

"I'll also ask our local Tory members what they thought of Alf's attack on hereditary peers. Moss Side's Frank Taylor is always good for a quote or two."

"Yes, that's important. Big Tom's bound to be taking a close interest in what you come up with and I don't have to remind you that he's going to be insistent on seeing balance. Make sure that you cover all angles and opinions."

Larry worked hard over the following week. Submitting his finished article, he felt rather pleased with the result. It wasn't long however, before he was brought back down to earth. Called in by Bill, it was made clear to Larry that it just wouldn't do.

"Big Tom's not happy and I'm afraid he's right. The article lacks balance and you're going to have to change it."

"Lacks balance? In what way?" asked Larry, clearly surprised.

"It reads like a manifesto for Tribune. You've hardly given any serious consideration to arguments supporting the retention of the hereditary principle."

That's not true," insisted Larry. "I've pointed out that hereditary peers make up some of the most active members of the House; that they have more potential to be independently minded than political appointees and that they're a link with tradition."

"Yes, but then you undermine those arguments, making it clear that in your opinion, they aren't valid. You're well aware Larry, that you shouldn't have done that. Stick to the details of the arguments for both sides. Our job at the *Evening News* is to present the facts and details and let the readers decide for themselves."

"I don't see how that's entirely possible when dealing with an issue such as this," argued Larry. "If I have put my opinions across, I don't see it as a problem. After all, it's only what our readers think. Mancunians don't hold with the notion that the will of the people should be held back by belted earls and others of their ilk."

"Some Mancunians do Larry and Big Tom won't have the paper becoming overtly political. You've done well since you joined us. Don't spoil a promising career by failing to work within the parameters set by the proprietors and the editor-in-chief. Make the necessary changes, re-submit the article and reassure Big Tom that you can follow instructions."

Bill had ended the conversation with some positive words of encouragement, nevertheless it had been a stark reminder to Larry that there were strict limits to what he was allowed to write. He had forgotten the golden rule. Just like the leader writers, political correspondents were being employed to use their literary skills to represent the attitudes and values of the newspaper's proprietors and they had to adapt to that reality if they wanted their career to progress. Larry enjoyed his job and certainly had no wish to put it at risk. Nevertheless, the incident made him all the more determined to work in an environment where he would have more freedom to express his own social and political observations and pursue the issues that he cared about. As yet however, it was clear that the chance of being able to do that, lay well in the future.

Chapter 81

Kay's baby was born in Park Hospital in the early hours of Friday morning, February 4th, 1966. A boy, it was only natural that Kay would name him Bernard in memory of his father.

Ethel and Anne had persuaded Kay that she should give up work a couple of weeks before she was due. Ethel had gone to stay with her, insistent that her daughter shouldn't be alone at such a potentially difficult time. It had been Ethel who had called the ambulance when Kay's waters had broken. She had accompanied her daughter to the hospital and had been present in the delivery room when the birth had taken place. It was a strange experience for Ethel. Having twice gone through the process of delivery herself, she could empathise with her daughter's situation, yet without having to physically suffer any of the pain and stresses of labour herself. With the delivery suffering no complications and the midwife satisfied with the condition of both mother and son, the pair of them were quickly back on the ward.

Eager to return home and with little Bernard healthy and content, Kay persuaded the ward doctor to discharge her three days after her admission. His agreement was based on the knowledge that, although this was her first baby and she was an inexperienced mother, Kay wouldn't be alone in caring for him. This was because Ethel had insisted on staying with her for the foreseeable future, overcoming the concerns that Kay had expressed about such an arrangement.

"What about Dad?" Kay had asked.

"It was his idea that I should stay. He doesn't like the thought of you being left all alone."

"But who's going to look after him if you're not there."

Ethel laughed.

"Your dad's not like other men. He's not useless. He can cook and tidy up. He's managed well enough over the last couple of weeks."

"Couldn't he come with you?"

"No, love. How would he get to work? It's not just around the corner from here, is it now?"

Ernest's shifts had meant that he was unable to get to the hospital during visiting hours, whilst Violet, although desperate to see her new grandson, said that she and Norman would wait until Kay was settled back at home. Anne, Larry and Robert had all been to see the new arrival before Kay was discharged. The former, having decided some time ago that she would never marry, now had another young child upon whom she could dote, to add to her beloved nieces and nephews. Only briefly did Anne reflect upon her childless state, but as she told Kay, she had the advantage of being able to indulge little Bernard without the parental pressure of responsibility. For Larry and Robert, the birth brought an understanding, not fully realised after her marriage, that Kay's situation was different to their own. She was still the beautiful, kind, happy and determined young woman that they had admired for so long, but now she was a mother and unlike them, her focus and aspirations would be on her son's future, rather than her own. Having known Kay for so long, Robert recognised that her responsibilities as a mother, brought his own situation sharply into focus. Whilst Kay had always been selfless; he remained stubbornly selfish.

It had been a happy occasion the following Sunday when Norman and Violet arrived to see little Bernard. In fact, it was quite a gathering. Ernest, who wasn't working, had been able to make his way to Church Road, as had Larry, who was also taking the opportunity to see his parents. Later in the afternoon, Joan and Colin had turned up to congratulate Kay on her little arrival too and just before tea, Robert, his mam and gran, came to pay their respects. Organised as ever, Ethel had laid on a fine spread for Kay's visitors. Endless drinks of tea, plates of pies, cakes and sandwiches.

Holding her grandson for the first time, Violet couldn't help shedding a tear. In little Bernard had returned the spirit of her son and she cradled him carefully in her arms. Through him, came hope. A belief that his life would help soften the sense of loss she had suffered when her son had been so cruelly taken from her.

"Come on now," said Norman gently. "You'll be upsetting the little chap."

"Oh, he won't mind," said Ethel, quietly. "He knows that they're only tears of joy."

Calm and contented, little Bernard was passed from one person to another without any hint of objection. Ethel and Violet couldn't have agreed more on how good natured he was; so much more than their own babies had been.

"We can't all have been that bad," said Kay, smiling. "I always thought that with the passage of time, memories became more positive."

"I think it's just because Nanny and Grandma have been mesmerized by their new grandson," suggested Larry.

"No, I don't think so," insisted Violet. "You always needed to be picked up as a baby, or you wouldn't shut up."

"Well, there you are. You can't argue with that," said Robert, laughing.

"You were no different lad," noted Edna. "You were always a windy baby. Why, the times me or your mam have had to march round the kitchen for hours on end, patting your back."

"He's still full of wind now," added Larry

As the room erupted into laughter, Robert and Larry thought it best to blend into the background. They'd learned that their elders were every bit as sharp as themselves and they had no wish to suffer further embarrassment. As they listened to the chatter around them, the pair were quietly amused at the constant comments referring to various parts of little Bernard's appearance, in terms of their resemblance to one or both of their parents.

"Don't people always do that?" asked Larry. "Insist that a baby is just like their parents, even though their features will change so much over a relatively short period of time."

"Yes, I suppose they do," replied Robert. "It's almost as if they want to reassure themselves that the parents were given the right baby when they came out of the hospital."

"Well, it's a bit late by then to start worrying about it."

"It certainly is, but I don't have to worry about that," remarked Robert.

"Why?"

"I was born at home of course. They couldn't have mixed me up."

"That must have been a disappointment for them," noted Larry, with a chuckle.

All the time that Robert had been chatting to Larry his eyes kept being drawn across the room towards Joan, who was deep in conversation with her sister. She looked as gorgeous as ever, wearing a beautiful two-piece, yellow pencil dress that hugged her figure tightly. She still held with the fashion of wearing long white gloves, which complemented her white hat and heels. He hadn't seen her since their liaison at the Grosvenor Hotel and the memory of that afternoon had his pulse racing momentarily. As Kay went to hand Bernard to her sister, Joan insisted on taking off her gloves, laying them carefully on a small occasional table to the side. Robert noticed how uncomfortable Joan had become, finding it awkward to hold her little nephew next to her. Unlike her sister, Joan certainly wasn't the maternal type and once again, Robert recognised that she was much like himself. Aware that parenthood would require to some degree, the sacrifice of self, for Joan, children were simply not an option. Giving her little nephew back to his mam, Joan made her way towards the refreshments. Making his apologies to Larry, Robert followed her.

Speaking to Joan quietly in the corner of the room, Robert posed a cheeky question.

"Seeing little Bernard hasn't got you all broody then?"

"I should think not."

"Well, Kay seems to have fallen into motherhood very easily. Being a parent must have some merits."

"And I'm sure you really believe that," replied Joan, laughing.

"Well, I suppose not," said Robert, smiling. "Kay's different to the two of us though and the little lad will always remind her of Bernard."

"Yes, our Kay's always put others first, so caring for a baby comes naturally to her. I suppose it's what annoyed me so much when I was growing up. She was always so helpful and considerate, even when I was horrible to her."

"But you two are okay now, aren't you?"

"Kay's always been fine. I was the one that needed to grow up and accept that the two of us are so very different. She chose her way and I chose mine. As you know, I'm not like you. I don't find the time to meet up with Kay that often, but when I do, I'm always pleased to see her."

Robert nodded and smiled. It pleased him to hear Joan talking so positively about her sister. His reaction didn't go unnoticed.

"You're still in love with her, aren't you Robert?"

The words surprised him. The conversation had taken a more serious turn and he struggled to reply.

"I thought so," continued Joan.

Robert looked at her closely. There didn't seem much point in denying the obvious.

"I always have and I suppose I always will. But I've had to accept that we'll never be together. Bernard was perfect for her. Loyal and steadfast. You knew all those years ago, didn't you, that I was too weak to be the same."

"Does it ever make you unhappy?" asked Joan.

"Not really. I've always been quick to accept reality. I have ambitions in the job and I'm happy to have casual relationships and no commitments. Most of all, I know that Kay will always be my best friend. We just have a different type of relationship. That's all."

Time was getting on and soon the guests began to leave. First, were Joan and Colin, followed by Robert, his mam and gran. Larry and Anne then departed leaving Kay, Bernard and both sets of his grandparents. It wasn't long after opening hours, that Ernest suggested that he and Norman should go to the pub. Happy to talk freely among themselves, the three women offered no objections.

Kay was delighted with how well Ethel and Ernest, Norman and Violet, continued to get on with one another. She had seen so many examples of families where the poor relationships between in-laws had caused arguments and division. Kay was grateful that little Bernard would be able to draw on the love, knowledge and experience of two sets of grandparents, who came from such very different backgrounds. When Norman and Violet returned home the following day, Kay reminded them that they were welcome back at any time. She also told them that when little Bernard was old enough to cope with the travelling, Larry had told her that he would accompany her down to Kent for a weekend's visit.

Over the next few weeks, Kay got well into the routine of caring for her son. After dealing with the household chores in the morning, after dinner she and Ethel would take him out in his pram to the shops and walk him around Chassen Park or take him a little further to Flixton Park and Gardens.

"It's far better having a baby in the summer," Ethel had told her. "At the moment the weather's cold and you can't have him outside in the garden for very long, without stopping what you're doing. You'd better tidy up your flowerbeds and get your seeds and bulbs planted, before I've gone home."

As Bernard's christening approached, Kay felt comfortable with the idea that it was time for her to begin to cope on her own. She was feeling increasingly guilty that her dad was having to manage alone, yet she could see how attached her mam was towards her grandson and feared that if she suggested that it was time for her to return home, she would get upset. In reality, Kay needn't have worried. When she indicated that she and little Bernard would be able to manage after the christening, Ethel had expressed her satisfaction at Kay's decision.

"Yes, I'm sure you'll be fine. It'll give me a chance to get straight again. I know your dad tries his best, but I've no doubt that the place has been going to wreck and ruin whilst I've not been there."

"But you told me that dad would be fine. That he could look after himself."

"You forget love. He's a man. He tries his best but just like most men, he's gormless, bless him."

Kay burst out laughing. It was an amusing outcome to a potentially tricky situation.

Chapter 82

On Sunday morning, March 20th, Kay was stood beside the font of St Paul's. She was holding little Bernard in her arms, ready to pass him over to the vicar. Her son was now six weeks old and it was time for his christening. Anne Martin, Robert and Larry, the chosen godparents, were ready to make their commitments to the child as friends, family and members of the congregation, looked on.

There was never any question that Bernard Junior wouldn't be baptised. Both his parents had been and Kay herself was a young woman of faith. She also knew that both Nanny Ethel and Grandma Violet wished him to be, although neither tried to exert any influence on her decision. As Kay's connection with St Paul's went back over many years, there was never a chance that she would choose to have the service at the local parish church in Urmston.

Robert and Larry were amused when Kay had asked them to be two of Bernard's godparents. At first, they thought that she was joking; an error on their part as Kay made it clear that she would never treat lightly, any serious decision about her son. When they found out that the christening service required them to affirm that they would encourage their godson to 'walk with them in the way of Christ,' their concerns were raised.

"But surely, Larry and I aren't what you're looking for Kay," suggested Robert. "We're not Christians."

"Well, I beg to differ," replied Kay, with a smile. "Whether you like it or not, you both hold Christian values. In most things, you'll set a good example for Bernard."

"Yes, but …"

"No buts," said Kay, cutting Larry off. "I've already discussed it with the vicar and he says that in this day and age, with the decline in the number of communicant members of the Church, good moral character is what they expect in a godparent. I assured him that you met the criteria."

"Are you sure?" asked Larry, smiling. "What about Robert and his girlfriends."

"Hey," replied Robert. "That was below the belt."

The pair of them broke out into laughter, before a sharp reprimand from Kay, brought them to heel.

"Enough! This is serious."

Chastened, both looked at her apologetically.

"Honestly. The two of you. You're just like a couple of kids."

She fixed them both with a steely stare. Although a number of witty responses had immediately entered their heads, neither dared utter a word. They knew well enough not to antagonise Kay any further.

Circulating among the guests in the church after the conclusion of the service, Larry and Robert were approached by Peter Jardine, who introduced himself to them.

"I wanted to say hello. Kay's a good friend and she's done some excellent work with young people through St Paul's for many years now. All of us here think a lot of her."

"We do too," replied Robert. "No one else could have persuaded us that we'd be suitable choices for godparents."

"That's certainly true," added Larry, smiling.

"I'm sure Kay told you that shared values are what's important for the role. We're realistic here and I hope you don't mind me saying that if someone so good and kind as Kay has chosen you as her closest friends, then you must both be of very good character. Being a godparent can be as much or as little of a commitment as you choose to make it. We see how the world is changing. There are those that say religion has had its day. I don't agree, but diminishing congregations, here and throughout the country, can suggest otherwise. As journalists, you have to be aware of how few of your pages are now filled with church matters."

"Well, certainly in the nationals and large regional papers like the *Evening News*. But the small, local weekly papers still have a healthy concentration on local parish matters," replied Robert.

"The nationals will be quick to jump on any hint of scandal though. Catholic or protestant. It'll get plenty of copy," remarked Larry.

"Not the kind of coverage that's ideal though," observed Peter.

Larry, nodded in response.

"As well as godparents," continued Peter, "You'll be uncles to Bernard too. You're going to be important in providing him with a fatherly presence."

Larry looked confused. Robert quickly explained Peter's words.

"When he says 'uncles', he's using the term loosely, as we do in Manchester. When kids are growing up, neighbours keep an eye on them. They become just like aunties and uncles who look after them if their parents aren't around. It's what makes me Bernard's uncle too."

It was now Peter's turn to look confused.

"As you can tell by his accent, Larry's a Southerner," explained Robert. "A bit of a toff too. I'm always having to explain the Mancunian heritage to him."

Peter laughed.

"Well, I'm sure you'll both do your best for Kay."

Looking across the church, the three men watched the beautiful young mother as she mingled with the guests. They knew that Kay must have felt deep sorrow that her husband wasn't there to share this moment, yet she put on the bravest of faces, giving time and consideration to all. Kay had learned to be pragmatic. She had a son to care for and imperfect as this world now was for her, his future was her most important priority.

Chapter 83

Nineteen sixty-six had brought with it the safe arrival of Kay's son, but just like other mothers, she was well aware of the dark clouds that had been hanging over the Manchester region since the arrest of Ian Brady and Myra Hindley. It was back in October that the shocking details about the Moors Murders began to be revealed to the public. Horrific in their nature, the terrible crimes not only impacted on the fears and emotions of the people of Manchester, but on those across the country and overseas too.

Employed on the *Evening News*, Robert and Larry couldn't help but be affected by the emerging story, but the latter, who had steadfastly stuck to his role as a political writer, wasn't connected to the articles and features related to it, as was the case with Robert. Having already spent time attached to the crime desk, Robert found himself part of a small team dealing exclusively with the police investigation, Ian Brady and Myra Hindley, the victims and their families and finally, coverage of the trial itself. Running from April 19th to May 6th the trial, held at a special court room at Chester Assizes, led to the conviction of Brady and Hindley for the murders of Edward Evans and Leslie Anne Downey. Brady alone, was found guilty of the murder of John Kilbride.

Given the importance of the story, Robert had been engaged on research and outdoor assignments around the clock. This had given Larry little chance to speak to him about the case. Through other members of the team however, he learned that unknown to his bosses, Robert had been interviewing many with close connections to the victims and their families and had been passing on the information to contacts in Fleet Street. Larry was well aware that local journalists would often freelance for the national dailies or the Sunday tabloids; especially when they came across shocking or salacious stories that their own editors would refuse to handle. Court proceedings were the most lucrative area for this kind of opportunity and in the past, Larry knew that when covering trials dealing with matters of public decency, prostitution and houses of ill repute, Robert had submitted short, sanitised accounts to the crime desk, whilst sending full, unadulterated copy to Fleet Street. This contained all the smutty details needed for the titillation of the readers and Robert was paid handsomely for his efforts.

With the extraordinary and serious circumstances surrounding the case against Brady and Hindley, Larry was concerned about his friend's behaviour. Not only was Robert acting in a way that may endanger his job, but just as importantly, Larry was concerned that Robert's actions and those of others like him, may be undermining the Crown's case against the accused. Larry's fears increased when, at the start of the trial, it emerged that David Smith, the key prosecution witness, had been offered £1000 by the *News of the World* for an exclusive following the expected conviction of Brady and Hindley. For a time, the revelation threatened to undermine Smith's evidence. Justice Atkinson however, concluded that the evidence given in court under cross-examination, wasn't significantly different to that Smith had originally given to the police. Smith's evidence remained admissible, but Atkinson condemned the newspaper's "gross interference with the course of justice."

After the trial, when Robert and Larry finally had a chance to go for a drink together, the latter raised the issue of David Smith and the *News of the World*. The resulting conversation proved difficult. They were long-time friends, yet both held strong opinions which, at times, seemed almost irreconcilable. As they both put forward their views on what they considered to be responsible journalism, it became very clear just how far their careers and aspirations had diverged.

It was Larry who began.

"Paying off Smith like that. The *News of the World* could have undermined the whole case against Brady and Hindley. What did you think when the matter was raised in court?"

"I thought we were coming out for a quiet drink," replied Robert. "I've been working non-stop on the case for weeks. I want to forget about it now."

"But it's important, Robert. I want to know what you think."

Robert realised that his friend wasn't going to let the matter drop and somewhat reluctantly, he gave his response.

"I don't think the *News of the World* did anything wrong. Justice Atkinson himself said that it didn't make any difference to Smith's evidence. I don't really see what your point is."

"But surely you must recognise that it could have done. Don't you think that the *News of the World* should have held off approaching him until after the trial?"

"No, I don't," insisted Robert, who was starting to find Larry a little irritating. "If they'd done that, they'd have lost out on the story to a rival. Smith was already considering other offers. Do you think those editors would have held back on a deal, if they'd been given the chance to make it?"

"No, of course not. But that's only because they think that they can act with impunity. Atkinson had a chance to order proceedings against the *News of the World*, but he didn't. If he had done so, there would be far less chance of the press trying to interfere in criminal trials in future."

"You sound like you'd support those demanding statutory regulation of the press."

"Well, perhaps that's the answer."

"I'm sure you don't believe that," replied Robert, somewhat dismissively. "No self-respecting journalist would."

"I suppose not," said Larry, with a sigh. "The Press Council's no use though, is it? We're hardly likely to be enthusiastic about supervising ourselves. The industry always puts its own interests above those of the public."

"Not always. The *News of the World* were taking a big risk signing up Smith when they did and they were supporting the public's right to know more about Brady and Hindley, from someone who had a real insight into their characters and backgrounds. If the public weren't interested, then the *News of the World* would never have acted."

"Oh, come on Robert, you know very well that the only consideration that mattered to the *News of the World*, was money. Profit. That's what's driving them. They don't give a damn about the trauma that the victims' families have had to go through."

Larry's withering broadside wasn't appreciated by his friend. Angrily, he decided that he should let Larry hear some home truths.

"Ultimately, that's the business we're in," replied Robert. "It's less about winning a Hannen Swaffer Award than plugging into the mains circuit of public emotion and so selling copy. If you want to succeed in this business Larry, it's what you have to do. The World as you'd like it to be, just doesn't exist. You need to start dealing with the reality of the industry and with your ability, you can go all the way."

"I can't accept that," replied Larry, quietly. "We're here to serve a greater purpose."

"Oh? What's that then?"

"To pursue truth and stand up for justice. Not to exploit our sources, but treat them fairly and with respect."

"Ah, I see. I understand now. I know what this is all about," replied Robert, somewhat abrasively. "People have been talking. Haven't they? You think that I was wrong to approach the friends and family of the victims. Don't you?"

There was a pause as Larry looked uneasily at his friend. He was beginning to regret ever starting the conversation, but now that Robert had brought out into the open, the matter that was really at the centre of his concerns, he knew that they would have to continue. Thankfully Robert, now feeling a little guilty at his rather brusque manner, offered him some reassurance.

"Go on Larry. It's okay. We need to get it all out in the open. It's the Northern thing to do," he added, with a smile. "You never know, you may find out that you and others have misjudged me."

Larry nodded. He was pleased that their friendship didn't seem to have been compromised.

"I think Robert, that sometimes you need to take a step back so that you're able to see what's morally right. It was a misjudgement on your part to push them for information."

"You've got me all wrong Larry. No money changed hands. It wasn't like with Smith. And you've been too quick to judge my motives. They're not what you think they are. In fact, my concern has been, as you call it, the search for justice. To do my little bit to help ensure that Pauline Reade, John Kilbride, Keith Bennett, Lesley Ann Downey and Edward Evans got that. They were kids and those two animals needed to pay the price."

"Okay," replied Larry. "Explain to me what you've been doing then."

"It started with my CID contacts from Bootle Street when we were having a drink in the 'Abercrombie'. They've given me some good stories whilst I've been working on the crime desk and they like how I've complimented them on various collars. They said their colleagues in Cheshire had Brady and Hindley bang to rights. They wanted to make sure that the two of them would never see the light of day again. They suggested that if they gave me the names of those who were close contacts to the victims and their families, that I could write articles which would bring home the devastation that those two bastards have caused."

"The intention might be good, but what you've done is still wrong and your connections in the CID should have known that," noted Larry. "If the evidence against the pair was overwhelming, why risk publishing information and comment that might sway a judge or jury? At the very least, it risked handing the defence the opportunity to claim that their clients could never get a fair trial."

"You say that what I did was wrong, but what Brady and Hindley did was more than wrong; it was pure evil. People had to be left in no doubt that the cell door needed to be slammed shut and the keys thrown away. Public opinion can make sure that they will never, ever be set free. I'd have no hesitation in doing it all again."

"I understand Robert," replied Larry, sympathetically. "Surely though, you were putting your own career at risk by using information from potential witnesses."

"The biggest risk, was ensuring I kept the bosses at work in the dark, not letting them find out what I was doing. To create a bigger impact, my contacts wanted the information I gained to get a national audience, so I was freelancing and sending material to Fleet Street. Obviously, I made sure none of it was attributed to me."

Larry breathed in deeply, taking time to consider what Robert had told him. Perhaps, after all, he'd misjudged his friend. Yet he wasn't naïve enough to think that Robert's behaviour had been entirely altruistic.

"Nevertheless, you must have put some credit in the bank, if you're determined on that move to Fleet Street," suggested Larry.

"I'm not the only journalist whose worked on the murders. There's been lots up here, scratching around for all the major titles."

"Yes, true. Not many of them have your advantages though, given your local knowledge and connections."

"I won't lie to you Larry. If the fact that I've provided information does help to get me the move to London that I've always wanted, then I'll grab it with both hands. Yet," Robert emphasised, "my motives over this case were always to nail Brady and Hindley as hard as I could. Whether you believe me or not, is up to you. But I know that I don't have a problem looking at myself in the mirror."

As far as Larry was concerned, Robert's acknowledgement of his ambitions, made the account of his actions all the more convincing. He recognised that his friend was at a crossroads in his career. For some time, Robert had been growing restless at the *Evening News* and although there were opportunities to advance his career by working for one of the Northern editions of the national dailies, he was increasingly drawn towards Fleet Street. Robert had never lost his childhood ambition to explore the world beyond Manchester and the perceived bright lights of London were an attraction that he found impossible to resist. Not long after the trial, Robert's wish was fulfilled. By providing copy to one of the Fleet Street teams investigating the murders, Robert had aroused the interest of their paper's editorial team. Once aware of the varied roles he'd successfully taken on at the *Evening News*, Robert was invited down for a rather informal interview. Offered a post as a senior journalist, initially focusing on celebrities and entertainment, Robert enthusiastically accepted. Finally, he had his opportunity to show that he could make good outside his native city.

Chapter 84

Monday morning, August 1st. Robert walked on to the concourse at Piccadilly Station and made his way to the ticket office to pick up his first-class single to Euston. The *Daily Gazette* had paid for him to travel on the new Manchester Pullman service. It was a generous gesture and one that suggested that his new employers were trying to impress him.

Moving along the platform, carrying his rather battered suitcase, Robert watched as a number of business types, wearing expensive suits and rain coats, were approached by uniformed stewards asking to carry their bags. The conduct of the latter, bordering on being obsequious, proved embarrassing to a working-class lad like Robert, who had grown up detesting the advantages of privilege. He was well aware that their attitudes were shaped by their desire for recompense. The Pullman was the train that bright and early whisked businessmen away to their deals in the 'City' and returned local politicians to Westminster. Well-heeled passengers, they tended to tip big. Robert was eyed dismissively as he made his way along to his carriage door. Smiling to himself, he realised that there would be no one coming to help him get his case on to the train.

During the journey, Robert left his compartment to stretch his legs along the corridor outside. Reaching the end of the carriage, he saw an old steward taking the opportunity to smoke a quick cigarette. Nodding towards Robert, the two of them had soon struck up a conversation.

"You're not a regular on here lad, are you?"

"Is it that obvious?"

"Your suit tells us you haven't got much. You've not paid a lot for that, have you?"

"You're not far wrong there" replied Robert, grinning. "It hasn't the cut of the cloth of most of your passengers. I could tell that the other stewards weren't impressed, by the way they were weighing me up on the platform before I boarded the train."

"Don't take it personally, but they wouldn't want to waste time lugging your bags around for nothing."

"Oh. Thanks."

"Well, it's the way things are. You don't get a fortune from the Railways for doing this job. You have to supplement it with tips and thankfully, a lot of these gents are pretty generous. Not because they necessarily like us or appreciate our help, but giving us a good tip, confirms their status. It reassures them that everything remains nicely in its place. Them up there and us down here," he added, raising and then lowering his hand for additional effect.

Robert was impressed. He recognised a keen wit, sharpened through years of experience observing his so-called betters. No doubt he'd left school at thirteen; probably whilst the Great War had still to run its full course and had grafted hard ever since.

"But don't you get sick of kow-towing to them? It's got to be difficult at times. I saw how arrogant and dismissive a lot of them were. I don't think I could take it."

"No lad. You don't understand. There's only ever one winner between us and them and for all their money and fancy jobs and titles, we'll always come out on top. Don't get me wrong, a fair few of our regulars are decent. Take the Lever brothers, Harold and Leslie. Genuine blokes fighting for us at Westminster. On here most Monday mornings and always speak to us with respect."

Robert was intrigued.

"Why did you say that you always win? It doesn't look like it."

"You're slow on the uptake lad. For us, it's a game. The stuck-up ones are being played and the silly bastards don't realise it. All that matters to us is the tip. What's a few words and the odd little bow when in return, we're getting a nice juicy tip? You see, they can't control what you're thinking. Whilst I'm smiling at them, my mind's telling them what complete arseholes we all think they are. But of course, they'll never know that. Afterwards, we all have a good laugh about it."

"I see," said Robert. "I suppose I can't argue with that."

"You wouldn't believe the gifts I've been able to get for the missus and decent presents for the kids at Christmas, thanks to those tips. Given the shifts I have to work and the hours away from home, it helps keep the wife happy too."

Robert nodded.

"Well, I suppose it all comes down to how well-off you are," continued the steward. "If you've a well-paid job and plenty of money, then you can afford to be more selective about how you treat people. Those such as us, don't get that luxury. As our old pal Lenin used to say, it's a means to an end!"

Robert chuckled.

"So then, I suppose you're all flying the red flag out on the Manchester Pullman?"

"Too right. Long live the Workers' revolution. Not that it'll come in my lifetime."

"Probably not," replied Robert.

"The times passed; the enthusiasm's gone," noted the steward. "When I came back from Hamburg at the end of the War, we were full of enthusiasm. A Labour landslide and we were going to create a Worker's paradise. But where is it? They didn't even do half the job. Don't get me wrong, it's better than it was, but our so-called leaders cosied up to the bosses and they're the ones still in control and calling the shots. It wasn't just Beeching who ripped the guts out of our industry. There were lines being closed down right from the start of nationalisation and Attlee's lot were in on it. Over 240,000 jobs have gone on the railways since 1948; no bright new world for those lads hey?"

Robert nodded sympathetically.

Taking a final draw on his cigarette, the steward pulled down the window and threw it outside.

"Well, I'd best be getting back before I'm missed."

"Okay" said Robert, nodding a quick farewell.

Yes, things were changing, but in a way that neither the steward or Robert's own father had anticipated when they had started out in their fight against fascism. The former had learned to adapt and he was more than just managing to get by. It was true that things were better now, but the brave new socialist world that he and his comrades had dreamed of, was still well out of reach. And now a young generation of bright, aspirational working-class men like Robert, less idealistic than their fathers, saw the chance of creating their own new world. Yet theirs would be one in which the individual would grasp the opportunities for personal advancement and material fulfilment, rather than fight for collective class responsibility and security. Robert wasn't going to Fleet Street to exercise an altruistic desire to influence national opinion in the fight for a fairer society. His purpose was to pursue wealth and social standing. Robert had spent his childhood in the streets of Ardwick and for all that it had shaped his character, his academic and vocational success, had begun to distance him from the community he'd valued so much. Leaving behind his life in Manchester had proved an easy decision. He was heading for the big city; the centre of everything. There were exciting opportunities ahead and he was determined to take them.

Chapter 85

Arriving at the *Daily Gazette*, Robert was taken straight to the office of Frank Mellis, the paper's editor-in-chief. When Mellis had interviewed him, Robert realised that he was in the presence of a man who had a very different personality to that possessed by his boss at the *Evening News*. Whereas Big Tom's exacting manner could easily strike fear into his subordinates, his new editor seemed good natured, relaxed and approachable. That impression was quickly reinforced as Mellis warmly shook Robert's hand and invited him to take a seat.

Frank was in his early fifties and like Robert, was the product of a working-class background. His grandfather had been employed by *J. T. Morton* in Aberdeen and had then moved south to London to work for the company when they opened up a new cannery on the Isle of Dogs. Frank's father had found employment in the docks, but his son became a copy boy on the *East End News* and established himself as a senior journalist before moving on to Fleet Street. Frank's reputation had been made during the War when, as a fearless front-line reporter, he had accompanied the troops from the Normandy beaches to the river Elbe. Although he came from hardy stock, Frank was slight of stature. He still possessed a full head of hair, but it had long since turned grey and his kind smile and gentle, blue eyes suggested a docility that was far from the truth. Frank was a tough character who had worked hard to make it to the top. He possessed an instinctive understanding of the shifting interests of his readers, against the backdrop of an ever-changing world and he had the capacity to take tough decisions. Frank prided himself on being a fair boss, but he expected hard graft and loyalty in return and he wasn't one to suffer fools gladly.

"We're expecting a lot from you son. I phoned Big Tom before we invited you for interview. He was very complimentary. I realised that you must be good, if Tom Henry thought you had promise. So, I think I've backed a winner and now you've got to show me that I'm right. I can tell you one thing; succeed and you'll have every chance of advancement here at the *Gazette*. And remember. Any problems and my door's always open."

Robert nodded. His new editor's approach seemed so different to those he'd worked under at the *Chronicle* and *Evening News*. He suspected that it would take some getting used to.

"Thank you, Mr Mellis."

"Call me Frank. I don't need any fawning minions to convince me that I'm still the boss. We're all in this together and when I delegate authority, I want to give it to confident, independent thinkers who aren't afraid to show initiative."

Frank paused and looked closely at Robert, before continuing.

"But make no mistake. If I think you deserve a rollicking, then you'll get one."

Robert laughed. He couldn't help it, but had no reason to fear his boss's reaction. Frank approved. In their meeting, Robert was alert and attentive and clearly looking forward to the new environment he would be working in.

"You've got a big opportunity son. At one time we'd cover stories on the odd entertainer or film star and only rarely would we give them any prominence. Now everything's changing. Our readers, especially the younger ones, can't get enough of these new celebrities. It's your role to keep your finger on the pulse; spot emerging trends, get us meaningful interviews and produce the best features. Music, film, television, even football. I want you spotting the upcoming stars and getting them in the *Gazette*. We've got to be ahead of the competition on this one."

"Football?" asked Robert. "Wouldn't that be in the remit of the sports desk?"

"You didn't think that at the *Evening News*."

"Well, I'd already worked in the sports department. It seemed acceptable for me to produce articles on the exciting talents that City and United were producing."

"Yes, but you also saw that a new type of young, celebrity footballer was emerging, who reflected the trends and fashions off the field, as well as performing on it. Lots of our female readers couldn't care less about the latter, but are fascinated with the former. That's why I've given you a free hand to approach any players you like. We all work for the common good at the

Gazette. You'll not find any problems from colleagues on the sports desk."

Robert nodded, clearly pleased with Frank's reassurance.

"You've managed to fix yourself up with somewhere to live then?" asked Frank, changing the subject.

"Yes, I managed to find a small terrace in Barking. Suffolk Road near to Upney tube station, so it's handy to get in," replied Robert. "I wouldn't mind, but I could have rented three houses in Manchester for the same money."

Frank laughed.

"You Northerners are all the same, aren't you? Desperate to get value for money. You can say goodbye to that. As you've found out, your money doesn't go anywhere near as far down here. That's why you get paid a lot more than your colleagues in Manchester."

"Oh well. I suppose that lets me know that the wage increase you offered me wasn't because you thought I was anything special."

Frank chuckled. He liked the young man. He was confident and assured, but he also had a good sense of humour and certainly didn't take himself too seriously. The signs were promising. The editor-in-chief of the *Gazette*, felt sure that his new employee was going to prove a successful addition to the team.

Chapter 86

Just over six months later, Robert was back in Manchester. Since moving to London, he'd already returned to the city to visit his family and friends, but this was the first time he'd been back in a professional capacity.

Robert's visit was occasioned by the announcement that George Best would be opening a boutique in Sale, with his friend and business partner, City's Mike Summerbee. The event provided an ideal opportunity to approach the young Irishman for an exclusive interview, in return for a feature article that would give national exposure to the new venture. The fact that Robert knew George from the time he'd reported on United for the *Evening News*, had helped the *Gazette* secure access to the young star. Given that association, it seemed clear that if the assignment were to be a guaranteed success, Robert couldn't delegate it to anyone else.

Known as *Edwardia*, the new boutique was located on Cross Street, part of the busy A56 that made its way to Old Trafford and central Manchester. The opening was scheduled for Wednesday, March 15th and when Robert arrived with a photographer, well before George was due, the pavements were already packed with spectators. The police were hard pressed to control the expectant and excited crowds, as the event threatened to bring the traffic to a standstill. As his photographer busily snapped away, Robert realised just how huge a star the boy from Belfast, still only twenty years old, had become. It was just a year since George had exploded on to the international football stage, when he had scored twice against the Portuguese giants Benfica and run their defence ragged as United thrashed them 5-1. With his 'mop top' haircut and good looks, the press dubbed him 'El Beatle'. It was a turning point for the game, as George became the first footballer to enter the world of celebrity.

George had certainly become an icon for the young. Although it was a school day, many kids had decided that the prospect of being punished for wagging school was worth it, as they strained for a sight of their hero. Young, female shop assistants too, had deserted their posts, eager to get close to their heartthrob. When Best and Summerbee finally arrived, accompanied by United stars Pat Crerand, Denis Law and Shay Brennan, as well as City's assistant manager, Malcolm Allison, there was pandemonium. With scenes reminiscent of the 'fab four', girls chanted, screamed and fainted.

Questioned about his manager's attitude towards the venture, George remarked that he was keen for his boys to have outside interests, particularly as it would provide them with something to fall back on when their playing days were over. It was an eminently sensible response from the young man, but there was no hint of conservatism about the items that the boutique would be selling. George and his partner were keen to be at the cutting-edge of contemporary fashion. The boutique's collection was aimed at 'the extrovert male', offering items such as tweed jackets, purple and mustard trousers, fur caps and skinny ties.

When George had dealt with the formalities of the grand opening and had mixed good naturedly with his fans, Robert talked to him and his partner about their hopes for the business. Importantly, he reaffirmed his previous promise that the boutique would be given full and positive coverage in his article. Yet Robert knew that the real interest of his readers lay in gaining an insight into the glamorous lifestyle of the young star and he hoped to get a more personal insight into the rewards and potential pitfalls of life in the spotlight, when he was invited to accompany George out that evening to *Time and Place*, one of the player's favourite haunts on Cathedral Street in town.

After arriving at the night club, Robert found that there was little chance for a detailed conversation with his subject. It didn't prove disappointing however, as he learned plenty by simple observation. He could see that George was no longer the shy teenager who had spent his spare time with his fellow apprentices in the Chorlton Snooker Hall. Now, he was happy to be the life and soul of the party. Robert couldn't help but feel envious as he watched a succession of young, beautiful women surround the Irishman, almost desperate for his attention. When he remarked to George that it seemed so easy for him to pick up any woman he wanted, the latter merely shrugged his shoulders and gave a cheeky grin. Yet despite the heavy mental and physical demands that were placed on the young footballer when he took to the field, George seemed oblivious of the need for any period of respite. He was happy to push himself to the limit in everything he did and Robert had learned from his local contacts, that nights such as these weren't isolated occurrences.

Back in London, Robert made good on his promise, producing a positive write-up on *Edwardia*. He'd also managed to strike a balance between his two audiences. Younger readers were fascinated to look through the window into George's world, whilst the suggestion of excess, although not criticised by the writer, was sure to elicit the grumbling disapproval of most of the older generation. The letters page certainly reflected the interest in Robert's article. George's conduct, both on and off the field, being applauded and condemned in equal measure. Importantly, Frank was delighted by the outcome and it put the final seal of approval on his satisfaction at the progress of his new senior journalist. George was just one of a number of celebrities that Robert had featured in the *Gazette* and the paper's entertainment section was gaining a growing reputation for the depth and quality of its content.

When Robert returned to Manchester to visit his family over the Easter weekend, he found that Larry was far from complimentary about his article.

"Couldn't you have paid less attention to what happened in the night club and focused more on the opening of the boutique? It would have left readers with a far more positive impression of George if you'd done that."

"What do you mean?"

"Well, all the references to George enjoying a drink and being surrounded by gorgeous young women. It was music to the ears of those ready to pounce on the profligacy of youth."

"But that's what he was doing. You're always the one insisting that we tell it how it is. And, so what? He was relaxing. People can accept that he's got a right to enjoy himself."

"You don't really believe that, do you Robert? You wanted a whiff of scandal; something that would make your older readers morally indignant. Overpaid and oversexed young footballers. How terrible."

"Believe me," replied Robert, laughing. "You've just described George to a tee."

"But he's a young man; a working-class lad like yourself. He's found himself in a new world with opportunities he could never have dreamed of. He's an inspiration to those from similar backgrounds. Leave it to others to peddle the petty criticisms."

"But he's in the public eye and people have a right to know what he gets up to. It's my responsibility to make sure that they do. George invited me. He was happy to let me see him on a night out and I gave him loads of free publicity for *Edwardia*."

"But it doesn't end up being free if it damages his personal reputation and makes him a target of negative media attention, does it?"

"Oh dear. I think you're the one trying to take the moral high ground now," replied Robert, laughing.

"I'm being serious," insisted Larry. "At one time you'd have championed George; admired his achievement, like you did with Stanley Baker and the Beatles. Celebrated him as a working-class hero."

"Well, those days are gone now Larry. Nothing's straightforward anymore, but one thing I am certain of, is that George is no hero. In fact, heroes don't exist."

"Did you believe that when the two of us interviewed Yuri?"

"A great man. I've no doubts about that. But we understood at the time that he was being used. He was part of a Soviet charm offensive. And did we ever get to know the real man beneath the uniform? I'm not sure that we did."

"But the small details aren't important. What counts is what men like George and Yuri represent. Heroes inspire; they can give us hope."

"And too often they can be dangerous. Pick the wrong hero to venerate and it's not long before you're faced with the prospect of a Hitler or a Stalin."

"You've become far too cynical Robert. You've changed so much. It seems as if you just don't believe in anything, or anyone, anymore."

"That's not quite true Larry. I just understand that all of us have limitations. That's why there can be no heroes. Take George. On the field he has no equal; he's a true genius. But off it, he's got feet of clay and the danger is that the bigger you build him up, the further he has to fall."

As usual, Robert always had a logical and reasonable explanation for his apparent cynicism. Nevertheless, it was increasingly obvious to Larry that his friend's relocation to London had accelerated his ambition to make it to the top. When the two of them had worked on the *News Bulletin* at Owens, they had shared so many of their hopes for the future. Now however, their ambitions seemed a world apart. Nevertheless, the two of them had shared so much together, that they felt almost like brothers. For all their differences, both of them knew that there was nothing that could undermine their friendship.

Chapter 87

Having spent over twelve months caring for her son, it was time for Kay to return to work. She knew that it would be a wrench to leave him, but if she wanted to maintain her financial independence, there was no alternative. Kay was however, well prepared to meet the new demands placed upon her. She had learned to drive and had used some of her husband's savings to buy a second-hand, blue Ford Anglia. It meant that it would be easier for her to drop Bernard Jr off to her mam in Bennett Street before continuing on to work.

She was particularly gratified that she had got her old job back. She had remained in touch with Anne throughout her absence, especially as the latter took her role as a godparent so seriously. As Anne had predicted, the department's recruitment issues had continued and so in early February, it was agreed that Kay would return at the start of the following month. Anne helped further by allowing her time to adjust back to working life. For the first few weeks, Kay spent much of her time in the office, compiling case histories and updating the client records. If out in the field, she was assigned the task of locating absent fathers for the non-payment of maintenance, or to ascertain the feelings of parents about the custody or adoption of their children.

By the start of April, Kay was thankful to be picking up the usual case load that she'd had before her maternity leave. This was mainly because it provided the variety of tasks and challenges that she found so interesting. Yet Kay had also become aware of the murmurings of discontent that some colleagues were making behind her back. They suggested that she was receiving preferential treatment. A high turnover in staff before Kay's return, meant that many of them hadn't experienced the generosity and support she gave to her colleagues. At the very least, being out more in the field meant that she could avoid any underlying currents of unpleasantness.

Having Ethel's support was a godsend. Kay would have found it impossible to function without her. Crisis intervention didn't respect normal working hours and it made up a significant portion of Kay's responsibilities. At any point, for a variety of reasons, children could be left without the care of their parents. It was Kay's job to track down relatives to help, or secure emergency foster parents or temporary beds in care. It all took time and knowing that Ethel would simply put Bernard to bed and look after him overnight, allowed Kay to focus as calmly as possible on the task in hand.

Despite the fact that Kay had coped effectively with many potentially upsetting assignments, one of her new cases proved very difficult to manage. Rita Webster was twenty-five and lived on Birch Street in West Gorton, opposite the old Imperial Brewery. Rita had approached Manchester Children's Services Department and made an application for care. She had a two years old son and daughters aged three and four. Her husband, a joiner, had deserted her three months ago and she had no idea where he was. It had proved difficult for Rita to obtain any benefits, as she was unable to prove that she had done everything possible to find him. Whilst her case was being considered, matters had come to a head. Unable to pay any rent, Rita's landlord was threatening to evict her and the concerned mother saw little option but to ask for her children to be placed in care.

When Kay had gone to visit, it was clear that although the family's situation was desperate, Rita was looking after the children the best she could. She refused to be beaten and had a defiant manner about her that was as striking as her long, auburn hair. Unlike other women in her situation, Rita's features showed no signs of stress or premature ageing. She was still a pretty young woman. It was clear that she had never truly trusted her husband. For quite some time she had been putting small amounts from her housekeeping allowance into a post office account, in case of an emergency. Unfortunately, it had only been enough to buy food and Rita was facing a crisis. She wanted to go out to work but couldn't earn enough money to pay someone to look after the kids. Kay wondered why she hadn't approached either her own or her husband's parents for help. Rita explained that she had no idea where the latter were. As for the former, they had disapproved of her marriage and had cut off all contact with her. Nevertheless, Kay pushed Rita for their address. Perhaps under the circumstances, they would react differently. If they could at least offer a temporary home to the children, it would give Rita more time to finally secure the benefits the family were entitled to.

The parents, who owned a handsome 'semi' in Whalley Range, had been exceptionally reluctant to let Kay into the house when she had turned up that evening. Her persistence on the doorstep, which risked attracting the attention of the neighbours, had finally gained her the access she sought. Sat in the freshly decorated front room, with its attractive Axminster carpet, Kay studied her hosts carefully. The couple, Arthur and Margaret Copley, were in their late fifties. They gave the impression of being scrupulously clean and tidy. Arthur, with his brilliant white shirt and tie, had sharply pressed creases in his trousers. His wife was wearing a neat, green two-piece suit, perfect for the AGM at the local WI. Rita was their final child, born some years later than her three older siblings. A portrait of Pope Paul VI and a picture of Mary and baby Jesus, were hung on either side of the fireplace. Kay soon realised that they were the key to understanding the inflexible attitudes that Margaret, in particular, had towards her daughter.

"I know that there's been some difficulties in your relationship with Rita. She's conscious of that and didn't feel that she could impose on you. Your grandchildren are facing an uncertain time and I insisted that she should give me your address, so that I could make you aware of the situation and see if you could help."

Kay had been diplomatic. She hoped that it would open the door to a frank discussion of Rita's problems, but her mother sat there stony faced and unmoved. Turning her gaze towards Rita's father, Kay looked at him closely, searching for some kind of response. Conscious of her attention, he began to soften.

"Well, perhaps you can explain Rita's situation a little more," he suggested.

Kay went into the full details of why the children were in danger of being put out on the street. She suggested that the couple could help by offering temporary financial support to enable the rent and arrears to be paid, until Rita's benefits came through. If they weren't keen to do that, perhaps they could allow the children to stay with them until Rita could resolve her difficulties.

"It's out of the question," replied Margaret. "We made it clear that we were finished with her when she got herself pregnant. We never wanted her to have anything to do with that thing!"

Her words were venomous. She almost spat them out.

"And then she had no choice but to marry him and now, this!"

It was a difficult situation for Kay, but she wasn't yet ready to concede defeat. She looked at Arthur. He appeared uneasy. Kay sensed that he wasn't quite as prepared to give up on his daughter.

"We can agree to a care order," said Kay, "but when there are relatives, we hope that they can help. The children normally respond far better and it avoids a situation where it might be more difficult for Rita to get her children back in the future."

"But why would that be?" asked Arthur, surprised.

"Because children's services would have to investigate Rita's new situation to see if she passes the 'fit and proper person' test. If we can't recommend that she does, your daughter would have to apply to the court for custody."

Kay had chosen her words carefully. She wasn't averse to a little exaggeration in order to get Arthur on Rita's side. Her use of legal parlance had impressed upon Arthur that serious consequences could follow, if they didn't help their grandchildren. Yet before he had a chance to respond, Margaret reaffirmed her position. She was dead set against her daughter and determined that they wouldn't help her.

"When she went from here, I told her that she'd made her bed and she had to lie in it," insisted Margaret. "There's a price to pay and this is it. It's God's will and she'll just have to deal with the consequences."

Kay watched as Arthur looked down at the floor. She knew that he felt ashamed; embarrassed that he couldn't stand up to his wife. He'd wanted a quiet life for so long that now he was completely unable to assert himself. It was therefore up to Kay herself to fight to help his daughter. Although she knew that questioning Margaret's personal religious beliefs would be completely against department policy, she was determined to challenge her.

"I don't think that God would agree with you Mrs Copley. Didn't Jesus say 'suffer the little children, let them come to me'? Isn't it the Christian thing to do to love your grandchildren and help them through difficult times?"

"They aren't my grandchildren. The only ones I have are from my first three children's marriages."

"But surely Mrs Copley, whatever your feelings are about Rita, you can't take it out on her children. They haven't done anything to hurt or upset you. They need your help. Surely if you talked to your parish priest, he would agree with what I'm saying."

"I think that's quite enough!" replied Margaret, fiercely. "You've absolutely no right to come into my house and say such terrible things. I want you out. *Now!*"

Kay knew that she had already gone too far and if Mrs Copley complained, she would be facing a serious reprimand. Getting up from her chair, Kay picked up her bag and started to move towards the front room door.

"I'm sure that you didn't mean to cause us any upset, did you? Just got a little carried away worrying about the children."

Arthur had finally stepped into the breach. He knew how vindictive his wife could be and had no wish for her to lodge a complaint against their visitor. He could see that Kay was genuinely concerned for the welfare of his grandchildren and he felt guilty that he had been too weak to stand up for them himself.

Kay nodded, but felt unable to offer any words of apology. Being two-faced wasn't a quality that was much admired in Bennett Street.

"I'll show you to the front door," continued Arthur.

Moving out into the hallway, they left Margaret to sit in silence. Opening the front door, Arthur followed Kay outside. Pulling the door too, he spoke to her quietly.

"Have you a card dear?" he asked.

"Yes, of course."

Kay rummaged in her bag and produced one for him.

"I should like to meet you again and see if I can help. It can't be here though. You've seen Margaret's attitude and I'm afraid she just won't budge. I know that she's too hard, but she's my wife and I have to appear to be standing by her. If you talk to the landlord, I can give you the money to cover the arrears and any rent till Rita's benefits come through. I'll have to do it without Margaret finding out, but that won't be too difficult, as I'm often working in town."

"The sooner, the better," Kay replied. "I'm not sure how much longer I can hold the landlord off."

"Will tomorrow morning at ten, be all right? I'll need to go to the bank first."

"Yes. That's great. Rita will be so relieved."

Arthur smiled. It looked as if a great weight had been lifted from his shoulders.

"Perhaps, she'll want to thank you herself," suggested Kay.

"Perhaps," agreed Arthur. "But I think it's best to take things steadily. I wouldn't blame her for wanting nothing to do with me. She must have felt let down these last few years."

"Never mind," said Kay. "At least it's a start."

Walking back to her car, Kay considered the strange attitudes that were held by Mrs Copley. During their conversation, she hadn't once referred to her daughter by name. In her mother's eyes, Rita had been lost the moment she had committed the terrible sin of fornication. Margaret despised Rita and her husband. As a result, in her world, their children simply didn't exist. Kay couldn't help but think that the real issues went far deeper. Margaret professed to be a Christian and yet she hadn't one shred of forgiveness in her. Kay wondered if it was the case that Margaret had been jealous of her daughter. Rita had been prepared to follow her heart and fly in the face of convention. By doing so she had experienced full sexual gratification and obtained that fulfilment about which, her mother had secretly fantasised. Rigid and uncompromising, Margaret had concealed her passion and desire behind religious dogma. If she were to soften in her attitude towards Rita and the children, her own years of sacrifice, living in her moral straightjacket, would have been in vain.

The following morning, Arthur made good on his promise and at ten o'clock, on the dot, he turned up at Kay's office to hand over more than enough money to take care of the rent, the arrears and food for the following month. Kay immediately contacted the landlord, who agreed that he would halt the eviction. His agent would go to Rita's home and receive the outstanding rent from Kay at five that afternoon.

Once the arrangements had been settled, Kay went to tell Rita the good news. The young mother was shocked; she certainly hadn't expected any help from her parents. The overriding emotion was one of relief. She had been on the edge of the precipice, certain that she would fall into the abyss. With Kay pushing hard to get her benefits, Rita could now see a way ahead.

"This is just the start," predicted Rita. "I'll have to wait a couple of years, but once all the kids are in school, I intend to get a job. I don't want social security. I know I have to take it now, I've no option, but I'm determined to get away from relying on anyone else."

"Sometimes we have to," said Kay. "There's no shame in it."

"I wouldn't be too sure about that."

"I was surprised to find out that you had three brothers and sisters," said Kay, changing the subject. "Why didn't you tell me? Perhaps one of them could have helped with the kids."

"No. I've had no contact with them since I got married. They wouldn't risk falling out with their mam on my account."

"Well, you never know," suggested Kay. "Your dad came good for you. I could contact them if you like. I don't see why you couldn't have a relationship with them separate to your mam. It happens all the time. Family members lose touch and then aren't aware when their relatives are in trouble. You'd be surprised how many, once we contact them, are ready to help and make amends."

"Perhaps, in the future," suggested Rita. "I think I'd rather take it slowly."

"What about your dad? I'm sure he would like to see his grandchildren. Make up for the time he's lost with you and them."

"Let me think about it. I am grateful, but bad things have happened and I need to be sure that I can put them behind me."

It was a sensible approach and at least Rita hadn't shut the door on it entirely. Kay knew that Arthur's continued support for his daughter, would help her over what would still be, difficult times. Nevertheless, she understood that Rita wouldn't want to feel beholden to him. They would have to work out a relationship satisfactory to both of them.

When reporting back to Anne, Kay was firm in her belief that the case file shouldn't be closed on Rita and her family.

"She's still got potential difficulties in front of her. We have to treat this as preventive work; take away any need for any further crisis intervention."

"Are you sure that it's not just a personal interest you have. It's clear from the file that you've got a lot of admiration for Rita."

"Yes, I do, but I think we can help Rita develop a closer relationship with her father and siblings. It can help provide a safety net for her and she won't need our help again."

"I can see your point Kay, but I'm afraid the file will be closed. She's kept her house, is receiving benefits and her children are safe. All reports show that she's a very good mother. I can't justify putting any more staff hours into this. You know that we have so many families in desperate need. We have to prioritise them. You need to tell Rita that you won't be seeing her anymore."

Anne could see that Kay was disappointed.

"Remember what I said when you first started here," continued Anne. "If you want to survive in the job, you have to be able to switch off; forget everything once you've gone home. If you get too involved, you lose your ability to see things clearly. And then, you're no good to anyone."

Kay knew that she couldn't argue with Anne's logic and so duly informed Rita that the department was now happy with her circumstances and would be taking no further action in terms of her family.

Chapter 88

It was often said in the department that no matter how long you had been in the job and how much you may have seen, there was always something that would come along and surprise you. This definitely proved to be the case when in early June, children's services received a complaint that the children of a one-parent family living on Gotha Street in Ardwick, were being neglected. With Kay's intimate knowledge of the area, it was no surprise when the case was allocated to her and she was charged with the task of going out to evaluate the situation. Reading the file in the office, Kay discovered that it was the children's father who had contacted them to make the allegations. He was adamant that his children weren't being properly looked after; they were living in a filthy house and going hungry, as there was never any food in the cupboards for them to eat.

With her car in the garage for repairs, Kay caught the 92 from Parker Street at four. The bus progressed steadily down London Road and Downing Street before the rush hour traffic had started to build. Kay was soon passing Ardwick Green and then was across the roundabout to be deposited on the pavement outside the ABC. Walking past the cinema, she advanced along Stockport Road, glancing into the windows of the shops that lined its route, before turning left into Marshall Street. Gotha Street was off to the right, but following convention, Kay nipped down the ginnel to the rear. Entering through the gate to the back yard, Kay was immediately struck by how clean and tidy it was. The yard was well swept and around the drain she could smell the unmistakable odour of 'San Izal' disinfectant. The half net at the kitchen window, itself clean and bright, was sparkling white. With smart, brown stoned steps leading to the back door, Kay knew that she had been sent on a wild goose chase. The mother who lived here, like most of her contemporaries, was incredibly house proud. She worked tirelessly to ensure that her neighbours would have no cause to call her for failing in her domestic duties.

Kay knocked on the back door. It was opened by a freckle-faced girl with long brown hair that, being wet, lay limply at the sides of her face. The girl was tidily dressed in a school blouse, skirt and cardigan. Her clothes showed few signs of wear and tear. From her reading of the file, Kay recognised that it was Janice. She was twelve and attended Ardwick Girls Secondary. Janice soon impressed Kay as being grown-up and confident. She was eager to help care for her younger siblings and so relieve the burden on her mother.

"Hello. I'm looking for Mrs Holmes. Is she in?"

"She's just washing our Jane's hair."

"Oh" replied Kay, taken back by the answer.

"Yes. We've all had to have it done."

Janice stepped back slightly and peering to the side called across to her mam.

"Mam. There's a lady here to see you."

"Well, tell her to come in. I'm nearly done."

"My Mam says come in."

"Thank you."

Kay stepped through the back door and into the kitchen. She looked around and could see a drop leaf table and chairs pushed under the window. It had an attractive green table cloth draped over it, with place mats and cutlery set ready for tea. A long settee covered the nearside wall, upon which was sat a young boy holding a copy of the *Dandy*. Looking at Janice, he called over to her.

"Will you read to me Janice?"

"Oh, not again!"

"Aw, go on our Janice."

His sister tutted, then broke into a smile.

"All right then, I suppose I'll have to. I can't wait until you've learned to read properly, then you won't be mithering me all the time."

Kay smiled. She knew full well that Janice's words were merely for effect. In reality, she could never turn down the cute little lad with his appealing smile.

"Thanks Janice."

Sitting down on the settee, Janice put her arm around him and cuddled him to her. As she opened the comic and started to read, he leaned his head into her arm, safe and secure.

By the kitchen sink, sat up on a chair, a second, younger girl was having her wet hair combed through by her Mam. Kay shuddered. The scene reminded her of the all too familiar ritual that she herself had dreaded going through in her childhood. The unmistakably pungent smell of 'Derbac' soap was in the air and Mrs Holmes was tugging on a metal comb, as she pulled it stutteringly through her daughter's hair.

"Ow Mam! It hurts!"

"Stop being mard. Of course, it doesn't hurt! Our Janice never complained. Would you rather have 'Nitty Nora' doing it? She will, if you've got any when she comes back to school to check everyone."

Kay was full of sympathy for the young girl, but it had to be done.

"There. That'll do. You can go and sit down now."

Satisfied, Mrs Holmes washed and dried her hands and then replaced the chair back beside the table. She turned towards Kay who had been waiting patiently for her to finish.

"Wouldn't you know it. They've got nits at the school again. I'm not taking any chances with any of the kids getting them."

"No. You can't be too careful. That's what my mam always said when I was a kid and she's used the Derbac soap on me quite a few times."

Kay's words, simple as they were, made a strong impression on her host. The Mancunian 'mam' and reference to being disinfected with Derbac soap, made it clear that Kay wasn't like the teachers and social workers she'd dealt with in the past. To Mrs Holmes they were all of a similar ilk; middle-class do-gooders. Posh and with a superior attitude. Kay appeared authentic. She'd grown up in these streets and was comfortable in them, unlike her colleagues who would breathe a sigh of relief when they returned to suburbia after their work was done.

Kay was impressed with Mrs Holmes too. There was no doubt that she was an excellent mother. The kitchen was spotlessly clean. Her children were well clothed, happy and healthy. Kay began to feel slightly embarrassed that she should be here at all.

Still, she knew that she had to act on the information received. It was her job to officially verify that everything was as it should be.

"You're lucky you caught me in. It's my day off. Normally my mam would be here taking care of them. What did you want?"

"I'm sorry to take up your time Mrs Holmes. I can see that you've got a lot on your plate right now ..."

Kay hesitated. She was clearly nervous, concerned that her forthcoming questions would unleash a barrage of vitriol from their intended recipient. It had happened so many times before and just for a moment, Kay began to question whether she had been wise to come out here without the support of one of her colleagues. In reality, she had very little choice. The department was short staffed. Several colleagues were absent, no doubt due to the cumulative effects of pressure and stress.

"Call me Shirley," said her host, smiling. "And don't worry. I think I know what you're going to say."

"Oh?"

Kay felt a sense of relief, yet was surprised by Shirley's response.

"You're here from children's services, aren't you?"

"Yes, how did you know?"

"Well, I could say that you've got that look about you, although you do have a little bit more style than visitors I've had in the past. You've got to admit, women from there are a bit dowdy, aren't they?"

Kay laughed. She shouldn't have. Her female colleagues certainly wouldn't have appreciated it had they known. But she liked Shirley, so typical of the hard-working and down to earth mothers from the city. These women took all the obstacles their tough existence could throw at them, completely in their stride and with humour and determination.

"It's him, the kids' dad, isn't it? He's made a complaint, hasn't he? I was wondering when someone would come round."

Kay nodded.

Shirley sighed.

"It's okay. Ask your questions and we can get it over with."

"Wouldn't you like us to talk privately?"

Kay motioned her heads towards the kids, conscious that their conversation may prove embarrassing.

"No. It's nothing that'll upset me or the kids. They know how barmy their dad is. When they do see him, which is rare, he's always asking them if I'm being a good mother. Not that the tight beggar ever pays any maintenance for them, or gives them anything when he does see them."

"Fair enough. I'm Kay Thompson by the way."

"Nice to meet you, Kay."

"Anyone can see that you've got a lovely house and the kids are a credit to you. I only need to ask you if I can see your food cupboard, please."

"Of course."

Shirley smiled and walked over to the wall cupboard built into the alcove by the fire place and beckoned Kay towards her. Opening the doors, she stood back with a proud and satisfied look.

"Will that do?"

Kay could see that there were numerous tins of baked beans, corned beef, soup and other items.

Opening the door to the top of the cellar steps, a cool place for perishables, for those without a fridge, Shirley pointed out the milk, butter and cheese and also the nearby bread bin. There was no way that these children had ever gone hungry.

"That's great," said Kay smiling. "Thanks for being understanding. I'm afraid we have to follow up when we receive a complaint, but I think from now on you'll be one of our exceptions. You had no way of knowing that I'd be calling today. What I've seen is a true picture of how well your family is being looked after. I just don't understand your husband. He should be pleased that you're taking responsibility for his kids. Why did he complain?"

"It's what they do. Other women face the same problem," continued Shirley. "I'm surprised you've not come across it before. Our hubbies may have cleared off, but even though they live over the brush with someone else, they still want to control you. I'm working now and he knows that I'm meeting other men. A couple of times, when my mam has been able to watch the kids, I've had a night out with the girls. He finds out and gets jealous."

"But he moved out, didn't he? Decided not to live with you. Why interfere in your life now?"

"Because I've had his children and I'm still married to him. It's all right for him to carry on as he wants, but he thinks I should stay in the house looking after the kids. He won't accept any other man moving in here, but he's no worries there though."

"Oh?"

"Yes," continued Shirley, her eyes blazing fiercely. "I'm not daft enough to want any man living in this house again. We're better off on our own. That's right, isn't it girls?" she asked, looking at her daughters. "Your mam doesn't need another man in the house, does she?"

"What about Andrew. He's alright Mam," remarked Jane.

"Course he is, the little tinker" replied Shirley, smiling fondly at her son.

"It's a shame," she continued, turning back towards her visitor. "They're so loving when they're young like Andrew, but then they go and grow up and all we can hope is that they don't turn into their fathers."

Kay laughed but she recognised the seriousness of Shirley's words.

"Anyway, even if I did meet someone special, what man out there would want to take on three kids? It's the price I've to pay. We women have to be responsible, seeing as too many men can't be. It's up to us to make the sacrifices. But I don't mind. I wouldn't swop these little terrors for anything."

"I'm sure we'd be able to help you pursue maintenance for the kids. If your husband paid up, surely that would help."

Shirley laughed dismissively.

"We'd be wasting our time. I tried that when he first cleared off, but after the court made me an award, he gave up his job. He claimed that he'd become unemployed and the court cancelled the order. They said he couldn't afford it and as I had a job, it was my responsibility to look after them. He was soon working again, but he didn't send the kids as much as a brass farthing. I then found out that his fancy woman was expecting. I thought that might give her some sympathy for the kids. Hard faced cow didn't care. I felt like lamping her one, but in her condition, I couldn't. Anyway, he walked out on her, just before she had the kid. She got paid back, didn't she? Eighteen and a single mother. She's too embarrassed to let on to me now."

"Well," said Kay, "they do say 'what goes around, comes around', don't they?"

"Yes, they do," replied Shirley. "By the way," she continued. "What did you say happens if he complains again?"

"Well," said Kay, "I'll be putting a positive report on file and I'll mention how vindictive he is. Without anyone else contacting us, he's most likely to be ignored."

"Good. I'd like to divorce him, but it's not easy and I suppose there's no real need to at the moment. It wouldn't stop him being silly anyway, would it?"

"No. I don't suppose it would."

As she walked back towards Stockport Road, Kay thought about the events of the afternoon. It had been surprising to discover just how vindictive Shirley's husband could be. Holmes couldn't be satisfied with the fact that he'd got away scot-free when it came to paying maintenance for his children. He was jealous that his abandoned spouse was now building a new life for herself. These selfish, feckless fathers, thought Kay. They were so eager to move on to pastures new, find another gullible woman and leave their onerous responsibilities behind them. They were a disgrace. Their actions should have put off any reasonable young woman from being involved with them. Yet, it didn't. Kay felt so angry. It was education that was needed. Too many women, especially in the working-class areas she had lived and worked in, readily accepted the notion that it was a man's world. They had learned that they should accept their lot, however bad it may be, without complaint. It needed to change, thought Kay, but with the overwhelming conservatism of convention, would it ever?

Chapter 89

The physical landscape of Ardwick, that Kay and Robert had been so familiar with as they were growing up, was certainly changing. It was down to the effects of the vast demolition programme that was being rolled out in many parts of the city, as the Corporation embarked on its unfortunately named, slum clearance programme. Like most of the area's residents, Kay would have preferred to have seen local politicians and planners respond to calls for the modernisation of the existing terraced houses. Not only would it have proved a far cheaper option than the wholesale construction of new homes, but it would also have left Ardwick's residents living alongside their long-time friends and neighbours.

In January 1969, Kay had visited a family who lived in a newly built council property, contained within a terrace of five homes, located on Rostron Close. The latter was the new designation for Rostron Street, which Kay had once passed daily, as she had walked down Bennett Street towards Hyde Road. Now, although Heywood House was still standing, all the familiar terraced streets around it, had been flattened by the bulldozers. There had been great optimism that the construction of new houses and estates would help bring about a new era in which poverty would finally be eliminated and equal opportunities open up for working-class children. As a member of children's services, Kay knew that such expectations were misplaced; a fact her visit to Rostron Close had confirmed. The much-lauded new homes had made little impact on the ever-growing list of crisis families that she and her colleagues were having to deal with. The issue had been very much on Kay's mind and one she was keen to discuss with Robert and Larry on their upcoming visit.

Kay had been surprised at how seriously her friends had taken to their role as uncles to Bernard Jr. The pair of them had been to see him regularly and at the start of February, they had come to stay for a couple of days, bringing him presents for his third birthday. Bernard was a lively and happy little boy, loved dearly by his mam and doted on by his nanny and grandma. He'd inherited his father's soft, brown eyes and his fondness for action and excitement.

"He's a little bugger, you can't take your eyes off him for a second," Kay's father had exclaimed, after watching him in the garden one Saturday afternoon, whilst Kay and Ethel had been out at the shops.

"Ernest!" replied Ethel, angrily. "Don't you dare use that language in front of our Bernard."

"He's your grandson and he's only little," said Kay, laughing. "Surely he can't have been that difficult to handle."

"Humph."

Ernest shrugged his shoulders and said no more.

"He's just completely gormless," continued Ethel, turning to Kay. "He thinks the lad should be like you girls were at his age. Well, he's going to have to get used to it. It won't be long before Bernard will be big enough to go and play football with him in the park."

Kay looked sympathetically at her dad. He was always destined for a telling off when he fell short of his wife's exacting standards.

"Don't worry, Dad. He can be a handful at times. He just seems to have so much energy. I'm thankful we've got the garden. It does tire him out. Eventually," she added, with a smile. "I have to say, that there are nights when I breathe a sigh of relief, when he's finally nodded off to sleep."

When his uncles arrived, rang the doorbell and Kay answered the door, Bernard, trotting behind her, squealed with delight. Robert picked Bernard up by his arms and swung him around in the hallway, whilst Larry entered carrying the presents.

"They've been wrapped nicely," observed Kay. "Attractive paper and string."

"Robert's gran did it for us. There's a present here from her and Irene too."

"If you put them on the sideboard in the lounge, they'll be out of Bernard's reach until I can take them upstairs. He's a bit giddy at the moment. He'll be more able to appreciate what you've got for him in the morning."

"Yes, I can see and Robert's not helping, is he?"

Robert had decided that he and Bernard should play aeroplanes and holding his 'nephew' out in front of him, was sweeping the little lad through the air, bringing a mixture of screams and laughter.

"Come on. That's enough," said Kay, firmly. "I don't know which one of you is the biggest kid."

Placed back on the floor, Bernard groaned in disappointment and held out his arms, his little face pleading for Robert to launch him through the air once more.

"No, Bernard," said Kay, firmly. "That's enough."

Lowering his eyes, Bernard thrust out his lip in disappointment. Robert smiled. He had seen Kay do the same on so many occasions when they were kids. Bernard knew, from the tone of his mam's voice, that she expected him to behave and he quickly settled down. Noting his reaction, Larry was impressed.

"I don't know Kay. You've still got that authority, haven't you? Just like when you used to sort Robert and I out when we were at Owens."

"I didn't sort you out," replied Kay, surprised.

Larry and Robert laughed.

"Yes, you did," confirmed Robert. "We always knew we had to shut up and behave, if we were annoying you."

"Well, I suppose I did," said Kay, smiling

"And still do," suggested Larry.

"It has to be said," continued Kay, "that men and little boys," she added, looking at Bernard, "need firm direction, if they're to be kept out of mischief."

Moving into the lounge, Robert and Larry sat on opposite ends of the settee with Bernard in between. It wasn't long before he was clambering all over them and Uncles 'Lahwee' and 'Bobs' ended up on their hands and knees playing cars on the floor with their nephew. The excitement of the occasion however, soon began to catch up with Bernard. It had been a long day for the little boy and Kay could see that he was getting tired. Knowing that Bernard would get upset if she took him upstairs to bed, she encouraged him to lay down on the settee and covered him with a blanket. It wasn't long before he had fallen asleep and the adults could sit back and finally relax.

"He's a real little chatterbox, isn't he?" remarked Larry.

"And such energy. He never stops," added Robert. "How do you keep up with him?"

Kay looked fondly at Bernard sleeping peacefully on the settee. Looking at him now, there was no sign of the bundle of energy that had taken centre stage from the moment her friends had arrived.

"With the greatest of difficulty," replied Kay, with a chuckle. "He's into everything and fascinated when he meets new people."

"It must be hard work, looking after him. I can't imagine myself ever being able to cope with bringing up children," remarked Robert.

"Obviously not," observed Larry, laughing. "You'd just leave it all to the 'little woman', wouldn't you?"

"And you'd be leaving it to the nanny," replied Robert. "Just like a typical toff."

"I don't know, you two," said Kay, shaking her head. "The older you get, the worse you are at ridiculing one another."

"Oh, you know we don't really mean it," replied Larry.

"I don't know about that," insisted Robert.

The two of them burst out laughing. Kay sighed. She wondered whether they would ever grow up. It seemed impossible to envisage either of them settling down with a wife and family.

"Bernard does help me to forget the pressures at work," said Kay. "I can't dwell on things too long at home when I've got a little boy to see to. Although there are some issues that I can't stop feeling strongly about."

"Such as?" asked Larry.

"How poverty and distress just don't go away. I'm forever visiting the new houses they've built in Ardwick and Chorlton-on-Medlock. There seems to be more children at risk than ever before. The old communities are gone and families are isolated. Besides those of us at children's services, there's no one else to help. The new estates were supposed to improve children's lives, yet they've actually made them worse."

"Why do you think it's all gone wrong?" asked Larry.

"Because the changes were never properly thought through," replied Kay. "They made the decision to bulldoze the terraces in the 'Manchester Plan' of 1945. The Corporation never offered residents the option of staying put and having their houses improved. That would have left the communities intact and less vulnerable children for us to deal with."

"Slum clearance and building new estates had cross-party support across the country," replied Larry, "not just in Manchester. I can't think of any of our local MPs, or councillors, who aren't genuine about wanting to improve the lives of working-class families. In hindsight, they could have looked at other options, but is it fair to be so critical?"

"Yes, it is," insisted Kay. "Politicians and planners have failed because they're arrogant and condescending. You can see it in the Housing Committee. Residents in Greenheys and Moss Side have put forward detailed refurbishment plans. They want to modernise properties in order to keep their communities together. It's a viable and far cheaper option, but the proposals have been dismissed. And why? Because the planners and politicians are adamant that they know what's best, rather than the people themselves."

"I think you might have just suggested that housing policy has been dictated by something more than just arrogance," observed Larry.

"Well, perhaps so. It is strange how there's so little questioning of the huge contracts that are generated by the clearance programme and the building of new estates. And this comes at a time when public finances are seriously challenged. If there's any hint of corruption mixed up in all of this, I think that's a question for someone else to investigate."

Kay looked directly at Larry. It was clear that she hoped he would do so.

"Well," said Larry, "the Tories may control the city council at the moment, but it was Labour who were in charge when all these housing decisions were made. You have to understand their thinking. They wanted a modern world and new solutions to old problems and that's why they were so invested in the idea of contemporary housing and flagship estates. Most believed that you could only give the working-classes a brighter future by cutting their connection to the past. Perhaps they weren't arrogant Kay, but just blinkered. Nevertheless, I can accept that some individuals could have been susceptible to accepting inducements to support the awarding of big contracts. It wouldn't be the first time it's happened in the realm of local government."

Kay nodded in agreement.

"You see Larry, as a girl from Ardwick, I can't help thinking that the building of these new estates was essentially a middle-class solution to a working-class problem. It showed no understanding of the culture, feelings and expectations of our community. You can only gain that empathy, by living there and experiencing it for yourself."

"Well, perhaps some of what you say is right. In fact, now that the slum clearance programme is well under way, a feature on its progress would seem justified."

"All-told Larry, this desire for modernity is effectively an appeal for the votes of the liberal-minded, middle classes," asserted Kay. "Those are what politicians of all persuasions need, in order to secure and maintain their power. Slum clearance has become a policy that allows the middle classes to feel good about themselves, without any understanding of the feelings of the people who actually live in those areas and want to remain there."

"I can see your point," said Larry. "I think this whole housing issue is something that the *Evening News* should be looking into. Suspicions of corruption would definitely be hard to substantiate, but looking at the ongoing social problems that still exist, despite the creation of the new estates, is something that can easily be investigated."

"I'm not sure you'll find too much enthusiasm for it," suggested Robert, who'd remained quiet until this point. "There's always been suspicions of shady dealings in terms of public contracts. It's true the world over. If there is anything going on and I'm certainly not suggesting that there is, you'll never get to the bottom of it and you won't be appreciated for trying."

Robert's words were unsurprising. His friends had long realised that the socialist principles of the young idealist were no longer visible in the pragmatic, older man. Robert had learned the importance of compromise and was prepared to embrace any opportunity to further his career. The notion of crusading journalism, so close as it was to Larry's heart, no longer held any value for him. Yet Kay, closer than anyone to Robert, would never be judgemental. She understood the passion that drove him to succeed; to prove that he could mix with the best of them. And she sympathised, recognising that he didn't have the social connections that someone like Larry could take advantage of, should he have chosen to do so. Yet if he did reach the top, where he would be able to rub shoulders with the elite, Kay feared that Robert would always be regarded as an outsider. If that were to occur, it would be a painful lesson for the lad from Ardwick to learn.

Chapter 90

Larry's conversation with Kay had certainly captured his attention and as he'd suggested to her, he was soon approaching Bill Young about writing a series of articles on the city's house clearance programme.

"The reality is," he pointed out, "for all the investment in new properties with inside bathrooms and central heating, in terms of other aspects of social deprivation, there hasn't been any improvement. My contact at children's services has told me that they're actually dealing with more problem families and vulnerable children, than ever before. All told, it's a very poor return for the huge investment that the Corporation has made on behalf of the ratepayers."

"But isn't it a little soon Larry, to make such sweeping judgements? After all, slum clearance is far from being completed. Perhaps we should give the Corporation chance to adjust its programme in light of any issues that may have arisen."

"Langley was built in the fifties; Darnhill, Hattersley and Mottram at the start of this decade. There are key social issues on all those estates. Surely the Corporation has had long enough to address them. We need to be holding them to account."

"I still think that we should wait Larry. Let's give these new system-built schemes a chance. The ones they're building at Wellington Road, Beswick and the crescents planned in Hulme. Now, you can't deny that they're all about creating community spirit; deck access and 'streets in the sky'. The plans are favoured by the architectural community and they've been highly commended by many of our competitors."

"Yes, I'm aware of that. Our colleagues on the *Guardian* seem to be particularly keen on the idea. Journalists and architects aren't the ones who are going to be living in them though, are they?"

"Obviously not, but that doesn't mean anything. I'm sorry Larry, but at this moment in time, I think it would be difficult to persuade Big Tom of the merits of covering this."

"But there's a bigger issue that I haven't mentioned yet."

"Such as?"

"The contracts."

"What about the contracts?"

"I've been looking into them. System-built housing isn't a cheap option. The old housing stock could have been kept and modernised at a third to a quarter of the price. I've the figures to prove it. Shouldn't we be concerned that the Corporation has agreed to expensive contracts whilst other, cheaper options, have been ignored. Surely, we need to investigate this. How exactly were the contracts awarded? Who negotiated them? Was the process transparent? Our readers have a right to know the answers."

"Whoa! Hold on!" exclaimed Bill. "I admire your enthusiasm Larry, but you must know that what you're suggesting would put us in dangerous waters. The solicitors just wouldn't wear it, even if we could sell Big Tom on the idea. Any hint of an allegation against any individual and we'd be drowning in writs. We have to back off on this one."

"But I'm convinced there's a story here."

"There may be, but proving it is another matter. We couldn't take the risk and neither should you. I've told you before Larry, you have to know when to compromise. It's going to keep holding you back, if you don't."

"That's the problem, I don't want to. I still believe that we have a role to play in fighting for truth and social justice."

"Yes, we do," replied Bill, "but there comes a point where we have to draw the line in order to protect the newspaper. You know we operate in an imperfect world. There are powerful individuals and organisations out there and we can't simply ignore them. And neither can you. If you want a freer hand to espouse social justice and attack vested interests, you'll have to work for a lower profile publication. One with a small circulation that isn't taken too seriously. You might be happier if you did, but your talents would be wasted and any influence that you could have had, will be gone."

The disappointing outcome of the conversation with Bill, brought in to focus Larry's growing frustration with his situation at the *Evening News*. For some time, he had been looking for the opportunity to write articles that were closer to his own political beliefs and he had recently been made aware that a vacancy existed for a senior journalist at *The Workers' Vanguard*, a left-wing daily based in London. Applying for the position, Larry was successful and by Easter had relocated to the capital. He was now working for a national publication, but the paper he represented had only a modest circulation; smaller in fact than the *Evening News*. Yet Larry was content. Unlike Robert, his ambitions went no further than having the opportunity to 'tell it how it is.'

Chapter 91

As the new year dawned it was clear that nineteen seventy would usher in a period of great change as far as the organisation of social services was concerned. When she had first met with Leslie Lever, in her early days working in children's services, Kay had identified the problem created by the lack of co-ordination between the provision of services for children, the elderly and those suffering with mental health issues and learning difficulties. Her concern was shared by many working within social services, as well as politicians of all persuasions at Westminster.

Over the next few years, the media had provided upsetting revelations about the abusive treatment of the elderly and mentally ill by the NHS, who were responsible for their care. It had led to the setting up of the Seebohm Committee that was tasked to investigate the organisation of social services. Its recommendations concluded that there should be only one service that would meet all the needs of the family. Consequently, legislation was drawn up which brought together the separate children's, mental health and welfare departments in local authorities. Receiving its royal assent on May 29th, the Local Authority Social Services Act finally delivered what Kay had requested of Leslie Lever and the Labour government, all those years ago.

The act ordered each local authority to set up a social services committee which would appoint a director of social services to manage the new department's responsibilities. The change meant an expanded role for the local authority, which now assumed oversight of aspects of the work of the NHS. In order to meet the new demands placed upon them, it was clear that there would have to be a reorganisation of social services departments and that this would include a restructuring of management. Having worked for some time as a senior child care officer, Kay had been increasingly drawn into assuming management responsibilities. She did expect that at some point she would move into a more advanced leadership role, for it seemed the next logical step in her career. Nevertheless, she wasn't expecting her opportunity to come so quickly.

Arriving at work on Monday morning, following the confirmation of the new act, Kay was met by Anne, who asked her to come to her office. Kay knew that she was about to be told something confidential and immediately assumed it must be information relating to one of her ongoing cases.

"I'm sure you're aware Kay, that the new act is going to require some big changes. There has to be more co-ordination between the different aspects of the work we do and new management structures are being put in place to try to ensure that it happens. I've asked you in Kay, to see you if you'd be prepared to take on the role of Assistant Director of Children's Services."

Kay was shocked and unable to answer. The offer had come completely out of the blue. Furthermore, the job had such a grand sounding title that she couldn't quite see herself in it. Noting her reaction, Anne laughed.

"It's a serious offer, if that's what you're wondering," said Anne. "It's all right. You can take your time."

Kay nodded, quietly considering the offer.

"Surely there are others, senior to me, that have more experience for the post. Aren't they in the running too?" asked Kay.

"I recommended that we went for someone younger and more adaptable," replied Anne. "These changes are going to bring a lot of upheaval and even more demands on the service. Whoever takes the post is going to have to be comfortable with the new arrangements and be reliable, resourceful and resilient. I know Kay, that you'll be able to handle the pressure. You're going to have to be very supportive of the team, because all of them are feeling uncertain about the future and no doubt you'll be the one who has to deal with the unhappiness at their new responsibilities."

Kay understood Anne's appraisal of the qualities that the new post would require. Working in social services had always proved stressful and the job entailed even more pressure with the increasing scrutiny of the profession by politicians and the media. When Kay had first entered children's services, the wider public had generally looked with sympathy on those they perceived to be working within a caring profession. Now, with publicity given to their failings, social workers were too easily categorised as incompetent and uncaring. Consequently, most of Kay's colleagues felt undervalued and many were questioning whether they should remain in the profession. It would certainly be a demanding task, guiding and supporting staff through the forthcoming changes.

"Times are certainly going to be difficult," continued Anne. "We've already been notified by some colleagues that they intend to hand in their notice and not just those that are getting closer to retirement. It looks like we're going to have a higher proportion of new and inexperienced staff coming in. I need someone with optimism and enthusiasm like you, to oversee their induction and mentor them through their difficulties. It's a big task Kay, but I'm confident you can do it."

"Will you be remaining as Head of Children's Services?" asked Kay.

"Yes, for the moment," replied Anne. "Is that important?"

"Well, for my first senior management position, I'd rather be responsible to someone I know and can trust."

"Flattery, will get you everywhere," said Anne, laughing. "I assume you're accepting the job then?"

"Yes, of course, but don't I need to have a formal interview?"

"No. You've just had it. The decision was mine to make and the paperwork confirming your new contract, will be ready to sign tomorrow."

Kay's career was moving onwards and upwards. She was facing a stiff challenge, but was confident that she would get through it and working under Anne, she knew that support and understanding would be available should she need it. Kay felt certain that Bernard would be proud of her achievements. She was bringing up their son and providing him with a secure home through her intelligence and industry. She only hoped that she would prove as much of an inspiration to little Bernard, as she knew his father would have done.

Chapter 92

When Kay accepted her new position, Robert had been working at the *Gazette* for four years and in that time, he had been making rapid progress. Initially a senior reporter in the entertainment section, Frank Mellis had seen his potential and quickly promoted him to features editor when the post's incumbent had moved on to pastures new. Still continuing to produce his own outstanding articles, Robert showed a willingness to roll up his sleeves and sub the work of his colleagues, in order to ensure the quality of their reports. Impressed by his energy and initiative, Frank knew that just like himself, Robert understood that no stone should remain unturned in order to ensure that each edition of the paper was of the highest possible standard.

Robert's continued success at the *Gazette* seemed inevitable and confirmation came when Frank handed him the chance to become the paper's leader writer, initially on a trial basis.

"It's going to require a lot of reading around," advised Frank, "you're going to have to know your stuff. Government policy, politics, economics; they could all be relevant to what you have to write about and you'll have to work quickly. With your academic background, I'm sure you'll be up to the challenge. If you do a good job, you'll be well renumerated."

Robert understood what a huge opportunity he'd been given and how highly Frank trusted him to produce lucid opinions that would fit with the views of the newspaper's proprietor. And the editor's judgement was sound. Robert realised that his responsibility was to express that viewpoint, his own personal opinions being of no consequence in terms of the issues he was addressing. Consequently, his period of probation was soon at an end and Robert was handed the role on a permanent basis. When Frank's deputy announced his intention to retire in July, 1970, the editor-in-chief had no intention of looking beyond his young protégé in order to fill the vacancy. At thirty years of age, Robert had become managing editor of the *Gazette*.

Harold Whittaker, the paper's proprietor, was the son of a collier, born and raised in Ashton-in-Makerfield just after the Great War. The youngest of five children, he left school at fourteen and became a sheet metal worker. Conscripted into the Royal Electrical and Mechanical Engineers, he returned home to Lancashire and built up his own steel stock holding company that became the industry's largest private business. Selling it to British Steel, Whittaker used the capital to diversify his interests into property development and the aeronautical industry. Finally, he'd branched out into the media, taking control of the *Gazette* and investing in two regional independent television companies.

Whittaker was generally content to leave the running of the *Gazette* to his editor. Under Frank's leadership, the paper had steadily increased its circulation and profitability and so he had little reason to question his judgement. Nevertheless, the proprietor had a keen interest in his investment and met his editor every Friday morning at eleven o'clock, so that he could be kept abreast of developments at the newspaper.

Neither pompous nor arrogant, Harold Whittaker seemed to possess none of the unpleasant traits that were often attributed to a self-made man. Small and stocky, with a round, pleasant face, when he arrived outside Frank's office, he always wore a cheeky grin as he winked at Alice, Frank's pretty young secretary. Although Robert had seen Whittaker in the building, he hadn't yet met him, but after his elevation to managing editor, Frank called him into his office so that he could meet the boss. As the two shook hands, Whittaker looked his employee up and down.

"So, you're the rising star that Frank's been full of. You're going to help him drive the *Gazette* onwards and upwards and make me even more money. Is that right lad?"

Robert smiled. Down in London, it was good to hear a Lancastrian accent and even more pleasing that Whittaker, unlike many others who relocated to the capital, hadn't tried to lose it.

"I hope so," replied Robert, with a chuckle.

"Good. That's what I like. A bit of confidence never goes amiss, does it?"

"No. As long as it's not misplaced," suggested Frank.

"Oh, I'm sure it's not," replied Whittaker. "I don't think a crafty old fox like you Frank, would put trust in anyone you didn't feel certain would deliver."

Frank nodded and smiled.

"So, you're from Manchester then lad. Whereabouts?"

"Ardwick," replied Robert, proudly.

"A self-made man like me and Frank then?"

"Well, getting there, I hope."

"Good answer. It's someone wanting to get there who'll try his damnedest to bring us success. That's right, isn't it?" asked Whittaker, turning to Frank.

"I can't disagree."

"Well, the reason I wanted to see you lad, is because I'm having a few guests around tomorrow night and you're invited. I'm out at Wimbledon. West Side Common. Frank knows the address. Be there at seven. He'll let you off early."

With that, Whittaker said farewell, leaving Frank and Robert alone in the office.

"You look surprised," said Frank, smiling.

"Well," noted Robert, with a sharp intake of breath. "I wasn't expecting that. Especially as I've never really met Mr Whittaker before today."

"But that's how it is now," replied Frank. "You're senior in the organisation. You have a face and a name and the boss is interested in what you have to say."

"Oh," replied Robert, slightly concerned.

"It's nothing to worry about. It's mainly a social occasion. Just be yourself Robert. Use that Mancunian charm and you'll be fine. And you'll get an insight into the lives of the rich and famous. I'll guarantee that you'll be impressed. Harold Whittaker and his wife aren't short of a bob or two."

Robert recognised that his recent promotion meant that his aspirations were now far closer to being realised. If he was a success as Frank's deputy, then a chance to become editor of one of the nationals was certainly not beyond him. It had proved reassuring to meet Whittaker. It showed that a working-class Northerner like himself, could make it to the very top. Yet Robert couldn't become complacent, for he knew that he still had a long way to go. Tomorrow, after he'd left the rented terraced house

that he lived at in Barking, he would be making his way to
Wimbledon Common and no doubt to a grand property that
would bring into focus the reality of his current situation.

Chapter 93

Leaving the office at five on Saturday afternoon, Robert walked the short distance to Temple tube station and travelled on the District Line out to its terminus at Wimbledon. From there, Robert took a taxi the relatively short distance to Whittaker's home. As the vehicle crossed over the Common, passing Rushmere Pond and the open heathland, Robert found it remarkable that such an untouched space, with dog walkers and horse riders roaming freely around them, could exist so close to the heart of the city. It wasn't surprising that properties here were at a premium and very expensive.

West Side Common was a long and in parts, tree lined road, behind which were a collection of mainly large and attractive detached houses. Reaching Whittaker's residence, Robert was impressed by a beautiful, double fronted building. It was enclosed behind a long brick wall which extended around the large grounds attached to the property. Entering through the open gates to the driveway, he walked towards the front door and rang the bell. Whilst he waited, Robert prepared himself for a guarded evening in which he would prove agreeable to his boss's associates and their wives. Yet when the door opened, he was in for a shock. There, in all her glory, stood a vision of loveliness.

"I assume you're Robert."

Her lashes fluttered, drawing his attention to her deep, brown eyes, soft and inviting.

Robert was quiet, unable to respond. Her presence had stunned him; literally taken his breath away. His heart was thumping and unconsciously he gulped in the air.

She laughed, then smiled, her ripe, moist lips parting to reveal her pretty white teeth. Her golden, chestnut hair was long and luxuriant, curling away from her graceful cheekbones.

"Well?" she asked, turning her head slightly to one side.

She was enjoying his embarrassment. She had made a conquest and knew it.

"Yes, that's right," answered Robert, uncertainly.

"Good. For one moment I thought you'd forgotten your name."

Robert shook his head and laughed, a reaction that steadied his nerves and restored his composure. He could now look more closely at her and admire how pretty she looked in the lacy black, V neck floral dress, that hugged her slender waist and revealed the soft, silken skin on her arms and neck.

"I'm Trudy by the way. Father's been expecting you. His other guests are already here."

"Oh," replied Robert, surprised. "I didn't know Mr Whittaker had a daughter."

"Should you have?"

"Well, if she…"

Robert paused and fell silent. He realised that a corny chat-up line would never impress a sophisticated woman like her. Tonight, the rules of seduction would have to be different.

"Yes?" asked Trudy, who was waiting for him to continue.

"Oh, nothing."

"Well, you'd better come in then."

Trudy turned smartly around on her black stilettos, the skirt of her dress swinging seductively around her. Robert followed as she walked through the inner door of the porch and into the spacious entrance hall, with its impressive sweeping staircase rising up towards the first floor.

"Ah, Robert. You've arrived then?"

Robert looked round, to see his host emerging from a door to the side.

"Yes, Mr Whittaker."

"I said to Trudy that you'd be the last one here. You wouldn't leave the office too early. We've too much of a work ethic us Northern lads, hey?"

"I hope so," replied Robert.

"Yes, not like us languid, Southern softies," remarked Trudy, somewhat dismissively.

"Well, I can let you off love. If I can't indulge my little girl, then what's the point of having all this?"

"I'm hardly your little girl anymore and besides, as I've pointed out many times, there are lots of ways of making money and they don't all conform to your quaint Northern homilies!"

"What do you mean?" asked her father.

"Well," she replied, before attempting what she believed to be a generic, Northern accent. "Tha'll never get owt for nowt. A hard day's work for a hard day's pay. Ee ba gum, where there's muck there's brass!"

Shaking his head, Whittaker sighed.

"I don't know. The way you make fun of your poor father. Determined to disown your Lancastrian heritage."

"Well, no disrespect intended to our distinguished guest, but I'm afraid I can't see how I could possibly have any connection to 'wild and woolly' land."

Robert laughed. The contrast between her refined accent, very posh, he would have thought as a kid in Manchester and her terrible 'Northern' accent, more from Yorkshire than Lancashire, had tickled him. Trudy was confident, sexy, funny and he suspected, more than a little dangerous too.

"Perhaps Trudy," suggested Whittaker, "you can show Robert around the rest of the house and then bring him out to the garden for something to eat."

"Why not? He's probably dying to know how the other half lives. That's right, isn't it Robert?"

Trudy winked at him and smiled.

"Will you stop trying to embarrass the lad and be serious," said Whittaker, vainly attempting to appear in control.

"Lad! He's not been that for a considerable amount of time. I think you're the one not being serious."

"Do you see what I have to put up with Robert? Criticised in my own home," observed Whittaker, with a shake of his head.

"You might be in charge out there, in your little business empire, father dear, but here with mother and I, it just won't do."

Robert watched fascinated as Whittaker, a man feared and ruthless in his business dealings, threw up his hands in desperation, sighed and walked away.

Left alone together, Trudy and Robert made their way slowly around the house, starting with the upstairs. The bedrooms were impressive; large, light and airy, with fabulous furnishings. Landings and corridors led to the several extensions that had been added to the property in the years since its original construction in the late eighteenth century. Externally, the house certainly maintained its period charm, but internally it was very much at the cutting edge of contemporary design. Back downstairs in the reception hall, Robert couldn't resist making reference to the highly polished, wooden parquet floor.

"It looks nice but if my mam and gran were here, they'd be wondering whether your dad couldn't afford to buy a carpet."

"Really?" asked Trudy.

"Oh yes," replied Robert, trying very hard to keep a straight face. "Carpets are fancy, lots of houses back home in Manchester still don't have them. They'd think that this was just like having a bit of old lino on the floor."

Trudy burst out laughing. Robert was pleased. He'd judged the mood perfectly. The two of them had been happily chatting away as she'd been showing him around and he'd judged correctly that she'd appreciate his sense of humour.

"We're laughing, but what you said is true, isn't it?" asked Trudy

"Yes. Some might have a couple of carpets downstairs, where the neighbours can see that you can afford them, but most don't have them upstairs yet. They've still got cheap lino down and perhaps a small rug near the bed, so it's warmer on your feet when you get up."

"My father goes on about his childhood all the time. How hard it was and how they had nothing."

"Yes, that's true and it was worse for him back in the thirties."

"But from what you're saying, it sounds like it hasn't really changed."

"Well, there's always been poverty."

"It's a world I don't know anything about and to be honest," said Trudy, "I'm glad that I don't."

"Is that why you were ridiculing your dad earlier?"

"Yes. I suppose so. I'm my mother's, rather than my father's daughter. I've been brought up like her; wanting for nothing. The best schools; the best of everything. You'd like to say I've been cosseted and spoiled."

"I see," said Robert

"Do you?" asked Trudy, "I'm not a tough, grimy working-class urchin like you Robert, but you still fascinate me."

"Oh?"

"Yes, most definitely. You aren't like the men I know. They haven't had to fight for what they've got and then worry that it could be taken away at any time. It gives you an edge that's so exciting."

Robert looked at her in silence. Her words had surprised him and he was unsure whether she was joking, or if she really meant it. But it didn't matter, for when he caught the mischievous glint in her eye and the way she ever so slightly pouted her lips, he knew only that he wanted her.

"Well, we'd best move on. Father will wonder just what we're getting up to."

She smiled once more, knowing that the hint of innuendo would send Robert's pulse racing further. Walking through into the elegant drawing room, Trudy pointed out the open fire place with its exquisite marble surround, before leading him through the French doors and out into the large garden.

"I'm afraid I won't be able to show you inside the annexe. We have guests staying there. I'd best hand you over to father."

Outside, her manner had become cooler and more distant. Robert wondered if she'd simply been leading him on, or perhaps he'd misunderstood her intentions. Or was she just keeping him eager, having him straining at the leash to jump to her every whim and command? Nevertheless, he was excited. Robert was experiencing emotions that were new to him. He wasn't in control of what may happen between them. It was just as Trudy intended.

"Yes, I suppose you'd better," he replied. "He'll think I've no manners, ignoring him."

"I wouldn't expect so. You pushy Northerners are all like that, aren't you?"

Trudy raised her eyebrows and gave him a wicked smile. Robert laughed. She was toying with him and he loved it. Having taken him over to her father, she slipped away to mingle with the other guests.

"I see you two have been getting on all right," remarked Whittaker.

"Yes. Trudy's shown me what a lovely home you've got. It's very nice around here, a lot different from where I am in Barking."

"Well, you never know lad, one day you might have something similar yourself. I can see you're ambitious and you obviously work hard. Remember, in this life, you get what you deserve."

Robert resisted the urge to smile, conscious that he was on the receiving end of one of those Northern homilies that Trudy had mentioned her father was so fond of.

"It's a grand place," continued Whittaker. "I've spent a lot of brass on it, but then you have to when you come from our background. I needed something besides the wife's house in Belgravia, so I could entertain properly. Oh yes, that's a prestige address and its worth a bob or two more than this, but here is like being in the country and I've got the big garden for my guests to mingle. It's somewhere a bit different and so close to the city."

"Yes, it certainly is," replied Robert.

"You have to do it. I can't do business with the partners I have now, in a two-up, two-down in Wigan, can I lad?"

"No. I don't suspect you could," said Robert, laughing.

"All this, is just for show. It's not real. Be careful you don't get too obsessed with chasing it lad. But I do love it when I get these 'toffs' coming here cap in hand to the collier's son."

Whittaker chuckled and Robert smiled. It seemed clear that regardless of his success, Whittaker's background meant that he would never feel socially secure among his upper-class associates.

"Anyway lad, it's time I took you around and introduced you to people. Be yourself. You don't need to put on any airs and graces."

It was advice that Robert didn't need. He could be polite and respectful, but a proud lad from Ardwick would never kowtow to anyone.

Chapter 94

Trudy Whittaker was twenty-eight; two years younger than Robert. She was rich, privileged and spoilt. Married and divorced twice already, she had an insatiable appetite for fun and as she continued her way through a number of intimate relationships, there was no sign of her slowing down. Exciting, sensual and flirtatious, her exceptional looks meant that there was no shortage of eager suitors. Together with her wealthy and fashionable, upper-class friends, Trudy had, without fear of embarrassment or disapproval, eagerly embraced the sexual freedoms of the so-called swinging sixties. Attracted to the handsome Mancunian, with his appealing rough edges, Trudy decided that she would seduce Robert and add him to her collection of admirers.

With the outside lights in the garden beginning to replace the illumination of the Sun, as it slipped down beyond the horizon, Robert was becoming tired of the somewhat meaningless conversations he had been having with a succession of Whittaker's esteemed guests. Now that the temperature had dropped and a gentle, cool breeze began to rustle the leaves on the plants and trees, most of the company were disappearing back into the more convivial atmosphere of the drawing room. Appreciative of the opportunity to be alone, Robert began to consider just when it would appear appropriate to make his apologies and return home.

"You look bored to death."

Robert turned round. It was Trudy.

"I don't blame you," she continued. "No one would willingly choose to spend their evening with that collection of old relics."

"They're not all old," replied Robert, with a chuckle.

"Well, you can't imagine any of them having a bit of excitement in their lives, can you? Or perhaps you're so busy pursuing your career, that you're no longer interested in such things. Is that right Robert?"

Trudy looked at him closely. Her words sounded like a challenge. She was willing him not to disappoint her.

"No, it isn't."

"Well then, let's get out of here. We can go back to my place."

"But what about your dad. I'll need to let him know I'm going."

"That's right. Make sure you're a good boy and don't go upsetting the boss."

Part ridicule and part rebuke, her words were pressing him to give up all thoughts of safety and compliance and ignore the consequences of leaving unannounced with the boss's daughter.

"Easy for you to say," insisted Robert. "I don't have the luxury you have. Us grimy working-class urchins have to think carefully, so that we don't throw away the chance of a future that we've worked so hard for."

She liked his answer. He'd been insistent and confident; stood up to her and shown his independence. He would be more of a challenge than most men who tried to resist her, but she knew that he would be hers before the night was over.

"Don't worry about father. You've shown your face. He's happy enough. You can say your goodbyes and I'll tell him I'm running you back home."

"Won't he worry that I might try to take advantage of you?"

Trudy laughed.

"You taking advantage of me," she said, dismissively. "Father knows that would never happen. There's no man alive that could control me. Anyway, my life's my own. He and mother know better than to try and interfere."

And she was right. When they approached Whittaker to say farewell, there was no reaction when he knew that they were leaving the party together. Walking outside into the well-lit driveway, Trudy led Robert towards a racing green, Mark III Triumph Spitfire. Classically proportioned, deceptively powerful and ascetically pleasing, the sports car fitted well the personality of its owner.

"Get in," ordered Trudy.

With the hood in place, it proved a tight squeeze for Robert as he manoeuvred himself into the passenger seat. Having opened the driver's door, Trudy paused to hitch up her dress, before she eased her legs gracefully into the car. Seeing her lithe limbs so exposed, a thrill of excitement ran through Robert's body. As she turned the ignition, the engine burst into life. Releasing the handbrake, Trudy drove the car slowly out of the driveway and then as they emerged on to the road beyond, she suddenly pressed down the accelerator and the car roared off along the side of the Common. Close to the ground, it was exhilarating but, even with the hood down, it was noisy and as the Spitfire raced forward, Robert could feel every bump and hole in the road. Soon they had dropped down into Wimbledon, travelling along Church Road and past the All England Club. Trudy was a good, confident driver, but whenever afforded the opportunity of an open stretch of road, she was keen to put the car through its paces.

It was quite dark now. The passing streetlights periodically illuminating the interior of the vehicle, allowing Robert to cast furtive glances at the captivating woman to his side. She had an overwhelming presence; powerful and provocative. Sat so close together, Robert was savouring every moment they were sharing in the intimacy of the tight, two-seater Spitfire. He could see the concentration etched on her pretty face and the outline of her beautiful breasts. Looking down, he was almost mesmerised by the movement of her legs as her feet operated the pedals. With the hem of her dress, pulled over her knees, he felt an almost overwhelming desire to place his hand between them.

"Do you think I can't see?" asked Trudy, suddenly.

Taken by surprise, Robert hesitated before replying.

"What?"

"You're getting all hot and bothered, aren't you?"

Robert felt his cheeks burning. He was thankful that in the gloom she couldn't see his embarrassment.

"No," he replied, somewhat unconvincingly.

Trudy laughed

"It's all right," she continued. "You don't have to hold back on my account."

Her words were electric; a promise of things to come that had Robert's heart pounding and his pulse racing. Excited and aroused, he wanted her now. That was impossible. Having to wait was unbearable and Robert groaned softly in frustration. Trudy understood and smiled. She wanted him to wait; desperate to give her everything and to ensure that he did, she hadn't finished teasing and tormenting him yet.

Approaching Battersea Bridge, Trudy slowed the car as they encountered some heavy traffic. Inching across the Thames there were cars and revellers all around them. Ignoring their proximity, Trudy reached across and without warning placed her hand in Robert's lap.

"I see," she said with a smile, "you're getting a little excited, aren't you Robert?"

Taken by surprise, Robert gasped.

"Someone will see us," he exclaimed.

"But you like it, don't you?" she asked, in smooth, velvet tones.

Overtaken with desire, Robert pushed hard against her hand, desperate for release. He no longer cared where they were. He would willingly risk the shame of discovery and let Trudy do whatever she pleased. But his relief wasn't what she desired. Taking her hand away, she wagged an admonishing finger and smiled.

"No. You're just going to have to wait."

Robert's frustration knew no bounds. He was desperate. She was tantalisingly close. Teasing and tormenting, she had taken him to the very threshold of ecstasy. In his mind she had sown confusion, for he didn't know if he was experiencing pain or pleasure. No woman had ever played so fast and loose with his emotions. Robert was spellbound, unable and unwilling to free himself from her control.

"Oh good," said Trudy. "Finally, it's moving."

She was referring, of course, to the queue of cars in front of them. Yet Robert hadn't noticed, his awareness of anything other than her presence, had long faded from his sensibilities. As they crossed the bridge, passed the Chelsea Embankment and made their way over to Gloucester Road, Robert's heart was pounding, his pulse was racing, his breathing short and hurried.

"Not much longer now," promised Trudy.

Turning towards her, Robert thought he saw the trace of a wicked smile, but all too quickly, the image was gone and he couldn't be sure that in his desperation and excitement, his imagination hadn't run away with him.

"Here we are, Cornwall Gardens."

Pulling into the long, narrow square, they travelled halfway down the row of imposing mid-Victorian houses, before Trudy parked the Spitfire. Getting out of the car, Robert followed her towards an impressive portico, topped by a stone balustrade, that contained the steps leading to a front door. Once inside, they made their way up to the fourth floor, the location of Trudy's flat. Turning her key in the door, Trudy pushed it open, stood to the side and looked at Robert.

"In."

Eager to obey, Robert passed through and into the hallway, Trudy quickly closing the door behind her.

Chapter 95

Awaking early the next morning, Robert slipped quietly out of bed. Looking down at Trudy, he couldn't help but smile, for as she peacefully lay there, breathing softly in her sleep, he saw a picture of innocence that belied the wild, untamed lover, who long into the night had driven him to the heights of passion and taken everything he had to give. Trudy was the best lover he'd ever had and he was sure that she knew it.

Picking up his clothes from the bedroom floor, Robert walked out into the hallway, had a quick wash in the bathroom and got dressed. When he returned to the bedroom Trudy was awake, stood beside the bed in her dressing gown.

"Silly boy. You should have used the ensuite."

Robert looked confused.

"The shower room, behind me."

Robert noticed a door, slightly ajar. He walked towards it and peeked inside, where he could see a shower cubicle, sink, toilet and bidet.

"Oh."

"Oh?" asked Trudy, laughing. "What's that supposed to mean?"

"Just that I didn't expect it to be there."

"Obviously not," replied Trudy. "I suppose they don't have them in Manchester or Barking, do they?"

"Well, only if you've got money," noted Robert.

"Yes, indeed," replied Trudy. "Come on, I suppose you could do with a coffee."

"I'd prefer tea."

"Of course. How very working-class," observed Trudy, shaking her head.

Robert followed her into the hallway and through to the living room. His first impressions left him gazing in wonder. Beautifully decorated walls, covered in original art work. Axminster carpets on the floor and in the front room, expensive furniture and furnishings. It was no different to what he'd seen at Whittaker's but somehow, he hadn't expected it here. Observing his reaction, Trudy laughed.

"Is it a bit too grand for you? Are you feeling uncomfortable?"

"No. It's just a surprise to see a flat looking so luxurious."

"Oh, really," replied Trudy, feeling slightly confused.

"Yes."

"Ah, I see," continued Trudy, "it's obvious to me now. You thought that it would be like the flats inside one of those tenements or high-rise blocks. The ones they've thrown up to house the people from slum clearance."

Not for the first time, Robert couldn't be sure whether she was being serious or simply teasing him. With most women, he wouldn't have bothered to work it out; he would have simply walked away. With Trudy, that wasn't going to happen. She was authentic; part of the social elite. Trudy was opening the door to a world which he was ambitious to be part of. Absolutely stunning, her dismissive reprimands excited him all the more. It fulfilled his fantasies to have her in control, doing to him whatever she wanted.

I suppose I'd better show you the rest of the flat and satisfy your curiosity."

Taking him back into the hallway, Trudy showed him three ample bedrooms, each one exquisitely furnished and decorated and the luxury bathroom that Robert had used earlier. Making their way back into the lounge, Trudy opened a pair of sliding doors behind which was a large kitchen diner, fitted out with expensive white oak cabinets and the latest appliances. In the centre, a fashionable island completed the stylish, contemporary look. Noticing a smile on Robert's face, Trudy was intrigued.

"What's so amusing?" she asked.

"All this equipment", he replied, gesturing to the appliances placed all around the tops.

"Why?"

"Well, I can see how my mam or my gran would love it here. They'd be dead keen to try out all this gadgetry, but you Trudy?" He paused and looked at her with a cheeky, boyish grin. "I can't imagine you cooking up a storm in the kitchen."

Trudy couldn't help laughing. Robert had a rough, rogue like charm, that she found attractive. He said what he thought and he didn't hold back. He was a man who would test her and until she broke him, he would have all her attention.

"That's quite right, Robert. I only usually have breakfast when I'm here. Normally I eat out at restaurants or at friends' houses. Occasionally, if I'm entertaining, my domestic will stay over and cook for my guests."

"Had I better make the drinks then?" suggested Robert.

"Don't worry, I'm quite capable of doing it myself."

Whilst Trudy dealt with the drinks, Robert walked back into the living room and wandered over to one of the large sash windows to look outside. Four floors up, he was afforded a view over the attractive private gardens that ran the full length of the grand terraces on either side of them. It was a haven of greenery, peace and respite in the heart of the West End and reserved exclusively for the use of the privileged and wealthy residents of Cornwall Gardens.

"Come on, your tea's ready."

Robert walked back into the kitchen. Trudy was sat on a tall stool on one side of the island and she beckoned to Robert to sit down opposite. Between them, on top of the island were cereals, milk, sugar and some toast, butter and marmalade.

"Very nice," observed Robert.

"Well, don't get used to it," replied Trudy. "I'll make sure that you do it in future."

Her words were interesting. They made clear to Robert that she didn't regard what had happened between them as just a one-night stand. He had made a positive impression upon her and she was intent on allowing him to see her again. And in the weeks that followed, Robert and Trudy found themselves spending increasing amounts of time together and invariably, when they went out in the evening, the pair of them would end up back in Cornwall Gardens for a night of unrestrained passion. For the first time in his life, Robert found himself in a steady and serious relationship and surprising as it may be, it was one that was increasingly showing signs, that it could become permanent.

Chapter 96

At the beginning of August, Kay arranged to take a week's holiday from work. Bernard was now four and a half and Kay had arranged for the pair of them to go and stay with his grandparents in Kent for a few days, before he started school in September. Kay had ensured that Violet and Norman had been invited regularly to stay at Church Road as their grandson was growing up. Violet, in particular, treasured her time with Bernard Jr, as he was a happy reminder of the son she had so cruelly lost. Kay worked hard to maintain the close relationship between Bernard, his grandparents and his Uncle Larry. Only in this way would her son be able to develop an appreciation of his father's life as a boy and young man, in the days before he met his mother.

Kay had decided that it was better for Bernard that they went on the train. The journey down from Piccadilly was straightforward enough, but knowing that Kay would be nervous about travelling across London, Larry had offered to meet her at Euston and accompany her on to Faversham. Larry was as good as his word and was waiting by the barrier as they left the platform. Suddenly noticing his uncle, Bernard squealed in delight.

"Uncle Lahwee!"

Holding out his arms, Bernard ran forward.

"Airplane!"

Larry took him by the arms and looking quickly around him to see there was no one close by, he lifted Bernard and swung him around through the air.

"Wheeeeee!"

Watching them, Kay shook her head. Spinning around, it was clear that they'd soon become dizzy.

"Right. That's enough."

It was the voice of command. One not raised, yet cutting through with the unmistakable timbre of authority. Quickly, Larry stopped and Bernard was back on the ground.

"More! More!" insisted Bernard, arms outstretched and jumping up and down.

"Bernard!"

Kay's tone was sharp. Chastened, Bernard looked sheepishly at the floor.

"Oh, no. I feel a bit woozy," observed Larry, shaking his head.

"It serves you right," replied Kay, unsympathetically. "You shouldn't be so gormless, should you?"

Like Bernard, Larry found himself looking at the floor. He'd been well and truly told off. He hadn't seen her for a while and was pleased to recognise the Kay of old, reigning her friends in when they were being foolish. It was clear too, that as Bernard grew older, he would find it wise to do as he was asked and understand that his mam usually knew best.

"Never mind," continued Kay, gently. "It's good to see you, Larry."

Kay moved towards Larry and threw her arms around him. Giving him a hug, she kissed him on the cheek and then stepped away. Smiling, Larry looked at her. Kay was now thirty years of age and she looked more beautiful than ever. He longed to tell her so, but it seemed such an inappropriate thing to do.

"Give me your case Kay and we'll set off."

"No, Larry. I'll carry it. You hold on to Bernard and make sure he's safe."

"Right you are. Come on then Junior."

Larry held out his hand and Bernard took it eagerly. As his uncle started walking, his nephew skipped excitedly after him, Kay following closely behind. The passing years certainly hadn't reduced her sense of trepidation as they made their way down the steps and escalators to the Northern Line. Bernard, on the other hand, couldn't hide his sense of wonder and fascination, as he bombarded his 'Uncle Lahwee' with question after question about all the new sights and sounds he was experiencing. Reaching the platform, it wasn't long before they were sat on the train. As Bernard continued to occupy all of Larry's attention, Kay sat quietly, remembering how, many years ago, she had clung on to Larry as he had guided her through the frightening depths of the underground. She couldn't say that she felt any more comfortable now and when they'd changed to the District

Line at Charing Cross and finally emerged in the daylight at Victoria, she breathed a great sigh of relief.

Settled into their seats on the train to Faversham, Bernard was becoming unusually quiet. It had already been a long and exciting day and as the train began its journey, the swaying of the carriage and the soothing, rhythmic rolling of the wheels, soon closed his tired eyes. Larry looked fondly at his little nephew and smiled.

"He's so inquisitive. He never stops asking questions and he's such a bundle of energy. A little human dynamo, isn't he?"

"You can say that again. He's a little rip. You need eyes in the back of your head when he's out anywhere."

"Ah, but you know you love him."

"Of course, I do," replied Kay, proudly.

"He's going to be really clever like his mam but I think he'd rather be Action Man, just like his dad," observed Larry.

The pair of them laughed.

"How's work?" asked Kay, changing the subject. "Are you still pleased you left the *Evening News*."

"Yes, it's turned out really well. It was the best move I could have made," replied Larry, enthusiastically. "I'm now the senior international correspondent at the *Vanguard* and in a couple of weeks, I'm going out to cover the war of liberation in Mozambique."

"Isn't that dangerous? I can't imagine the Portuguese authorities looking kindly on a journalist from a left-wing paper moving freely around the liberated zones."

"No. I'll be fine."

"You won't be from what I've been reading," continued Kay, expressing her concern. "Haven't the Portuguese army just launched an all-out offensive against the guerrillas? They've been pretty brutal, I understand. What will they do to you when you arrive there?"

"Don't worry. I'm not travelling by the normal channels. I'll be flying out to Dar es Salaam and joining up with the guerrillas in Southern Tanzania and crossing over the border into Northern Mozambique. That's where the liberated zones are. The Liberation Front needs international support and so they'll make sure that sympathetic reporters like me, won't be put in any danger."

"I hope so," replied Kay, sounding unconvinced. "Don't be reckless, Larry. Bernard's already lost his father; he doesn't want to lose his uncle."

Larry nodded. He could see that Kay looked uneasy and tactfully he changed the subject, telling her about how excited his mother was about seeing her grandson and reminiscing over their visit to his parents' house when they were at Owens.

Over the course of the week that followed, Bernard Jr enjoyed himself immensely. Blessed with hot, sunny weather, he was able to play out every day. Staying in the middle of the countryside, Kay's son was experiencing a completely different way of life to that he was used to in Manchester. Furthermore, being near to the coast, Norman and Violet were able to take him to the seaside and Kay finally got to see the amusements and attractions in Margate. It wasn't just Larry's parents who were delighted to see Kay and Bernard. Alice was still very much a part of the Foster household and she made an immense fuss over the little boy. When Kay had arrived, she had put an arm around her and hugged her tightly and as the days passed and she observed the happy and playful young boy, she insisted that it was just like having his father back in the house once more.

The afternoon before she and Bernard returned home, Kay and Violet were sat in the garden enjoying the sunshine. Norman and Larry had taken young Bernard to Faversham and after a busy week, it was the first real opportunity for the two women to have a long and private conversation. The friendship between them, established on Kay's first visit had, over the years, developed into the strongest of relationships. It had been fortified by the joy of Kay's marriage to Bernard and the birth of their son and also through the shared sense of loss as a result of Bernard's passing. Violet was grateful that Kay had been so insistent that she and Norman played a key role in their grandson's life and appreciated that such a close bond between a wife and mother-in-law was rarely the norm.

"Little Bernard's such a credit to you Kay. His father would be so proud of him. But are you making sure that you're looking after yourself?"

"Yes, of course."

"I don't know how you possibly do it all. You look after Bernard and you have all that responsibility at work and then you have the house to attend to as well."

"No, I can't take the credit for all that. I get lots of help from my mam. She's the one who's looked after Bernard whilst I've been at work. Now he's starting school, I've persuaded my parents to leave Bennett Street and move in with me. I couldn't expect Mam to travel from Ardwick every afternoon to collect him from school."

"They've lived there since they've been married, haven't they?"

"Yes, that's right."

"It must have proved a bit of a wrench for them. Every home contains a lot of memories."

"Yes, I was concerned about that, but Mam said that life was all about creating new ones. It could have been awkward for my dad, but he's been moved to a new depot much nearer to Church Road."

"Still for all the support that Ethel and Ernest give you …"

"And you and Norman too," insisted Kay.

"You've worked so hard," Violet continued. "It's you all over Kay. Always self-deprecating. And you shouldn't be, you know."

"But I don't think I work anywhere near as hard as women had to in the War. They worked longer shifts and still had houses and kids to look after."

"I can see that you're just not going to allow me to give you any credit," said Violet, shaking her head.

"No, I suppose not," replied Kay, laughing.

"Seriously though, do you get enough time for yourself? It worries me, Kay. You give so much to everyone else, perhaps it would be nice for you to be on the receiving end for once."

Kay looked confused, unsure of what Violet was alluding to.

"You're a very beautiful woman Kay. I'm sure if Bernard could, he would tell you that if you have a chance of being happy with someone else, then you should take it."

It was a most generous suggestion and underlined the intimacy of the relationship between the two women. Kay reached across and squeezed Violet's hand softly.

"Thank you. You're so kind, but there can never be anyone else. Bernard is the only man I could ever love. It was fate that brought us together. So many circumstances, that if just one had been different, the two of us could never have met. If Larry had gone to Cambridge; if he and Robert weren't both reading history; if Larry hadn't invited us here; if Bernard hadn't been on leave and the list goes on. It had to be fate; we were destined to meet. I've accepted that we've only had a short time together. It's hard, but far better than us never having met and my life remaining unfulfilled."

Violet was lost for words. They had always been able to talk about anything, but her daughter-in-law's revelation of the deep and true love she felt for her husband, was intensely personal. Yet Kay felt no embarrassment at revealing the deep feelings in her heart and soul. She loved Bernard desperately and she was prepared to let everyone know it.

"No," continued Kay, "little Bernard and I are quite settled."

"I understand," replied Violet. "As long as you're happy."

"Don't worry, we are."

There was a pause before Violet turned the conversation towards Larry. It was clear that she was becoming concerned about him.

"Kay, how have you found Larry? Does he seem settled now he's back in London?"

"He appears to be and he's certainly made up at the moment over his new role at the *Vanguard*. He was getting very frustrated at the *Evening News*. You know Larry, he'll never give up on his principles and he was becoming unhappy at not being able to investigate the issues that mattered to him. Now, at the *Vanguard*, he's able to do that."

"It's funny, isn't it? All those years ago when he set off for Owens, Norman and I were so worried about him being far away in Manchester, but now I'm concerned because he's no longer there."

"But why?" asked Kay.

"Because when he was at the *Evening News*, we knew that you were close by to help him if he needed support. Now he's lost that."

"We're always in contact with one another and he's already been back several times to stay over. He and little Bernard are best pals. A pair of real tearaways. I'm sure he wouldn't hesitate to ring me to ask for help and advice if he wanted it. Besides," she added reassuringly, "he's got Robert close by in London. I know the two of them see each other all the time."

"Yes, I know and Robert is a good friend, but you were most responsible for helping him settle safely in Manchester. When Norman and I first met you, it was obvious that you were the glue that held all three of you together."

"Well, perhaps at the time, that was mainly due to the foolishness of young men. Larry and Robert are far more dependable now and both of them will always look out for each other."

"I suppose so," replied Violet, with a sigh. "I did hope that Larry would find someone to settle down with and have a family of his own. I'm not sure that will ever happen though."

"I suppose that at the moment, Larry's overriding concern is his job," suggested Kay. "A steady relationship would be hard to maintain when he'll be travelling all around the World. Things may change. You never know."

As Kay finished speaking, the women heard the rising sound of a car's engine, followed by the crunching of gravel on the drive way, indicating that the men had returned. It was a welcome interruption which effectively curtailed the conversation, for Kay knew that there was no more she could say to remove Violet's concerns about Larry. Kay was however, certain that Larry's upcoming assignment had given him a new lease of life; one that would help him face the future with purpose and confidence.

Chapter 97

Having dismissed the chances of Larry getting married in the near future, at the end of September, Kay received a letter containing an invitation to attend the wedding of Robert and Trudy Whittaker. The ceremony was to take place at Kensington and Chelsea Register Office on the first Friday in December. The news was surprising, as Kay had recently spoken to Robert on the telephone and he had made no reference to his intended. As long as Kay had known him, Robert had never made any important decisions without due thought and consideration. He was disinclined to act with impetuosity. Furthermore, Kay had believed that her friend would remain a confirmed bachelor, happy to gratify his amorous desires with a succession of brief dalliances. Kay was therefore intrigued by his decision to get married. As unlikely as it seemed, could it be that he'd fallen hopelessly in love?

There was no question of Robert being a victim of love. His decision to marry Trudy had been a matter for the head and not the heart. Certainly, his intended was attractive and as a couple, they were more than sexually compatible, but what made Trudy so different to all the others, was that she had real pedigree. Robert had enjoyed his brief flings with the young middle-class women he'd met since his days at Owens. A self-centred, working-class lad, Robert saw his series of successful seductions as evidence that he was climbing the social ladder. As soon as he'd met Trudy, he'd recognised that she was the genuine article; there was no affected accent or pretence of gentility. Rich, gorgeous and sophisticated, she would be his trophy wife. Trudy offered him the social connections that would give him access to powerful figures in business and the media and in return he was determined to do what he'd never done for any other woman; he would remain faithful.

Yet the decision for marriage hadn't initially been Robert's to make, for the driving force in their relationship, from the moment they had met, had been Trudy. Passionate and impulsive, since

her late teens Trudy had worked her way through a number of unsatisfactory relationships, leaving two ex-husbands trailing in her wake. As yet, no man had been able to tame her tempestuous nature and she now believed it was because they were effete members of her own class; spoilt and privileged, weak and spineless. She thus became determined to find herself a 'real man' and when she met the upstart Mancunian, rough and ready, but curiously handsome, who would deny her to the point of ridicule, she believed that she was falling in love. Yet unlike Robert, her desire to get married was based firmly in the present. Trudy had little idea of how she was going to commit to their relationship in the future.

It fell to Kay to organise the travel of the invited guests from Manchester, down to London. On the day before the wedding, Kay, Ethel and Bernard Jr met up with Irene and Edna, early in the morning at Piccadilly station and the party travelled to Euston, where Larry was waiting to greet them. They were then whisked away in a couple of taxis, the short distance to the *Imperial*, a luxury five-star hotel on the east side of Russell Square. Only recently rebuilt, it had been designed in a brutalist, modern style. As they emerged from their taxi, the choice of accommodation didn't make a great impression on the mature ladies from Manchester.

"It's awful, isn't it?" asked Edna, not noted for holding back on her opinions.

"Another monstrosity," observed Irene. "It's just like the Hotel Piccadilly."

"I'm sure it's very nice inside though," remarked Ethel who, aware that she was Robert's guest, hesitated to join in with the criticism that she clearly agreed with.

"Oh, it most certainly is," responded Larry, reassuringly. "And I can tell you that it's cost Robert and Trudy, a pretty penny to put you up here."

Edna and Irene made no response, then as they walked away towards the hotel's entrance, Larry could hear them quietly tutting and mumbling about a 'waste of money.' Followed by Ethel and Bernard, the two women made their way inside. Kay and Larry looked at each other and smiled.

"I should have known there was no point in trying to impress them with the cost," said Larry.

"It's just unfamiliar to them," said Kay, "a different world. They want to hold on to the certainties and simplicity of their youth. It's all just a little too modern for them. The Sixties have done for so many of their generation and they certainly won't be swinging along with the times."

"Yes, I suppose Robert would have been better off booking them in it at the *Russell*."

Larry motioned towards the other great hotel on Russell Square, that could be seen nearby. Unlike the *Imperial*, it hadn't been knocked down and rebuilt and so it still retained its appearance from the time of its construction at the turn of the century. Clad in decorative terra cotta, the building provided a stately example of late Victorian, renaissance style architecture.

"Yes, I'm sure he would," replied Kay, looking towards it and clearly impressed. "It's far closer to somewhere like the *Midland*. I'm afraid that to Edna and Irene and to my mam too, the *Imperial* reminds them of being back home in Heywood House. London can be such a disappointment."

"How so?" asked Larry.

"Because most Northerners who have never been here are a bit like Dick Whittington and imagine that when they go to London, they'll find themselves somewhere magical. They don't understand that away from the famous tourist spots, it's just like any other city, only much bigger."

Fortunately, once settled in their rooms, the ladies began to mellow and when Robert popped in to see them later, there was no hint of any dissatisfaction at the arrangements that had been made for them.

"Oh, it's smashing love," said Edna. "You shouldn't have gone to all this trouble. Haven't you done well for yourself, putting us up in a place like this."

"He certainly has Mam," added Irene, proudly.

Larry looked bewildered. Smiling, Kay leaned over and whispered quietly in his ear.

"He's their pride and joy, Larry. They'd never upset him by voicing any misgivings about the accommodation."

"I thought you Northerners were always so blunt," replied Larry.

"Not if it could really upset someone close to you," explained Kay. "I thought you would have known that."

Chapter 98

The next morning, just after ten, Larry returned to the hotel to ensure the arrival of the taxis for the journey to the register office. Honoured to be Robert's best man, Larry was taking his responsibilities very seriously. Importantly, he was conscious of the fact that Irene and Edna had yet to meet Trudy or her family and he was determined that he would stay with them until the ceremony began, so that they wouldn't feel at all isolated in the gathering of Trudy's own friends and family.

The Kensington and Chelsea Register Office was situated within Chelsea Old Town Hall, which was located on the fashionable Kings Road. A neo-classical, Grade II listed building, its external appearance created a favourable impression on the Mancunian party when they arrived just before quarter to eleven. As they waited outside for the couple to arrive, Larry attempted to pass the time by recounting a few details about the historic nature of the wedding venue.

"Robert and Trudy have chosen a very fashionable location to get married," remarked Larry. "Some very famous people have been married here."

"Did you hear that, Mam?" asked Irene. "It seems our Robert's in good company getting married here."

"Like who?" asked Edna, looking expectantly at Larry.

"Well, James Joyce for instance."

The two women looked blankly at one another. It was clear that they had never heard of him. Kay resisted the urge to laugh. For all the years he'd lived in Manchester and was now working on a left-wing newspaper, Larry had no understanding of the world of celebrity for the working-classes.

"Who's he?" asked Ethel, who was equally confused.

"Well, he's a writer."

"Is that all?" replied Edna, witheringly dismissive.

Clearly disappointed that he had failed to impress, Larry conjured up another name.

"Well, there's Marc Bolan. He was married here back in January."

"Oh yes, love. We know him," replied Edna.

"Yes, he's that pop star, isn't he? I've read all about him and his shenanigans in the *News of the World*. He could do with a haircut," observed Irene.

This time Kay couldn't hold back and broke out into peals of laughter, with which all bar Larry and a bewildered little Bernard, joined in.

"Well, he's just one of many," continued Larry, desperate to prove his point. "Judy Garland got married here last year and you can go right back to Wallis Simpson who tied the knot with her second husband, Ernest Simpson, here."

"I hope our Robert's marriage lasts longer than theirs did," remarked Edna.

"Mam! Think what you're saying. Our Robert's not like them. He'd never marry carelessly. Now, would he?" asked Irene, reproachfully.

Kay wondered if Edna hadn't inadvertently voiced an underlying suspicion that Robert's decision to marry a rich Southerner, who they had still to meet, may not have been one to which he had given adequate consideration. Whether or not Irene shared such misgivings, she was determined that she would be supportive of her son and welcoming to his wife in keeping with the spirit of the day.

Certainly, when Trudy arrived and Edna and Irene saw her for the first time, they couldn't question the fact that Robert was marrying a beautiful, elegant and graceful bride; a woman of real sophistication. Trudy had chosen a thoroughly modern outfit. Ivory in colour, it was a beautiful silk pencil dress, the top of which hugged her impressive figure, with the skirt reaching just below the knee. To add the classy finishing touches, Trudy wore a matching jacket, gloves and heels.

During the formality of the ceremony and the taking of the photographs, Robert's mam and gran had little chance to talk to Trudy and her family, but at the reception, Robert was finally able to introduce them to one another. Trudy was charming, seemingly appreciating that her acerbic wit would be misunderstood and unappreciated by her new in-laws. Significantly, Whittaker and his wife were particularly welcoming and the former spent much of the afternoon chatting to Edna, Irene and Ethel, whilst his wife mingled with the other guests. It was as if the lad from Ashton-in-Makerfield was happy to be back among his own.

When he arrived at Chelsea Old Town Hall, Robert was pleased to see that Kay was there as expected. Moreover, he couldn't help but notice how absolutely gorgeous she looked in her light blue, two-piece suit and her matching white hat, gloves and heels. Yet as the afternoon unfolded, he became frustrated that the demands of circulating among Trudy's friends and relations and engaging in polite, but meaningless conversation, was delaying his chance to introduce his new wife to his closest and dearest friend.

"Don't you think that we should talk to Kay?" asked Trudy. "After all, she has come all this way and she is one of your dearest friends."

"Well, yes," replied Robert, somewhat hesitantly.

Trudy laughed. She could see that Robert was embarrassed, for he knew that she had noticed the way his eyes had been following Kay all around the room.

"Don't be silly Robert. I know how much she means to you and yes, she is very pretty."

It was Trudy all over. Robert should have known that he had no need to feel any embarrassment. Confident in her own good looks, she had no inclination towards jealousy. The exact nature of Robert's relationship with Kay intrigued her, but in no way did she feel at all threatened by it. With Robert in tow, Trudy made her way across the room to where Kay was talking to Larry. Seeing them approach, Kay turned towards them and smiled.

"Hello, Trudy, I'm Kay. It's nice to meet you."

"And you too."

Trudy turned to Robert.

"Why don't you give Kay and I a chance to have a chat. Take Larry to meet some of father's associates. I'm sure he'll find them interesting. You journalists always like talking shop, don't you?"

"Yes, that's a good idea. In my exalted position, I rarely get a chance to mix with the barons," remarked Larry, laughing.

With the two men departing, Kay and Trudy had an opportunity to get to know one another.

"Robert told me that you work in social services and that you have quite a lot of responsibility."

"Well, I wouldn't quite say that," replied Kay.

"You're too modest. Robert's very proud of your achievements. I already know that he thinks the world of you."

"It's just that we've known each other for so long," explained Kay. "We lived in the same streets, went to the same junior school and then to Owens together. Growing up, there were so few of us taking that journey, so we depended on one another to be able to get through all the challenges."

"Yes. I suppose it's such a struggle for the working-classes to get on, isn't it?"

Kay smiled. She wasn't sure whether or not there was a hint of condescension in Trudy's voice, but she wouldn't have reacted even if there was. Kay had never commented on, or interfered in, any of Robert's relationships. The two of them had determined that his love life would never be allowed to undermine their friendship.

"I do admire you for being able to do something important," continued Trudy. "I'd never be able to tolerate the rigours of work; it would interfere with my routines and make too many demands on my time. Of course, I'm fortunate that I have means and can exist quite adequately. I don't have to concern myself about finding employment, or taking a wealthy husband."

"Yes, no doubt that helps," replied Kay, diplomatically.

"And you have a little boy too, don't you Kay?"

"Yes. Bernard."

"I don't know how you manage. I can't imagine having a child myself, not that I suppose Robert wants one."

Kay was surprised. Whilst she and Bernard were courting, the two of them had discussed the question of children quite early in their relationship and both of them were clear about wanting a family. It seemed strange that Trudy and Robert had married without knowing each other's wishes in that regard. It reinforced the impression that the wedding had taken place in rather a hurry.

"I can't imagine life without him," replied Kay. "He's certainly a big responsibility and he can be a little rip, but I get lots of support. Mam looks after him whilst I'm at work and all his grandparents spoil him rotten, as do Uncle Bobs and Uncle Lahwee."

"Bobs and Lahwee?" asked Trudy, looking confused.

"Yes. It's what Bernard calls Robert and Larry. It's how he first pronounced their names and they've never felt inclined to try and correct him," answered Kay, smiling.

"I see."

The note of uncertainty in Trudy's voice indicated that she had no appreciation of the endearing quirks of personality exhibited by young children.

"It's clear to see that he means the world to you," continued Trudy.

"Yes, he does."

"Well, I suppose we'd best go and find the men," suggested Trudy.

"Yes, I suppose so."

Their conversation hadn't lasted long but each of them had gained a clearer understanding of the personality of the other. Kay could see that Trudy had little interest in starting a family. She was very much like Robert in the sense that they were both inclined to pursue their own interests. It was uncertain however, whether this would provide a satisfactory basis for a long-term relationship. Importantly, Trudy instinctively understood that Kay treasured her son, because of her deep, undying love for her husband. Unlike Trudy herself, Kay had been faithful to one partner alone and much as Robert obviously cherished her, Kay would never be other than his dearest friend.

Chapter 99

In early January 1972, Robert made a short trip to Manchester to visit his family. Edna and Irene had been living in Bennett Street flats since early 1965, just before the houses on Armitage Street had been demolished. Neither had wanted to leave Ardwick and had been fortunate that one of Ethel and Ernest's neighbours were willing to exchange their flat, for the house with a garden that the Corporation had offered them in Hattersley. Yet Robert wouldn't be staying overnight in Ardwick, but with Kay in Urmston.

Robert's relationship with his dearest friend was as strong as ever. The two of them spoke regularly on the telephone and Robert had been back to see her a couple of times since the wedding. Travelling with him was Larry who, having been given a break from his international duties, had just completed a special assignment on the failures of slum clearance. The visit was also welcome as it would give them the chance to check on the progress of their nephew. Bernard Jr was now almost six and growing up fast. He'd settled in well at school and although his command of language continued to grow apace, he still insisted on referring to his uncles as 'Bobs' and 'Lahwee'. Always excited when he saw them, it was clear to Kay that the bond between Bernard Jr and his uncles would only grow stronger with the passage of time.

On the first night, after Bernard Jr had been put to bed, the adults settled down in the lounge. It had been a long time since they'd had a chance to catch-up with one another. Kay told Larry that she had read his recent articles on the new housing programmes, but was unhappy at their political bias.

"Well, I'm just pleased to know that you've read them," said Larry.

"I read all your articles and I keep an eye on what's been covered by Robert's paper too. I have the *Vanguard* and the *Gazette* delivered every day and I look through them when I get home. I'm proud of you both, but it doesn't mean that I won't have a go at you when I think you're wrong."

"Well, I'm not a star reporter like Larry," remarked Robert, "so anything I've had a hand in, won't be attributed to me."

"Yes, but you're a key member of the editorial team and you oversee the content, so I'm not letting you off that easily," insisted Kay.

"Fair enough, I suppose," replied Robert, somewhat reluctantly.

"As for your article," continued Kay, looking back at Larry, "I was disappointed. You focused solely on allegations of corruption in order to attack capitalism. You made scant reference to the consequences following on from the destruction of long-standing communities and their shared values. When you were still at the *Evening News*, you wanted to deal with both. It seems to me that you're still being restricted by what you're actually allowed to write."

"Come on Kay," said Robert. "You know that all newspapers push an agenda. Proprietors and their editors put a slant on the news to support their own opinions."

"Yes, but it leads to stereotypical reporting and that can't be good."

"Not necessarily," said Larry. "What may appear to be a stereotype can, in reality, be the truth. Sometimes things are exactly as they appear. When everything seems so obvious and creates the impression that it fits too perfectly, you shouldn't assume that it's necessarily subjective. In that case, you're the one not being objective."

Robert laughed.

"Oh my, Larry. Do you have to make everything so complicated? Or is that you've drunk too much wine?"

"Seriously," continued Kay. "I get so frustrated at how the media covers issues involving social services. When I was a child care officer, I only occasionally spoke to the press, but since I've been assistant director, I've had to deal with them on a regular basis. Whether they're from the local or national press, or television and radio for that matter, journalists are the same…"

"Now you're stereotyping," observed Larry.

"Let me finish."

Kay looked at him reproachfully, before continuing.

"Journalists want to sensationalise every story and we're in the firing line. When you work with difficult and vulnerable families like we do, there are bound to be problems and incidents. But when I talk to members of the press and try to deal with matters of fact, they don't want to know. All they're interested in is a whiff of scandal. They love to show our department's incompetence; portray us as careless and uncaring. Arouse public condemnation and emotion; a furore that will fan the flames of the story. Then they'll target an individual under our care; portray them as monsters, dangers to society, when they're not. We and those we care for, are such an easy target and so journalists aren't interested in reporting the truth."

"That's not always the case," suggested Larry. "Surely you can accept that sometimes the press has helped. If not for investigative journalists exposing the shortcomings in social care, there wouldn't have been a focus on integrating family services. You've got to say that has been a benefit."

"Fair enough, in that case," agreed Kay, "but there's so many times when press coverage has treated us unfairly and has helped undermine our work."

"Such as when?" asked Robert.

"Well, a recent case for example. Our department were made out to have been negligent to the point where a whole family almost died. The reality was that the responsibility lay squarely on the shoulders of the mother."

Kay hesitated. Robert and Larry were intrigued, eager to hear more.

"Go on," said Robert.

"I shouldn't. I'm not supposed to breach the confidentiality of our files."

"Oh, come on Kay! It's us," said Larry. "As if we would betray your confidence."

"Or ever do anything to compromise you," added Robert.

Kay sensed their disappointment. She was their best friend, yet hadn't treated them accordingly.

"I know, I'm sorry. Since I got this job, I've got used to being so careful. At work, I can't relax my guard for a moment. Yet, if not you, then who can I trust?"

"It's all right. You don't need to tell us anything more. We understand," said Larry.

"No, it's not. I want to tell you. It was a family in Ancoats. They had a fire late at night. The front room curtains were set alight, but the neighbours were alerted and they got the four kids out. The fire brigade arrived quickly and there wasn't too much damage. Next morning, the reporters were out to talk to the mother, a woman called Aileen. The fire officer had told her that a lit candle had fallen against the curtains. Aileen explained that she had no money to pay her electric bill and so it had been cut off. That's why they were using candles. She said that she'd contacted social services and the DHSS and been ignored; that no one would help her. When the *Evening News* report came out, they blamed us. Aileen had two teenage girls, seventeen and fifteen and two boys, nine and three. We were accused of deserting them in their hour of need. We hadn't. We had a case worker assigned to them in the past. The eldest daughter had been caught soliciting in town and we'd worked with her and helped find her a job. What the papers weren't interested in, was the fact that Aileen worked and her ex-husband paid maintenance. She had plenty of money, but she preferred to spend it on expensive clothes and going out. That's why she couldn't pay the electric and had also got behind on the rent. All the neighbours knew that she was in the pub when the house set on fire, but the *Evening News* never printed that. Neither did they mention that the DHSS couldn't help her because her income was too high."

"That's understandable," said Robert, "it's the newspaper business. At the *Gazette* we would have likely done the same. If you take Aileen's version of events, you've got a real human-interest story. Far more mileage in doing that, than just reporting on what actually happened."

Kay sighed.

"The worst thing about it wasn't the criticism we received, but the fact that Aileen faced no consequences for ignoring her responsibilities. Once she had the press on her side, there was no chance of opening a new case file on the family. Could you imagine the howls of protest? We'd have been portrayed as being vindictive. The upshot of it all was that an anonymous benefactor, who'd read about the case, came forward and covered the arrears on both the electric and the rent and paid for the house to be refurnished and decorated."

"Well, I suppose what you have to say, is that this Aileen woman, is a real survivor," suggested Larry. "She's certainly resourceful."

"And a constant reminder, that there's no real justice in the world. I look at all the mothers we deal with, who do try to remain decent and honest, despite the hard times they've fallen on and I think how much more they could have benefitted from that money."

"It's the job you chose Kay," said Robert. "It's tough. But you'll still do it, because you care. That's the difference between us. I could have written that *Evening News* article quite easily, even though, like you, I would have seen right through Aileen. Unlike Larry, I have no illusions about the working-classes."

"Illusions? What do you mean?" asked Larry.

"Well, you radical 'toffs' on the far left, can't bring yourselves to portray members of the working-class as anything other than paragons of virtue. You'd be bound to sympathise with Aileen and condemn the bourgeois institutions that abandoned her family. There's so much to admire about the types of communities that Kay and I grew up in, but we both know that they contained some 'wrong uns' too. There were quite a few like Aileen when we were growing up and there are lots more since the new estates have been built. You see Larry, there aren't the same social expectations on people since the old neighbourhoods disappeared."

"He's right," added Kay. "I've started to notice it more and more."

"Yet even though Aileen is a waste of space," continued Robert, "I'd still be happy to write her up as some unfortunate, struggling heroine. Unlike Kay, I have to admit that I no longer really care about standing by the old communal values. That difference makes us perfect for the different jobs we've chosen. Kay has her sense of morality intact, whereas I lost it a long time ago. Moving to Fleet Street and working to reach the top of the profession, has made sure of that."

"I think you're being a little harsh on yourself," suggested Larry.

"No, I'm not and I'm perfectly comfortable with it. You're different again Larry, because you still believe. You're still searching for the truth, albeit your version of it. Writing is, for you, an end in itself. You've kept your sense of morality because you don't seek the material rewards that I do."

"Well, that may be true Robert," remarked Kay, "but we still love you."

The three of them burst out laughing. It was only because they had continued to remain so close, that they felt comfortable enough to expose their innermost feelings. Even though their geographical separation brought long periods when they were apart, a bond had been formed between three friends at Owens, that would prove almost impossible to break.

Chapter 100

As the first signs of Spring began to appear in 1973, Robert realised that for some time he and his wife had been slowly drifting apart and it was his fault as much as hers. The fact was that for all his ambition to mix with the social elite, Robert's attempts to get there were firmly rooted in his belief in the value of hard work and perseverance. Robert had never abandoned his faith in meritocracy and thus found it challenging that in marrying Trudy, he came into contact with a circle of friends that included effete and ineffectual young men, who frittered away their days in frivolous and extravagant entertainments. Robert could accept his wife's privileged life of leisure, but he expected her male friends to be industrious and useful. He understood however, that if he wanted to retain his wife's approval and gain acceptance from the 'smart set' that surrounded her, his attitudes would have to change. If that didn't happen, then his marriage had no chance of surviving.

There was no doubting the growing sense of disharmony between Robert and his wife. This had become apparent after he had taken Trudy to visit Edna and Irene at Heywood House, shortly after their wedding. Throughout the visit, Trudy had felt uncomfortable and was eager to return to the *Midland*. On the following day, rather than returning to her in-laws' flat, Trudy had insisted that Robert should go and collect his mam and gran, so that they could have lunch in the more genteel surroundings of the hotel, before returning to London. When, some months later, Robert had suggested that they ought to visit Manchester again, Trudy had dismissed the idea out of hand.

"Oh, you just go Robert. I've got so much on at the moment."

"But it would be nice for them to see you as well. They hardly know you."

"Why not bring them down here instead?" asked Trudy. "Put them up in a hotel and I'll pay. You'll be able to take them out and show them the sights. They didn't get a chance to do that when they came for the wedding. They'll enjoy it."

Robert realised that his wife wanted to spend as little time as possible with his family and it was abundantly clear that even though they had plenty of room, she didn't want them staying at Cornwall Gardens.

"No, it's okay," replied Robert. "I'll just go to Manchester on my own. Mam and gran will understand that you've got things you have to do."

"Perhaps that's for the best," replied Trudy, trying hard to hide her sense of relief. "You can take the opportunity to drop in on Kay and her little boy too, can't you?"

"Yes, I suppose I can."

As they entered their second year of marriage, Robert focused increasingly on his work, much to his wife's frustration. Trudy was used to being the centre of attention; popular with her friends and surrounded by a host of prospective lovers. She had made it clear to Robert that their relationship was not living up to her expectations.

"When I met you Robert, I didn't expect to end up living with my father."

"What do you mean?"

"You're becoming just like him. Obsessed with work. I wanted you because you seemed so different. I thought that you were rebellious; but I was wrong. You're grey, dull and boring."

Robert had promised that he would do better and to an extent he had, believing that matters were improving between them. Then he decided that he would get hold of some tickets for a West End show and return home early to surprise her. Arriving at their flat however, it was Robert who would encounter the unexpected. Entering the hallway, he halted in disbelief. Coming from the bedroom were the unmistakable sounds of a couple making love. For several moments he felt numb, unable to face the truth, hoping that somehow, it wasn't his wife that was in their bed. Realising that inaction wasn't an option, Robert reluctantly made his way to the open bedroom door. Stood there, they were oblivious to his presence and he continued to watch as Trudy moaned in pleasure as her skilful lover satisfied her needs.

And then it happened. He was jealous; felt rage and anger that a lover could satisfy her more than himself. He rushed over to the bed and pulled them apart. Grabbing her paramour, Robert flung him across the room. Colliding with the wall, the man slumped to the floor. Moving deliberately towards him, Robert raised his fist, ready to strike, only for Trudy to dive in front of him, her naked body protecting her lover from any further punishment.

"Don't you dare!"

Robert looked at her and he knew that it was over. Her nakedness underlined the fact that she had been prepared to give everything to her lover; an acknowledgement that her husband had nothing left to offer.

Unclenching his fist, Robert was silent. He breathed deeply and began to shake his head. He had never been violent and it had shocked him to see the look of fear in his wife's eyes as she had screamed at him to stop. Looking down at her lover, Robert realised that they had met before. It was Tobias Brooke, one of Trudy's childhood friends. Suddenly, although perhaps he shouldn't have, Robert began to feel ashamed of what he had done.

"Is he alright?" asked Robert, looking at Trudy.

"He will be, if you just leave him alone."

Robert moved away and watched as Trudy fussed over his rival, getting him to his feet and sitting him back on the edge of the bed. Looking at him, Robert could see that Tobias hadn't suffered any serious physical damage. It was only the fact that he had been unexpectedly thrown across the room that had disorientated him.

"You just can't leave Manchester behind, can you Robert? You had to act like a thug, didn't you?"

Robert was quiet, but to reassure Tobias that he had calmed down, he left the bedroom and walked through to the lounge. It wasn't long before he could hear whispering in the hallway and then the sound of the front door opening and closing. Her lover having departed, Trudy returned to her husband.

"Robert. We need to talk. Matters need sorting out."

Her words were direct and demanding. Trudy had clearly recovered from the shock of Robert's behaviour.

"You acted outrageously. You had no right to lay your hands on Tobias."

"I'm not condoning my actions, but I did catch the guy having it off with my wife."

"That wasn't his fault. You weren't supposed to be at home."

Robert laughed. He could hardly believe what he was hearing.

"Oh, so it was fine as long as I didn't find out about it? Is that right then?" Robert asked, clearly annoyed.

"And I suppose you've never done the same yourself, have you Robert?"

Her words could have been disarming, for Robert immediately recalled how he and Joan had cheated on Colin. Nevertheless, he pushed such thoughts to the back of his mind, ignoring her question.

"So, I don't have a right to be angry, then?"

"The fact is Robert, that there's a correct way to behave. If you'd been brought up properly, you would know that."

"Oh, excuse me. I'm very sorry," replied Robert, his voice laced with sarcasm. "I'm afraid we in Ardwick call a spade, a spade. When we come across a cheating bastard, good manners go out of the window. If your Tobias had breeding, he wouldn't be skulking around knocking my wife off behind my back, would he?"

"Do you have to lower the tone?" replied Trudy, dismissively. "Can't you act civilised for one moment?"

"I think, I've been very civilised. Vey understanding where you're concerned."

"No, you haven't. You're such a prude. I decided I wanted another man. So what? Why shouldn't I? You should have an open mind; understand my needs. But you can't escape your petty, small-minded, working-class hypocrisy, can you? Your wife mustn't seek satisfaction in the arms of another, but it's fine for her husband to cheat, isn't it? Don't tell me that you haven't done it since we were married. All those pretty young things at work?"

"I haven't."

"Look me in the eyes and tell me that."

Robert stared straight back at her. There was no question that he was telling the truth.

"I admit it. I enjoy the sight of a beautiful woman as much as any man does. I'm married though and I've been faithful to you. If I hadn't, I'd tell you."

"Well, more fool you. I wish you had done. If you'd felt guilty when we were making love, it might have spiced things up a bit. Provided some excitement for once."

Robert winced. Her words had hurt him and she knew it.

"I know what it is. I've bruised your ego, haven't I? The great lover, Robert Wilson, can't satisfy his wife. It's ages since you have done. To be honest, I'd become fed up of acting; pretending to enjoy it when you tried to make love to me. I should have been up for an Oscar. Why do you think that I turned to Tobias?"

Robert was subdued. He had no answer, although he didn't entirely believe that she hadn't responded to him for as long as she had claimed. Trudy looked at him with disdain.

"Haven't you got anything to say?"

Robert held his silence.

"I did have respect for you," continued Trudy, "but now I see you for what you are. You're pathetic!"

It was clear to Robert that she intended to provoke him, but he was calmer now and had his mind focused firmly on the bigger picture. He was no longer the boy who had stood his ground in defiance of Ruby in the classroom at Armitage Street School. Robert now had a promising career to protect; one to which Trudy's father held the key. Holding his tongue and temper in order to protect his future prospects, was now far more important to him than any principles he may once have had.

"I want you out of here," demanded Trudy.

"Don't worry, I'll find a hotel."

"Oh, I certainly won't worry and tomorrow you'll be hearing from my solicitor. I want a divorce."

"Yes, you're good at that, aren't you?" remarked Robert. "You won't find any objections from me."

By the weekend, Robert had found himself another terraced house to rent, back on Suffolk Road in Barking. It was strange how little he'd had to collect from the flat in Cornwall Gardens. Besides a few clothes, he really had no personal items there. It seemed to sum up the lack of commitment that he and Trudy had shown towards their marriage. The unpalatable truth was that Trudy had regarded him as nothing more than her little plaything and she'd expected that he would come running at her beck and call. But he had his own ambitions, determined to answer to the demands of his job. In a relatively short time, Trudy had become bored of him and was ready to move on to someone else. The fact that he'd caught her cheating with Tobias, had simply speeded up their inevitable separation.

Robert understood that with Trudy, he had never really been in love. He had lusted after her, dazzled by her carefree, almost dangerous attitude towards life. She had excited him and making love to her had been intense. In fact, theirs had been a purely sexual relationship, for there had developed no deep affections or shared interests to place their marriage on firmer foundations. Strong minded and confident as he was, it didn't take Robert long to put his love life back on a familiar footing. He was soon enjoying the freedom of being single and decided that even if he were to live together with someone again, their relationship would never be on the basis of marriage. There was only one woman who Robert knew that he could truly love; his beautiful Kay. She was however, beyond his reach and seemingly destined to never be more than his best friend.

Chapter 101

There was no doubt that Robert had concerns about his situation at work and for the following few weeks he felt uncertain about his position. Robert was convinced that Whittaker would look unfavourably on the breakdown of his daughter's marriage and as proprietor of the *Daily Gazette*, would demand his dismissal. With his father-in-law's influence within the industry, Robert feared that he would lose his chance of reaching the top in Fleet Street, or becoming editor of a significant provincial daily. He may well be forced to return to Manchester, with his dreams at an end and his career in tatters.

What made matters worse was that although Trudy's solicitor had been in touch, her father had not made any contact with him, even though he'd been in to see Frank Mellis on a couple of occasions since the separation. Powerless to address the situation, Robert became convinced that he was being made to suffer. He believed that Whittaker had his career dangling by a thread, leaving him with the forlorn hope that somehow, he may be spared. Finally, at the start of June, Whittaker came to the *Gazette* once more and this time sent word to Robert that he wanted to see him.

With the greatest sense of trepidation, Robert knocked on the open door to the editor's office, where Frank and his father-in-law were engaged in light-hearted conversation.

"Ah, Robert," said Whittaker, cheerily. "I wanted to see you. Could you give us a bit of privacy Frank?"

"Yes, of course. I'm sure you two have lots to discuss."

As Robert moved aside, Frank gave him a reassuring smile, before exiting his office and closing the door behind him. Certain that Frank would take no pleasure from his dismissal, Robert relaxed a little.

"Sit down lad. I want to talk to you," said Whittaker, motioning to the chair in front of the editor's desk.

Robert did as he was asked and watched as his father-in-law sat down in Frank's chair opposite. He felt certain that Whittaker would open the conversation by making some reference to his marital breakdown, but he was wrong.

"I've had an offer accepted for *The Examiner*. What do you think? Could it be a goer?"

Robert was taken by surprise. It was the last thing that he'd expected to hear and he found it slightly confusing that Whittaker was interested in his opinion. Nevertheless, he was pleased to have the opportunity to discuss a subject other than Trudy.

"Not in its present state," answered Robert. "Its sales are dropping like a stone. It was a bad decision to launch it as a broadsheet. There were too many in the market already. It had no chance of taking readers away from the *Telegraph*, *Guardian* or *The Times*."

"So, if you had the *Examiner* lad, what would you do with it?"

"The only way to get success is to re-launch it as a tabloid. It has to look different. A new, red mast head, to bring it in line with the *Mirror*. It needs to have a familiar look for their readers. After all, they're the audience that you should be aiming for. I'd reign in the length and prominence of serious news. Focus on scandal, sport and entertainment; that's what most people want. Ordinary folks read a newspaper to be entertained and they like a laugh. I'd go further than the *Gazette* and spice up the pictures and the content. The people that you and I grew up with, want their politics simple; issues laid out in black and white. Find out what they're thinking and then reflect their opinions. Then they'll trust you and you can influence them in short editorials. It's a big task, but society is constantly changing and the new paper can move with it and get ahead of the competition. It's a huge opportunity."

Robert had spoken with passion and enthusiasm about Whittaker's potential investment, but he did have a word of warning for him.

"I assume you know that you'll inherit a huge problem with the print unions. They've been able to hold the paper's management to ransom for years. That's something you're going to have to deal with if you decide to go ahead and take it on."

"That's why I've been offered it on the cheap," replied Whittaker. "Don't worry, I've met with the main man, Bill Pritchard, already. I'm sure I can get him on side. After all, if I don't buy the *Examiner*, it's going to the wall, along with hundreds of his members jobs."

"He's a crafty one. You'll need to watch him."

"So am I," replied Whittaker, laughing.

Robert smiled.

"Well, lad. It seems as if your ideas about the *Examiner*, are the same as mine. I expected that they would be, but I needed to satisfy myself."

Pausing, Whittaker looked closely at Robert. He was weighing him up and down; satisfying himself that he was content with the offer he was about to make.

"I've had my eye on you for a while lad. Frank's certain that you're ready and I'm happy to back his judgement. It's time for you to move up. I want you to be the new editor-in- chief of the *Examiner*. What do you say?"

Robert was shocked. The offer was completely unexpected and unsurprisingly, he struggled to respond. Whittaker had a reputation for being unorthodox, but what industry analysts had seen as questionable decision making in the past, had quickly established him as a key player in the national media.

"You do well with the *Examiner* and I can guarantee you that you'll be a wealthy man. As an incentive, I'm offering you 5% of the shares and bonuses for hitting circulation targets."

"You're not concerned that I'm still relatively young for the job?" asked Robert.

"Not at all, because I know that you have the ability to do it and you're desperate to prove yourself. I don't regard your appointment as any kind of gamble. The *Examiner* needs someone young with ideas and energy; it has to be totally transformed. I don't think that an older head, with established ways of thinking, is going to be able to pull it off."

"I assume that you've considered that by bringing someone in like me, there's bound to be resentment among the senior editors and staff."

"No there won't," insisted Whittaker, "because I've already held meetings with them and I've made it clear that I'm backing you one hundred per cent. Any nonsense from anyone and you fire them!"

Robert saw the steely, determined look in Whittaker's eyes. His father-in-law was deadly serious.

"So, what do you say lad?"

Robert was quiet for a moment. He was desperate to accept, but he knew that in order to throw himself wholeheartedly into the challenge, he must address his situation with Trudy first. He had to know that their impending divorce wouldn't become a future point of contention between the two men.

"But what about Trudy?" he asked.

"Well, what about Trudy?"

"She must have told you that she's applied for a divorce. In the circumstances, I'm not sure that she'll be enthusiastic about your plans for me."

"Yes," replied Whittaker, before pausing slightly. "I understand what you're thinking. You've seen how I indulge her. Trudy's still my little girl, but Robert, I'll never allow her to get in the way of business and I certainly won't take the chance of losing you to a rival. I'm well aware of how challenging my daughter can be. Your divorce has no bearing at all on our working relationship. In any case, I'm not a man who holds a grudge. It's not good for business."

Whittaker paused, giving Robert time to digest his words.

"And by the way," he continued, "that Tobias character, he's another waster. You should have hit him harder!"

"Oh," said Robert, surprised.

"The problem with our Trudy, is that she's still not sensible enough for marriage. Her mother and I tried to talk some sense into her when she told us she intended to get married again after she was divorced the first time. But she was having none of it and I'm sure our advice only made her more determined to do as she pleased. What could we do? She was twenty-one. When she told us she intended to marry you, we obviously thought that she should have waited, but we knew it was best not to interfere. We hoped that this time, she might perhaps have come to realise the responsibilities of marriage, but obviously that hasn't been the case. A privilege of wealth, is that you never have to grow up, if you decide you don't want to. Unfortunate as it is, that's the situation Trudy finds herself in."

"I see."

For a moment Robert wished that he and Whittaker could have had this conversation before the wedding. Certainly, it would have saved him from the embarrassment of all and sundry being witness to the sorry sight of him being used and discarded by his spouse. Then he realised that Whittaker had shown him respect. By not having the conversation, his father-in-law had made sure that he hadn't given Robert the impression that he wasn't good enough for his daughter.

"But let's get it straight now lad. I might sympathise with you for the way our Trudy's behaved, but you'll still get nowt out of this divorce. Her money comes from me and her mother. She gets an allowance and the flats ours too. We've never been daft enough to put any assets in her name, as the first pair of comedians she married, found out to their cost."

"I didn't expect to," said Robert, amused by Whittaker's disdain for his daughter's former partners. "The best thing for us both, is that we go our separate ways as quickly as possible."

"Don't take it personally," replied Whittaker, reassuringly. "When I married her mother, I accepted that her fortune was no concern of mine. Anything I've got, I've had to earn myself. Her father insisted on that and it's still the same now. You see lad, they'll never accept us. We can marry into their families and be successful in business, but they'll never let us join their clubs. For them, we'll always be nothing more than a peasant, only convenient to them when they need us to make them some money, or get them out of the mire."

Robert nodded, his experiences with Trudy's friends meant that he knew exactly what Whittaker was talking about. He had learned that there was a limit to just how far up the social ladder you could climb. Yet in terms of wealth and his status within the media, Robert could see no limits. As the new editor-in-chief of the *Examiner*, Robert was determined to achieve the success that would take him to the very top.

Chapter 102

In June 1975, on the morning of the second anniversary of his takeover at the *Examiner*, Robert was asleep in his mam's flat in Heywood House. He'd driven up from London the previous day, arriving unannounced and rather late in the evening. Irene and Edna, were of course, delighted to see him, but the latter had no hesitation in telling him off for not allowing them to provide a hot meal for him on his arrival. Suggesting that he could take them all into town for something to eat, his idea had been given short shrift.

"That might be what you fancy Londoners do, but you can save your money. It's not for wasting on our account," remarked Irene, sternly.

"And you don't know what you'll be eating," added Edna. "A week doesn't go by without the *Evening News* reporting that one of those new, fancy restaurants has been shut down by the health inspectors."

"But I'll take you somewhere nice, I promise."

"Hmm, I'm sure," replied Edna, unconvinced.

Opening a tin of best corned beef, that she'd been saving for a special occasion, Irene proceeded to make sandwiches for her son, whilst Edna made a brew and got out an unopened packet of McVitie's chocolate digestives. Sitting down with Robert at the kitchen table, the women looked on contentedly as he eagerly tucked in.

Robert's mam and gran hadn't asked him the purpose of his visit. For family and friends, their door was always open and since moving south, he had continued to come home regularly to see them. It was a fact commented on favourably by the neighbours. Knowing how far Robert's career had progressed, they respected him for keeping in touch with his family; a trait not necessarily shared by others in his situation. As they spent the rest of the evening asking Robert about his work at *The Examiner*, Edna and Irene had no idea that he had come to deliver a real surprise. On the following day, he would reveal the news that would transform their lives.

Woken by a knock on the door from his gran, half in a daze, Robert shouted to her that he was awake and slowly, sitting up in bed, he reached out to grab his watch on the bedside cabinet. It was already nine o'clock and hurriedly he jumped out of bed, went to get washed and changed and was soon in the kitchen with its welcoming smell of bacon and eggs.

"Sit down love. I bet you could do with this," said Irene, holding out a plate of bacon, eggs and tomatoes.

"Oh, Mam. You didn't need to have gone to so much trouble. A bit of toast would have been fine."

"Tell your gran, she's the one who nipped out to the butchers to get the bacon."

"You shouldn't have gone putting yourself out gran," said Robert, turning to Edna.

"Putting myself out? Do you think I'm too old to go to the shops, you cheeky mare?"

"No," replied Robert, flustered. "I didn't mean it like that. It's just that …"

"Just nothing. Trying to tell me that I can't spoil my grandson."

"I'm sorry, gran."

"And you should be. Now there's an end to it. Sit down and get it eaten before it goes cold."

Obediently, Robert did as he was told. It hadn't taken him long to readjust to the stark reality that within the Mancunian household, it was the women who were in charge.

"Well, are you ready?" asked Robert, after finishing his mug of tea.

"What for?" asked Irene.

"I'm taking you out in the car."

"Where?" asked Edna

"Oh, you'll see. It's a surprise."

Eager not to disappoint him, Edna and Irene quickly got ready and they were soon sat in the back of the car, as Robert drove down Bennett Street and on to Hyde Road. Passing along Brunswick Street and through the University, Robert turned left down Oxford Road, continuing into Wilmslow Road, with Platt

Fields visible on the right as they moved through Rusholme and into Fallowfield, where Robert turned right and drove on into Wilbraham Road. The journey now seemed a familiar one to his passengers.

"This is the way to Kay's," observed Irene.

"Yes," replied Robert.

"Is that where we're going?"

"Well, nearby," replied Robert. "You're just going to have to wait and see."

As they travelled into Stretford and drove across Chester Road, the two women were convinced that Kay's house in Urmston was in fact their destination. Yet, when they eventually reached Church Road, Robert turned off to the right.

"Where's this?" asked Irene.

"It's Mansfield Road," replied Robert.

As he drove the car up the road, Irene and Edna admired the neat suburban semis, which were soon replaced by a series of modest, but attractive, detached houses. Slowing down, Robert pulled the car over to the right and halted across the driveway to one of them. Having applied the hand brake, Robert turned off the engine.

"Well, what do you think?"

"About what?" asked Edna.

Robert turned round and looked at his mam and gran. The pair of them appeared confused; they didn't have a clue what he was up to. Robert smiled. It was just the reaction he had hoped for. They didn't have an inkling about the surprise that he was about to spring on them and it gave him a feeling of real satisfaction.

"Do you know," said Robert, "you two are so special. You've always stood by me. Without you, I wouldn't be where I am today. Finally, I can thank you by giving you something more than words."

"Don't be daft. What are you on about?" asked Irene.

"He's puddled," added Edna. "That London air has befuddled his brain."

The reality was that both women were feeling a little uncomfortable. Robert had never been particularly demonstrative with his affections and his behaviour seemed bizarre. It had occurred to both of them that perhaps the stresses of running a national newspaper, was beginning to prove a bit too much for him.

Smiling, Robert picked up a large, bulky envelope and handed it to his mam.

"Here you are. This will explain everything."

"What is it?"

"Open it and find out."

Irene continued to look at the envelope, unable to act.

"Give it here," said Edna, taking it from her. "Let's just humour the lad."

Opening the flap of the envelope, Edna turned it upside down to take out the contents. Before she could do so, a bunch of keys fell into her lap.

"What are these?" asked Edna, as she picked them up.

"What do they look like?" asked Robert, chuckling.

"Stop playing at silly buggers and tell us what's going on."

"Mam!" said Irene, shocked at her language.

"So, help me Robert Wilson, you might be a fancy editor on Fleet Street, but you're not too big to get a smacked arse."

Robert burst out laughing, but realising that he risked the ire of his gran, recognised that it was now time to reveal all.

"Alright. I'm sorry," said Robert, looking suitably contrite.

"I should hope so," said Irene, sternly. "Now, what's this all about?"

"Do you see the house there?" asked Robert, pointing at the driveway to the side of them.

The two women turned and looked.

"Well, those keys are for that house and the papers inside the envelope are the deeds to the property. It's ours now."

"What do you mean, ours?" asked Edna.

"The three of us own it. Me, you and my mam. I've bought it outright and our names are on the deeds. It's all ready for you to move in. We just need to let the Corporation know that you'll be moving out of Heywood House and organise a removals firm to bring everything here. I've already sorted out the utilities and the rates."

Edna and Irene were stunned. Robert realised that it would take a little more time for them to fully comprehend the situation.

Patiently, he sat waiting for the inevitable questions that would come his way.

"But surely, you can't afford it," said Irene, eventually.

"Yes. We appreciate what you've done, but can't you give it back?" asked Edna. "We don't want you in lots of debt on our account."

"I'm not in debt," insisted Robert. "Since the time I was made assistant editor, I've been very well paid. My rent isn't expensive and I've been able to put lots away. I've earned some big bonuses over the last twelve months and buying this house is an investment. It's ours. No more throwing money at Manchester Corporation."

"But we're happy in Ardwick. You didn't need to worry about us," replied Edna.

Robert knew that his mam and gran were feeling guilty. They had always looked after him and couldn't conceive of a situation in which he would effectively be supporting them. He understood that adjusting to a different kind of family relationship would, at first, prove awkward. Robert therefore focused on the fact that their move to Urmston was entirely logical.

"Gran," said Robert. "I loved living in Ardwick too, but you and I both know that it's nothing like it was when we lived on Armitage Street. And it won't be long before Heywood House will be coming down too. Isn't it far better to move here, then end up on one of the new estates in a couple of years' time?"

"Yes Mam," said Irene, sighing, "our Robert's got a point there, hasn't he?"

Edna nodded and Robert realised that he was starting to win them over.

"I chose here, because, Kay, Ethel and Ernest are just around the corner. That means you have friends nearby and the neighbours are nice anyway. There's Chassen Park just a couple of roads away and the local shops are nearby. There are plenty of buses into town too. You'll love it here. I promise."

Silent, Robert looked closely at the two women, his eyes imploring them for their blessing. Finally, his mam and gran smiled.

"Come on then," said Edna, brandishing the keys. "Let's have a look at our new house."

Opening the back door of the car, Edna got out on to the pavement, followed closely by Irene. As they walked up the drive and towards the front door, Robert was eagerly explaining the key features of their new home.

"There's a lovely garden at the back and a garage. Inside there are three bedrooms, two of them doubles. Central heating, a smart kitchen and bathroom. A good-sized lounge and dining room."

"It's alright," said Irene, laughing. "We won't change our minds. We're coming here to stay. You don't need to tell us what we're quite capable of seeing with our own eyes."

"Aw, the lad's just excited, bless him."

Edna threw her arms around Robert and squeezed him tightly. It was the final seal of approval.

Chapter 103

Over the next couple of years, Robert's star continued to rise. There was no question that he had now become a key figure on Fleet Street. Under his leadership, the *Examiner* had quickly proved popular and established itself with impressive circulation figures that were second only to the *Daily Mirror*. Analysts widely expected that it wouldn't be long before the *Examiner* would overtake its rival. The paper's rise had not come without controversy however. The sensationalist brand of journalism championed by Robert and the paper's focus on nude pin-ups and salacious scandals, were roundly condemned. Critics lamented the fall in journalistic standards and accused Robert and Whittaker of dragging the national press through the gutter. Yet both major political parties were eager to gain the paper's endorsement and the prime minister had remarked that he only ever worried about what the *Times* and the *Examiner* were writing about his government. It was a clear acknowledgement of the fact that the opinions of Whittaker's publication, held great influence over the minds of the 'ordinary, hard-working people,' who Robert identified as the backbone of its readers. Financially, Robert's success had seen him rewarded generously. Whittaker had also appointed Robert as a consultant on a regional television company in which he had a major interest. A man in demand, always ready to provide a controversial opinion, Robert had become a regular guest on current affairs programmes and hosted a weekly review of the papers.

Since travelling to Mozambique on his first commission for *The Workers Vanguard*, Larry had worked on a number of dangerous, foreign assignments. He'd been present in Uganda, in the aftermath of Idi Amin's coup in 1971 and then had been posted to Indo-China, where he had reported on the final year of American involvement in Vietnam. He had remained to witness the collapse of South Vietnam and the reunification of the country. In his last assignment he had covered the civil war in Angola between the communist MPLA, favoured by the

Vanguard and UNITA, backed by the US and South Africa. Larry's journalistic career hadn't taken him to the dizzy heights of fame and fortune, as it had his friend. The fact that he was writing for a niche publication with a small circulation, meant that his excellent articles didn't receive the plaudits or exposure that they deserved. Nevertheless, Larry couldn't have been more content. He believed that he was free to write as he wanted and about situations and issues that were of real importance.

Kay would often reflect on the pleasant fact that despite the passage of time, she, Larry and Robert had remained the closest of friends. With the changes that they had experienced in their lives and the relocation of Larry and Robert away from Manchester, it would have been easy for them to have slowly drifted apart. The fact that they hadn't done so, was in no small measure due to Kay's influence. As Violet had noted, Kay was the glue that held the three of them together and her deep affection and concern for her friends had created bonds that couldn't be broken. As such it was no surprise when Larry and Robert arrived at Church Road in early August 1977, to congratulate Kay on her recent promotion. With Anne's elevation to Head of Social Services, Kay would be placed in charge of the children's department. Yet they hadn't only come to see Kay. Bernard Junior had passed the eleven plus and would soon be starting at Urmston Boys Grammar and his uncles were keen to find out about his new school and pass on some advice.

"So, there's no girls at the school then?"

"No, uncle Robert."

"That's a shame."

Kay shook her head.

"What?" asked Robert, with a wounded expression.

"You know what," replied Kay, firmly. "He's only eleven. He's got plenty of time for girls in the future."

Bernard Junior looked at his mam, confused. He was already five feet tall; big for his age. He had his father's brown eyes, a pleasant countenance and a cheerful disposition that appealed to both adults and children alike. At school, Bernard had shown an aptitude for physical education. He shared his parents' intelligence and his mother's quality of showing kindness and consideration towards others. The fact that he no longer referred to his uncles as 'Bobs' and 'Lahwee' was a clear indication to them, if they needed it, of just how he and they were all getting older.

"I didn't mean that," ventured Robert. "I just think that mixed schools are better in educational terms."

"Yes, I'm sure you do," replied Kay, trying not to laugh.

"Well, I certainly wouldn't disagree with you there Robert," remarked Larry. "Girls are a civilising influence. We could have done with them at King's."

"Originally, Larry's school was mixed," noted Kay, "but apparently the student numbers had grown too big and at the start of the sixties, the education committee created two single sex schools on separate sites."

"I'm sure you'll work hard and do well whatever kind of school you go to, won't you Bernard?" asked Larry.

"Yes and at least you'll know that you've had to graft for it," noted Robert. "A good Northern grammar, not the soft option of a privileged, Southern independent school, like Uncle Larry went to."

Bernard smiled. He loved listening to the banter between his uncles. He was ready to be entertained, that is, unless his mam stepped in and stopped it.

"You two," said Kay, with a sigh. "I've not seen you for a while and when I do, you can't avoid your childish bickering."

"I haven't said anything. It's Robert" said Larry, sounding hurt.

"That's because I haven't given you a chance to," replied Kay. "You're both as bad as one another!"

Bernard grinned as he watched his uncles, just like chastened schoolboys, looking meekly at his mam.

"Anyway Bernard, it's time for bed," said Kay. "You need a good night's sleep with your uncles taking you out tomorrow."

With Bernard's departure, Robert and Kay began to talk about their respective parents' relocation to Urmston and how it had impacted on their perceptions about their own Ardwick heritage.

"Like my mam and dad, Irene and Edna love it round here," observed Kay. "You must be pleased Robert, to see them so happy."

"Yes, I am. I was worried at first. I knew that the flats would be coming down and I thought that mam and gran were only staying there as they were so used to living in Ardwick. I didn't think that they would be able to see the benefits of moving somewhere else."

"It was the same with my mam and dad," agreed Kay. "They decided to move in so that they could help me to look after Bernard, but it was a big change for them. The fact is though, that the old Ardwick disappeared back in sixty-five, when the terraces were being demolished."

"You know Kay, the last time I was at my mam's, in Heywood House, I had a good walk round. It's all new flats and houses now, but most of the streets have different names and the people aren't the same. Like you told us all those years ago, the old sense of community is gone. There was a rough edge to the area; it didn't have the welcoming feel that I remember as a kid. Ardwick seems alien to me now. It's almost as if you and I are from a different world that no longer exists."

"But surely, it's still very much a working-class area," noted Larry.

"It depends on how you define working-class," said Kay. "Our department deals with so many families in the area and I have to say that you'd be hard pressed to find many of the values held by the communities that we grew up with in the sixties."

"Such as?"

"Such as the proud independence that everyone had. The desire to sort out your own problems if you possibly could. A belief in honesty and hard work and the value of being a good neighbour."

"Surely you're looking at your childhood through rose-tinted glasses," suggested Larry.

"No, I'm not," insisted Kay. "You can see the difference with the old folks we try to help. It's hard at times to get them to accept any benefits or assistance. They think its scrounging and demeaning to do so. On the other hand, many of the younger ones are well versed in the knowledge of their entitlements. Times are hard; the city has got massive economic problems and it's tough for youngsters, but so many of them are content to do nothing; take their benefits and not bother to find a job. And once you have an older sibling with that attitude, the younger ones in the family follow suit. Without acceptance of personal responsibility, the next step is for some to be drawn into a life of crime and then of course, we have to come in and try to pick up the pieces."

"But that won't happen to Bernard," said Larry. "He's from a middle-class family living in a more affluent area and so you have to accept that you're being too hard on some of the young people you work with. Being working-class is still a big disadvantage when you're young and trying to get on in life."

"Yes, it always will be," said Robert, "but Kay's original point remains. The so-called working classes of today are far different to those of the thirties and the post-war generation. They simply don't have the same values and aspirations. In fact, I'm not sure that the term working-class has any real relevance any more. A different terminology needs to be applied to those in the nation's lowest socio-economic groups."

"Perhaps so," conceded Larry. "Nevertheless, we can't deny that in Manchester and elsewhere, there are problems experienced by the poorest members of society that aren't going away and for the benefit of everyone, they have to be addressed."

"I think I can safely say, that all of us can agree on that," said Kay.

"Very much so, but the manner in which we do it is, I suspect, one on which disagreement is far more likely," concluded Robert.

Chapter 104

Robert's assessment was a frank admission of how far his own political views had changed since the days when, as an idealistic sixth former, he had truanted from school in order to attend the anti-Suez demonstrations in Albert Square. As his career progressed, Robert's material aspirations grew with it. The lad from Ardwick found that his old socialist principles were being diluted to such an extent, that by the time he was editor of the *Examiner*, it could be argued that they had ceased to exist.

Prior to the announcement of the general election in March 1979, Whittaker was already directing the *Examiner* towards support for the Tory Party and its new leader, Margaret Thatcher. It was a decision that Robert, as editor, had no difficulty in supporting. He was now a man of means and the chaos of 'the winter of discontent' had persuaded him that a change of political direction was necessary. Robert took personal responsibility for writing his paper's leaders and as election day approached, sensational front-page stories portrayed a state of national collapse under Callaghan's Labour government. Robert was comfortable fighting a negative, even 'dirty' campaign against Labour. After all, Callaghan's team was clearly attempting to exploit Thatcher's femininity. They were playing on the prejudice that judged any woman incapable of handling the pressures of high office. When the election results came in and the Tories were returned with a forty-four seats majority, there was no doubt that the *Examiner* had played a key role in switching the allegiance of many of its readers away from Labour.

One aspect of the Conservative manifesto that had seemed particularly pertinent to Robert, as editor of the *Examiner*, was the pledge to strike 'a fair balance between the rights and duties of the trade union movement'. Before Whittaker had taken control of the paper, Robert had warned him about the potential difficulties that the unions could provide for them. At first, relieved that their jobs had been saved, the various union leaders worked harmoniously with management and one another, in ensuring the uninterrupted production of the paper. Yet once the *Examiner* had become firmly established in the market, the long-standing disputes between the different 'chapels', in terms of demarcation and pay differentials, re-emerged. The result was a series of walkouts and threats to the production and distribution of the newspaper. Further problems emerged with Whittaker's desire to see the gradual introduction of computer assisted typesetting. It was controversial as it threatened the jobs of the Linotype operators, who set the type and the compositors, who made up the pages. Robert had got his boss to agree to a phased introduction of the new technology, with assurances that the men most affected, would be guaranteed a job for life. Nevertheless, on the instructions of their national leaders, the changes were rejected. Neither the *Examiner*, nor any other newspaper, was able to introduce the use of computers on Fleet Street.

Robert's most persistent opponent, when it came to the matter of working practices, was Bill Pritchard, leader of the unskilled casual workers who helped to operate the basement presses. Just before Christmas, Robert arranged a meeting with his nemesis. It was due to the fact that checks had revealed that wage packets were being collected for men who weren't present and working in the building. Pritchard had swept unannounced into the office, as he usually did. Sitting down on the other side of Robert's desk, he leaned lazily back in his chair. With his small, round lens glasses, unkempt hair and goatee beard, Robert could almost imagine that he was negotiating with a latter-day Leon Trotsky.

"We issue five hundred pay packets to your members every week," Robert began, "but we've carried out several daily checks on the staffing in the basement and there's never been more than two hundred and fifty men down there. It seems that wages are being claimed under false pretences."

Pritchard sat bolt upright in his chair. He was furious.

"Who gave management the right to take unilateral action? It's a disgrace. You should have consulted with me before taking such liberties with our members. Checking on them, behind their backs, the men would be fully justified in walking out."

"Well, if we'd done that, it would have defeated the exercise, wouldn't it? As they say, forewarned is forearmed."

"I'd advise you, that casting aspersions on our members, isn't likely to go down very well with them."

Pritchard spoke slowly and precisely. He was in a position of strength and he knew it.

"Management has every right to know that when men are being paid wages, they're receiving them because they've actually done an honest day's work," insisted Robert.

"And they have. Are you saying that my members don't have the right to a break? When your checks were being carried out, that's where those men were."

Both he and Robert knew that his answer was ridiculous, but it was up to management to prove beyond any doubt, that it was. In reality, claiming wage packets for phantom workers, was one of the many 'Spanish practices' that was tolerated by all the newspapers on Fleet Street.

"It was established well before you arrived, that high print runs couldn't be achieved without a minimum of five hundred men working on the presses," continued Pritchard. "If there were only the number of men present that you claim, there would have been gaps in production and we both know that there weren't any."

"Don't you see that these old, outdated practices won't help anyone?" asked Robert. "Certainly, not your genuine members."

"And certainly not your boss Whittaker," snapped Pritchard.

"You're wrong. I persuaded him to try and work with the unions on change, but his goodwill won't last for ever. Whether you like it or not, modernisation is coming to the industry and we're all going to have to learn to adapt. Ultimately, we can't hold back new technology and outdated practices will have to change. It can't have escaped your notice that there's a different political climate now; there's a real will to curb union power and not only from the Tories. Here on the *Examiner*, I'm trying to negotiate a way through it in order to help all of us. I've worked my way up in the industry and I've no wish to put genuine workers out of a job. You and the other chapels should work with us and so avoid draconian solutions being imposed by a new breed of proprietors, who aren't prepared to accept the abuses of the past."

"Oh, I know all about your background," said Pritchard, dismissively. "How you were a working-class lad from Manchester who worked on the local papers and made good here on Fleet Street. But that doesn't mean a thing, because when men like you have made it, you can't wait to turn your back on your heritage. You'll happily cosy up to the bosses and sell out the men that you've grown up with. Does it make you feel ashamed to look the men you would have once called brothers, in the eye?"

Hurt by Pritchard's stinging rebuke, Robert fought hard to keep his temper. In reality he was fully aware that his career had removed him from his old, working-class environment, but he still believed that he held to its values and those weren't ones that would tolerate the lies and corruption that were being practised by Pritchard and his acolytes.

"I'm trying hard Pritchard, to see any evidence that you really are concerned for your members. In Manchester, we all worked together; whether it be on the locals or the Northern dailies. We were all part of a team; proud to put out the paper. There was no nonsense over demarcation, or any of the petty disputes that bring production to a halt down here. The only taboo was that journalists never touched the metal type in the composing room. Other than that, we all mucked in together. There's unity in the North, because we all knew that every one of us depends on getting the paper out on time. Your petty squabbles, between the various chapels, hurt one another. There's no brotherhood that I can see, either here or anywhere on Fleet Street. Now, in the spirit of co-operation, what are we going to do about these phantom workers?"

Pritchard looked at him and sneered. Robert's words meant nothing to him, for he was certain that his members' power to halt production, meant that Robert would have to accept the status quo.

"As I've said, unless you want to jeopardise production, existing staffing levels must be maintained."

Pritchard got out of his chair and walked towards the door. Opening it, he halted and turned to face Robert.

"It might help," he said, with a smile, "if you communicate with us before acting so provocatively in the future. I can't be responsible for the goodwill of my members if you're intent on insulting their integrity."

For the moment, the unions in Fleet Street were in the ascendancy. There was a belief that the old Spanish practices were so deeply rooted in the industry, that they could never be challenged. And with that confidence had come union intransigence; a resistance to any kind of change. As Robert had noted however, a new breed of proprietors had emerged and men like Whittaker wouldn't tolerate the situation for too much longer. In reality, the obduracy of union leaders like Pritchard, was only hastening the end for their members.

Chapter 105

After Bernard Jr was born, Kay feared that the absence of his father may leave a void in his life that, as a woman, she would find difficult to fill. Her fears were unfounded however, as Ernest soon developed a close bond with his grandson. Furthermore, Larry and Robert showed a genuine concern for the welfare of their nephew. Even after moving to London, they had regularly visited Bernard and taken a serious interest in his progress at school. When Robert had visited in February 1980, on the occasion of Bernard's fourteenth birthday, he found his nephew full of questions about his role as editor of the *Examiner*.

"Uncle Larry's a journalist, so it's obvious what he does, but what exactly are your responsibilities?" asked Bernard. "I've tried looking in the school and local libraries and I know that you're in overall charge of the newspaper, but I can't find out any real details about what you have to do on a day-to-day basis."

Robert smiled. His nephew's words brought back memories of the visits he and Kay had made to Ardwick Library, all those years ago.

"You and Larry have really ignited his interest in the media," said Kay. "He's already thinking about it as a possible career."

"Yes, I am," confirmed Bernard. "That's why I wanted to know more about what you actually do."

"Well, I'll tell you what," said Robert, "if it's all right with your mam, you could come and stay for a week in the summer holidays and I'll take you into work with me. Then you'll be able to find out what I do and just what it takes in order to produce the *Examiner*."

"Oh Mam!" said Bernard, excitedly. "Can I?"

"We'll have to see," said Kay, firmly.

It wasn't the response that he'd hoped for, but Bernard knew better than to express his disappointment.

"It all depends on you continuing to work hard at school and getting a good report at the end of the year."

Kay looked closely at Bernard, emphasising the importance of her words.

"Now, go and sit with your nanny and granddad for a bit, they've not seen you all day."

Bernard nodded and left the room.

"You still scare the life out of me," said Robert. "When you're in that serious mood, we all know that we have to do as we're told."

"Of course, because it's for your own good," replied Kay.

"Perhaps, I should have asked you first, before making the offer, but the kid was excited and I wanted to reward his enthusiasm," explained Robert.

"Don't worry," said Kay, "I understand. I just want him to appreciate the opportunity you're giving him and if he knows he's going to have to get an excellent report, then he's having to earn it."

"I see. It's a shame that I can't come up with similar ideas to motivate the print unions," replied Robert, laughing.

"You know Robert," continued Kay, "Bernard really admires you and Larry. He tells everyone about you. At the last parent's evening, his English teacher said that Bernard had offered your services for a school careers evening."

"That was good of him. I wouldn't have had to come very far, would I?"

"Well, you needn't worry, because once the governors knew that you were editor of the *Examiner*, they decided that you weren't suitable."

"No doubt because of our nude pin-ups," suggested Robert, laughing. "I don't suppose it stops them looking at them though."

"Probably not," said Kay.

"Well, wasn't Larry suitable?" asked Robert.

"Unfortunately, not. They didn't think it wise to expose the boys to a communist propagandist from *The Workers Vanguard*. I'm only thankful that I wasn't asked to remove Bernard from the school, given his association with you undesirables!"

The two of them burst out laughing.

"Seriously though Robert, if I let him come and stay, you will be able to look after him, won't you?"

"Of course. I'll have moved in to my new house on the edge of Wimbledon Common by then. It's near Whittaker's place and you'll love this, it's close to where Stanley Baker used to live."

"Oh," replied Kay, surprised.

"Yes. Stanley made a big impression on you, didn't he?"

Kay smiled, but said nothing.

"At the time I felt jealous," observed Robert, "especially as I could tell that he was quite taken with you."

"But he was devoted to his wife," noted Kay.

"Yes, that's true. He was."

"You're sure," asked Kay, changing the subject, "that if Bernard does come in the summer, he won't be getting in the way?"

Robert looked confused. He was unsure what she meant.

"It was just that your mam mentioned that you'd met someone and she thought it might be serious."

Robert laughed.

"I don't know. That's just like Mam. She and my gran are always ready to marry me off, whenever I happen to mention some woman's name."

"They only want to see you settled," said Kay.

"I'm happy enough. I'm not ready for another serious relationship."

"Well, if that means you've gone back to your carefree teenage years, make sure that Bernard doesn't get any similar ideas."

"He won't," insisted Robert. "You've nothing to worry about."

"I don't want my son being introduced to another Pauline," continued Kay.

Robert looked surprised.

"I was aware that you knew about the other girls back then, but I didn't think that you knew about Pauline."

"There's a lot I know about," replied Kay.

"Such as?"

"I'm not telling you."

"Well, if you're really concerned about me looking after Bernard properly, why don't you come down too?"

"No, it's fine. I'm sure that I can trust you. Just as long as you remember what you've been told."

"I will."

Kay smiled, a suggestion to Robert that perhaps, she had been teasing him all along.

Chapter 106

Robert hadn't been totally open with Kay when he told her that he hadn't been looking for a long-term relationship. The reality was that he'd only recently parted from Karen, who had lived with him for several months in his home in Barking. She was just nineteen; less than half his age. Robert had first noticed her as a pretty and feisty assistant in the office library, yet he had waited until she was eighteen before he began to pay her close attention. Flattered by the advances of her boss, Karen found him curiously handsome and far more sophisticated than the numerous young men, who were so desperate to take her out. Yet having moved in with him, Karen became frustrated. Robert's obsession with work left her lonely and disillusioned. A fun-loving girl, she was soon reconnecting with old friends and recognising the impossibility of bridging the differences between herself and Robert. When it had inevitably come, their parting had been acrimonious. Just as with Trudy, Robert had returned home to find his partner in bed with another man.

When she had left, Karen had dismissed Robert as old fashioned and pathetic. Her words had hurt him, but they were enlightening too and made him reconsider his approach to the pretty, young women he'd been so eager to pursue in the past. He recognised that in his position, he needed stability. His two attempts to find a loving relationship had failed and there was no need, for the foreseeable future, to try again. He knew that his mam and gran wanted to see him settled with a family and have the opportunity to spoil his children, but for Robert, that wasn't important. Besides, both he and Larry had enjoyed the time they had spent together with their nephew. It seemed quite possible that for both of them, Bernard Jr would end up being the son they never had.

With Bernard having obtained an excellent school report, Kay was happy to confirm to Robert that the visit could go ahead. An official letter from the offices of the *Examiner* duly arrived at Church Road, containing a ticket for the Manchester Pullman service to London on the following Monday morning. Bernard was informed that the editor-in-chief would be waiting for him at Euston, from where he would be taken to the offices of the newspaper. It was a thoughtful touch; exciting for Bernard and much appreciated by Kay.

When Bernard arrived, Robert greeted him warmly and then the two of them took a taxi to the *Examiner*. As they chatted, Robert had a suggestion for his nephew.

"As you've come here to work this week, perhaps we can dispense with you having to call me uncle all the time. Robert will be fine. What do you think?"

Bernard was quiet, he was obviously giving careful consideration to Robert's suggestion.

"I don't think I should," said Bernard, eventually. "My mam might not like it if I don't call you uncle Robert."

"You used to call me 'Bobs' when you were a toddler and anyway, your mam isn't here, so she won't know, will she?"

"But if I forget myself when you next come to visit and just call you Robert, she won't be pleased."

Robert smiled.

"Fair enough. It does sound like your mam. Your uncle Larry and I are just like you. We know better than to get on the wrong side of her. She gave us many a telling off when we were at Owens. It's not a good idea to annoy your mam."

The visit started well and over the course of the week, Robert was as good as his word, allowing his nephew to get an insight into all aspects of the newspaper business. Furthermore, Robert insisted that Bernard shadow him throughout the week, which meant that he was able to observe the discussions and decisions that took place during daily editorial meetings. Even Whittaker was happy for Bernard to attend his weekly get-together with Robert, having humorously insisted that the lad must be sworn to secrecy over anything he heard. It was an exceptionally busy and tiring week, but one that Bernard found extremely enjoyable and inspiring. On Saturday evening, Robert and his nephew finally had chance to review how the week had gone.

"Well then Bernard, do you still want to be a newspaper man?"

"Oh yes. More than ever."

"So, we at the *Examiner* haven't put you off then?"

"No, not at all. It's so exciting. I never realised how many different departments of a newspaper there are and how every one of them have to work together to get the editions out on time."

"That's right," replied Robert. "But remember that everyone is under a lot of pressure and you've got to be thick-skinned if you want to work in our business. You'll get called out if you've not done your job properly. I often got cursed at in my early days at the *Chronicle*."

"I saw plenty of that when I was in the subs office," said Bernard.

"Yes, you would have," replied Robert. "Subs have to reduce a story to its most essential information and that's tough when you have to hit a word limit in a very short period of time. The chief-sub and his deputy are hard taskmasters on any newspaper and they don't suffer fools gladly."

"I know," noted Bernard, chuckling. "I've learned quite a few new swear words this week."

"Well, don't let your mam hear you using them."

"Don't worry. There's no chance of that."

Robert laughed. He was pleased at how well the visit had gone and appreciative of the fact that Bernard had shown such an interest in following his uncles into the media.

"I've been thinking," continued Bernard. "I've found it so interesting being at the *Examiner* and I've learned so much more than I ever do at school. Would it be better for me to try and get a job on a local newspaper when I'm sixteen and forget about the sixth form?"

"No," replied Robert. "The days are long gone when men like Frank Mellis could join a newspaper as a copy boy and make their way up to becoming a Fleet Street editor. They want graduates now, so my advice is that you stay on and take your 'A' levels. Then go to university, like Uncle Larry, your mam and I did. Besides, in the future you may decide that you want to do something else. With a good degree, you can keep most options open."

It was sound advice and Robert could tell that Bernard had accepted it as such. He was an exceptionally bright and confident young man, a reflection of and a credit to, his mam.

Chapter 107

At the start of January 1981, Larry was sent on assignment to Vietnam. He'd been tasked with putting together a series of articles relating to how the unified nation was recovering following the war against the United States. His editor expected that his star writer would produce an uplifting account of how socialism was triumphantly rebuilding the nation, despite seemingly insurmountable odds. Larry was told that the current disagreements between Vietnam and her neighbour, communist China, were not part of his remit.

Larry found this instruction strange, for it seemed difficult to write about the present state of the country, without reference to the Sino-Vietnamese War of 1979 and the ongoing tensions created by the continued presence of Vietnamese forces in Cambodia. In fact, it had only recently been deemed safe to travel in the border areas, given the Chinese Army's shelling of Vietnam's Cao Bang Province during the summer of 1980 and incursions across the border by both sides in October. Vietnam had offered a ceasefire in the new year but when Larry arrived, it still hadn't been officially accepted by the Chinese. Nevertheless, the situation seemed relatively calm and as the Vietnamese authorities were happy with his socialist credentials, Larry was able to travel freely around the country, collecting the information he needed for his articles.

Circumstances were soon about to change. On May 5th 1981, Larry was present in the Cao Loc district of Lang Son Province, when Chinese forces attacked the Vietnamese positions around Hill 400. Entering the combat zone, Larry bore witness to the atrocities carried out against Vietnamese civilians. He also tried to verify reports that Chinese civilians had been killed in retaliation by Vietnamese forces crossing the border into Guangxi Province. Returning to Hanoi, government officials were keen for Larry to contact the *Vanguard* with details about the Chinese atrocities. Informing his editor that he had photographic evidence to support his story, Larry was shocked when he was ordered to return to London immediately. Although the *Vanguard* had published all his articles on Vietnam's social and economic health, it was clear that they wouldn't carry any reports that he intended to file on the border crisis.

Back in London, Larry immediately sought a meeting with his editor. He was determined to clear the air and insist that his article must be published. Despite his years of experience, Larry's strong sense of justice wouldn't allow him to accept the practical realities of editorial decision making.

The editor of the *Vanguard*, James Green, was in his late sixties and an old school Marxist. He had grown up in the Stalinist era and as an enthusiastic teenager was captivated by the vision of a socialist utopia, that he believed was being created under the Five-Year Plans. Even the revelations of Khrushchev about the evils of the Great Terror had not shaken his faith in the soviet dictator. Green still had a framed photo of Stalin on the wall behind his desk, insisting that the portrait of his hero would stay there as long as he was editor of the paper. For Green, loyalty to socialism and the Party was everything and that meant that the operation of the *Vanguard*, could never be allowed to bring the movement into disrepute. It was a point that he immediately made clear to his reporter.

"It's not only because your article needs further verification, that I rejected it. What you've written doesn't serve the interests of international socialism. You've created a picture of disharmony between key communist states. The difficulties along the Sino-Vietnamese border are a temporary fallout between friends and it won't be long before the situation is resolved."

"That's not true and you know it," insisted Larry, trying hard not to lose his temper. "I have the photos here to give you all the verification you need."

Larry picked up a large envelope that he had placed on his editor's desk and proceeded to pull out the incriminating photos that substantiated his allegations of Chinese atrocities.

"Here," insisted Larry, offering the photos. "Look at them. What more proof do you need?"

Taking the photos, Green gave them no more than a cursory glance before returning them to Larry.

"It isn't the intention of the *Vanguard* to play into the hands of the capitalist media. If we were to publish your article, they'd love it. 'Just look at how evil the soviet system is', they'll write in their leaders. Without any effort on their part, you're handing them a story that could prove a serious blow to the worldwide revolutionary cause."

"That's not the reason," insisted Larry. "It's our 'comrades' from Moscow, isn't it? They're unhappy that I'm highlighting the conflict, as it may be taken as a criticism that they aren't doing enough to support their ally, Vietnam. It's money that's talking here. You're afraid that if we publish, we'll lose their financial support."

Green was silent. He couldn't deny the fact that Moscow wouldn't be happy if they published the article. Furthermore, sales of the *Vanguard* to the Soviet Union and eastern Europe, helped keep the paper solvent. Moscow alone agreed to take six thousand copies daily. Nevertheless, he wasn't about to acknowledge that to Larry.

"If you don't publish," continued Larry, "then you're no better than the editors on Fleet Street; the 'lackeys and lapdogs of capitalism', as you love to call them. We at the *Vanguard* would be selling our souls for money. Instead of speaking the truth, we'd be remaining silent so as not to embarrass our Russian paymasters."

Green's expression remained impassive. Had anyone else spoken to him in such a way, he would have fired them. Larry however, was a talented and determined journalist and he had no wish to lose him. Green hoped that it still wasn't too late for Larry to understand his point of view.

"The journey to socialism can never follow a straightforward path," remarked the editor. "Comrade Lenin taught us that."

"Yet you're proposing that we go backwards," replied Larry. "Back to the days of Harry Pollitt and George Matthews, when the British socialist movement was expected to support the Soviet Union, regardless. Even the atrocities of Joe Stalin had to be overlooked; for all that was important was the ultimate triumph of the Workers."

"That's the truth of it," insisted Green. "Ultimately, we have to be prepared for bumps in the road, like this business between

Vietnam and China and find a way around them. We must, first and foremost, protect the interests of socialism."

"No, I can't accept that," continued Larry. "We have to acknowledge a higher truth. It doesn't mean that socialism's dead because flawed leaders and governments lose their way. That's natural. What's important is staying true to the message. Don't you see? Only by exposing flaws within the movement, both here and abroad, can we ensure the purity of the message. My article serves the cause of socialism, it doesn't destroy it."

Green shook his head slowly and sighed.

"It doesn't have to be like this Larry. Just accept that sometimes we all have to compromise. In time, you'll realise that. We've such an important job to do. No one else is fighting for justice for the working-classes. The *Vanguard* is the only true socialist voice out there and you're part of it. We need your heart and passion. You came here because we allowed you to express your socialist aspirations. You know that being with us is your only hope of making a difference."

Larry was quiet. Green coughed uneasily. For all his brilliance, Larry could prove difficult and it now seemed that he'd reached the point where he was contemplating resignation.

"Take a few days off," suggested Green. "You've had a tough time in Vietnam. It's been a tricky assignment. You need a break. Things will look better when you've rested and had a chance to reflect."

"No, I'll not change my mind," insisted Larry. "If you can't, or won't publish the article, then I can't see a future for me at the *Vanguard*."

"And where do you think you'll be able to go?" asked Green. "For all that you're an excellent journalist, none of the nationals will be keen to take you on after you've worked here. I can tolerate the fact that you want to be your own man, but other editors will expect you to be far more compliant. You already know that from your time in Manchester."

Larry was quiet. He knew that Green was right, but his desire for the truth was becoming nothing short of an obsession.

"Look Larry, take some time off and come back a week on Monday. I'll hold your job open until then. I'm not going to change my mind on the article, so it's up to you."

Larry nodded his acknowledgement, picked up his envelope and walked from the room. It seemed unlikely that he would be returning to the *Vanguard*, for Green knew how strongly his reporter felt about the issue and that his commitment to his principles would ultimately overcome his concerns for his professional security.

Chapter 108

Convinced that his article should be published, for the next few days Larry agonised over whether he should take the story about the Chinese atrocities to Fleet Street. It was a difficult decision, for he had to be certain that the truth was more important to him than avoiding the impression that he was betraying his colleagues at the *Vanguard*. Having decided that it was, it seemed logical that he should first approach Robert at the *Examiner*. When they met however, his friend declined the offer of the story and quickly explained why.

"I'm sorry Larry, but our readers aren't interested in that part of the World. Since the Americans left, Vietnam is just a distant memory. To do it justice, your article needs to be presented as a major feature and I can't give it that kind of treatment."

"Surely, you're underestimating your readers," replied Larry. "There's a basic decency in most people that's bound to be affected by their knowledge of the atrocities that are going on out there. People need to know and then they'll demand that the government joins with other countries to help negotiate an end to the conflict."

"As an editor," explained Robert, "I'm no different to James Green. I have to work within the parameters set by the expectations of the readers and my boss too. We carry short, straightforward political articles. It suits our audience. Your story is too complex."

"There was a time," insisted Larry, "when you wouldn't have taken that attitude. When you edited the *News Bulletin* at Owens, you fought tooth and nail for the right to print the truth and stand up for justice. I'm giving you the chance to do the right thing and you should take it."

Robert was surprised by Larry's criticism. He understood his friend's emotional investment in the article, but was confused by Larry's inability to accept the realities of the newspaper industry, when he had worked in it for so long. Larry's words had stung him and it was unsurprising when he hit back.

"The character you talk about at Owens, is long gone and do you know what was initially responsible for that happening?"

Robert paused and looked intently at Larry.

"Our visit with Kay to see your parents, all those years ago. You see Larry, it opened my eyes. I experienced the lifestyle. The wonderful house and gardens, the beautiful possessions and I realised that's what I wanted. You've always been secure; a rich family to support you. If you were from my background, then you'd understand. For so many, life was uncertain. Fearing the knock on the door of the rent man or the tallyman and sometimes kids having to lie and say that their Mam wasn't in, because that week she didn't have enough to pay them. People beaten down, kids wearing hand-me-downs and not having proper food. Have you ever eaten sugar butties?"

"Well, no," replied Larry.

"Actually, we enjoyed them at the time, but meeting your family gave me a chance to understand that it was possible to transform my life. The money I have now, gives me the independence that few who went to Armitage Street School have ever managed to achieve. You see Larry, I really don't care about your moral judgements."

Larry was quiet. His friend's revelation had shocked him.

"Look. Be sensible," continued Robert. "It's clear that Green wants you at the *Vanguard*. Go back. He won't know that you offered me the story. It's the best place for you."

"I can't," replied Larry. "I'd be allowing them to take away my moral conscience."

"How can you be so naïve?" asked Robert, in frustration. "You've been working for a Soviet funded newspaper for years. Don't you think that in all that time you haven't been a cat's paw of Moscow? No journalist is ever completely free to write what they want."

"But I can't just forget what I've seen. Women, children and old men murdered and brutalised. The story has to be told."

"War is brutal. It always has been," insisted Robert. "Your criticism of the Chinese can be levelled at any country in any conflict. We saw the reports from Malaya in the Fifties and Aden in the Sixties, about the atrocities carried out by our own troops. We know of the Yanks and My Lai and the Soviets in

Afghanistan. All governments try to cover up atrocities; fabricate evidence to support their cause and deny everything. We just have to live with it. It's certainly not worth throwing away your livelihood over. For all your good intentions, you'll be a casualty that no one in the business will give a second thought to."

"Yet your own father was part of the retreat to Dunkirk. He witnessed the SS atrocities. You told me about it and how he was almost butchered by them himself. And you always insisted on telling his story Robert; exposing those criminals for what they did. Back then you weren't thinking about upsetting German susceptibilities, but I suppose that now, you'd think twice about putting it in the *Examiner*. You've sold out Robert. You aren't the angry, opinionated, working-class lad I first met at Owens. The industry has taken your soul."

"I'm proud of my dad and what he did," replied Robert. "He believed that he was fighting against evil and tyranny; for a world of equality and humanity. He helped secure the time to evacuate the beaches at Dunkirk and got back across the channel. Yet he died from his wounds, leaving Mam and I alone. And what did the Establishment do for the hundreds of thousands like us? A pittance of a widow's pension; mothers forced to take two or three jobs to eke out enough for their families. And Dad's socialist dreams? Nothing! Still the same people getting rich off the backs of everyone else. Well, I saw the light. If you can't beat them, then you have to try and join them. I did just that and of course, I compromised. Perhaps went so far, as you put it, to 'sell out.' Yet to see the look in Mam's eyes and the smile on her face when I took her to the house in Mansfield Road and handed over the keys, it was worth it. I could never have done that without getting here and becoming editor of the *Examiner*. What my dad's death taught me, was that you can't wait around. You have to seize what you can in life, for the opportunity may never come again. However much we'd like it to, nothing in society ever really changes. Not fundamentally."

"I can't accept that," said Larry, quietly. "There always has to be a chance to make things better for everyone."

"No. There's no chance," replied Robert. "It's the way things are. Live with it. What I've achieved is by accepting reality; the world as it is, not how I'd like it to be. Before I left Manchester,

I remember telling you that it was always easier for you to moralise. You had money, privilege and the security of a wealthy family. I had no such luxury. If ever I was going to amount to anything, I had to learn to play the game. To get to sit in this office, I had to compromise. Court the rich and powerful and then make sure that I never forget how easily they can break me. I won't throw that away Larry, much as you're my friend and I would love to help you. I just won't take a chance on running your article."

Larry nodded. He finally understood. He hadn't intended that his visit to Robert would prove so difficult. The conversation had become heated, almost acrimonious and Larry realised that his criticisms had been harsh, even unfair. Although disappointed by his friend's decision, Larry didn't want to leave without knowing that Robert still regarded him as his close friend.

"I'm sorry, Robert. I haven't been fair. I can only say that I've become too attached to the story. I wasn't thinking straight. Everything's still okay between us, isn't it?"

Robert smiled. Larry's words had hurt him, but they had been the closest of friends for so long and he had no intention of changing that.

"All the time you spent in Manchester and you still think like a bloody Southerner!" he joked. "Being friends is all about knowing that you can have a right go at one another and then it's all forgotten."

"Thanks," replied Larry.

"Kay would tell you the same."

"Yes. I suppose she would call me gormless, wouldn't she?"

The two of them started laughing.

"Well, I'd best let you get on," said Larry.

Robert walked over to his friend and patted him affectionately on the shoulder.

"Yes. I'll see you soon."

When Larry had left his office, Robert couldn't help feeling uneasy. His friend was an emotional man with deeply held convictions and it was clear that what he had seen out in Vietnam had profoundly affected him. He doubted whether Larry would be able to exercise the necessary detachment to continue working at the *Vanguard*, given that they had turned their backs on the suffering of both Chinese and Vietnamese civilians. Robert knew that it would be difficult for Larry to find another editor prepared to publish his article and more importantly, for him to secure alternative employment.

Later that night, Robert had the chance to go over their conversation. At the time, he had robustly defended himself against Larry's criticisms, but since his initial anger had subsided, he began to consider whether some of what his friend had said, was true. Furthermore, Robert began to wonder what his father would have felt about his actions. Sergeant Billy Wilson had been a staunch trade unionist and Labour man. It wasn't likely that he would have approved of his refusal to back Larry.

Worried about Larry's state of mind, Robert began to feel guilty. Was there anything more that he could do to help him? It was then that he recalled hearing about *The Clarion*, a weekly left-wing newspaper that was on the point of closure. The publication was in serious financial difficulties and would clearly not survive unless it could quickly find a buyer. Over the next few days, Robert made contact with its owner, examined the accounts and the premises. Meeting with its small, but dedicated staff, he discovered that their editor had already departed. It meant that Robert would have less difficulty in installing Larry as his replacement. Now established as a successful editor and businessman, with a portfolio that included investments in various media outlets, Robert was sure that he would be able to cut the publication's overheads. Furthermore, it was clear to him that with its left-wing leanings, the current ownership had seriously ignored the potential for raising advertising revenues. Robert was sure that under his supervision, the paper could, at the very least, break even. It was enough for him to drive a hard bargain with the current owner and take over as the new proprietor. All he had to do now was tell Larry the good news.

Chapter 109

Larry understood the logic of Robert's advice, but after their meeting he knew that he could no longer work for the *Vanguard*. He was convinced that he must do everything possible to see his story published and running out of options, he decided that he would approach the Tory press; those who Green had dismissed as 'the lackeys and lapdogs of capitalism'.

Invited to bring in his story to the first paper he contacted, Larry was taken to the editor's office by a pretty, young secretary. It seemed to him that the top men in Fleet Street were all the same. Like Robert, they had to surround themselves with good looking women. Watching the editor's eyes wandering all over her impressive figure and seeing the young woman flutter her eyelashes at him in return, Larry wondered whether her role was less about work and more to do with pleasure. After all, Robert had told him in the past, that he had slept with several of his young, female assistants.

After reading through Larry's article and carefully examining his photos, the editor handed them back to him.

"Sorry, it's not really the type of thing we're after."

A look of incredulity crossed Larry's face. He couldn't believe what he was hearing.

"But surely, the revelations of Chinese atrocities can only undermine the reputation of one of the most important socialist powers. I can't believe that you, or your proprietor, don't want that."

"Yet, I have to ask myself, why do you?" replied the editor, fixing Larry with a quizzical look. "I was intrigued when you contacted us, given that the profile of this paper hardly matches your own political leanings. Your reputation precedes you, Foster. A brilliant journalist who could have made a fortune on Fleet Street, yet your aspirations start and end with writing for a 'tin pot' little journal, aimed at the weirdos and wasters on the left. No one reads it, but you believe in the cause and have steadfastly stuck to the task. Why do you now want us to damage a government that you have supported so strongly in the past?"

"Because, I have to tell the truth. I can't allow it to be buried and when Beijing are aware of the criticism of those actions, the ones responsible will be held accountable."

The editor laughed quietly and shook his head in disbelief at the foolhardy soul he saw in front of him. Despite all the horrors he had seen and the duplicity of the countless politicians he'd interviewed, Foster refused to abandon his idealism. He steadfastly believed that somewhere, somehow, a perfect, free and egalitarian society could be established and he would be one of the torch bearers who would help it to become a reality.

"That's an incredibly naïve point of view for someone as hard-bitten as you," the editor observed. "Even if we did publish, I'd guarantee that Peking, or sorry, Beijing as you and they insist we call it nowadays, would deny it. They would be adamant that the evidence had been fabricated by the Vietnamese and handed to the western press in order to discredit them."

"But we don't know that for sure," replied Larry. "At the very least, the crimes can no longer be hidden from the leadership by those in charge of the responsible PLA units."

"Perhaps," replied the editor, "but I couldn't help you with the story, even if I wanted."

He paused, Larry waiting for him to continue.

"The fact is that we've been warned off this one."

"Warned off?"

"Yes. We were forewarned about your article before you approached us. The Foreign and Commonwealth Office have made it clear that it's not in the country's interest to upset the Chinese at the moment."

"Why?"

"It seems that secret negotiations have been going on for a couple of years about the status of Hong Kong. The lease on the new territories runs out in 1997 and there's a need to secure stability for our investments out there. Too much criticism in the British media could well undermine the talks. The Chinese could respond to our hostility by threatening to 'pull the plug' on them. Our own government doesn't want to be embarrassed by any revelations about the atrocities in Vietnam either."

"Embarrassed?"

"Yes. The official line, when the negotiations are made public, has to be that Beijing can be relied upon to look after Hong Kong's residents. The government wants to avoid mass protests and dissension towards any future agreement. You can see how your article could stimulate panic, when most of the Chinese community would prefer to stay under British rule. The reality is that Beijing will never allow that to happen."

"So, as usual," replied Larry, "it all comes down to money."

There was a real bitterness in his voice, that he made no attempt to hide.

"Of course. There are billions tied up out there in business and property and from what I understand, Deng wants to take advantage of Hong Kong's economic resources and find an accommodation with capitalist interests. Perhaps that's the real reason that your own editor doesn't want to publish and put any talks in jeopardy."

"Effectively," observed Larry, "you're saying that there's little point in me approaching anyone on Fleet Street."

"That's about the size of it. You know yourself. No publication can afford to ignore a directive from the FCO. I'll tell you what though Foster. This meeting today didn't happen. I've no intention of letting the *Vanguard* know about it. My advice is that you go back there. Forget about this and get on with your job."

"Why would you do that?" asked Larry. "Why would you want to help me?"

"Because although you're naïve and inflexible and can be a pain in the arse, it's still good to have someone in the industry that we can all look at as a reminder of what we, when we first started out, intended to be."

His words were generous, but in his disappointment, Larry could only regard them as an expression of pity. As he left the building, Larry was acutely aware of his impotence. He'd always believed that as an investigative journalist, he had the capacity to make a difference. Now it was clear that he was fighting forces that were far more powerful than himself. It seemed almost inevitable that his article would never see the light of day. The question he had to ask himself now, was what would he do next?

Chapter 110

Over the next few days, Larry had remained at home. Contemplating his future, he had fallen into despair. He was determined that he wouldn't return to the *Vanguard* and even if he'd wanted to, there was no chance of securing a job on Fleet Street. Having operated with a large degree of freedom at the *Vanguard*, Larry wanted to continue to write about the issues that mattered to him. It meant that there was no chance that he could work on a provincial newspaper and revert to being a run-of-the-mill, general reporter. His only possible option would be to operate as a freelance journalist. To be successful however, his work would have to be commercial and he would have little opportunity to write the articles he wanted. It seemed obvious to Larry that in his current circumstances, he no longer had a voice that could make a difference.

A few weeks later, at the start of July, with his purchase of the *Clarion* nearing completion, Robert telephoned Larry at his flat in Kentish Town. His friend had sounded rather subdued, but Robert was sure that when he turned up and offered him the editorship of the paper, he would soon cheer up. Entering the flat, Robert was in for a shock. It was still early evening and light outside, but Larry's front room curtains were drawn and the room was in a mess. Robert was sure that the curtains hadn't been opened for some time and when he looked at Larry, unkempt and unshaven, it seemed that his friend was in danger of turning into a recluse. Deciding to act as normally as possible, Robert moved directly on to the point of his visit.

"I've got some good news Larry. I'm close to finalising a deal to buy the *Clarion* and I'd like you to be my partner and the paper's new editor."

Larry stared at him. Robert was unsure whether he'd understood his offer.

"Well? What do you think? Can the pair of us make a success of it?"

Again, there was no response.

"I want it to stay just as radical as it's always been and as editor, you've got a free hand to run it as you please," Robert continued. "All I'll do, is put someone in to supervise the books and raise the advertising revenues. I've costed everything and with you leading from the front, I'm betting that the paper can gain the reputation of being the only true voice of the left."

"I don't understand," said Larry, confused. "Why would you of all people want to buy the *Clarion* and then have me run it? I've got no editorial experience. Surely, if you're serious about making a go of it, you should choose someone else."

"After we spoke at the *Examiner*, it made me stop and think," replied Robert. "I had to face some unpleasant home truths, because you were right to say that I'd lost touch with my younger self. I'd conveniently forgotten that there was still so much injustice in the world and that there had to be a voice to speak out against it. Buying the *Clarion* allows me the chance to give something back; to give a different message to the ones that I've put out at the *Gazette* and the *Examiner*."

"But why not edit it yourself?"

"Because I understand my limitations. I can't be like you, Larry. I live in the material world. I won't give up the wealth and status that I've worked so hard for. Call me egotistical, but I'm staying at the *Examiner*. The *Clarion* needs someone incorruptible and honest to edit the paper. It needs to be kept on a straight road. I can't think of anyone more qualified to ensure that than you. Now, you'll be able to print what you want; get your Vietnam article out there. The FCO may be able to intimidate Fleet Street but with you in charge, they'll never frighten the *Clarion*!"

Robert smiled, but Larry had still not shown any enthusiasm for his friend's proposal and it became clear that there was something that was bothering him.

"I have to ask. Did you already know about the FCO directive when I came to see you?"

"No. Only afterwards."

"And you didn't contact them about my article?"

"Of course not."

"Are you sure?" asked Larry, suspiciously.

"You shouldn't need to ask me that. Remember, I was concerned that you were burning your bridges with the *Vanguard* by approaching other newspapers. If I'd already received the FCO directive, I would have told you and made sure that you didn't needlessly risk compromising yourself with Green, by going to see anyone else."

"But how did the FCO know about my article?"

"Come on Larry, you know yourself that intelligence gathering is going on all the time. As soon as you contacted Green from Hanoi, the FCO would have known about it. You're tired and not thinking straight."

Robert looked closely at his friend. It was clear that he felt the world was against him and most concerning of all, he seemed to be losing his enthusiasm for the struggle.

"All right," muttered Larry, unconvincingly. "Fair enough."

"Look Larry, why don't you come and stay with me whilst we're getting the *Clarion* up and running. We'll have lots of decisions to make, so it makes sense for you to be close at hand. I've a housekeeper who looks after me. She sorts everything out: meals, cleaning and washing. It'll give you a break from here. Why don't you get some clothes together and whatever else you need and you can come back with me now."

"No. I'm fine right here," insisted Larry.

"Well, what about the *Clarion*? You are going to help me out, aren't you Larry? I'm depending on you."

"Yes, all right. Let me know when the contracts are signed and the paper is yours."

Larry sounded disinterested, but Robert accepted his words at face value, not wanting to push his friend any further.

"Good," said Robert. "I'll get off and I'll be back in touch in a couple of days."

As he drove home, Robert was deeply concerned. His friend exhibited all the signs of having fallen into a deep depression. He had wanted to insist on Larry coming with him, but he had been uncertain of how his friend would react. Larry had lost his sense of vocation and seemed on the verge of turning his back on his friends and family. He was anxious, exhausted and alone and what the consequences of that would be, Robert dreaded to think.

Chapter 111

Back home, Robert immediately telephoned Kay. It was what he always did when he was facing a crisis. Yet as the line continued to ring, Robert began to worry that perhaps there was no one in. Eventually though, the call was answered and Robert's spirits immediately lifted as he heard Kay's voice on the end of the line.

"I'm sorry for phoning you so late, but I need your help," explained Robert.

"That's all right," replied Kay. "What can I do?"

"It's not for me. It's Larry."

"Ah. You're worried about him as well, aren't you?"

"Yes. How did you know?"

"Instinct. I received a strange letter from him yesterday. He was reminiscing about the old days at Owens and wishing Bernard well for the future. I had the impression that he wasn't expecting to see us again. I've been trying to contact him ever since. His phone's just ringing and at the *Vanguard*, they said he was on leave. I thought of contacting Violet, to see if she'd heard anything from him, but I didn't want to worry her. I was going to ring you tomorrow morning and ask you to go to his flat, to see if he was there."

"That's where I've just been," replied Robert. "He's there, but he's in a bad way."

Robert told Kay about his visit and how he felt uneasy about leaving him on his own.

"The thing is Kay, that I don't know what to do. He doesn't seem to want me to help him. That's why I contacted you."

"I'm coming down. I'll get the Pullman from Piccadilly and I'll be at Euston just after ten. Be there to meet me Robert and you can take me straight to Larry's flat."

"Yes. Of course."

"Right, I'll need to pack my case and get some sleep. I'll see you in the morning."

And that was it. She was gone.

Robert felt relieved. Kay had taken control and a plan was in place. Realising the dangerous state that Larry was in, she hadn't hesitated and once moved to action, she was an irresistible force. Larry loved and admired his sister-in-law and Robert felt confident that she would be able to rescue him from his misery and isolation and set him on the road to recovery.

Up at the crack of dawn, Kay appreciated the value of the support that her mam and dad were always on hand to provide. She knew that Bernard would be well looked after, with there being no need to alter his routine. Furthermore, Ethel could be relied on to inform children's services that due to family reasons, her daughter would be absent from work and pass on the instructions that Kay had left for her deputy. Ernest, not on shift until the following day, was also able to drive Kay down to Piccadilly Station in good time for the train.

Arriving at Euston, Kay was pleased to see that Robert was waiting for her at the end of the platform. Dropping her case, she threw her arms around him and gave him a big hug. Taking a taxi from outside the station, they were soon on their way to Larry's flat.

"It's not very far from here," said Robert, "We'll soon be there. There's just one thing though. You need to be prepared for the state of the flat. As I said last night, the front room is in a mess. It told me straightaway that something was wrong."

"Don't worry. I'm here to help, not to get upset."

"I know," replied Robert. "You're far better at dealing with these situations than I am. Nevertheless, I think you'll find it difficult to see the condition that Larry's got himself into."

Larry's flat was on the ground floor and his friends could see that his curtains were still closed. Approaching the front door, Kay rang the bell. There was no answer. After ringing it several times without any response, Robert walked over to the front window and began to tap on the glass.

"Kay, come over here and shout through to Larry. If he's in there and hears you, I'm sure he'll open the door."

Kay did as Robert asked. Eventually, the curtains parted and Larry's face stared out through the window.

Robert's warning had been right for when Larry opened the front door, Kay was shocked. Standing before her was a stooping, broken man. Bearded, his hair unkempt, he'd clearly not changed his clothes in days. His eyes seemed to have sunk back into his head and he appeared utterly exhausted.

"Hello Larry."

Larry was silent.

"Well," said Kay, sharply. "I've come all this way and you haven't even asked me in and offered me a cup of tea. Have you forgotten the good manners we taught you in Manchester?"

Her approach was perfect. It was the Kay with whom Larry was so familiar. Decisive, in charge and telling him off for acting gormless. Shaken by her rebuke, his eyes lit up and he held open the door.

"Come in," said Larry, weakly.

Kay and Robert walked into the hall and waited as Larry closed the door behind them. Turning to see Kay's smile, Larry instinctively put his arms around her and rested his head on her shoulder. Without warning, he burst into uncontrollable sobbing. Squeezing him gently, Kay waited for the tears to subside.

"It's all right Larry. Don't worry. It'll be fine. You'll see."

Taking Larry into the front room, Kay sat him down on the settee.

"Right Larry, Robert and I are desperate for a brew. Have you got everything we need in the kitchen?"

"I think so."

"Well, you can sit here with Robert and I'll make us all a drink."

The kitchen wasn't too bad. The tops, sink and draining board were clear and reasonably clean, as was the floor. It gave Kay the impression that Larry hadn't been preparing any meals and this had probably contributed to his listlessness. Unable to find any milk in the fridge, Kay searched through the cupboards for mugs, tea and sugar. What she found, concerned her. Behind the mugs were several boxes of aspirins. In all the time she'd known him, Larry had never been one to bother over aches and pains, colds or viruses. In his present depressed state, her immediate fear was that he may have been contemplating an overdose. It was now more important than ever that they get Larry out of the flat and under their supervision. Returning to the front room, Kay asked Robert if he would go to the shops for some milk and biscuits.

Once he had left, Kay set to work persuading Larry that he needed a break.

"It must be a long time since you've had a proper rest from work, Larry. Robert mentioned that you were leaving the *Vanguard* and that the two of you were setting up your own newspaper. That's going to require some effort, isn't it? It's a good idea to recharge the batteries before you start. Don't you think so?"

Larry was silent, but nodded his head obediently. Kay's arrival on his doorstep, had shaken him out of his stupor. Seeing his caring and beautiful friend, Larry realised that if he continued to follow his negative and suicidal thoughts, it would have terrible consequences for others besides himself. His sister-in-law had already lost her husband and his parents, their son. How would they cope if he were to be so selfish? And what would his nephew and Robert think? The latter was trying hard to help him and he had simply dismissed him. Suddenly, Larry felt ashamed.

"I'm so sorry Kay," said Larry, weakly. "You shouldn't have had to come all this way. The flat's a mess. I've nothing to offer you…"

Larry's voice quietly tailed off and once more he started to cry. Sat beside him, Kay put her arm around his shoulders. It was what he had needed; the chance to release all the anguish that he'd been bottling up since his return from Vietnam.

Once Larry had settled down, Kay gently explained to him what they were going to do.

"When Robert comes back, we'll have a brew and tidy up. Then, you're going to pack your suitcase because tonight we'll be staying at Robert's. I'm going to give your mam a ring later and let her know that we'll be there tomorrow. You're going to have a good rest in the fresh air. We'll soon have you fighting fit and ready to take on your new job."

"But don't you have to be at work?" asked Larry.

"I'm on leave. I've not had a holiday in ages, so I'm going to be staying too," explained Kay.

"Oh, good."

Larry felt relieved. It seemed like an enormous weight had been lifted from his shoulders. Unlike last night, he had no objection to accepting the help of his friends and after Robert had returned, he sat contentedly drinking his tea and munching on some chocolate digestives, whilst Kay told him all about how young Bernard was getting on at school.

That evening, Kay called Anne. The latter insisted that she take as much time off as she needed. It only remained for Kay to telephone Violet and explain, as carefully as possible, the situation with Larry and that Robert would be driving them down in the morning. Grateful for Kay's intervention, Violet told her that everything would be ready for their arrival.

Chapter 112

Setting off after the early morning rush hour, it was a straightforward journey down to Faversham and they arrived just before noon. As Robert drove the car slowly around the bend of the driveway, past the trees and flower beds, Kay heard the familiar sound of the wheels crunching on the gravel and waited expectantly for the house to appear before them. When it did, she could see Violet and Norman waiting outside to greet them. Kay knew how relieved they would be to see their son safe and sound. Sensibly, when Larry got out of the car, his parents reacted as usual. Violet hugged and kissed him, whilst Norman patted him on the shoulder.

"It's lovely to see you all. You're in the usual rooms," said Violet, smiling. "Do you want to go and get settled whilst I start on lunch?"

"Do you need a hand?" asked Kay.

"No, it's all right. I can manage."

Whilst Robert got their cases out of the boot, Violet and Norman went inside.

"Go and help your mam in the kitchen," suggested Kay to Larry. "She'll be pleased with the help. You don't have to mention anything."

"But what about my bags?"

"I'll take them over with mine," said Robert.

With Larry insisting on carrying her case, Kay followed him into the main house and upstairs to her bedroom at the top of the oast house. After Larry had gone to the kitchen, Kay made her way outside and walked over to the cottage where he and Robert were staying. Overnight she had given much thought to her friends' new venture and had come up with an idea that she believed would better secure Larry's commitment to it. Now, she needed to explain her thoughts to Robert.

"The *Clarion* sounds like an exciting project Robert, although it seems an unusual publication for you to take over."

"Yes, normally it would have been, but I think that with careful management, we can make a go of it."

"Nevertheless, it's a big commitment that you're making."

"At first, it will be. Once we start raising some advertising revenues and we get the finances into the black, then I can put in an accounts manager to ensure that everything continues to run smoothly."

"So, you're not expecting to make much of a profit then?"

"Hardly."

"Why did you really want to buy the *Clarion* then?"

"Do I have to say? I'm sure that you've already got a good idea."

"Yes, but I want to hear it from you."

"I feel responsible for what's happened to Larry," explained Robert. "I could have done more to help him. He wanted me to publish an article he'd written on Vietnam and I turned him down. When I was younger, I wouldn't have hesitated; it would have been a case of publish and be damned. He's my friend and through the *Clarion*, I'm giving him a voice. Never again will anyone be able to silence him."

"You mustn't blame yourself Robert. You had no choice but to act in the interests of the *Examiner*. Larry understands that. What happened in Vietnam deeply affected him. He was already struggling to cope with it before he came to see you. Don't be too hard on yourself and by making him editor, it's going to be easier to keep an eye on him."

"As long as he doesn't want to go back on his travels."

"I doubt he'll be looking to do that. There are plenty of causes for him to get passionate about here at home. What's important is to encourage his enthusiasm for editing the paper and I think that I may have a way of helping with that."

"Go on," said Robert.

"Well, once the sale has gone through, let more of us buy into the paper. Bernard, myself, Norman and Violet. They don't have to be big shares, it's just that it would make the venture into a family enterprise. Then Larry knows that we all believe in him and he'll be committed to producing the best quality newspaper that he can. It's the thing that will keep him focused and healthy."

"I'm not sure that you should all be risking your money," replied Robert, concerned.

"Why not? I've got full confidence in you and Larry to make a go of it. Bernard and I have savings and investments. I'm sure Bernard will be keen. Since he stayed with you last summer, he's been obsessed with working in the media."

"Well, I don't mind young Bernard getting involved during the holidays, but I draw the line at any prospect of you considering a career change. You'd be taking over in no time," joked Robert.

"By the way," continued Kay. "As the paper is getting relaunched, shouldn't it be called *The New Clarion*?"

"Yes, I was considering that myself and your idea," said Robert, "seems a good one, although I'll only let you put in a token amount. I'll take on most of the risk. I'm better able to afford it."

"Okay. I'll talk to Violet later. I'm sure she and Norman will want to get behind the idea."

Later that afternoon, whilst Norman and 'the boys' were outside in the garden, Kay and Violet had a chance to talk openly about Larry's situation. Kay explained to her the reasons why Larry had become depressed and what she and Robert had planned in order to get him positive and healthy once more. Importantly, Violet confirmed that she and Norman would be happy to invest in *The New Clarion*.

"I realise now that his letter to me, was a cry for help," said Kay. "When Robert and I went to see him yesterday, it allowed him to release all the emotions that he'd been holding on to since he was in Vietnam. He must have seen some terrible things and he was angry and frustrated because he wanted to help, but everywhere he turned, it seemed as if his voice was being silenced."

"Larry's always been so sensitive," observed Violet. "He seemed fine when he was with me in the kitchen, although I never mentioned to him that I knew anything about the state he was in."

"When I saw him," continued Kay, "it was obvious that he needed time to rest and recuperate and so I persuaded him to come and stay here, whilst Robert handled the details of setting up the launch of the paper. I'll stay for a couple of weeks, if that's all right and when school has finished, Bernard can come too."

"Of course, you can stay. You know that you're always welcome and we've not seen Bernard since Easter. He and Larry get on like a house on fire. Norman and I love having him here, waking up us old-timers with his youthful enthusiasm."

"You're not old-timers," insisted Kay. "You're only as old as you feel and you and Norman have been open-minded and forward thinking for as long as I've known you."

"That's very kind Kay, but we are getting older. We're both well in our seventies now and I know that I speak for Norman too, when I say that we're so grateful that you have always been around to give Larry your love and support. You're almost like his guardian angel and it's reassuring to know that when we're no longer here, Larry can always turn to you, as he's done ever since he went to Manchester."

"You mustn't talk like that," said Kay. "You're both going to be here for a lot longer yet."

Not wanting to upset her, Violet became more optimistic.

"Well, let's hope so. We wouldn't want to miss out on seeing what our grandson gets up too. I know how proud his father would be of him. Young Bernard has an advantage though; he has you as a mum. You've done a wonderful job bringing him up Kay."

The following week, the school holidays having begun, Bernard Jr joined them. For the first time, Kay had allowed him to make the journey to Kent alone. His presence came at exactly the right time. Having taken it easy for several days, Larry was beginning to feel that he should return to London. His nephew's presence however, changed that. Larry enjoyed sharing with Bernard, his plans as editor for *The New Clarion* and advising him about how best to set about entering the world of journalism. Furthermore, Larry was keen to spend time on the tennis court with his nephew. Being a natural athlete, Bernard quickly reaped the benefits of his uncle's coaching. Soon, there was nothing between them in terms of their playing ability. With trips to Canterbury, the seaside and walks in the country, Larry was kept busy entertaining his nephew. At the end of August, rested and recuperated, Larry travelled with Bernard to Euston to see him off on the train to Manchester and then made his way to Wimbledon. As they were now business partners, Robert had been able to convince Larry to give up his flat and move into the annexe attached to his home. The purchase of the newspaper was complete and Robert was in the process of organising the allocation of new shares in the company, as Kay had asked him. *The New Clarion* was now ready to be launched and expectations were high that it was going to be a success.

Chapter 113

On Saturday August 28th 1982, Larry, Robert, Kay and Bernard were back in Kent to celebrate the anniversary of the launch of *The New Clarion*. The attendance of Roger and Barbara, their sons George and William, along with their wives and children, signified the presence of four generations of the Foster family. The weather was hot and sunny; perfect for the outside festivities. It was a happy and hectic day, Violet and Norman sparing no expense in laying on an impressive spread for their family and friends.

A year on, the paper was proving the success that Robert had predicted. Zealous in pursuit of the truth, Larry had established a reputation as a crusading editor whose journalists were always looking to champion the cause of the unfortunate and the weak, whilst exposing the rich and powerful. *The New Clarion* had found its niche in the market; the publication of relevance for students, left-wing intellectuals and liberals alike. It was shifting enough copies to cover its costs and with companies recognising the unique elements of its readership, sales of advertising space had increased dramatically, so allowing the paper to turn a profit. As such, both major partners had played their own crucial role in the *Clarion's* success.

With the lunch time buffet out of the way, Larry organised a tennis tournament. Knowing his ability, Robert and Roger made their excuses, but Bernard, George and William were keen to take on the challenge. With Larry and Bernard comfortably winning through to the final, the pair returned to the court, eager to prove their superiority. As the match progressed, it was clear that Larry was struggling to keep pace with his younger, more agile opponent. Sat together, on a bench a little distant from the others, Kay and Robert couldn't help laughing at Larry's exasperation.

"Larry's finding it very different to when you played him," observed Kay.

"Well, Bernard's got far more talent than I had."

"You didn't say that at the time. You kept making up excuses and trying to put Larry off."

"Well, I wasn't going to admit it to Larry and let a Southern 'toff' get one up on me."

"I don't know," said Kay, laughing. "You two never stop having a go at each other, do you?"

"It's only healthy competition," insisted Robert.

Kay smiled. She put her arm around Robert and gave him a hug.

"What was that for?" asked Robert, surprised.

"Because you've a good heart. You've been so kind to Larry."

"But he's helping me too. I love what he's doing with the *Clarion*. When I'm getting hammered on all sides for running the 'sleazy, sensational *Examiner*', I can still look at myself in the mirror."

"I can't believe for one moment, that all the criticism isn't anything other than water off a duck's back, as far as you're concerned," observed Kay.

"Well, yes," conceded Robert, "but I think you understand what I mean."

Kay nodded and the two of them spent a few moments in silence watching Larry being dragged around the court, as Bernard went through a whole range of cultured and impressive shots.

"The kid's got real ability, Kay. Larry's pretty good, but Junior's making him look like a mug."

"He's always been good at sport," replied Kay. "He's got that from his dad."

"It's exciting, isn't it? Bernard's got the whole world in front of him and I'm looking forward to watching his journey, for I know that he'll do well for himself," observed Robert.

"Do you remember back to when we did?" asked Kay. "When we had the world in front of us."

"Yes, I do," said Robert, smiling. "I often think about the dreams we both had growing up. Do you remember Mr. Chandler showing us that old pupil register and telling us to make the most of our talents like Charlie Chaplin did?"

"Yes, of course I do," said Kay. "Were you inspired by knowing that Charlie had gone to our school? I was."

"Yes, me too. It made me think that if we worked hard, we really could achieve anything."

"And do you remember that time when we were under the railway bridge on Hyde Road?" asked Kay. "When you said that one day you wanted to board the train and let it take you away, whilst I said that I would never leave Manchester. It's all come to pass, hasn't it?"

"I suppose it has."

Again, the pair of them fell silent. As they watched the tennis, they knew that it was only a matter of time before Bernard would be victorious. Reaching into his pocket, Robert pulled out his wallet and then took out a small black and white photo and showed it to Kay.

"Do you remember this?" asked Robert.

"Of course," replied Kay. "It's from the photo booth in 'Woolies'. We had it taken just before we went to the Ritz to celebrate our 'O' Level results. I've still got my two copies, including the one you made a silly face on. I showed it to Bernard and he said that you look completely gormless on it."

They both laughed, but Kay was touched to see that he valued the photo so much, that he carried it with him in his wallet.

"I've got the other at home, just in case anything happens to this one," said Robert.

"You didn't have it in your wallet when you were married to Trudy, did you?"

"Of course, I did. Why shouldn't I?" asked Robert, genuinely surprised by her question.

"She didn't see it, did she?"

"I don't think so, but I don't care if she did."

"Oh Robert," sighed Kay. "Are you ever going to understand how most women think?"

"I do Kay. I've learned to. But you and I have always been so close and anyone I become serious about, has to accept that. If they can't, then it just won't work."

"That's asking a lot of someone. We all feel a little vulnerable at times and carrying our photo around with you, might make your wife or girlfriend feel insecure."

"If I ever find the right one, then I know they'll accept it and won't be jealous. You should see it as a test of their understanding and the sincerity of their commitment."

"And what about you, Robert? Do you appreciate the need to be sincere?"

"I believe I do. I've finally understood the conversation that you and I had in 'Caf', when I told you about Joan and the times I'd been with other women. I sensed that sex provided satisfaction, but no lasting fulfilment. You were right in telling me that I was still too young. That I couldn't truly comprehend what I was saying, because I was driven towards wanting the next woman; the next encounter. I now realise that right from the beginning with Pauline, I've had no emotional investment in any woman I've been with and that includes Trudy. So, I'm not surprised that I haven't found love."

"You may, Robert. it's not too late," said Kay, softly.

"No, I don't think so," replied Robert. "I'll never have that woman who can truly touch my soul."

Once more, there was silence, for Robert could go no further. Kay was the one that he had always been in love with and he was sure that she knew it. Nevertheless, Kay would remain true to the memory of her husband and would never marry again. Long ago, Robert had learned to banish all thoughts of what might have been, grateful for Kay's continued presence in his life. She had accepted him, with all his faults, ever since the day she had rescued him from the bullies on the Black Brook. She would always be there for him, just as she was now. He felt so fortunate to have her love and friendship but he knew, as did she, that more than that, he could never have.

Hearing a whoop of delight, Robert and Kay turned their attention back towards the tennis. Running to the net, an exuberant Bernard, thrust out his hand and waited for Larry to come and congratulate him on his victory.

"Oh dear," said Kay. "I hope that's not going to put Uncle Lahwee in a bad mood."

"Well, on the tennis court, he'll just have to accept that he's yesterday's man," replied Robert, with a chuckle.

Walking over, they could see the look of disappointment on Larry's face, as Bernard took the plaudits for his dominant performance.

"Come on everybody," said Violet, breaking into the celebrations. "We need to be getting back inside for dinner."

As the others drifted towards the house, Kay and Robert offered their commiserations to Larry.

"Never mind," said Kay. "Your nephew's quite the sportsman now."

"I can see that," replied Larry. "He's become really good, very quickly."

"Well, it's your own fault. After you taught him to play last summer, he enjoyed it so much that he joined the local tennis club. He's been getting lots of coaching and turning out for them in league matches."

"I should have known," said Larry, shaking his head. "It felt like his dad had come back to torment me. He always beat me too."

"But come on, Larry," said Robert. "It was to be expected. You're not that good, are you?"

"What do you mean?" asked Larry.

"Well," replied Robert, dismissively. "You couldn't beat me all those years ago, could you?"

Robert struggled hard to keep a straight face, as he witnessed Larry's annoyance and frustration. He was intent on prolonging the banter.

"Couldn't beat me? You, who never won a single game and kept wasting time so that we couldn't play to a finish. I don't think so."

"I wanted to finish," replied Robert. "You could tell that I was getting the hang of it. You were the one who walked off the court."

"Yes, because it was obvious that you were just making a mockery out of the whole game."

"That's enough. The pair of you!"

Her words were sharp. Bernard, walking slowly back to the house, turned round. He could see his mam gesticulating at the pair of them and smiled. It was a comical scene as his two uncles bowed their heads, uncomfortable at facing her displeasure. As he got nearer, Bernard could hear her final words on the subject.

"Now, let's forget it. We need to get inside."

As the sun dipped below the trees, Bernard watched as the three of them began to walk towards him.

"I'm sorry, Kay," said Robert.

"Me too," added Larry. "We were only having a bit of fun."

"Hmm, I'm sure," replied Kay.

"Come on, Kay," said Robert. "You know you love us really."

"Yes, you know we can't help it," added Larry.

Shaking her head, Kay smiled.

"After all this time, I still have no idea what I'm going to do with you two."

"You'll look after us, as you always have done," said Robert.

"Yes. Keep us on the straight and narrow," added Larry.

Moving either side of Kay, Larry and Robert linked arms with her and together, they walked slowly towards the house, three friends whose unbreakable bonds of affection had seen them through the tragedy and triumphs of such changing times.

www.ingramcontent.com/pod-product-compliance
Lightning Source LLC
Chambersburg PA
CBHW070336170726
48291CB00001B/64